Stay in Your Lane

ELLE F. SUN

THE EVERSON VALLEY SERIES
BOOK ONE

TABLE OF CONTENTS

The following is a list of subjects that are discussed within *Stay in Your Lane:*

- Abuse (Physical, Verbal, Emotional)
- Death (On and Off Page)
- Violence and Assault (On Page)
- Alcoholism, Drunk Driving
- Sexual Content
- Explicit Language
- Grief, Loss
- PTSD

Please take these topics into consideration before reading and do what is best for your heart and mental health. This book is intended for audiences 18+

AUTHOR'S NOTE

Stay in Your Lane is full of love, wit, pain, laughter, and tears. While it is pure fiction, it is based on a reality that many have been through and are still going through.

In this novel, abuse is directly addressed and considered graphic, among other sensitive matters. While I did my best to write with care, I also did not want to shy away from the reality of these struggles.

Please take your heart and mind into consideration before reading this story. The content warnings are to protect you and I understand this book may not be for everyone. It's real, raw, and written as something that could happen because it's something that does happen.

This is a romance book, but it also a book of realism, not escapism. I dearly ask that you consider your heart and your mental health before and while reading this. If you find at any point during the book you cannot continue, I support you stepping away for your wellbeing.

Xx, Elle

FOREWORD

Approximately 12 million people every year are affected by intimate partner violence (IPV) and sadly, that's 1 of every 4 women in their lifetime.

While *Stay in Your Lane* is a work of fiction, it was inspired by my own story and one that unfortunately many others have lived through.

If you, or someone you know finds themselves in a situation where your safety is compromised, please seek help.

You can reach the National Domestic Violence Hotline 24/7 by calling 1-800-799-7233 or by texting the word BEGIN to 88788

For the person who needs to realize they deserve far better than what they've been getting.

I hope this finds you in time.

PROLOGUE

FIVE WEEKS AGO

HARLOW

Being nervous isn't something I'm unfamiliar with.

I've had swim meets riding on me, on *my* wins. I've raced against national title holding swimmers. Over the last three years, my team has relied on me to uphold my own title as one of the highest ranked collegiate female swimmers in the southeast. And each time I've found myself in those situations, I've never faltered or choked. I thrived. I rose to the occasion.

Every. Single. Time.

But right now? Right now I can't say the same. I can't find that fearless swimmer inside of me. My nerves are so far from under control. I would dare say my nerves are controlling me.

I tap my foot while I wait for my coach to come into his office. I sent an email this morning letting him know we needed to meet as soon as possible. The last thing he's probably expecting on this early Sunday morning is his top swimmer waiting with her arm in a sling.

The door swings open, startling me. "Sutherland! What can I do for y—"

Coach Bradford stops in his tracks and the exact moment I was dreading begins to unfold before my eyes. His face is hardening. His eyes are narrowing. He glances at the sling, then back at me before sighing and walking over to his own chair. It creaks as he sits and leans back, crossing his arms. I've never seen him like this—so distant, cold, reserved.

"Well," he starts, then stops to pinch the bridge of his nose, letting out a large exhale. He meets my gaze again. "What the hell happened?"

"I had an accident," I barely mutter out. I can feel heat rushing into my cheeks. My ears are starting to ring and my chest is tightening.

"You…had an accident," he repeats, doing absolutely nothing to mask his skepticism.

"Yes. Last night. I was with some of the team at the Chi Kappa house and I fell." My words are coming out robotic as guilt starts to consume me.

I know I didn't do anything wrong by being at the fraternity house, but I still feel all the blame in the world crushing me right now. As long as we don't appear on social media with alcohol, the athletic director said it's fine if we go out or to some parties. I'm not an idiot either to think he doesn't know about the party so there's no point in trying to hide where I was.

I didn't even want to go to the stupid fucking thing, but my best friend, Lennon, wouldn't stop telling me that we couldn't break tradition and skip it. The back to school block party happens every August before classes start, and because we're seniors this year, she said it was *a requirement.* Clearly I should've gone with my gut and screwed tradition this time around.

"The student health center did an X-ray and it's dislocated. They were able to put it back in place though." I shiver, trying not to recall the *clunk* sound it made. "It's minor. But I know this means I can't swim. " The last few words leave my lips with a small croak and my eyes begin to sting.

"Minor?" He laughs sarcastically. "Minor my…Tell me something, Sutherland?"

My heart starts to thump loudly in my chest as my worst nightmare comes to life and Coach Bradford asks the question I knew he probably would.

"Were you drinking?" He sits up, resting his hands on the desk.

"I was, but—" He cuts me off mid-sentence by holding up a hand.

"That's enough. Make an appointment with the athletic trainer to be evaluated. I want you to get X-rays from our sports medicine department, and when I get the scans and notes from your appointments, I'll email you a plan. I estimate you'll be out for at least six to eight weeks. You're lucky you didn't need surgery."

Just when I think it's over and I can breathe, he hits the desk with his hands, causing me to flinch in my chair. He stands up and starts pacing around his cold, gray office. Seems it's not the only thing that's had the life sucked out of it today.

"What the hell were you thinking? You're my top athlete, Sutherland! And your *shoulder*? I know you understand as a swimmer how devastating a shoulder injury is." Stopping in his tracks, he turns and faces me. I can't stand the way he's looking at me with such disappointment.

"Coach, c'mon. It's not like I did it on purpose!" I want to fight back. I want to stand up for myself but as he narrows his eyes, likely thinking I'm just feeding him some bullshit I lose my courage. "I'm sorry, but if you'd just let me explain—" I'm interrupted yet again.

"I don't need your excuses. I need you to not be injured." Sitting back down and burying his face in his hands, he lets out a groan. Then he reaches for his phone and starts to make a call. Is he calling the dean? Am I going to get in trouble? I'm about to say something when he starts talking.

"Hey, Tom…Yeah, I'm good. Well, I could be better." He shoots me a glare.

I could be better too, Coach.

I have no idea who Tom is or why he needed to be brought into this uncomfortable conversation but I guess it's better than the alternatives.

"Yeah, well listen, Tom, I need a favor. I've got an injured swimmer here who's going to be starting rehab and physical therapy in the next two weeks, hopefully. You have a time during the day when I could trouble you to reserve a lane for her? It'll be a Monday through Friday schedule, likely for six weeks."

More garbled words come from the other side of the phone. I don't even realize I'm craning forward, trying to make out the conversation. But Coach does and shoots me another glare as he leans away from me.

Once the call ends, his demeanor shifts to calm and collected. Honestly, it might be even scarier than when he was upset.

"Well, Sutherland, it's settled. You'll be doing your practices at the campus rec center for the next six weeks, starting the first week of September."

"Wait, what?!" I shoot out of the chair, raising my voice. "The rec center?"

Nodding his head, he motions for me to sit back down. I ignore his stupid gesture and step closer to his desk. "Why can't I do my rehab and PT at the student athlete center?"

"*Why?* Do you really need me to answer that?" The curtness in his voice is making my blood boil. I've swam for Coach Bradford since I started at Everson University as a freshman. Our relationship has always been great, but now he's treating me like some transfer who just started this year. Then it hits me.

"You don't want me with the team. You think my injury will cast a bad light on our program because I got hurt at a party. So, what, you're banishing me to the rec center?" I scoff as the words leave my mouth.

"You're lucky I don't just end your final season right now. You *are* the standard. You set the bar for the rest of your teammates. And this situation here?" He uses his pointer finger to draw circles in the air around my sling. "This 'accident' is unacceptable. Look, Sutherland, I'm sorry you're injured, but I expected better from you."

There it is. The final blow that has me cowering away from his desk towards the door. Coach doesn't try to stop me, but makes one more remark before I'm bursting out of his office into the hallway.

"Check in with Pierce Harding at the training center going forward. He'll be your point of contact, getting messages from me to you, and vice versa. I need some time to rework the upcoming meets." He shakes his head, turning to his computer and dismissing me.

I make it into the hallway before turning the corner, colliding with a trash can I desperately need. As I empty the contents of my stomach, tears burn my eyes. I've never felt like this before. I don't know what's happening to me.

How in the hell am I supposed to survive the next six weeks?

ONE

OFF MY GAME

SHEP

"Shep…Shep!" A voice startles me in my chair and I realize I must have dozed off for a few seconds. I straighten up and clear my throat before looking down, seeing one of my co-workers, Max, standing next to my lifeguard stand.

"Yeah, what's up?" I scan the pool area and thankfully nobody is in the water. Luckily, the rec center is pretty dead around this time of the day. But still, it's not like me to fall asleep on the job. It's also not like me to have night after night of tossing and turning, but here we are.

"Just wanted to let you know Tom is coming around today, so maybe you should get a Red Bull or something so you're not caught slacking on the job." A small smirk appears on Max's face before fading away then his tone becomes more serious. "What's going on? You haven't been on your game lately."

As I go to respond, the answer to his question walks out of the locker room and onto the pool deck. He follows my gaze before laughing. "Well, never mind the Red Bull. That right there is enough to keep you awake." He walks off, snickering, and I feel a burning in my chest. He isn't wrong, but it bothers me that my interest isn't the only one that's been piqued since Harlow Sutherland started practicing at our pool.

In my defense, I've never seen a body as perfect as Harlow's in that jet black race suit she wears to swim laps in. It also doesn't help that she has golden blonde hair and sparkling emerald eyes that you can see even from a distance. Okay sure, maybe I'm biased because I have a thing for female athletes, but she really is the most gorgeous girl on campus.

I watch as she gets ready to start her practice. She's been swimming here for three weeks now, yet every time she comes in, I still have to prevent myself from tracking her every movement to soak up her appearance.

Tom, the building manager, told all of us at the end of August that she'd be swimming here. She's rehabbing her shoulder and we were instructed to reserve a lane for her, Monday through Friday, 4:30 to 5:30 PM.

Rumor has it, she was drunk and fell. One of my buddies who lifeguards at the rec and the athletic center told me her coach basically exiled her here since so many people saw her at the party when it happened. The guy's probably trying to save face but kind of seems like a dick move. Especially for someone like Harlow.

I did my research after Tom made the announcement. I know her race times. She's crazy talented and one of the fastest on our college's team. She carries the team in the 200 Medley Relay as their third leg and butterfly swimmer. I was mesmerized as I watched footage of her previous races. The way she propels herself out of the water during her races shows incredible strength. So yeah I understand why the swim coach is pissed that she's hurt but still, he couldn't show her a little grace?

Somehow, all of my lifeguard shifts overlap with her practice schedule and now I feel like I know her better than anyone which is maybe why I wish someone would've shown her some kindness with all this. I have to see her struggle trying to swim again. I have to watch her get frustrated when she can't fully push herself out of the pool. Hell, I even caught her crying once during some of her physical therapy stretches. I've probably witnessed a more vulnerable side of her than most people in her life. Okay, well I don't know about that, but there's definitely something about seeing this worn down version of her that feels oddly intimate.

Especially because she's one of the black sheep on campus, always keeping to herself. Maybe that's what makes her so interesting. She's caught my eye on campus a few times over the last couple years and again when we had a lecture together once or twice. Not many people know too much about her, other than her role as a student athlete and Beckett's *sometimes* girlfriend. He's one of my fraternity brothers, and for the life of me, I can't figure out what she sees in that guy. But outside of all that, I really can't say too much about her.

So maybe it's a little bold of me to feel like I get her, but there's a connection there I just can't explain. Something drawing me to her.

"Can I help you?" a voice catches me off guard.

"Oh, shit. No, sorry," I reply quickly, shifting my weight in my lifeguarding chair before looking down only to be met with a burning stare from none other than Harlow herself.

"Well, you've been staring at me the entire time I've been here. It's kinda fucking creepy."

Leave it to me to zone out while staring at her during her practice. Not even realizing she's out of the pool and walking right up to my stand.

I'm definitely off my game.

TWO

I LOVE THIS

HARLOW

Five more laps. Five more laps and I'm one practice closer to being back with the team.

I touch the side of the pool and look up at the giant clock on the wall. I'm already twenty seconds ahead on my interval laps, so I take a moment to prop my arms up on the edge of the tile, pull my goggles onto my forehead, and reach for my bottle.

I pour a little water in my mouth and let the rest dribble down my chin and onto my chest. Despite swimming for almost an hour, the water doesn't feel cool anymore, making the contrast of the iced, bottled water refreshing. I close my eyes as the water around me sloshes and my mind starts to drift.

I remember my first swim lesson. My mom thought it would be a good idea if I found a fun little hobby because apparently I was a "busy child." Dad wasn't around much with his job, so I think Mom was just looking for a way to keep me out of the house for an extra hour after school. I chuckle to myself while the memories play in my head. Little Harlow, who never listened to the lifeguard's whistles and ran to jump into the pool head first every time I got there.

Mom got her wish, though. At eight years old I found my love for swimming, which turned into endless practices and hours out of the house. So much for just finding a hobby. Swimming became my life.

I take another sip of my water and return my mind to the present. The clock is coming up on the fifteen-second mark, so I set the bottle down and pull my goggles back on before taking a deep breath, sinking underwater. My feet find the wall and I push off into a streamline position. After a few dolphin kicks to further myself in the lane, I break the surface and take my first breath of air. I turn my head back into the water and start swimming freestyle to finish up my workout.

I toy with the idea of maybe trying my butterfly again, but I know that if I keep trying to rush it, it will only take longer for my shoulder to heal. Not to mention the last time I tried it was embarrassing, at best. I should just be grateful those miserable two weeks of being stuck in a sling are over. Not being able to do anything but minimal lower body strength training and cardio was torture.

I reach the end of the lane and do a few extra kicks before pulling my arms to my side and doing a flip turn, making my way to the other end of the pool. I love this. I love the quietness of the water, how it shuts out everything but my own breathing and thoughts. I can get lost in my own mind during these workouts and it only makes time go by faster.

After a few more strokes, I glide through the water to the wall and pull the rest of my body to the edge. Glancing up at the clock, I smirk to myself for finishing early yet again. Four laps later, my final touch of the smooth, tiled wall ends today's practice. I pull my goggles off and set them on the edge before taking a deep breath of air, going underwater. While submerged, I pull my swim cap off and let my long, blonde hair free.

This is another favorite feeling of mine. The rush of water through my hair is the best cool down. When I break the surface, I prop my arms up on the edge of the pool and look around to make sure no one has their eyes on me.

This is the part I don't like. This is the part I hate.

Among the other things I haven't been able to do recently, it's been a feat in itself to get out of the water. I used to be able to push myself up and out in one quick move, but now I have to use my good arm to start the process before basically lobbing the rest of my body forward and onto the pool deck.

When I realize nobody is paying attention to me, I toss my cap and goggles towards the base of the swim block and shimmy myself out. Once I make it onto the edge, I let my legs dangle in the water for a few more seconds.

I close my eyes, trying to shut out flashbacks from the last few weeks. The yelling of Coach Bradford when I told him I was injured. The looks from my teammates when Coach told them all I was going to be out from September to mid-October. The passing stares from the rec center workers when I showed up for my first week of rehab practices.

I know what they all think of me. I know what people say about me on campus. It's hard enough being a college athlete. Factor in being a female college athlete? Every misstep, every mistake, is put on an even bigger display. I think my favorite encounters, though, are with the people who are just innocently blunt and make comments like, "Aren't you that swimmer girl who got drunk at the Chi Kappa frat house and hurt your shoulder?"

At first it really bothered me. I kept experiencing the same feeling I had in Coach's office—heat rushing into my cheeks, my ears ringing, and my chest tightening. According to Google, it's a panic attack, but I refuse to accept that. So I've just told myself over and over that I don't care. It works. Sometimes. Until I find myself needing to throw up. But whatever, until I'm back with my team, my plan is to just dismiss the rumors, laugh at the comments, and ignore the stares.

Speaking of stares, how long has that stupid lifeguard been looking at me? I turn and glance over my shoulder to see if there's someone behind me or something else catching his eye, but nope. Just me.

This isn't the first time I've caught him watching me. At first I thought it was a coincidence that he'd already been looking at me when I looked his way. But no, it was not a coincidence. He's got a staring problem and today, I've had enough. Not to mention, he already saw me cry last week during some of my stretches for PT.

I grab my water bottle, swim cap, and goggles then stand up and walk over to the back wall where I put my swim bag and towel. I throw my items in the bag then wrap the towel around myself. Glancing back over at the lifeguard stand, *pool boy* is still glazed over, looking in my direction.

I huff and grab all of my belongings before marching up to his stand. I get to the base of the steps leading up to the chair and come straight out with it.

"Can I help you?"

He shifts quickly in his chair and blinks a few times as if coming back to reality. "Oh, shit. No, sorry. "

"Well, you've been staring at me the entire time I've been here. It's kinda fucking creepy." I cross my arms, eyeing him up and down.

"Staring? At you?" He stumbles over his words before running his hand through his dirty blonde hair. "No, I was definitely not staring at you."

I raise my eyebrows and let my arms fall down to my sides. "Right, okay. You could at least have some sort of excuse other than *no*." I turn to start walking away towards the locker room when I'm stopped in my tracks.

"It's Harlow, right?" His voice is soft, making me feel like I'm hearing my name for the first time. I'm so used to only being referred to by my last name when I'm swimming.

Spinning around on my heels, I take a few steps back towards his stand as he climbs down, meeting me on the pool deck.

"Yes?" I respond with an edge in my voice. Whatever he has to say about me, about why I'm swimming here, I'm not up for it. I may have just asked him to give me a reason for why he was staring, but I don't actually want to hear it.

Imagine my surprise when instead of offering me some

half-ass answer, he reaches out towards my shoulder before stopping about halfway, bringing his hand to his pocket.

My breath catches and I take a step back, needing some space from whoever this guy is. I don't know him. I've seen him around the fraternity house, so I assume he's also a brother. And unfortunately, he always works when I have to practice.

"Sorry," he mumbles before running his other hand down his face.

"For?" My heart's now pounding and the thin swimsuit I'm wearing likely isn't hiding the intense rise and fall of my chest. Luckily, my hard workout is an easy excuse for that.

"Honestly, I don't know what I'm doing." He laughs to himself and I can't help but notice the softest dimples in his cheeks. "I just wanted to say I'm sorry you're injured."

His words catch me off guard and my mouth falls open a little. Here I was assuming he was also a part of the rumor mill. "Wait, what?" I try to respond, but only a dry whisper comes out. The sincerity in his voice makes my legs feel weak.

He takes another step towards me, this time with more confidence. Not in an intimidating type of way, more like with a gentle determination. He reaches out and touches my injured shoulder. The second his skin grazes mine, I realize I'm holding my breath and also not moving away from him. Why am I not moving away from him?

"I said…" He stops and lightly runs his thumb over the curve of my shoulder before withdrawing his hand. I wince at his touch and he looks at me with a strange expression. It's not pity or judgment, it's almost like a genuine curiosity. "I'm sorry you hurt your shoulder. I saw some of your race videos. I know it can't be easy having to practice away from your team, on top of not being able to compete," he says.

My mind has gone blank. I think I've blinked now maybe four times in a row before I realize I need to respond. "Uh, thanks," I get out before looking down at his hand that was just on my shoulder and then back up to meet his eyes. "Wait, you know my name, why don't I know yours?" I reply quickly. *Smooth, Harlow. So smooth.*

He smirks then turns around, walking back towards his stand. I'm absolutely dumbfounded right now. He's just going to walk away? More importantly, why do I care?

He makes it up to his chair then turns to look at me. "Maybe because Harlow Sutherland doesn't know everything like she thinks she does," he says, grinning.

His response has me shaking my head as I turn around myself, making my way to the locker room to rinse off and change.

Was that real?

THREE

"DISASTEROLOGY" BY PIERCE THE VEIL

HARLOW

I let the water from the shower run over my body without even realizing it's essentially scalding my skin. My mind hasn't stopped reeling since that dumb lifeguard decided to touch me, let alone speak to me. Then to not tell me his name?

I decide I've let this man occupy my thoughts for long enough. Turning off the shower, I dry off then find my locker and grab my black overnight bag that doubles as my practice bag.

I wring out my hair, twisting it up into a bun before throwing on my jean shorts, Doc Marten boots, and an oversized Everson University sweatshirt and tossing everything else into my duffle. As I sling my bags over my good shoulder, my flippers poke me in the neck making me flinch and sending a shooting pain throughout my bad shoulder. Like a reflex, I drop all my bags.

Whispers come from behind me, so I close my eyes and

rest my forehead against the cool locker. I know what's happening and this is the last thing I want to deal with right now.

Spinning around, I smile at the few girls who are now murmuring amongst themselves and do a friendly wave. "I'm fine, thanks." I bend down and grab my bags again then quickly make my way out of the locker room.

Before the door shuts, I hear faintly from behind me, "Can you imagine? Going from, like, the top swimmer to not even being able to carry your own bags? All because you got too drunk at a party?"

I push myself off the wall I didn't know I was clinging to and make my way out to my car. Tears sting the edges of my eyes but I refuse to let them fall. I open the door of my gray Bronco, tossing my bags in before climbing into the driver's seat. Leaning against the headrest and closing my eyes, I reach out towards my passenger seat for the soft fabric of my childhood blanket that I drive with. If anyone asked, I'd tell them it's an old towel. But the truth is, after I got hurt, I started bringing it with me as a piece of comfort.

As much as I wanted to act like coming to the rec and swimming again was easy for me, in the beginning it wasn't. It made me uncomfortable to feel like some spectacle that people stopped and stared at. After the first week of rehab practices, I decided to do a deep dive online about getting through injuries as an athlete and read an article about the emotional damage it can cause as well. Not being able to do what you love is harmful enough, then factor in my circumstances and, yeah, let's just say I could definitely feel the damage. I'm not one to really pay attention to my feelings, but the stuff I read made sense.

The article mentioned having something tangible that brought me peace could be helpful. I'm sure they were referring to like a stress ball or whatever, not a childhood blankie, but oh well. Honestly, it doesn't even matter because right now it's not soothing me.

Opening my eyes, I let out a large exhale before glaring down at my arms then sit up and grip the steering wheel with my good hand, letting out a strangled scream. I rest my forehead against where my horn is and hit it out of frustration, a few honks sounding off in rhythmic response. Chuckling, to myself, I pop back up to look around and see a few heads turning my direction. *Fuck this.*

I clip my seatbelt into place before peeling out of the parking lot. I roll down my window and press play on the only song I know will help me express these feelings. "Disasterology" by Pierce the Veil blares through the speakers and I allow myself to sink into the lyrics during the short drive home and forget about all the bullshit from the last hour.

As I pull into the Overlook Apartments, I look around and take in the mountain scenery. Everson University is known for a lot of things but being nestled in the North Carolina mountains is definitely at the top of the list. I'm not complaining, it certainly is pleasing to the eye.

I shut off my Bronco and grab my bags before making my way to my unit. As I slide my key into the lock, I hear movement beyond the door letting me know my best friend is home too. I push into the apartment and am greeted with a very loud, "LOW-LOW!"

I don't know how many times I can argue against that nickname but if it makes my best friend happy, then I will continue to let it roll off my shoulders, among many other things.

"Lennyyy…" I whimper out in a failed attempt to match her enthusiasm as I kick the door shut behind me and walk into the kitchen to meet her.

"Uh, that's it?" She stands there with her hands up in the air—a spatula in one, a glass of wine in the other.

"Yes, Lennon. That's it." I turn out of the kitchen and start towards my room, dropping my bags on the floor in the process.

"Whoa, no way José. What's wrong?"

Apparently I didn't get out all my frustration in the car ride home because I spin around and force out between clenched teeth, "They were talking about me again in the locker room."

Lennon drops her hands, setting down her wine glass and the spatula before rushing over, wrapping her arms around me without hesitation. "Those bitches. Who was it? Do you know?"

I groan at the pressure she puts on my shoulder. She steps back and leans to kiss me on the forehead. "I'm sorry. It's just a few more weeks at the rec center then you will be back with me and the rest of the team."

I shrug my shoulders as best as I can then turn back around and walk into my room. Lennon is right. The only thing standing between me and the much needed end of all this gossip is just a few more weeks. Well, that's if I pass my PT evaluations.

Lennon must be back at it in the kitchen because I hear a crackling sound and a small shriek. I close my eyes and laugh to myself. Lennon is a lot of things; my best friend, my roommate, my teammate, my confidant, but she's NOT a good cook. She tries though, I'll give her that, but most of the time it ends like it will tonight—me taking over and her hopping up onto our counter, sitting criss-cross applesauce, drinking her glass of wine while watching.

What's really funny about Lennon not being able to cook is that she's Italian. She grew up in a house where home cooking was introduced to her when she was basically a toddler. She does know how to boil noodles and add jarred pasta sauce to a dish, but that's about the extent of her cooking knowledge.

Me? My dad taught me to cook when I was in high school and had to start following meal plans during race season. At first it felt like a chore, but it quickly became something I looked forward to when I realized all the different variations of meals I could make. Even though I'm less than an hour away from home, I still miss him, and being able to cook some of the meals we made together gives me the feeling that I'm back with him in the kitchen.

Lennon has been benefiting from my cooking skills since high school, when we first met. We didn't attend the same school because she lived just outside of Everson Valley, but I was fortunate enough to have met her on our year round swim team when we were fourteen. We've been inseparable since.

I start to walk into my bathroom and pull out the messy bun on top of my head, when my phone goes off. I roll my eyes. This is the last person I have patience for, but if I ignore them, it'll only make things worse.

BECKETT

You still coming to our party tomorrow
night?

I need a date

I place my phone down on the counter and get back to work on my tangled hair. I know I shouldn't even be going over to the Chi Kappa house with all the gossip of my injury but I also know that Beckett won't take no for an answer. Not another second passes and I'm texting back as if operating on auto-pilot.

Yeah, sure.

I toss my phone behind me onto the cream comforter that encases my bed and take in my reflection in the mirror.

I look at myself, my shoulder, and tears start to prick the surface again. As if Lennon can sense what's going on, she pops her head into my room. "Hey Low—oh, hey, shhh." She rushes over and pushes my knotty hair out of my face before running her thumb over my cheek where a single tear has betrayed me. "What's going on?" Her voice is so tender it makes me want to cry harder.

I reach up, putting my hand over hers and move it off, giving it a small squeeze. "Nothing," I offer, but she doesn't seem convinced so I add on, "Today's practice was just hard and hearing those girls talk about me getting hurt just made the sting worse. And then *he* had to touch me and apol—"

"I'm sorry, back up. *He?*" She looks at me with wide brown eyes.

Shit.

I stumble over my words trying to cover my slip up but Lennon stands in front of me now with crossed arms, tapping her foot.

"Try again," she responds with a bite to her tone.

I look around the room searching for anything to focus on other than my best friend who is growing more impatient at my lack of response. Side stepping her, I make it to the edge of my bed and plop down.

"Do you know that blonde lifeguard at the rec center?" I groan.

This gets her attention and before I can blink, she's next to me on the bed. "Oh my gosh."

"I'll take that as a yes," I retort before laying back on my comforter and staring at the ceiling.

Long brown hair is now dangling in my face as she hovers over me with the most demanding look. I swat at her hair before sitting back up and facing the wall.

"He's always staring at me and today I decided I was done with it. He was basically watching me the entire time I was there so when I finished my practice, I walked over to his stand to confront him."

This has Lennon jumping off my bed and turning on me faster than a cheetah going after its prey. "You did, WHAT?!" The last word echoes in my room as her voice raises to a shrill pitch.

"I confronted him!" I say before lifting my hands up and slapping them down on the tops of my thighs, falling back onto my bed again.

"I heard you! But what did you say?!" The urgency in her tone makes me laugh. I peer up over my nose and she's standing in front of me now with her hands on her hips in a way that says, *Uh hello? I'm waiting!*

"I asked him if I could help him with something because he was clearly staring at me and it was creeping me out." I squint as I finish my sentence, bracing myself for her response, as it likely won't be gentle.

"Harlow! For heaven's sake! You can't just march up to people and accuse them of things like that!" She pushes her hands through her hair before looking at me, the smirk reappearing on her face. "Well, what did he say?"

"He denied looking at me," I say with a blank expression. "But then he got off his stand and…" My voice trails off as the memory flashes in my mind again.

"And, what? Harlow! Get out with it!" Lennon claps her hands in my direction.

"He said he was sorry!" I roll over on my stomach, burying my face into my comforter in hopes I can hide the blush creeping into my cheeks as I finish my sentence. "He said he was sorry I was injured and then rubbed his thumb over my hurt shoulder." The confession is muffled by my mattress but doesn't prevent Lennon from hearing every single word.

I feel a light tap on my butt and roll back over as Lennon sits next to me and looks down at my flushed cheeks. "Low, babe. That's…"

"Shocking?" I fill in for her, sitting up but not meeting her gaze. "Freakish?"

"Well, it's those things for sure, but what I was going to say was kind. Thoughtful?" Lennon lays down and we turn on our sides to face each other.

"Don't get ahead of yourself, because when I asked him

for his name after I realized I didn't know it, even though he clearly knew mine, he wouldn't tell me." I huff.

"Wait, what do you mean he knows your name but you don't know his?" Lennon raises her eyebrow.

"That was how he started the conversation after I confronted him on his stand! He hopped down and followed after me, then said, 'You're Harlow, right?' Which actually, now that I think about it, tells you right there he *is* watching me."

"Or he knows who you are because everyone on campus knows who you are?" Lennon offers in response.

I scowl back at her. "Okay, fine. Well either way, after he made that oddly kind gesture, I asked for his name and he wouldn't give it to me."

Lennon stands up and for a moment I think she's about to join me in my little rage fest. Instead, she's the second person to shock me today. "Good," she says, then walks towards the kitchen before calling out, "Come on Harlow, dinner won't finish itself and we both know I'm done cooking."

My mouth falls open, just like it did only an hour or so before, but I stand up and follow her into the kitchen.

FOUR

"DADDY'S HOME."

SHEP

I look down at my watch and sigh in relief that I only have thirty more minutes left of my shift before I get to go home and act like I didn't touch *the* Harlow Sutherland today after her practice. Mondays typically drag, but this one in particular is taking its sweet fucking time.

I don't know what possessed me to follow her off my stand but then to *touch* her? I couldn't help it though, it's like my arm moved on its own. It probably confirmed every thought in her mind that I'm some creep who just sits here and watches her. I meant what I said about being sorry she was hurt and couldn't race, but I had no intention of then reaching out to touch her injured shoulder.

I blame the doe-like eyes she gave me after I made my apology. She looked so sad and delicate, which was quite the contrast to her fiery comments. Her subtle wince as I grazed over her soft skin was enough to let me know I made a mistake.

"Hey, Shep!" a gruff voice calls out behind me. I turn around to see Wes walking up to me. If there's anything that eases the torture that is Mondays, it's sharing a shift with one of my best friends.

"Yeah man, what's going on?" I shoot back.

"You going to the date party tomorrow for your frat?" He makes it to the edge of my stand and whips my calf with the rope of his whistle.

"FU—" I rub at my now stinging leg. "I haven't decided yet. Why, you wanna go?"

Wes didn't rush our freshman year because he's attending Everson on scholarship, but we got paired as roommates and he became my forever plus-one after I got initiated into Chi Kappa. Sophomore year we lived together again on campus and the man became more of a brother than my fraternity ones. Then junior year was an absolute shit show. I tried to live at the fraternity house and quickly realized I only liked seeing those guys during our events and not every day, so I threw in the towel on that and decided to get a place with Wes for our last year of college. Best decision I ever made.

"Yeah, actually. I heard some of the swim team is going to be there and I've had my eye on a brunette I saw at the meet last month who happens to be in my senior thesis group." He smirks.

My ears perk up at this, wondering if that means Harlow will be there. I considered she might because of Beckett, but now there's an even higher chance. All too quickly-and loudly-I reply, "Yes. Yeah, let's go."

Wes gives me a funny look before another sly grin

appears on his face. "Your sudden enthusiasm wouldn't have anything to do with a certain *blonde* swimmer would it?"

"Good one," I deadpan.

Wes cocks an eyebrow and I know he doesn't believe me, but he chooses not to argue, chuckling instead as he heads back over to his stand across the pool.

———

I pull into the driveway of my townhouse and turn off the ignition. Do I really want to see Harlow tomorrow? I haven't stopped replaying our conversation and the more I think about it, the more I feel like an idiot. I don't know if not telling her my name was my best move. She could actually not care.

My thoughts are interrupted by the ringing of my phone.

"Hey Mom, perfect timing."

"Oh? How's that, Son?"

"I was lost in thought and you called me just in time to stop it. What's going on? Everything okay?"

"Yes, I was just calling to see if you had figured out your senior thesis yet. Your father and I were talking about it last night over dinner."

"Thanks, Momma, but I haven't decided on anything yet. I just know that I need to find something by December."

"Alright sweetie, well if you need me you just call."

"Okay, I will. Love you, Mom."

"I love you, my Shepherd boy."

The line clicks and my head feels clear already. A text message pops up almost instantly.

MOM

Oh, and you stay out of that head of yours.

Tell Wesley that I send my love.

I shake my head. That woman would claim Wes as her own if she could. Grabbing my bag, I jump out of my truck and slam the door behind me. That sound alone grants me a small howl from beyond the front door. "Yes, yes. Daddy's home," I call out, opening the door to be greeted by the sweetest fur baby I know.

I set my stuff down then kneel to Dahlia's level and give her much needed pets and rubs. At the beginning of the year, the fraternity hosted a giveback with the local shelter and this little lady caught my eye. The organization told me she was their longest resident, having been brought in when she was two and is now four years old.

It's not hard to figure out why. Dahlia may be mixed but she's mostly a pitbull. The reputation of her breed preceded any opportunity for someone to take the time to meet her and realize she's the most loving dog. Not to mention, a total baby. If she isn't sleeping with me, she's sleeping in Wes's bed. She craves physical affection and maybe that's why we get along so well.

I turn the corner into my bedroom and drop my stuff. Wes isn't home yet, but he let me know he was heading somewhere to prep for one of his exams after he finished up his shift. The guy never stops studying.

Dahlia jumps up on my bed and starts to whine, already

craving my attention again. "I know baby, just give me one second."

A huff comes from her floppy lips. Laughing, I turn back around and grab a pair of sweats from my drawer and change out of my swim trunks and lifeguarding shirt into the familiar soft material. I don't bother putting anything else on, sweatpants and no shirt is my natural state.

Running a hand through my wavy hair, I face Dahlia and her tail wags in anticipation for what's to come: the daily debrief.

"Alright, so let's see…" I head over to my bed and sit down next to her. She nuzzles into my side as I start to reel off the formalities. "Breakfast was fine, you know that, we ate together. Class wasn't bad. Work was, well, more interesting than normal. I actually talked to Harlow today."

I soften my voice as I say Harlow's name and my dog's ears perk up and she tilts her head. Of course Dahlia recognizes the change in my tone when I say Harlow. It's not like I talk about her almost every day or something.

"Yeah, I know don't give me that look." I gather her smooshy face in my hands and give her a kiss on her forehead. "Nobody will ever replace you. My first true love. My Dahlia girl."

As I'm continuing my baby talk, I hear the front door swing open and Wes calls out, "Daddy's home!"

Dahlia jumps off the bed to go greet him and I holler after her, "Traitor!"

Wes's laugh booms through the town house as he saunters towards the middle of the living room where I can see him through my door frame. Dahlia's rubbing against his calves like a damn cat.

"What's that about a traitor, hm? Don't be upset that Dahlia recognizes I'm the real man of the house."

"Oh fuck off." I walk out into our living room and plop down on the couch. "Where'd you end up at once you left the rec?"

Wes shifts uncomfortably and turns to go put his things down.

"Whoa, hold up. What aren't you telling me?" I lean forward, resting my elbows on my knees and study him pensively.

He spins around and lets out a loud sigh. "I went to Boulder Brewing Co. and Beckett was there with some of your frat brothers."

"Okay, and?" I raise my eyebrows as I await for whatever nugget of drama he has for me.

"He was talking about your girl." Wes walks over and mirrors my position on the opposite couch.

"First off, not my girl. Second off, why are you being so weird about this?"

He reaches out and starts rubbing Dahlia, which I know is his way of putting a buffer into the conversation.

"He was talking about the date party and, well, I guess Harlow is going with him."

"Right," I deadpan. "Well, they must be dating again. Maybe when they're on another break and he's entertaining his newest flavor of the week, I can see if she's into me. Besides, I just talked to her for the first time today, it's not like she'd just agree to go with me anyways."

Wes coughs like he's choking before stammering out, "I'm sorry? You talked to her today? And you didn't think to mention this to me at the pool? Honestly, man. It's like we're not even friends sometimes!"

"Don't be so dramatic. Yeah, we talked. She apparently finally caught onto the fact that I've got a habit of keeping an eye on her when she's at the rec center." I avoid looking at him.

Wes laughs, "Keeping an eye on her, is that what we're calling it? Talk about the understatement of the century."

"Oh, give it a rest. We get it. You know I'm into her. "

"Well I'm glad you're able to cut the bullshit about it with me. All I really wanted to say was, if I'm being honest, I'm with you about Beckett. The guy's a fucking prick and I don't know how you deal with him being in your fraternity."

"I don't. Remember?" I spread my arms out in front of me, gesturing to him that I'm here with him and not living at the frat house where I had a front row seat to Beckett's lack of loyalty. Wes nods his head in silent understanding.

"Oh, by the way," I start, " Momma Fords told me to give you her love."

Wes slaps his hand on his chest. "Be still my heart. I love that woman."

"Yeah, yeah. We know. You're her favorite." I roll my eyes.

"Hey! At least you know." He stands up and starts to head towards his room before looking back over his shoulder and giving me a wink. "Don't hate the player, hate the game. Hey by the way, were you planning to wear a suit tomorrow?"

"Uh, I hadn't really thought about it yet." Dahlia jumps up next to me on the couch and lays her head on my lap. "Why?"

"Oh, I just didn't know if you were planning on trying to impress Harlow or not." A sly grin sneaks up on his face.

"Or, you're trying to impress the brunette you mentioned earlier and don't want to get dressed up by yourself?" I shoot him a glare.

"I actually don't know what you're talking about and I resent that presumption." He puffs out his chest and leans against his door frame.

"Okay scholarship boy, cool it with the proper talk. I'll wear a suit with you tomorrow. But NO tie."

Wes closes his eyes and makes a fist before letting out a hushed, "Yes," as he shakes his hand in the air triumphantly.

He turns and goes back into his room, kicking the door shut behind him. Wes and I might argue like brothers, but he's my best friend and I'd do anything for that fucker, even wear a damn suit.

FIVE

NOPE

HARLOW

I wake up and my stomach's already in knots. The whining of my alarm in the background is nagging, but my mind is caught between reality and the dream I was just having of me swimming at the last national race I won. I can still hear the echoes and faint roar of the crowd cheering for me so I close my eyes, drifting back into some disoriented version of sleep, and feel the lull of nostalgia rocking me back into my dreams.

My memories envelop me and I can't escape how much I miss life before my injury. The last few weeks, while necessary, have been awful. Lennon and I don't get to spend as much time together and I didn't realize how much it's affecting me until this last week when I was driving home from the rec and the silence in my car was deafening.

Lennon and I had this routine. We would wake up, make breakfast together—eggs and a smoothie for me, coffee and a breakfast sandwich for her—then sit in the living room and go over our days while we ate. We both had morning classes, so we would ride together to campus. After they were over, we'd head to the athletic center early to do a light jog around the indoor track before making our way into the locker room to change for swim practice.

Lenny does her best to remind me that this is temporary, and while she doesn't contribute to the rumors and gossip, she also hasn't made an effort to ask me about that night. I think she knows the physical hurt is enough and doesn't want to add to any emotional hurt, but still, it would be nice if she asked.

The only person who has even remotely shown interest in how things might be affecting me is the lifeguard. Which is a train of thought I've been fighting. The few times I have though, left me in a state of heated disarray and confusion. Even now, the image of his face in my mind causes my heartbeat to move down between my legs.

NOPE.

I snap open my eyes and shut off my alarm. Swiping out of the screen, I go to the call button, deciding maybe it's time I made the effort to let someone know I'm not doing okay and also, maybe to distract myself from thinking about that certain lifeguard.

There's only one person fit for that job in this season of my life and that's my older sister, Margot.

We're just shy of five years apart and not only is Margot a good sister, it's a blessing and a half that she's also a licensed psychologist and therapist. She also attended Everson for undergrad and graduate school before moving to open her own counseling practice a few towns over. She's struggled with some stuff of her own in the past so I actually feel like maybe she'd understand what I'm going through.

I've only talked to her once since everything happened. I pleaded with her to be the one to break the news to Dad about my injury and that I wasn't going to be out for a few months. I knew he wouldn't be upset with me, but I also didn't want to risk hearing any disappointment from him either. Coach Bradford was more than enough.

The line rings once before I hear Margot's chipper voice on the other line.

"Happy Tuesday, my little fish! How's my favorite sister?"

A small chuckle leaves my lips, bringing a momentary lightness to my chest. "You only have one sister, Margot."

"Well no need to squash the mood when the sun's just come up. What's going on though? You okay?"

I contemplate my next words. If I don't choose them wisely, they'll come out in a croak instead of the indifference I'm hoping for and she'll try and psychoanalyze me or some shit.

"I think I'm just nervous. I have my first check-in with Coach Bradford today. It's almost been four weeks of rehab practices and PT and, well, I just don't feel very confident. I don't know what he's going to be looking for to measure my progress. Outside of my ability to not drown."

This warrants a choking sound from Margot, as I assume she's taking a sip of her signature morning matcha and trying to stifle her laugh.

"It's fine, Mar, you can laugh."

"Okay, well it's not funny—you drowning. But obviously, yes, we know that isn't going to happen because you can swim. He hasn't given you any markers? Any sort of progress report?"

"No. I actually haven't even talked to him since I told him I was injured back in the middle of August. He sent me off to the sports medicine clinic to make sure my shoulder was back in place and didn't need surgery. I've been working with the athletic trainer, uh, Pierce? Pierce Harding?"

"Oh." Her voice trails off.

"You know, he told me that my last name was familiar to him."

"Yeah, I know him from when I went there."

There's an emotion to her voice that I can't figure out but I don't think now's the time to ask.

"Anyways, he's had me on a good schedule for practices and PT. I'd rather have my check-in today with just him but I guess Coach Bradford really is the only one who can give me the green light to start swimming with the team again."

"Well, I say just go into it with an open mind. Where is it being held?"

"The rec center where I've been practicing. So I'm guessing he wants to evaluate my stroke and make an assessment based on that. I've been doing really well with my stretches and the other strokes, but I haven't swam butterfly yet."

"I see. I think you're going to be okay, little fishy. But, just in case you don't feel like you will be, I'll text you some mindfulness practices I've been using with my patients lately. Keep you in the now, all that jazz."

"I'd love that. Hey, I've got a pretty good team here. You and Pierce, helping me get through this."

"Do not EVER lump me into the same category as that meathead."

The edge in her tone catches me off guard, and while I don't want to push, I can't resist one more little nudge.

"I mean, he's pretty hot…" I laugh into the phone as Margot huffs.

"Alright, I'm not entertaining this. You good? Because I do have an appointment coming up."

"Yep, I'm good. Just ready to get back in the pool and put all this behind me."

"Soon enough. But hey, be gracious with yourself."

"I'm trying. Love you, sissy."

"More."

As the line clicks, relief begins to wash over me. Margot's right. I know I'm making good progress and today should be a breeze. The moment of confidence ends as quickly as it began when I remember the Chi Kappa date party is tonight, and suddenly I'm pulling my pillow over my face, screaming as loud as I can into it.

———

I pull into the parking lot of the rec center and hop out of my Bronco before grabbing my bags and kicking the door shut behind me. Tucking my head down, I start to lose myself in thought when out of the corner of my eye, I see a truck coming and jump out of the way to avoid being run over.

"What the hell!" I shout, heat rushing into my cheeks when I realize that I wasn't actually in any danger and just yelled at a stranger.

The truck pulls into a spot near mine and a voice rings out behind me.

"Hey! Are you okay?"

I turn to see the one and only lifeguard of my night-mares jogging towards me. My mouth dries up immediately and my heart starts to quicken. He makes it just a few inches in front of me before I realize I haven't spoken or moved.

"Hey," he reaches out and lightly rubs his thumb against my cheek. "Harlow. Are you okay?"

The touch of his skin on mine sends a spark down to my core, jolting me back into reality.

"No, I'm not fine. Please don't touch me." The words come out harsher than I intend.

He recoils his hand, then takes a step back. "Seriously, I'm so sorry. I didn't think I was even close to you but damn, you must have been really distracted."

Squinting in disbelief, I look him over and realize he appears more disheveled than normal. Not that I take the time to assess how he looks, but it's clear to me something's amiss.

"Right… Well, slow down next time." Hell will freeze over before I admit that he wasn't anywhere near hitting me. I turn on my heels and make my way towards the rec, my ponytail swishing against my back. Then it dawns on me.

"Are y—Are you coming into work right now?" I spin back around.

Pool boy walks towards his truck, grabbing a backpack, before heading in my direction again. "Yeah, I am. Why?" He smooths out his clothes and it seems he isn't prepared to be on shift right now.

A frantic feeling begins to course through my body. "You don't usually work this hour. You… You shouldn't be here."

He cocks his head and one side of his mouth turns up

into a subtle grin. "You have my work schedule memorized, Harlow?"

Hearing him say my name again sends shivers down my back. "No," I refute quickly. "I just know that your shifts have overlapped with my practices so I assume that's when you work."

"Right," he says, drawing out the word to let me know he doesn't believe a word I'm saying.

"I'm serious." Putting my hands on my hips, I lift my chin up some to appear in control of the matter. "I just didn't expect you to be here right now."

"Well surprise. Once again, Harlow Sutherland doesn't know everything like she thinks she does."

"What does that even mean?" I shoot back at him, my eyes narrowing. "Huh? You think you know so much about me? Well you don't. You know nothing about me. So while I might not know everything, neither do you."

I storm off towards the rec center, fuming that he's here right now. I know he watches me. I know he pays attention to me, and now I will be under his gaze while I meet with Coach Bradford for my first check-in. I don't know which of the two I'm more unnerved by, but this is not the time to be distracted.

I turn the corner, pushing into the locker room. Another group of girls who seem to be leaving stop and look at me. Fear and concern flood into their eyes before they grab their stuff and rush out as if I just brought the plague into the room or something. I collapse onto the bench in the middle of the room and let my things drop to the floor. I'm so fucking tired of this judgment.

I finish putting my bags into the locker, then grab my

towel, goggles, swim cap, and water bottle. I close my eyes and take a few deep breaths, recalling the little tip Margot sent me after we ended our call.

All she said I have to do is breathe in my intentions and breathe out my fears.

Taking a deep breath in, I think to myself, *I believe I'm a successful swimmer.*

As I exhale, I think to myself again, *I release the fear I'll never swim again.*

I do this a few more times, repeating the same thoughts with every inhale and exhale, then make my way to the door. Cracking it open, I peer out and see Coach Bradford and Pierce already waiting for me on the bleachers.

I do another glance across the pool and see my least favorite lifeguard getting adjusted on his stand. Why am I so nervous that he's here? This should be like any other practice I've had in the past, minus the fact I'm currently injured. Whatever, I can do this. I just need to get myself out of this damn locker room.

SIX

TWO THUMBS UP

SHEP

I heard her before I saw her, and even when I finally realized the blonde yelling at me was Harlow, nothing made sense.

I jogged over as quickly as I could but she stood there frozen as if in shock. I instantly thought, *Did she think I was going to hit her?* Trying to be gentle with her and bring her back to reality seemed like the wise choice, but, surprise, it backfired. Her freak out over my shift was just the icing on the whole fucking cake.

I continue musing to myself about the interaction from the parking lot as I put my stuff away in the office and make my way out to my stand.

It isn't until I make it to the ladder and climb up into my guarding chair that I see the reason why Harlow appeared so rattled in the parking lot. In the far corner, a man who I know to be Coach Bradford is sitting on the edge of one of the bleachers with some disgustingly buff looking guy who looks kinda familiar. They're talking to each other, looking at paperwork, then Coach Bradford checks the watch on his wrist.

When he looks up, I follow his stare to find a very sheepish looking Harlow about thirty feet from me, snaking her way out of the locker room onto the pool deck. Her eyes flit between the bleachers and me. She stops for a second, and I wonder if she's going to turn around. Then I see the rise and fall of her shoulders as she takes a deep breath, and her feet start moving in the direction of Coach Bradford and the other guy.

I have to admit, the contrast of this shy person in front of me versus the feisty one in the parking lot just minutes ago has me wondering if maybe the tough girl attitude is all a front. Maybe Harlow's attempts to be closed off is the armor she needs to protect herself. But from what?

She takes a few more steps, then stops one more time and glances back in my direction. I see panic and shame flooding her face. I screw my features up into a look of confusion, then it dawns on me a little too late. Her coach, the other guy—this must be some sort of evaluation and I'm here to see it.

I can't decide if I should just try and not pay attention or do something. I mean, I can't really do much other than leave my shift, but I got called in early for a double because someone else is sick so I know that's not actually an option. Guess I'll just try and ignore what's going on. After all, Harlow made it very clear in the parking lot that she wants me to leave her alone and stay in my lane.

And I'm about to do just that, except, when I glance

over again, there's a look of desperation in her green eyes that has me shaking my head, doing something I'm probably going to regret.

I blow my whistle and everyone looks in my direction, including Harlow. I motion for her to come over to my stand, her mouth falling open. I clear my throat and call out, "Excuse me, could you come over here please?"

Harlow whips her head around to ensure it's her I'm signaling to, then turns back in my direction and points her finger at herself. "Me?" she mouths.

I nod my head and look over at the direction of her coach and whoever else is with him. I couldn't care less what they think of me at this moment.

Harlow needs some rescuing and I just happen to be a lifeguard.

She looks over towards the bleachers, and her coach flicks his hand in the air giving her the go-ahead to come talk to me. Looking at me again, I can see the panic in her eyes, but she starts trudging towards me anyway.

I meet her at the bottom of the chair ladder and her face is twisted into a look of frustration and confusion.

"What the hell do you think you're doing?" Her voice comes out low as she clenches her teeth.

"I know," I say softly. "I know why you freaked out in the parking lot."

She straightens at this and crosses her arms. There's that armor. "Yeah, you almost hitting me—"

"Stop. Just stop, Harlow. We both know I wasn't even close to you. Something's happening today with your coach, isn't it? I know that's him over there."

I watch as the gears turn and it's like she's trying to

decide if she wants to fight me on this. I'm shocked though as her harsh expression falls and she whispers, "Yeah."

"And what? You don't want me here because…" I start.

"Because, nothing. I just wasn't expecting to see you here during all this." She waves her arm toward the water before meeting my gaze. "It's fine. I'm fine."

"No, you're not fine." I pause for a second, trying to gather my thoughts. "Harlow, you're right. I don't know everything about you, but the little I do know from observing you over the last few weeks leads me to believe you're off your game right now."

She glares, a devilish grin starting to form on her face. "So you have been watching me?" There's an edge in her tone that makes the blood rush straight between my legs.

"That isn't the point here." I move the bright red rescue buoy I wear around my shoulder to the front of my body, hiding what's growing in my shorts. "Look, I'm just trying to help you out. Can you tell me what's going on right now?"

She fidgets with the strap of her bathing suit, snapping the fabric on her skin. I can't help myself and reach out, stilling her hand with mine. She freezes, her eyes widening, and stares at me.

"Why do you do that? Always find a reason to touch me." I barely hear her soft voice. She looks down at my hand and then pries my fingers away.

"I'm sorry. I don't have an answer for you other than I just want to help. Is there anything I can do for you at this moment? Besides giving you these few minutes away from your Coach and…"

"Athletic trainer." She finishes my sentence for me.

"That's Pierce Harding. The A.T. for our swim team," she clarifies.

"Right, well, either way, can I help?"

As if she has a sudden realization her guard's been let down for too long, she snaps back into her cold demeanor and takes a step away from me.

"No. I'm fine. Thanks." She turns and walks back over to the bleachers.

"Whatever," I mutter under my breath as I climb back up onto my stand.

As I situate myself, I study her body language while she talks to her Coach and the athletic trainer. From where I am, it seems to be going well, but what do I really know?

Coach Bradford points to a piece of paper, Harlow nods her head, and Pierce stands up, moving towards her. I about jump off my stand when he places his palms on either side of her hips and runs his hands up her sides. She's looking up at the rafters, letting his hands touch her in ways I've only dreamt about.

She spins around and is now facing me. Pierce works his hands over her shoulder and down her arm. Her eyes feel like they're looking through me as he continues to massage her upper back and do small rotations with her arms. She looks so *lost*.

Pierce says something to Coach Bradford and he scribbles on his clipboard. Harlow looks scared and uncertain, sending an ache into my chest that I can't identify.

After a few more assisted stretches, she gets her cap and goggles before heading over to the swim block. She closes her eyes and her mouth is moving ever so slightly as if mumbling something to herself.

Coach Bradford stands up and walks to the edge of the pool with Pierce, then yells at Harlow to go ahead and get in the water. She flinches at his tone then looks my way again. I offer her a soft smile, giving her two thumbs up while nodding my head and, I'll be damned, her face softens and she nods her head in return.

Pulling her swim cap over her head, she slides her goggles on, and dives into the pool. I watch her streamline under the water for a few seconds before she breaks the surface and begins freestyle.

Her strokes are effortless and I'm lulled into a sense of peace watching her swim. It's like she was born to do this.

A few more minutes go by and Coach Bradford calls her to the edge of the pool. She wades over and her loud, "What?!" cuts through the silence of the rec center.

I can't help but lean forward, trying to make out the conversation between Harlow and her Coach. Even Pierce looks a little alarmed.

"You want to be back with the team?" I hear Coach Bradford respond, and it's less of a question than it is a threat.

Harlow shakes her head and smacks the water with her hand. What the hell?

Pierce steps forward and whispers something in Coach Bradford's ear. Offering no privacy for the conversation, Coach Bradford parrots what I imagine Pierce said, but in a louder voice. "Well, I need her ready!"

He's shaking his head now, walking back over to the bleachers grabbing his stuff. They've been here for maybe ten minutes and the guy is already calling it quits?

Pierce steps forward now and crouches down near

Harlow. I try to read his lips but it's no use. Harlow pulls off her cap and goggles, throwing them onto the pool deck, then sinks herself underwater.

I've watched her do this many times at the end of her practices, but she doesn't break the surface quickly like she usually does. Instead, I'm watching her sink lower and lower to the bottom of the pool from my chair. I stand up, peering out into the water. Pierce is also now looking over the edge into the pool, then looks back up at me. A flash of urgency strikes his face when the strangest noise emanates through the air. What sounds like a garbled scream rings out from under the water and bubbles quickly rise to the surface.

I'm not even thinking as I race down my ladder and charge towards these two assholes who have seemingly crushed Harlow's spirit.

"What the hell did you do, huh?" My voice is trembling with anger. I've never felt this level of protectiveness before except with my mom, and I'm still usually able to stay level-headed.

"Easy there, son. Who do you think you're talking to?" Coach Bradford snaps.

"You!" I shout back. "I'm talking to you!"

He walks up to me, just a few inches away from my face, puffing his chest out like he's some macho guy.

Pierce steps in between us, breaking the tension. "Whoa, hold on now. What's going on?"

"What's going on is whatever treatment you're showing your swimmer here is unacceptable!" I step away, walking to the edge of the pool just as Harlow's beautiful face pops out of the water.

I reach out and offer her my hand. To my surprise she

grabs on with her good arm, and lets me gently lift her out of the water. I guide her towards my chest, shielding her from the two dicks behind me. "Are you okay?"

Searching her face, I hope for some sort of emotion. Anything to let me know she's alright. Time stands still when she rests her forehead against my chest and quietly mumbles out, "No. He told me to swim butterfly and he knows I can't. It's way too soon."

Heat rises to my face as I turn back around, facing her coach and the A.T. again, keeping her hidden behind my frame. "I don't know what type of rehab plan this is, but I've been here every practice Harlow's had, and for her to work this hard to recover and be treated this way…"

"You're out of line," Coach Bradford barks at me. "What's your name, huh? I bet Tom would love to hear all about how one of his lifeguards is talking to a university coach. Don't think your boss will be too happy about that." He sticks his nose up after his remark, as if he thinks he has the upperhand.

Ha, if only he knew.

"Shep Fords," I respond with pride. He wants to try and bring Tom into this, I'll bring in someone even more important. "As in, Sheriff Ford's son. So yeah, go ahead and let Tom know about this and maybe I'll let my dad know about it too. I'd be happy to fill him in."

As I finish my sentence, a whisper tickles my back and I hear Harlow breathlessly mutter, "Shep."

The realization hits me, she still didn't know my name. What a perfect time for introductions.

My attention draws back to Coach Bradford who is

straightening up next to Pierce. "I see," he grits out. "Well I can still have a chat with Tom. Let's go, Harding."

The athletic trainer shifts his weight back and forth on his feet before turning and standing next to me. "Actually, I think I need to stay and work with Harlow some more. She's my priority and her recovery is my responsibility."

Coach Bradford's eyebrows raise almost to meet his hairline and he scoffs. "This has been a waste of my time. I told you she wasn't ready, Harding."

"And, I would just like to clarify once again, I never said she was ready to swim butterfly. I told you that I wanted to show you her progress, and, like Shep here has said, she's doing really well." Pierce finishes his sentence and Harlow moves out from behind the both of us to meet Coach Bradford's glare.

"I'm sorry the season hasn't started the way you thought it would. I know a lot of that's on me." Her voice waivers and it throws me off to see her usual sass nowhere to be found.

Coach Bradford shakes his head and walks past all three of us. Asshole.

"Harlow, I'm so sorry." Pierce is the first to speak up. "I had no idea he was going to ask you to swim fly. Even I know how ridiculous of an ask that is. I think starting the season with two losses already is just messing with him."

"I get it," Harlow clips, already pulling her mask back on. "We just need to train harder. I'll work on my stretches in the morning and night now, maybe double my swimming practices too." She turns to grab her belongings from the bleachers and pool deck, leaving her athletic trainer alone with me.

"Look, man," he starts.

"No, don't 'look man' me. I know you've been working with her outside the rec, but I've also been working every shift she's been here. What's her coach's deal? That was seriously fucked up." My temper is starting to rise again.

"I hear you. That's why I wanted to say, thank you." He responds quickly before I can cut him off. "I don't think Harlow has anyone in her corner through this besides me and maybe her sister. I don't know, she mentioned her a few times when I asked about her support system during one of our sessions." He stops and looks to make sure Harlow isn't within earshot. "I don't know if a lot of people have her back through this. I'm sure it's her doing, I think we can both agree she's got some serious walls up. Took me an entire week just to get her to tell me what her actual pain rating was." He shakes his head.

"I don't know her. At all, actually. But someone needed to be there for her just now." I'm coming down from the adrenaline and realizing exactly what I've done.

"Either way, man, she needed that. I'm Pierce Harding by the way," he offers his hand out to shake mine.

I grasp it and return the gesture, "Shep Fords, but you heard that."

"Yeah, your dad's a good man. I've met him a few times during board meetings. But look, you see Harlow pushing herself too hard, or something seems off? You let me know. I'm paired with her directly for her rehab and I'm on her side."

I nod my head, actually believing what he's saying. "Will do. Thanks."

He pats the side of my arm before walking in Harlow's

direction while I'm left to think over the last ten minutes and how I just went out of my way for a girl I hardly know, in a way I never have before.

What's going on with me? And why do I have no doubt I'd do it again?

SEVEN

COLD TILE

HARLOW

If I could sell my soul right now to disappear, I would. Seriously, who wants it?

Everything I feared might happen during this evaluation did, and then some. I'm starting to think I may be the unluckiest person alive.

Not only did Coach Bradford embarrass me, but my shadow who I now know is *Shep*, was present to witness all of it unfold.

"Hey, Sutherland?" Pierce catches up to me as I grab all my stuff.

"Hey! All good here." I'm sure the pep in my voice is less than convincing but at this current moment, I need to get the hell out of this rec center. I glance to the side to see Shep still in the same spot, looking me up and down as if I might fall apart at any given moment.

"Look, I just want to tell you again. I had no idea Bradford was going to pull that with you. It goes against the training and rehabilitation plan I wrote up for us, and you've seen that yourself, so I hope you believe me." A look of sadness washes over his face.

"I know," I say with a half smile. "You didn't fail me."

"Thanks, Sutherland."

Pierce drones on about our schedule for the next week following this shit show but all I can do is think about the small moment of time where I let my guard down and put my head against Shep's chest.

I know I'm allowed to be vulnerable and not be okay, but I didn't have it on my Harlow BINGO card that it would be with Shep. Especially after our previous little chats where he didn't even want to tell me his name.

"Does that work with you?" Pierce's voice cuts back in through my thoughts.

"Yeah, sounds good. Thanks." The words lazily leave my mouth as I push past him to approach the other person who came to my defense today.

"Shep, huh?" I cock my head to the side and pop my hip out as I wait for his response.

"Yeah," he laughs awkwardly, "not the best way to have introductions but now you know."

I cock my head the other way, taking in the guy standing before me. He isn't all that bad now that I'm not looking at him with darts shooting from my eyes.

He's definitely tall, probably 6'2". I continue scanning him over and damn, he's absolutely ripped. I'm talking abs cut by a chisel and a V-line peeking out from his swim trunks that makes my mouth go dry. His wavy hair looks soft and like it can't decide if it wants to be brown or blonde.

But what really has me raising an eyebrow is his soft blue eyes.

"Hello? Are you in there?" Shep's voice comes out muffled while I bring myself back to the present.

"Yep, all here. Anyways, thanks for," I turn around and draw circles in the air around the pool, "all that."

He laughs and runs a hand through his hair. The sound is comforting and for a moment, I find myself not annoyed by his presence or conversation and that sends warning signals quickly through my subconscious.

"You had me worried there for a second when you sank to the bottom of the pool. " His tone is cautious, like he knows he could be pushing it, but I can also see the worry in his eyes. "Is that something you do when you're over-whelmed?

How did he pick up on that?

"Only sometimes. Oddly enough, I've always enjoyed sitting at the bottom of the pool. Ever since I was a kid, it makes me feel like—"

"Nobody can get to you?" He finishes my sentence and my mouth hangs slack in shock.

"Yeah, something like that," I murmur before realizing it's been too long that my walls have been down. "Anyways, while it was nice what you did, I don't need you protecting me like that."

Shep scoffs and rolls his eyes. "Okay, Harlow. Back to this. I'll see you tonight." He turns around and walks back over to his stand and doesn't look my way again.

Tonight?

I close my eyes and let my head fall in defeat when I realize that, of course, Shep will be at the date party tonight.

Correction, I am definitely the unluckiest person alive. It's like I can't escape him and it both infuriates and interests me.

I start my walk back to the locker room when my stomach sinks. In the corner of the rec center is one of Beckett's friends and I know this isn't going to end well for me. I smile in his direction but he's already typing away on his phone and as soon as I make it into the locker room, I hear my own phone going off.

2 Missed Calls From Beckett

Perfect, just perfect. This is exactly what I need right now. I shoot him a text that I'll call him when I get home and pack all my shit up before walking out to my car. I sink into the driver's seat, the weight in my chest overwhelming me. I'm aching and not in the way I can just pop a few Tylenol.

I spend my drive back to the Overlook deep in thought over the last few weeks. I want to get home and talk to Lennon, but as I pull into the parking spaces in front of our building, I know none of that will happen. Beckett's already here, waiting for me.

I take a deep breath and get out of my car, walking in his direction. "Hey!" I try to muster up all the cheer I can. "What are you doing here? I thought we were going to meet at the Chi Kappa house for the date party tonight?"

"You have a lot of explaining to do," he deadpans.

"Alright… Want to talk here or—"

"Your room. Let's go." He interrupts me, then grabs my forearm, clearly forgetting I'm injured before pulling me up the stairs.

"Ow," I say, mostly out of annoyance but also because I don't need him manhandling me while I'm still recovering. I unlock the door and we're greeted by Lennon who's finishing some takeout in the living room.

"Oh, hey you two!" she says with a bright smile. "Beck, I didn't know you were coming here before the party tonight! Our girl must have forgotten to tell me, or I would have ordered dinner for you!"

Beckett lets out a dry laugh. "*Our girl* has been forgetting to tell us a lot of things lately it seems." He cuts me a glare. "It's good to see you, Lenn." Then he ushers me towards my room.

"You too! Low, I'll be in my room getting ready. Come in when you and Beck are done talking, unless he's staying?"

"No," I speak before he can. "He's not. Just having a quick chat then I'll get ready with you."

Beckett and I make it into my room and he shuts the door behind me. The knots in my stomach are growing tighter and I can feel the contents of my stomach threatening to rise up in my throat. *No…Not now.*

"Want to explain this to me?" Beckett turns his phone and my jaw drops. His stupid ass frat brother sent him a picture of Shep comforting me after he pulled me out of the pool.

"Well, first of all, what the fu—" I cut myself off and shake my head. "Why is someone taking pictures of me? And second of all, that's just the lifeguard who helped me out of the water and I was catching my breath there in the photo." I cross my arms in front of me. My mind is absolutely blown right now that I'm even having this conversation.

"I know who he is. He's in my damn fraternity. Do you know how that makes me look? Everyone knows you and I are together, and then you're over there cozying up to Shep fucking Fords?" His face is turning an unpleasant shade of red and I know I only have a few seconds to talk myself out of this before it turns bad.

For as long as I've known Beckett, he's had anger issues, but I always associated them with drinking. Some people are just angry drunks, at least that's what they say right?

I would see him tick here and there at different functions but the first time I really saw a different side of him was last year at one of his fraternity events. We had only been seeing each other a few months, but after knowing him since sophomore year, I didn't think he was a bad guy, despite his occasional outbursts when he would drink.

Beckett also could be so moody. There was some tension leading up to that event for whatever reason, but nothing I wasn't used to. He just kept telling me how it was a really important night which I could understand, so I made sure to have all my ducks in a row leading up to it but things fell apart the day of.

I had a dinner planned with my parents before the party and it ran late, so I drove straight to the Chi Kappa house. I texted Lennon asking if she'd bring my stuff so I could change when I got there. Well, she was also running late and Beckett was less than pleased that people saw in me my regular clothes. It's not like I looked sloppy or anything, I just wasn't wearing a cocktail dress and heels like everyone else. My hair was still curled. I had makeup on, and I was technically wearing a dress of sorts…just with Doc Martens.

Right after I got there, an already buzzed Beckett pulled me into one of the side rooms.

"What're you fucking wearing?" He grabbed at my oversized flannel then pushed me away from him. I stumbled a little before I caught myself on a chair and stood up straight.

"I'm sorry, I was at dinner with my parents and was going to——"

"Fuck your parents!" he slurred out, cutting me off in the process. "I invited you to be my date to this and you know how important tonight is for me. Not only are you late but you show up looking like this. How could you do this to me?"

His words stung and I realized tears were welling up in my eyes. I had never been talked to like this before, but instead of feeling defensive, I felt very self-conscious. I pulled my phone out and quickly dialed Lennon's number. As the line rang, Beckett stepped forward and gripped my wrist with a shocking force that made me drop my phone.

"Hello? Hello, Harlow?" I could hear Lennon's voice from the speaker as my phone lay on the floor. Beckett reached down, picked it up, and held it in front of my face, mouthing the words, "Go ahead."

"Hey, Lenny, sorry, I dropped my phone. I was wondering how close you were?" As I spoke, Beckett's eyes turned into beads of black and his grip tightened on my wrist.

"I'm just about to head out! What's up?"

"I wanted to make sure you saw my text. I'm already at the fraternity house and was wondering when you'd be here so I could change? You're still bringing my dress right, the black off-the-shoulder one?"

Beckett looked down at my feet and then back up at me. "Oh, and my black heels too."

"Yes! They're in my hand and I'm walking out the door now." She chimed back. "See you in ten, I'll text when I get there."

"Sounds good, drive safe." Beckett hung up the phone, then let go of my wrist, which was now throbbing and I could see a hand mark forming.

"Don't leave this room until you're in that damn dress. I'm sorry I'm so worked up, it's just, you're too beautiful to wear stuff like this at our events." He ran his thumb over my cheek and I half believed what he said.

"I wasn't going to wear this the whole night. I'm sorry." I whimpered out, unsure of exactly what I was apologizing for but feeling like I'd done something very wrong. "I'll come find you when I'm changed." I tried to smile but I was still confused over the last few minutes.

"Okay, babe." Beckett kissed my cheek and left me standing shell shocked in the middle of the room.

When Lennon got to the house, I changed and then found Beckett. He showered me with love and affection, complimented me to everyone we interacted with, and even mentioned me in his small speech he had to give in the middle of the night to thank everyone for coming. It made me feel special, but something still felt off.

It was like, once I slipped into the dress and immediately began playing the role of Beckett's date, I lost all sense of self. I shrunk into the shadows of that party and realized I was nobody to anyone in that room. I continued to play my part as the girl on Beckett's arm, but by the end of the night, he was so drunk I was able to slip out without him even noticing.

As I drove home, I shuddered at the thought of what he would do if I tried to end things with him. I then realized I needed to do whatever I could to make sure Beckett was happy with me. Because I never wanted to feel the way I did in that side room again.

The next morning, I woke up and Beckett hardly recalled the encounter. Instead he sent me multiple texts of high praise and made me feel so good about myself. He even showed up at my apartment with flowers, new heels, and some dresses. We spent the rest of the day together and had a great time. So, I shrugged off the encounter with his drinking and told myself I should've planned better, and that I'd make more of an effort for the events he invited me to.

A few weeks later, something similar happened again and I was about to throw the towel in all together because things were really starting to get to me. I was starting to feel scared. The presents, the flowers, the texts weren't doing it for me anymore and I thought maybe I could just call things off and we could go back to being familiar faces, but he was able to sweet talk his way into me giving us another try and now things were just the way they were—this uncomfortable but familiar routine. We shared friends, we had overlapping sched-ules, and he claimed he loved me. Surely everyone experienced rocky moments like we did.

"Harlow," Beckett snaps at me, pulling my mind from the past.

"I'm sorry. It didn't mean anything and if I'm being honest, I've told that lifeguard to leave me alone but he's always working when I have to practice and still tries to talk to me." I rush out.

He steps forward and grabs my jaw with his fingers. I can feel his grip tightening and I try to slap his hand off but he squeezes tighter, before pushing me away from him. I rub my jaw and walk over to my closet to try and put some space between us.

"That mouth of yours must've said something to make Fords think he can touch what's mine," Beckett sneers before walking over and spinning me back around to face him.

"I swear. I haven't had a real conversation with him other than today when Coach Bradford basically sabotaged my swimming evaluation." I roll my eyes thinking about the last few hours. What a shit show this day has been.

"Wait, what? What did Bradford do?" His voice becomes calmer and for a second, it's like he actually cares. I wish I could have this version of him all the time.

"Nothing. He's just pissed off that the team isn't doing well without me and he took it out on me." Pushing past him, I sit on my bed and rest my hands on my knees. "I know he wants me back but I can't just snap my fingers and swim butterfly again."

He walks over and sits down next to me, placing one of his hands over mine. His touch does nothing but make another wave of nausea roll through me. "Damn, that's so shitty, babe. Still can't believe you dislocated your shoulder."

"Right," I say, patting his hand. "Well, it's fine. Over and done with."

He grabs my jaw again, this time turning my face towards his and softly kisses my forehead. It bothers me that it almost makes me forget the last few minutes. He stands up and starts walking to my bedroom door. "I'm glad we got to talk before tonight. Wear something sexy, will ya?" He pushes out my door and calls out through the living room, "Always a pleasure, Lennon. See you two beautiful ladies later!" Then he leaves.

The way he's able to just turn on his charm is so unsettling. That coupled with the uneasiness I've been fighting since I left the rec center finally wins. I run to the bathroom and collide with the cold tile as I heave into the toilet. Wiping off my face after I flush, I sit against the edge of the tub and close my eyes. The ringing starts in my ears and my chest starts tightening. *Why does this keep happening!*

I reach for my phone off the counter and re-read Margot's texts to me. It momentarily pulls me out of the panic and I tell myself it's just a few hours. I can make it a few hours.

EIGHT

MY BEST BOOTY WIGGLE

HARLOW

"Let me guess, one of these is for me?"

I walk into Lennon's room and there's about ten different dresses laying on her bed. I glance over the beautiful pieces of clothing and smile. Lennon has impeccable fashion sense and thank heavens for it because I'd be lost without her.

"Yes! Of course!" she shrieks. "I thought maybe this one?"

She points to a long sleeve mini dress that's covered in black sequins. The neck is high in the front with a clasp resting at the nape, then opens up on the back until right above the waist.

"Is this not…a bit much?" I question, tilting my head to the side as I eye the dress up and down.

"No! It needs to be dressier because it's supposed to be like a seated dinner party! It's how they try to get people interested in rushing and stuff." She smiles and gets up from her vanity. "Don't ask me how I know so much. Those few dates with some of Beckett's friends actually gave me a little frat knowledge."

She picks up the dress and walks over in my direction before turning me to face her mirror. With both our reflections now in frame, she holds the dress up to me and smiles.

"See! Perfect dress for the perfect girl." She kisses the top of my shoulder.

I take the dress and spin around to hug her. Maybe just for a night I can play dress up with my best friend and pretend my life isn't such a disaster. "Thank you, Lenny. I don't know what I'd do without you."

"Aw, Low, all this over a dress?! Have I really almost converted you to be a fashion lover?" She squeezes me tight then steps back before sitting down in front of her vanity. "Hey, that was sweet of Beck to stop by before tonight!"

My body goes rigid. "Yeah, well, kinda." I walk over to her bed and plop down. "He came by because…" I let my words trail off, unsure if I really want to unpack all of this.

"Because?" Lennon quips, while leaning closer to the mirror, spreading a gloss on her lips.

"One of their fraternity brothers took a picture today of Shep and I, and sent it to Beckett." I glance over my shoulder to catch her reaction in the mirror. She draws her eyebrows together, then plunges the lip gloss wand back into the tube.

"A picture of what? Was he upset?" She tosses her hair over her shoulder then casts a look my way.

"Um," I realize if I tell her what the picture was, then I'll have to tell her all that led up to it. "Talking. We were just talking. But yeah, he was." I draw my bottom lip into my mouth. "Like, *really* upset."

She gets up and walks towards the bed, sinking down next to me. "What do you mean? He seemed fine when he was here. What did he say?"

"He just wanted to know why we were talking, I don't know. He just wasn't happy with me, and I don't think I did anything wrong." My stomach knots up as I admit this. Lennon and I don't talk much about Beckett, only because I know they're friends and she thinks he's a flawless guy.

"Well you know Beck, he's just super into you. Probably sees Shep as competition? Or maybe he was just having a bad day." She gives me a reassuring smile, shrugging her shoulders.

"Okay but—"

"Beck is crazy about you-anyone can see that. I'm sure he's not upset at all."

"Lenny, I'm telling you, he was." I try to press a little harder and hope she can hear the distress in my voice.

"Then the party tonight will be the perfect opportunity to make up. You guys are too cute together to fight." She winks but it's lost on me as I once again choke on my words.

"Okay, yeah," I mumble.

"Perfect." She gives my hand a light squeeze. "I don't know how much time we have, so you might need to throw your hair up into a ponytail."

"Right," I say numbly, before getting up and walking through her door back into my room with the dress. Laying it down on my bed, I head into my bathroom and run my brush through my hair. It amazes me after all these years that it's yet to turn green from the chlorine.

With a few mindless passes of the brush, I question myself and Beckett's behavior earlier. Maybe it did look bad? I mean, yeah, my head was on Shep's chest, but it was just for a second while I caught my breath. Would I be upset if I saw something like that of Beckett with another girl?

I shake off my thoughts as I gather up my hair and tie it off with a black scrunchie to match the dress. It doesn't look great, but it'll work. I put a little makeup on before shimmying the dress up onto my body.

Looking in the mirror, I softly smile at myself. I know I'm not ugly, but sometimes I forget how I look when I'm not in a swimsuit with my hair knotted into a bun. I walk into my closet and grab a pair of black heels, then sit on my bed to slide them on. My phone buzzes as I clasp the second one. It's my family group chat, which can only mean one thing. Margot talked to our parents.

> **MOM**
>
> Hi, Harlow
>
> How was your swim meeting today?

> **MARGOT-RITA**
>
> Sorry, I texted them both this morning after our call. Don't hate me.

> **DAD** 🤍
>
> You didn't do anything wrong, Margot. We're glad you told us. We miss you, fishy.

> It was fine. I still have more rehab to do. Why don't y'all come up this Sunday and we can grab lunch on Main Street somewhere?

MARGOT-RITA

Is your traitor sister included?

MOM

Margot, you are so dramatic. Of course you're coming. We haven't spent time, all four of us in a while.

DAD 🤍

You know I'll be there.

Great, well then I'll see you all Sunday. I love you for checking on me, and just because. I'm sorry I dropped the ball by getting injured.

DAD 🤍

Don't start. Text me or Mom tomorrow sometime if you want to talk more about the evaluation. We love you.

I set my phone down and try to not let my emotions get the best of me now that I'm thinking about seeing my family for the first time since I got hurt. I shake off whatever feeling is trying to settle in my chest and make my way into Lennon's room.

"Hey there sexy, planning to go home with anyone tonight?" I lean against her door frame and give my best booty wiggle in her direction.

She spins around and squeals. "Oh my GAH, you are so damn HOT! Wow! Yes, I will be going home with you!"

She flips her wavy, brown hair over her shoulders before spritzing some perfume on her collar bones. "What?!" she says to me, raising her eyebrows.

"Sorry, but, who are *you* actually trying to go home with

because that dress? Damn." I look her over and admire Lennon's figure in her own black dress. It has a lace bustier at the top then flares out into a silk mini dress. She's a little taller than me and has more of a model figure than I do. The dress is perfect for her.

She rolls her eyes. "Okay, please. As if."

"Uh huh, sure. Well, let's go before you and I just stand here and compliment each other back and forth for the next hour. I think our Uber should be here in about a minute." I grab a small purse off her dresser and stuff my phone and apartment key into it before heading to our front door.

NINE

WE LOOK LIKE EACH OTHER'S DATES

SHEP

Oomph.

The sound of my fist connecting to the punching bag reverberates throughout my room.

I'm about to go for a few more rounds to end my training and get ready for the date party, when I'm interrupted by a knock on my door.

"Come in!" I call out.

The door opens and Wes takes a few steps into my room. "How's it going?" He points at the punching bag.

"Good, I'm just trying to work off some stress before tonight." I start to unwrap my knuckles and walk over to my computer, pausing the music I had playing in the background.

"Something happen?" Wes inquires.

"Nah, it's all good. What's up?" I toss the wrap on my desk.

I've been boxing now for almost a year. It started when

Dad brought me with him to the precinct and some of the new cops were practicing self-defense. One of them mentioned how beneficial boxing had been for their fitness and overall health. It also doesn't hurt to know how to protect yourself. I'm not one for violence, especially growing up with someone like my dad who always advocated against it. But with boxing, it's really more about the work out than the fighting to me.

"I caught wind of what went down today, or at least I heard that something happened at the pool with Harlow."

The burning feeling in my chest is back and I try to not show how affected I am.

"She really can't catch a break." I huff out. "Honestly, I'm the one who caused a scene."

I continue to clean up my room from my workout while filling Wes in on what happened earlier. I do my best to leave out the moment shared between Harlow and I, while still making sure he understands how badly she got screwed over today.

After he makes sure I'm *actually* okay, he leaves my room so I can get ready for tonight. I walk back over to my laptop and press play on my music. "MAGNETIC" by Wage War starts up again and I get lost in the lyrics.

I think over the moment earlier when I drew Harlow to my chest. I wonder if she noticed how perfectly she fit against me. Probably not.

I continue getting ready for the night with her on my mind. If anyone knew how much I think about her they might be concerned, but I really can't help it. Weeks of observing her, then having her in my arms today, damn, I want to do that again.

I grab my suit jacket off the back of the chair and call out to my beloved Dahlia girl from my room, "Daddy needs you to come here please so we can get you settled before I head out." The light jingling of her collar lets me know she's on her way in so I open up the door to her crate before tossing a treat inside.

"Wes, are you ready? I'm putting Dahlia up now." My voice rings out into the townhouse while Dahlia is curling up inside her crate. Kneeling to the ground, I pull a blanket up over her, then lean into her crate plopping a kiss on top of her head. "Be good, my girl." She looks up at me with her sweet pittie eyes before returning my kiss with a sloppy wet one of her own.

As I lock her crate, Wes stands in my door frame. "Damn, we look pretty good."

I look over in his direction to realize we are dressed almost exactly the same. I roll my eyes while I grab my suit jacket and push past him, shutting my door behind me. I didn't even want to dress up but, of course, I agreed and now we look like each other's dates. Honestly, it's par for the course.

"You ready to see your girl tonight?" Wes uses a sing-songy voice as he trails behind me to the front door.

"I don't know, are you ready to see yours?" I snap at him but to my surprise he replies with a simple, "Yes, I am actually."

"Whatever, you're driving." I throw my keys at him before walking over to the passenger side of my truck. Maybe I am excited to see Harlow, but there's no way in hell I'm telling Wes that. "I'm also DJ-ing," I say before Wes can turn the radio on.

We drive listening to Noah Kahan and my stomach starts to knot up thinking about seeing Harlow again after how today went. Should I even talk to her? I need to think of some sort of game plan. I could just say hi to her in passing and play it cool, but that doesn't feel natural for me. I genuinely do care about the girl, yet she has made it pretty clear she wants nothing to do with me.

"Hello? Earth to Shep?" Wes raises his voice and I realize we are already at the Chi Kappa house. I get out of my truck and grab my suit jacket, sliding my arms into the sleeves and pulling it on over my all-black outfit. Pulling on the collar of my button down to make sure it's sitting nicely above my jacket, I turn to look at my reflection in the window of my truck.

Damn, I do look good.

Wes walks ahead of me towards the front of the house and the tight feeling in my chest is back. What if Harlow didn't even show up to this? All these nerves for literally nothing. A few brothers stop and shake my hand. We exchange minimal conversation while Wes also catches up with some of the friends he has made from attending so many of these functions with me.

I scour the crowd in the house for Harlow's blonde hair but don't see her yet. Wes however looks over at me and nods his head in the direction of the outdoor area, mouthing one word that has me nearly knocking over the people around me to get to where he is.

"Harlow."

I meet him at the edge of the grand french doors that lead from our main dining hall to the back of our house where another bar is set up by the pool. It takes all of two seconds for me to find her and when I do, my heart nearly stops.

Harlow's beautiful—there's no doubt about it—but the sight of her right now has me in awe. The heels she's wearing make her toned legs look like they could go on for miles. Her entire back is exposed in the sparkly little dress she's wearing. Her long blonde hair is tied up in a ponytail and for a moment I lose myself in the thought of pulling on it to have her fall back into my arms. I wonder what she tastes—

"Wait, Shep, that's the brunette I was telling you about." Wes interrupts my thoughts. I move my hips slightly to try and adjust myself in my pants then look back in the direction of Harlow and the girl next to her.

"Hold on. Like, the girl you're into? Is *with* Harlow?" I cock my head taking in the scene before me. The two girls are chatting, sipping wine, while looking around themselves. Harlow suddenly fixates past the pool. I follow her gaze to see Beckett looking at her, then me, then back to her.

Looks like it's my time to shine.

"Come on, let's go over there." I nudge Wes in the direction of the girls. He moves slowly like his brain isn't connecting with his feet, then snaps out of it and walks with confidence.

As I get closer to Harlow, the same smell that I remember from the first time I saw her at a date party dances in the air around me, sending me back in time.

We were hosting our annual charity event. I was in charge of helping with the door that night and I remember her showing up late. She flew past me, her blonde hair leaving behind a scent of vanilla spice and cherries that I wanted to envelop myself in, and beelined straight for Beckett.

She was wearing this oversized flannel and some black boots. At first it was strange to see, because everyone else was pretty dressed up. But I came to learn—that's Harlow.

I saw her again later and she had clearly changed at some point after breezing past me. She looked as breathtaking then as she does now. I don't think she ever left my sight that night until I noticed her slip out early. The second she left, I felt her absence.

It was then that I realized there would never be a moment that Harlow could escape my attention if we were ever in the same place at the same time again.

TEN

"HE'S HOT."

HARLOW

We get to the Chi Kappa house and I can already feel the panic in my stomach starting to build. I hate this new side of me. Yeah, this will be my first time back since the night of the injury, but shit used to not get to me like this.

Lenny takes my hand, holding it as we walk through the house. She flashes a bright smile at all the faces we pass. She hums various *hi*'s and *hey there's* to multiple people until we end up near the bar in the back of the house by the pool.

I look around and feel like everyone's eyes are on me. Is it because of what I'm wearing or because everyone knows what happened the last time I was seen at a party here? Lennon gets herself a glass of wine and water for me, then we settle into a spot, standing and watching as people start to arrive. She's mindlessly talking to me about the rest of the week and what we should do this weekend since there isn't a swim meet.

I'm trying to listen to her words but my mind is starting to wander back to the last time I was here. My eyes scan around me to the grand pool, the myriad of rock features, and then they lock with Beckett who's standing across the way with a few other frat brothers. His eyes turn into slits and I can tell his grip is tightening on his drink, but what on earth could I possibly have already done wrong tonight?

"Harlow." A voice behind me speaks softly and a shiver is sent down my spine.

"Oh my," Lennon speaks before I do and I turn to understand both Beckett's stare and Lennon's comment.

Standing behind me is one tall, blue-eyed, lifeguard. Except, he isn't a lifeguard at the moment. No, he's a mouth watering sight, wearing an all-black suit, with a matching black button down underneath. I'm trying to find words but it feels like they are stuck in my throat. Another guy steps forward, with darker hair and dark eyes in almost the same outfit and breaks the silence by extending his hand in my direction. When he does, I notice a few tattoos peeking out on his forearm.

"Hi, I'm Wesley Porter, Shep's best friend, but you can call me Wes." I shake his hand while he finishes his introduction but I can't help notice how he's really looking at Lennon and not me.

"Harlow. Um, but you probably already knew that if you're Shep's best friend." Suddenly, I feel the gaze of Shep burning into me so I grab Lennon and push her forward. "This is Lennon, my best friend."

"Geez, Low, bit rough there," she says over her shoulder, giving me her famous side eye, but then promptly sticks her hand out in Wes's direction. "Lennon, like she said. I think we have a class together?"

Wes's face lights up and I can't help feeling like Shep and I are now the ones who don't belong in this conversation.

"That's right," Wes chimes back. "You're on the swim team."

"I am!" Lennon smirks. "A guy who does his research? Go ahead and take me home now!" She laughs but Wes's face turns the most precious shade of pink.

"Oh gosh, she's kidding. Lenny, please." I blink in her direction with wide eyes, hoping she catches on to the awkwardness lingering in the air.

"What?" Lennon says under her breath. "He's hot."

I smile uncomfortably as Wes extends out his arm for Lennon to grab on. "Can I get you another drink?" He nods to her now empty wine glass. "I think these two have some things to discuss."

Lennon giggles before slipping her arm through Wes's and they wander off towards the bar again, but not before she can yell back over her shoulder for anyone nearby to hear, "Good luck!"

I try to laugh, but when I look at Shep his stare is locked on me. I feel the air being sucked from me and, for the second damn time in the span of a few minutes, I can't seem to find words.

"I just wanted to check on you," he states coolly. "I know today was hard for you and I'm not sure if it got any better based on some passing glares I'm receiving from your boy, Beckett, over there."

I turn and face Beckett again who's now withdrawn from his group and staring at Shep and me. My stomach knots up thinking about the conversation he and I had earlier at my apartment. I cannot have another confrontation with him so I try and pull a hail mary.

I push Shep away from me, dramatically enough that I notice Beckett's eyebrows raise. "Seriously, you need to leave me alone." I raise my voice a little now that I know Beckett is paying full attention.

Shep's mouth drops open a little and he furrows his eyebrows. "I'm sorry, what?"

"I mean it. I don't know why you keep talking to me but you need to stop. I'm here with Beckett." I cross my arms and take a step away from him.

Please take the hint, Shep. Please.

Shep looks around and realizes Beckett is now walking in our direction. "Whatever, Harlow. Enjoy your evening."

He turns to walk away and I can't help but feel bad. I know he really does mean well, so I move to the front of him, hiding my face from Beckett and mouth, *"I'm sorry."*

Shep moves away from me with an even more confused look on his face and I turn around and intercept Beckett, hoping my performance worked.

"Babe, I was starting to get worried you might be ditching me for Fords." His voice is loud enough to cause Shep to turn his head back in our direction.

Oh, for fuck's sake. I've had enough of this.

I interlace my fingers with Beckett's and nod my head in the direction of the house. He grips my hand and we make our way inside towards the formal dining room. Once there, we duck off into a hallway when he grabs me by the waist pressing my back against the wall. I can't discern the look on his face but I give him a soft smile.

"Hey, I'm sorry about that. I seriously don't know what his deal is." I kiss Beckett's cheek and look up at him hopefully, but that hope is fleeting as I feel his hands tightening around my sides, his fingers pressing into the exposed part of my back. They squeeze tighter and it feels like my ribs are being crushed from behind.

"Beckett," I choke out. From this angle, nobody would be able to tell what's going on because it merely looks like a couple having an intimate moment against the wall. I try to push his hands off me with mine but he doesn't react or move.

"Beckett," I call again, but his eyes are darkening and it's like his soul has left his body. "You're hurting me." His fingers are pressing so firmly into my skin, tears are springing to the edge of my eyes.

He finally speaks, his voice low and gravelly. "I thought I told you to leave Shep Fords alone."

"Did you not hear me? Hear what I said to him?" I squeak out. My breathing is becoming raspy and I don't know how long he's had me in this hold now. "Beckett!"

At this point I'm entering fight or flight. *Think, Harlow. Think.* I lift my heel ever so slightly before bringing it down on his foot.

"Shit!" he yelps as whatever dark trance he was in is now broken. I push him off of me and make a run for the closest bathroom, locking myself inside. I don't even bother to turn on the light as I shrink further away from the door, running into the edge of a counter.

"Harlow?" I hear his voice calling out eerily. "Harlow,

where are you?" I can hear his footsteps approaching but just as they stop by the door, someone calls out his name. "Yeah, be right there." I hold my breath and pray that he gives up on his hunt for me. I close my eyes, thinking he's gone but then I hear a low voice through the mere inch of wood, "We'll talk later, Harlow." Then he turns and walks away.

I can't fight it anymore. I collapse to the ground, covering my mouth with my hand as I try to stifle the sob that's now wracking through my body. How did things get this far?

After a minute or so passes, I gather the courage to stand up and turn the light on but my breath catches as pain radiates through my body. I look over my shoulder and my reflection in the mirror causes another sob to leave my mouth. On the middle of my back are two very distinguishable hand prints that are slowly changing from a bright red to a dark purple.

"I CAN'T DO THIS!" I scream, finally letting out all the emotions I've been harboring for what feels like the last few months. I slide down the wall, meeting the ground once again, and surrender to the ache in my chest. My shoulder, the fights with Beckett, the interactions with Shep, the judgment from Coach Bradford, all come crashing down on me. I feel like I can't breathe.

I kick my legs out from under me and unclasp my heels, throwing them across the small room. As I lay my head back against the wall, tears streaming down my face, another realization hits me. There's absolutely no way my swimsuit will cover up the bruises forming on my back. *You've gotta be fucking kidding me.*

"I give up," I say to myself, accepting the fact I'll be spending the rest of the night here until I can find a moment to slip out without anyone noticing me, or Beckett's handiwork.

ELEVEN

MR. CONFIDENCE

SHEP

I've been at the date party for less than thirty minutes and I already want to leave.

Talking to Harlow was a shit show. I knew Beckett would be here, but I didn't expect her to disappear with him in the middle of a simple conversation. That alone pisses me off because he was already slurring his words. No surprise there though, the guy might actually be a functioning alcoholic.

I didn't think for one second that she might actually be into him. Could I really have been that naive? Or was I ignorant to think she might be interested in me? Either way, I'm done with this night, especially after her confusing silent apology. Whatever.

I look around for Wes only to see him cuddling up to Harlow's best friend. She looks absolutely delighted with whatever he's telling her and for a brief second, envy flares up in me.

Why can't I have that? If not with Harlow, why not with

anyone? Maybe I just need to move past this crush or infatuation. I wish I knew how it even started and maybe that would help me squash it.

Approaching Wes and Lennon, I notice her hand resting on his but she quickly moves it away when she realizes I'm walking up to them. I glance at Wes who's radiating a sheepish red glow but is also smiling bigger than I've ever seen.

"So what's been going on between you two?" I signal to the barback for a beer while Wes and Lennon both look around like teenagers who've been caught in the basement.

"Lennon was just telling me about how she started swimming and oh, hey, where's Harlow?" I see it clicking in Wes's mind that he's the only one who successfully won over his interest of the evening.

Her friend straightens up as if she's also interested in my answer, so I decide to ignore Wes and see what that's about.

"Not sure. But, Lennon, right?"

She nods her head slightly and a wave from her brown hair falls over her shoulder. Wes brushes it out of the way for her and once again my mind is all over the place.

Focus, Shep. Fucking focus.

"Right, so, Lennon. Tell me, you seem to know who I am, but we've never officially met." Her cheeks flush as she sets down her wine glass. The barback hands me my beer over the counter, allowing her a few seconds to gather her thoughts. As I take a sip, the smooth liquid moves around in my mouth and cools me down from the events before this.

"Can we go over there?" She points to an area where

there's high top tables and people engaging in casual conversation around various ones.

"Sure. Wes, you coming?" Wes is already grabbing Lennon's wine glass for her and following us over to one of the open tables. I really feel like I missed something between these two but that conversation is for another time.

"So, before we talk, I'd also like to know where Harlow is?" Lennon looks around the back of the house before making eye contact with me again.

"Oh, you didn't see her push me away and tell me to leave her alone?" I roll my eyes and take another sip of my beer. I may be acting childish about this but I know for a fact I didn't do anything to deserve that. The look of shock on both their faces urges me to continue on before they can get a word in. "Yeah, told me to leave her alone, then went off somewhere with Beckett."

"Oh," Lennon deadpans. "Well, I mean they did come together. You know they're basically dating, right? You have to. You and Beckett are fraternity brothers and I'm sure you've seen Harlow with him plenty of times." *Yeah, her and a handful of other girls*, is what I want to say. She offers her words with a politeness that tells me she obviously likes Beckett and is friends with him or something.

"Yeah, I know. Everyone knows. And how that asshole maintains a relationship with Harlow is beyond me." A possessiveness burns in my chest again similar to the one I felt at the pool when Coach Bradford was making an example out of Harlow. "You know, I don't think I've seen him once at the rec center while she's been doing her practices—not dropping her off, not picking her up, sure as hell not checking on her."

Wes's eyes grow big and he shakes his head at me. Maybe I'm being over the top but the guy's a grade A dick. Nothing about him and Harlow being together makes sense.

"Well, I guess you're right about that." Lennon affirms, and for Harlow's best friend to agree feels like a small win. "But, it's been like this for over a year now. On and off, but in Beckett's eyes, always on."

I look at Wes again and hope that he will understand my silent plea for a moment alone with Lennon and he picks up on it. "I'm going to go grab a water, need anything?" I shake my head in sync with Lennon and Wes trails away from the high top towards the bar.

"Lennon, I'm going to be very honest with you. I'm interested in your best friend and judging by the way you've been acting since I walked up behind Harlow about thirty minutes ago, you know something, and I just need a little help here." As the words leave my mouth, regret nips at me, but being honest about the way I feel about Harlow also feels liberating.

"I know nothing," she quips. "But you're interested in my best friend, huh?" Lennon repeats my words with a smirk, then narrows her eyes. "Tell me, what do you even know about Harlow besides the fact you watch her swim every day?"

Fair question, but little does she know I'm prepared with an answer.

"I know she drives a Bronco and parks in almost the same place every day at the rec center which tells me she likes her routines. I know she keeps a blanket of some sort in her car because I've seen it on the passenger seat multiple times when I've parked near her. I know that she's disciplined because she always gets to the pool ten minutes before she starts swimming. I know she ends her practices by taking her cap and goggles off, then goes underwater and lets her hair out. It's one of the few moments I ever see her at peace. I know she works harder than anyone I've ever met. I know she always leaves the rec center in a sweatshirt with her hair in a bun and will always be wearing her black boots—which for some reason I really like. But most importantly, I know she deserves far more than Beckett could ever give her."

Lennon's jaw is slack and her eyes wide. The exact reaction I was hoping for. I take another sip of my beer before setting it down.

"I—wow. Harlow wasn't kidding." She shakes her head as if trying to come back to the present moment, lost in a thought.

"What do you mean?" I press.

"She told me she confronted you at the pool because you were staring at her. Is she right? Are you, like, obsessed with her or something?" Lennon steps away from me like suddenly I've done something very wrong. My confidence is diminishing now and I didn't think about the way saying all of that out loud might sound.

"Fuck me. No. I just thought maybe things changed a little today." I blurt out, frustrated now that this isn't going to plan. Lennon's look of confusion leads me to my next question. "She hasn't told you, has she?"

"Told me what?" Lennon leans in now and relief floods me that she doesn't know about Harlow and I's interaction and all this makes that much more sense.

"Coach Bradford sabotaged her today at the pool during

her check-in." I pocket my hands and try to not let the memory of earlier work me up.

"He what?!" Lennon's voice shakes and Wes is walking back over to the table.

"Oookay, bad timing." Wes pivots on his heel and turns back around to wait out the conversation.

"Speak!" Lennon shouts.

I'm so stunned by the sudden change in her demeanor, I forget what we're talking about. "Huh?"

"Oh my gosh. Coach Bradford! What happened today?" She's tapping her high heel now, crossing her arms.

"Oh, yeah. My shift got switched today for some reason. Harlow had her first check in—"

"I'm aware," she cuts in, "get to the point!"

"Damn, okay. Your coach told her to swim butterfly."

"That's insane!" she yells as if I'm at fault.

"Lennon, please." I place my hand on her arm. "Harlow told him she couldn't. Even her athletic trainer—"

"Pierce."

"Yes, Pierce. He was there and even he was shocked." I shake my head recalling the incident. "Harlow was so defeated, she sank to the bottom of the pool and for a second I didn't know if she was going to come back up to the surface."

Lennon's eyes well up and she moves a hand over her mouth.

"I could tell something was wrong when I got to the rec because I ran into Harlow in the parking lot. She was really flustered and when I put it together she was having an evaluation, I tried to talk to her beforehand but she assured me she was fine."

"Well, that's Harlow for you," Lennon interjects.

"So I've learned. When I realized what was going on, I got off my stand and confronted Coach Bradford." I take a step back from Lennon and put my hands in my pockets again. "I told him whatever program he was running was unacceptable and as I spoke to him, Harlow came out of the water, so I went to help her out. For a split second, she let me in. She told me she wasn't okay."

"Oh my gosh." A single tear runs down Lennon's cheek and Wes seems to notice because he quickly returns to the table.

"Is everything okay?" He looks between Lennon and me.

"I have to go find Harlow. Shep, I'm sorry I assumed the worst. Thank you. Genuinely." She places a hand on my cheek before turning towards the house, but stops and turns back around. "You know, I've always been team Beckett but maybe I'll consider team Shep."

My heart lightens as she disappears into the house.

"What the hell was all that?" Wes leans on the high top table and I don't know if I should fill him in or let him stay in his bubble of having a good night with Lennon.

"Nothing, man. Just realized Lennon and I needed to talk about a few things."

He nods his head in understanding. Before we can continue the conversation, a few of our coworkers walk over and start talking about the weekend coming up. I scan the crowd for Lennon, in hopes she might return with Harlow but it's been about fifteen minutes and neither of them are in sight.

A few more minutes pass and Lennon emerges from the

house and finds Wes and I. An expression of concern is all over her face. "I can't find her." She sighs and puts her face in her hands. "I don't typically worry about her but after the day she had and being back at the fraternity house since the party in August. I didn't think about how all of this might make her feel."

"Hey, I'm sure it's fine. You didn't know about the evaluation." Wes rubs a hand along her back. She smiles at him, but then steps away.

"Yeah, which bothers me even more. I'm sorry, this has been lovely but I need to find my friend. I'll see you in lecture tomorrow, Wes?" She smiles softly but I can tell things are getting awkward real fast.

"Yeah, sure. Of course. I hope everything works out." Wes nods his head at her and I wish I could yell at him to hug the girl or something but after another second, she frowns a little then walks away.

"Dude, a head nod?" I raise my eyebrows at Wes and his face loses all emotion. "What happened to Mr. Confidence I saw over by the bar?"

"I don't know. She makes me nervous and I can't really tell if she's into me or not. She was giving off that hot and cold flirting vibe. I don't know, it's all good really." He looks around the crowd. "Still no sign of Harlow?"

"No," I reply. "I guess I could go look for her but I also get the feeling that I would only be causing her more trouble." The thought hurts but maybe there's some truth to Lennon's first impression of me being obsessed with Harlow. Maybe it couldn't hurt to reel it in a little, let her do her own thing.

I signal to Wes that I'm going inside and notice he's

found Lennon again and he's going after her. Good on him. I head towards the main dining room and there aren't many people inside. Ducking off into one of the side rooms by the kitchen, I happen to catch sight of Beckett. I move behind one of the pillars, hoping he will lead me to Harlow, but he just walks back outside and rejoins everyone else.

I'm ready to give up and go home. I would love to be in bed with my dog and not worrying about anything else today.

I start to head down the hall when I hear a faint sniffling. Slowing my pace, I approach a bathroom where the sounds of soft cries leak out from under the door. I go to knock but hesitate, my fist hovering over the door. I've done my fair share of bathroom rescues at this fraternity house and more often than not, I'm shooed away by a friend. I decide to let this one go and keep walking towards the front door.

I get to my truck and pull out the breathalyzer my dad has me keep in my glovebox. I've only had one beer tonight but with my dad being in law enforcement and my desire to not ruin my life and someone else's, I know I can never be too careful. I use it and see that I'm more than okay to drive so I shoot Wes a text that I'm heading home but I can come back out and grab him if needed. He 'thumbs up' my text so with that, I start up my Tacoma and head home to the one girl I know will always love me and be there for me. My sweet, Dahlia.

TWELVE

CHARITY CASE

HARLOW

I'm looking at Shep across the pool and I can't help how exposed I feel in my swimsuit. I know my bruises are visible and his eyes are tracking me like a hawk surveying its prey. I try to avoid his gaze and make a beeline for the locker room but he's off his stand faster than I can make it to the door and barricades me against the wall.

"Where are you going, Harlow?" His voice is husky and the sheer fabric of my one piece does nothing to protect me from the heat I feel radiating from his body. "Turn around and let me see your back."

I gulp and shake my head no. I can't do this. I can't have this confrontation right now. Shep nods his head to counter my response and I find my feet turning as if they're not connected to me.

"That's a good girl," he praises in a voice that makes me shiver. "Now, who did this to you?" As the last word leaves his mouth, I feel his breath tickling my lower back where I know my skin's marred with purple and red splotches.

"I-I'm okay." I try to speak but the heat building inside of me is becoming too much. I'm at a loss for words and I can't stop him. The softest touch graces my back and I realize he's kissing where Beckett's hands left daunting traces. "Oh, Shep," I mumble.

"That's right, Harlow. Let me take care of you—"

BAM! BAM! BAM!

I startle awake as I hear a pounding on my bedroom door. "Low, are you coming to get coffee with me or not? I've been listening to your alarm go off for like the last thirty minutes." Lennon's voice adds to my disorientation and I look around my room in a panic. *It's not real. It's just a dream. Since when do I have dreams about Shep?*

"Yep, uh, just give me a minute! Sorry, deep sleep," I shout back through my door.

"Uh huh," Lennon responds, opening it. "Well let's go! Up and at 'em!"

I freeze, realizing I'm in a sports bra and Lennon might be able to see the bruises from Tuesday night. I've been hiding out in the apartment, telling everyone I've had food poisoning but it's Friday now and Lennon clearly thinks I'm recovered. *Hardly.* The marks on my lower back have only settled deeper, becoming even more noticeable.

"Okay, will you get me my Docs? They're by the door." If I can get her out of my room, I can throw a sweatshirt on before she notices.

"Only because I love you and you said you'd buy this round since I got the last trip to Boulder." She turns and marches out of my room, sighing dramatically.

I jump out of bed and grab my Everson sweatshirt from a pile of laundry on the floor, pulling it over my head carefully as it brushes past my shoulder then shimmy into a pair of jean shorts as Lennon walks back in, dropping my boots in front of me.

"Here you go, princess." She blows me a kiss then sits on my bed. As I slip into my Docs, I chuckle to myself at the stark difference between her and me. My typical wardrobe consists of shorts, my EU sweatshirt, and my boots. Whereas Lennon, being the fashion queen she is, always looks put together, even if she didn't try.

Her chestnut hair is slicked back into a bun, showing off her prominent cheekbones. Her tan skin causes her signature gold hoops to glow. She's sporting a matching black workout set and looks like she walked straight out of an athletic magazine. Anyone who doesn't know we are best friends and sees us having coffee together might assume I'm some sort of charity case or volunteer project that Lennon is helping out. It works though, and I love that about us.

"So," she starts. "Do you want to talk about Tuesday night yet?" She fidgets with the edges of my comforter. We still haven't really discussed where I went at the date party. I ended up slipping out and coming home, sending her a text that something upset my stomach and that I was sorry. The Uber ride back was like being in the twilight zone. Nothing that happened in those few hours felt real.

"What about it?" I ask casually while pulling my hair up into a ponytail and turning to go brush my teeth.

"Well, I had an interesting conversation with Shep while you were MIA." She stands up and walks over to me. As she leans against the door frame, she continues, "He told me what Coach Bradford did."

I freeze and wish she didn't wait to bring this up. My mind immediately starts to spin and panic wells up in my stomach. "What did he say?" I deadpan with my toothbrush half in my mouth.

Lennon sidesteps me and hops up on the counter. "Well, for starters, you could've told me about the evaluation. Why didn't you?"

I lean forward, spit into the sink then rinse my mouth out. Standing up to meet Lennon's face, I can tell she's asking out of concern, but recalling the event feels intrusive and like I'm being probed.

"Because it was a shit show, Len. I didn't know what to say about it." I turn to walk out and she uses the end of her shoe to nudge me in my back. It prods one of the bruised parts of my skin and I immediately gasp from the pain. "Don't just walk out," she says, having no idea what she's done.

Tears are welling up from the dull ache now radiating through my body. I can't risk her knowing something's wrong so I leave my room entirely and head for the living room.

"Harlow? What's wrong?" Her voice follows me.

I plop down on the couch. "Nothing. I just don't want to bring it back up. Why did Shep feel the need to talk to you about it, though?" I press.

"Oh, right. So, basically, okay don't freak out," she starts to say as she sits opposite me on a chair. My eyes feel like they might pop out of my head with how wide I'm opening them. "Shep might've admitted to having feelings for you." She bites down on her lip and looks around the room knowing she just opened the world's largest can of worms.

"I'm sorry, he *what*?!" I jump off the couch and start pacing. "Why on earth would he say that? He hardly even knows me!"

Lennon squeals out a laugh before slapping her hand over her mouth.

"Yes?" I urge her to continue.

"Nothing, just, he knows you well enough." She stands up and walks over to the counter where her purse is. Grabbing it, she walks towards our door. "Can we continue this over coffee? I'm going to need more caffeine to brace myself for your reactions from here on out."

As we pull into a spot on the street outside Boulder Brewing Co., I can feel Lennon's eyes boring into me. I know she's dying to tell me everything Shep said but I've also found lately that sometimes ignorance really is bliss.

We walk into Boulder and immediately see people we know. Being the social butterfly she is, Lennon darts over to them and waves at me to go ahead and order. I'm buying after all.

"Hi, yeah can I get one cold brew with some honey and your cold foam on top, please?" I scan the coffee shop to see who exactly is here and hope by some miracle Shep or Beckett is not lurking in the shadows. I don't have the patience for either of them right now. The barista clears her throat and I realize she's been waiting on me to finish my order. "Sorry, and can I please get an iced coffee with a splash of sweet cream?"

I pay and walk over to meet Lennon who has disbanded the group that was in the corner by the couches and is smiling eagerly at me. "Guess what I just found out?" Tapping her fingers on her knees as if playing an imaginary piano, she doesn't wait for me to answer. "Chi Kappa is finally hosting a fall formal in two weeks!" She squeals while I feel the color drain from my face.

"What?" She scrunches her eyebrows at my lack of enthusiasm. "This means we get to go dress shopping soon! You know that's like my love language. Speaking of shopping, we need to figure out what we're going to wear to their Halloween party too."

The barista saves me from the conversation, calling out our order. I stand up to walk over to the counter when the bell rings at the door and I hear a voice that I know all too well. I spin around and see Coach Bradford with Pierce walking in, my heart rate now skyrocketing. Before I can grab my drinks and run, I'm spotted.

"Hey! Sutherland! What's going on?" Pierce smiles and reaches out a hand to rub my good arm. I know my face right now is probably screaming "what the fuck," but I choose to force out a smile and look past him to Coach Bradford.

"Hi, Coach. I wanted to talk to you after my evaluation… Didn't expect it to be here at the coffee shop but," I look down at my feet, wanting to stand up for myself but instead two words that seem to weigh me down in all areas of my life spill out of me instead. "I'm sorry."

Coach raises an eyebrow before looking at Pierce,

nodding him off to go order, then looks back at me. "Things have not been great for the team, Harlow. While I know I shouldn't have pushed so hard for you to swim butterfly, I let the losses cloud my vision. I pushed too far and I'm the one who should be saying sorry."

My jaw falls open and I blink a few times trying to come back to the present moment. "Wait, what?" My words stumble out of my mouth, filtered through shock and disbelief.

Pierce walks back over with two hot black coffees and hands one to Coach. He takes it and smiles at me again. "A few more weeks, Sutherland. Pierce said you'll be cleared for meets. You may not be able to swim butterfly but at least we can throw you into the freestyle events again. Something is better than nothing. So keep up the good work and take care." He lifts up his fist and I awkwardly bump it with mine.

I follow him with wide eyes as he walks over to a chair and sits down before looking back at Pierce who has a shy look on his face. "Um, I'm sorry," I start, "Did I miss something?"

"I talked to him after what happened. It seriously pissed me off because I work just as hard to make sure my athletes are trained well. And, not just to recover, but to not re-injure themselves. He compromised our plan that I put a shit ton of time and effort into, so I told him that." He sips his coffee, giving me a moment to think.

"Huh. Well, I wasn't expecting that, to say the least." A genuine smile spreads across my face and for the first time since I got hurt, a glimmer of hope warms my soul.

"Yeah, I mean, Fords was really helpful. It meant a lot for him to come back—"

"I'm sorry, Shep was involved with this?" Another wave of disbelief knocks me over.

"Yeah, I mean he came with me to meet with Coach the next day, attesting to your practices, as well as the progress you've been making, and how the plan I wrote out for you seems to actually be helping."

"I can't believe it." Shaking my head, I glance over at Lennon who's watching the entire interaction like it's a new reality TV show. "Thank you, seriously. I'm here with my friend so I should probably get back to her."

"Alright, well I'm glad to see you out. Guess that means you're feeling better?"

I nod my head sheepishly, realizing I can't keep up the food poisoning ruse much longer.

"Good. Text me when you're back in the pool, but hey, don't go too long without practicing." Pierce may be all work no play, but at least I can trust he wants me to get better.

"I'm still doing my PT stretches, but yeah I'll keep you updated. See you, Pierce." I walk past him over to Lennon and slowly sit down, worried the second my ass touches the cushion there will be another reason for me to jump up and sprint out the door.

"So that looked juicy. Spill." Lennon grabs her iced coffee from my hand and takes a big gulp. "Ugh, sweet nectar. I'm alive again."

I snort out a laugh. At least I know Lennon will always be here to bring me joy even when life feels like one big cluster fuck. "Coach apologized for what happened at my evaluation."

"Oh?" Lennon's eyes widen. "And what did Hottie McTrainer have to say?"

"Good lord, Lennon. He's not even that hot." I look cautiously in the direction of Coach and Pierce then back to face Lennon. "Okay, he's kinda hot, but that's beside the point. He told me that the one and only thorn in my side, Shep Fords, went to Coach Bradford with him to talk about what happened." I roll my eyes and take a huge gulp of my cold brew.

Lennon chokes on her drink, "Wait, what? Shep was involved?"

"Do you understand now? He seriously can't stop inserting himself into my life. It's getting weird." I let out a loud sigh. Part of me did feel truly annoyed by his persistence but another part of me feels softened by his obvious care for me. It's a strange feeling, one that I don't have room for.

"Okay, so this is great because I can now marry what I wanted to say with what you've just told me. Yes, the boy has it bad for you. I mean, B-A-D. Which, typically I'd be coming at you with an all hands on deck attitude, but I know you're with Beckett. However…"

My stomach knots at the mention of his name and the handprints on my back start to burn like fresh brands. *Maybe this will be my moment.* I consider telling Lennon what's been going on but she cuts off my thought.

"At the date party, Shep mentioned that you 'let him in' for a moment after your evaluation went south." Her use of air quotes makes me flush with embarrassment. He told her? Who am I kidding? Of course he did.

Logic flies out the door and I blurt out, "I think everyone needs to mind their own business when it comes to me, my swimming, and my relationships."

A flash of hurt flickers in her brown eyes. "Harlow, that's not fair. I'm just trying to figure out what's going on since you don't talk to me anymore."

"Lennon, what do you want me to say? I'm the punch-line of most jokes when we go out together. Our team thinks I'm some irresponsible drunk. Shep continues to cause prob-lems for me. Beckett…" I pause and think over my next few words. "I don't think it's going to work out. Once I graduate, I know he and I will go our separate ways."

Do I really want to stay with Beckett for the rest of my senior year, though? Blips of Shep course through my mind and, once again, my chest tightens. This is all too much. I need to focus on what's always been the goal: get better and compete again.

Lennon still hasn't said anything and quietly sips on her coffee. I decide to remedy my harshness by flipping the girl-talk on her. "You and Wes looked pretty cozy on Tuesday."

Her face turns the deepest shade of red, which I've never seen happen to her before.

Bingo.

THIRTEEN

DEAR GOD, PLEASE, NO.

HARLOW

The rest of the weekend moves quickly and before I know it, Sunday is here and I'm getting ready to go meet my parents and Margot at Summit Sandwiches in downtown Everson. As it gets closer to October, the weather starts to drastically cool off in the mountains so I decide an oversized T-shirt, flannel, with my Docs and tights is the perfect look. Smoothing my hair down over my shoulders, I look at myself in the mirror.

I practice a smile. *There.* That looks like a girl who's doing just fine. A girl who is almost finished with her shoulder rehab and will be swimming with her teammates soon. The smile slips off my face. I hate how well I can play the part of *everything's great!* but at this point, I'm not just playing the part. I'm the lead role and I don't see the credits coming anytime soon.

I start to make my way out into the living room when I hear ringing from behind me. Turning around, I slap my comforter until my hands discover my phone. Beckett's name flashes across the screen. I hesitate, but like every time before, I know I can't avoid him so I lower to my bed and press answer.

"Hi, Beckett," I force out cheerfully.

"Where the hell have you been?"

"What do you mean? My apartment? Going to my classes?"

"Is there a reason I haven't seen you since Tuesday?"

"Did we have plans?"

"After the little stunt you pulled Tuesday, I thought you'd want to make it up to me and apologize."

"Me?!" I blurt out too quickly. "Me, apologize? Are we remembering the same Tuesday night?"

"Don't get an attitude with me. Once again, I invite you to an event and you make a fool out of me. Except this time, you involved another guy. Like c'mon, Harlow. Why can't you just let us have fun? We used to be so good together, baby."

"Fun… Right, well how can I make it up to you, Beckett, since I once again ruined your night?" The words hiss out of my mouth. My patience with him is seriously wearing thin.

"Well you could start by using that mouth for something else. Why haven't we hung out lately? I miss your body."

"Ha!" I scoff. "Did you forget I'm injured?"

"So? You could be on top. Then you wouldn't have to worry about your shoulder."

My jaw drops. The silence hangs in the air between us for about a minute before he speaks again.

"Well I guess I'll just take care of myself some other way."

"Okay." I deadpan.

It would not surprise me in the least if Beckett has been sleeping around since I got hurt. Not that he and I had much of a sex life, so he already probably wasn't "faithful," if you even want to call it that. We've never been official but I don't peg him as the loyal type.

"Actually, how about you make things better by coming to the fall formal with me? Get all beautiful like I know you can and we have a good night together. Just us, like old times. What do you say?"

I was waiting for this since Lennon told me about it at coffee.

"Beckett, can I ask you something?"

"Uh, I guess?"

"Why do we do this? You and me? I clearly can't do anything right and somehow you still find a reason to hang out and keep up with whatever *this* is. For the life of me, I can't figure out why."

When there's no reply, I think maybe he's hung up.

"Really, Harlow? Seriously?"

"Seriously."

"Fine. I remember when I first saw you and I thought you were the prettiest girl on campus. I'd never met anyone like you either. You were talented and we had fun together. Look, I know things haven't been great lately but we've been doing this thing for almost two years now. It would make me happy to be the guy who gets to have you on his arm at the formal. It's one of our last ones. Don't let me down."

Part of me softens when I think about the first few formals he and I went to when we first met. When everything was light and easy. Why couldn't they be like that again? Another part of me—the people pleaser one—doesn't want to upset him. Not to mention what his reaction might be if I did say no.

"Okay, Beckett. I'll go with you."

"Perfect. Let me know what you're planning on wearing and I'll see if I can coordinate. I'm sorry—"

I hold my breath. Is he actually about to apologize?

"—that you couldn't enjoy yourself with me on Tuesday. Formal will be better."

There it is.

"Yeah, okay. If you say so. Look, I gotta go. I'm meeting my family for lunch so I'll text you when I pick out my dress. Thanks for calling. But hey, one condition for the formal if we're going to go together?"

"And what's that?"

"Keep your hands to yourself this time."

I hang up before he can say anything else. Rolling my eyes, I turn my head and see Lennon through my doorway standing in the kitchen with a cup of coffee.

"What was that about?" she inquires.

I don't know what all she heard so I play dumb.

"What do you mean?" I get up off my bed and head into the kitchen to meet her.

"Who was that? Beckett?" She sips on her mug and leans against the counter.

"Yeah, he was calling to see how I was feeling and wanted to know if I'd go with him to the fall formal." I meander through the kitchen and living room, rummaging around for my purse.

"Well that's good, but I'm more curious about what you said to him before you hung up?" I hear her set the cup down and I freeze.

"Oh, about him keeping his hands to himself?" I respond quietly.

I turn around and Lennon has her arms crossed and she looks very concerned.

"Yeah," she starts, "Did something happen, or—"

"Oh gosh, no!" I interrupt her. "No, he was just so handsy on Tuesday and it made me uncomfortable. You know how I am about PDA. Plus, I still don't feel confident about certain things because of my shoulder. That's all." I smile and spot my purse by the door.

Lennon takes a step towards me and puts her hand on my arm. "Harlow?" Her voice is quiet. "You'd tell me if something was wrong, right? Between you and Beckett?"

I hold my breath. Is it finally happening? Am I finally going to say it out loud?

"Because I hope you know I love you both and just want you guys to be happy." She smiles and rubs my arm.

My shoulders sag and I accept the reality that maybe I've waited too long to even say something. I can imagine I'd get questioned about why I'm still with him, or why I haven't told anyone. If only it were as simple as just calling it quits. Besides, Lennon has waved off our past conversations with comments about how rough patches and growing pains are normal in a relationship.

"Right, thanks Lenny." I kiss her cheek, then grab my purse and dart out the door, feeling like the walls of our apartment are closing in on me.

I spend my drive to meet my family in silence. I think over the last few months and wonder if there even was a way to cut Beckett off when I knew things were getting bad. In reality, the night I got injured should have been the final nail in his coffin since he was so drunk he didn't even realize I was hurt.

As I pull into a parking spot outside of the sandwich shop, I see Mom and Dad with Margot already sitting down at a table. I observe them for a minute through the window like an outsider. In almost every aspect of my life, I feel like I don't really fit in anymore. Margot and my parents have always had what appears to be this seamless relationship.

There was some time in Margot's senior year of high school where we had to all go to counseling as a family, but even then, it didn't ever feel like my parents were let down by her. When I called Margot to tell her I was hurt, she told my parents for me. I didn't hear from them for a day, then I got a text from Mom telling me she was sorry. I'm sure she just didn't know what to say because she and I have never been that close to each other.

Dad called me the next day and we talked for a few minutes. He asked me for details and I avoided giving him specifics. He made a point to tell me that he wasn't disappointed in me and was just sad that I wouldn't be starting my season as early as I typically would, but he also chalked that up to how he loved coming to my meets.

I step out of my Bronco and make my way onto the sidewalk to head towards the shop door. Before I can make it there, someone lightly taps on my shoulder.

Dear God, please, no.

"Hey, Harlow."

I plaster a grin on my face and spin around on my heels to be greeted by Wes and for a moment, I'm distracted. Lennon wasn't wrong. He's hot.

He's got brown messy hair that looks like he runs his hands through it during the day. The tattoos I noticed peeking through his sleeve at the date party are on full display in the pale yellow T-shirt he's wearing with black jeans and Converse. *Alright, I get it, Lenny.*

"Oh, hey." I breathe a sigh of relief.

"Expecting someone else?" he says with a shy smile. "Maybe my best friend?"

"I just didn't know who it was. I've had lots of surprise encounters the last couple days." I laugh a little.

"I gotcha, well I just wanted to see if you're feeling better. Lennon was really worried about you Tuesday and I saw your text about getting sick and leaving." He tucks his hands into his pockets.

"Oh, yeah, something didn't sit right with me. But, you were with Lennon after I left?" I look over my shoulder and see my family has noticed me. They wave and I wave back, letting them know I'll be just another minute by holding up my pointer finger.

Wes smiles and nods. "Yeah, just for a little. We weren't like, *together*. I mean, we were together, but not like—"

I shake my head, sorry to have gotten him all worked up. "I think I asked the wrong question here. Hey, I'm meeting my family for lunch but thanks for checking on me. I'll let Lennon know I saw you?" I ask because it feels like something's going on and I'm not sure what mess I just stumbled into.

"No! No, I just mean, it's not a big deal. We don't talk like that or anything. We don't talk at all actually." He stops speaking for a second and a frantic look washes over his face. "I've also gotta go. I'm meeting my sister at Boulder! Have a nice lunch." Wes steps forward and I realize too late that he's a hugger so I'm caught with my arms slack by my sides while he lightly wraps his arms around me. I pat his back, then step away and shake my head, dumbfounded at this entire encounter while he turns to head off.

"Oh, hey!" I call after him. "Same goes for me, don't tell Shep you saw me."

He salutes then walks off in the opposite direction.

I open the door and finally head to the table my family is sitting at. Dad speaks first, "New friend?" and points at the window where Wes and I were just talking.

"Oh, no, well, kind of? I'm not sure actually, but he's a lifeguard at the rec center so I see him around." I bend down and hug him before walking over and hugging Mom too. Margot just extends her finger and I *boop* it with mine. Something we've done since we were kids, with no real meaning other than our way of just saying, *hey, love you.*

I sit down and don't pick up the menu. There's no need. I'm ordering grilled cheese with tomato soup. I don't care what anyone says, it's comfort food at its finest.

"So, how's everything been going?" Mom gets right to the point.

"I'm okay, just been busy with my rehab practices and then keeping up with classes. Nothing's really changed except I haven't had any meets yet." I smile at the waitress who walks over in the middle of our conversation and takes our orders.

As she walks away, Margot cuts in, "Well I'm glad to see you! You look great and I love the outfit."

"Thanks, sis." I offer her a shy smile. If only she knew what it was covering up.

"So what's your timeline looking like then? Until you can compete?" Dad sips his water after he asks his question and I can tell he's worried about pushing too far.

"I'm hoping for two more weeks, but Coach said maybe three to four. It just depends. We agreed that I'll start out doing some freestyle events before getting back to swimming fly." I reach out and put my hand on his. His eyes twinkle at me and I know he loves me but I still can't help feeling like I've disappointed him too.

"Well that's great news, dear!" Mom speaks, then looks at Margot and then back at me.

Margot smiles sheepishly and goes to open her mouth but our food arrives and takes the moment from her. I don't let it go though, and once everyone is settled with their orders, I start the conversation.

"Margot, is there something you wanted to talk about?" I raise an eyebrow at her and flash a look of skepticism.

"Kind of, but I didn't want this lunch to be about me." She takes a bite of her sandwich and relief floods my body.

God, PLEASE make this lunch about you.

"Oh, honey, don't start," Mom rolls her eyes. "Margot got offered a job at Everson!" The shrill in her voice makes me cringe and I look at Dad and then Margot who are both quietly chewing their food.

"That's—well, wait, is it good? What are you doing?" I ask while blowing on my soup to cool it down.

"They want to bring me on as an advisor and student counselor," Margot answers. "I wasn't sure about it but then I realized I would get to be close to everyone again and that could be good!"

Dad nods his head but doesn't say much. Why do I get the feeling there's more to this than they're letting on? Then it hits me.

"Oh my gosh, it's to keep an eye on me isn't it? Y'all are

worried I'm going to, what, get depressed or something? Stop swimming?" Exasperation fills my tone and I slouch down into my chair. "That's exactly what it is, isn't it?"

Now it's Dad who is quick to speak. "I told them," he glares at Mom and Margot, "you are doing just fine, but Margot wants to be there for you."

"I'm just glad both of my girls will be close by again," Mom says.

"I am FINE!" I raise my voice a little and a few heads turn our direction. "Why is everyone so concerned that I'm going to just fall apart or something? I'm not some fragile little thing. You guys have no idea what I've been dealing with and now you want to just rush in and keep tabs on me like a child?"

"No! Sissy, that's not it at all. I just, ugh," Margot sighs then looks at Mom. "I told you I shouldn't have brought this up today."

Mom rolls her eyes again, waving her hand in dismissal.

"I won't lie, I am worried. But I really took the job because it has great pay, benefits, and I miss Everson." Margot half smiles at me before looking down at her food.

There are so many ways I could respond at this moment. So many choice words that would continue to express how I'm feeling but I swallow my emotions and take a deep breath before smiling back. "Okay, when do you start?"

Her eyes light up. "The new year! I have to help transfer some of my own patients to other providers but then I'll be transitioning into my position with the school."

"Are you living nearby? Or what are you doing with your house?" Margot lives about an hour out of town in a sweet little house. She was so proud to afford it all on her own and she's put so much character into it since she bought it.

"I'm renting it out to a mom I connected with through someone at my office. I found another place right near here actually. I'll move out in January and the new tenants will take over in the spring." She reaches her hand out and I know she wants the assurance that I really am not upset with her.

I *boop* her finger and Dad interjects, "This is nice. I'm glad we did this." Then laughs dryly while looking at Mom who has a sour face.

We finish eating and have small talk about different events coming up, I mention the formal, Dad talks about the changes in our town, just the usual. As we get ready to leave, Mom and Margot go to use the restroom and I'm left alone with Dad.

"Hey, Harlow, listen to me for a second." Dad speaks softly and I turn to face him. "You take your time getting better, okay? You know I miss seeing you swim, but your healing is what matters to me and I'm sorry if I ever made you feel differently."

He reaches out and envelops me in a hug that I didn't know I needed. Tears immediately spring to my eyes and I nod my head yes into his burly chest. "It's okay, Dad. I'm sorry I let you down."

He pulls away from me and holds my face in his rough calloused hands. "You could never let me down. You are so much more to me than just my talented fishy." He kisses the top of my head and pulls me in for another hug.

We stay like this until Mom and Margot walk over and then we all say goodbye.

As I get into my car, I sit in the front seat and let the words of my dad wash over me. I wish I could agree with him. I wish I didn't feel like I was a let down. I wish I believed I was more than just the top swimmer at Everson. But when one thing has defined you for most of your life, and that one thing is momentarily stripped away…? A deep ache fills my chest and a question runs through my mind that's been haunting me since I got injured.

If I'm not Harlow, the swimmer, then who am I?

FOURTEEN

LEVERAGE

SHEP

It's almost been a week since I last saw Harlow. She disappeared from the date party and she hasn't been swimming at the rec center. Wes mentioned she got sick, but I don't know how much of that I believe.

I'm standing outside of the Everson Valley Sheriff's Office, which happens to be across from the local coffee shop, watching her interact with her little group of friends. Lennon and Beckett stand across from her on the sidewalk and she looks completely withdrawn. I try to make eye contact with her but the only person who seems to be aware of my presence is Lennon.

Harlow's playing with the ends of her dark denim jacket when she finally sees me. We hold each other's stares for a few seconds. Damn, has she always looked this sad? I offer her a small smile, but she dismisses it and leaves their group all together. I watch her for a few seconds before she gets into her Bronco and drives away.

I turn to head inside the precinct and the second I walk in, I'm greeted by a handful of employees. The first few years of my dad being Sheriff were pretty shitty. For a while, I stopped getting invited to different parties and everyone worried I was a narc. Eventually I just stopped going out and found I actually enjoy the comfort of staying home more anyways.

I turn the corner and find my father sitting at his desk. He looks up and immediately light fills his face.

"Son! What brings you in today?" He stands and walks around to shake my hand before embracing me.

I hug him back then sit down in one of his office chairs while he moves back around his desk. "Mom wanted me to check in with you for my senior thesis. I didn't know if there were any programs I could shadow and do some hours with."

He nods then types a little on his laptop before looking back at me. "It seems we have some openings with the evidence department. You'd be helping transfer old paper logs into our computer system."

"Pass."

"There's a few ride along opportunities, but I don't know how that would interfere with your job and classes. I'm also not thrilled about throwing you right into a patrol car." He lifts his coffee cup and sips before leaning his arms on the desk. "Son, what do *you* want to do?"

I sit there for a few seconds while my mind idles. I chose criminal justice as my major because I grew up around law enforcement. It fascinated me and I thought that with my dad's experience, it would be easy for me to fall into the ranks. However, I didn't really think about the fact that maybe I didn't want to be a police officer or sheriff. Sure, there were aspects about criminology that interested me but I knew if I wanted to really follow in my dad's footsteps, I'd be looking at more schooling in the Academy.

It's hard to really even think about what I want to do with my future when I've totally lost my vision for it. The few times I do think about it, one green-eyed, blonde-haired face pops into my mind. Everything has been thrown out of whack since I decided to insert myself into Harlow's life. I don't know what I expected to happen when we finally talked, but it certainly wasn't the rollercoaster I got strapped in to.

"Son?" My dad's voice cuts through my thoughts.

"How did you know you wanted to be a cop?" My words came out plainly, but at this point, I'm desperate for guidance.

He chuckles and leans back in his chair then spins around a photo of Mom.

"Mom?" I ask in disbelief. I thought it would have to do with some manly experience or his friends.

"Yep, your mother." He smiles and looks off into the distance as if lost in his own memories. "I remember one of the first dates we went on, we were leaving and someone tried to mug us."

My eyes go wide. He's never told me this before. "Why am I just now hearing about this? What happened?"

"Well, your mom got a little roughed up, nothing major. I took most of the beating, but the guy made off with our wallets and they never caught him. For a while, your mom was scared to go anywhere, not knowing if he was out there waiting to come back around, so I decided that I would become a part of the change to stop things like that from happening. Now, I'm sure that seems silly. There's far bigger things out there that I could never work hard enough to fix, but if I could start with your mom and make her feel safe, that motivated me at the time."

I sit in shock, thinking over the story I'd heard before of how they met and only dated for a few months before getting married. Dad quickly joined the Academy and in the first few years of their marriage, Mom got pregnant with me and then I grew up around police life. They've been together for twenty-seven years and are probably part of the reason why I'm so eager to settle down.

"So, you chose your career to make Mom feel safe? Did you ever catch the guy?"

"No, we didn't, but the effort I made to join the force and look for him made her feel secure and loved. I would have done anything for her." He smiles at the photo as he turns it back around to face him.

"That's interesting. I didn't know that." I scratch my head while I think about what else there is they haven't told me.

"Well, at the time it wasn't like it was worth bringing up because since I joined, I've done a lot more than look for low life muggers. But, now that you're asking, I figure this is as good a time as ever." He stands up and walks around his desk to be in front of me again.

I stand and meet his stare. "Whatever you choose to do, Shep, make sure it means something to you. I'll send over all these openings and you can choose the one you feel fits you best." He smiles and walks towards his door to let me know the time we have is up.

As I drive back to my house, I start thinking about any areas of my life that have had an impact on me and would push me towards a certain career path. Unfortunately, the only thing I can really think of is adopting Dahlia and how much peace she brings me and Wes.

I'm fortunate to have two loving parents in my life and while I don't have any siblings, I've always been able to find meaningful relationships with people around me. Yet, something in me started shifting around the time I got Dahlia. I started to feel like something was missing in my life. I've had a few serious girlfriends but most of them ended because I couldn't see a future with them, at least, not one that I thought would be successful.

Wes however grew up in a broken home. His parents fought a lot when he was a kid and after his mom had his younger sister, she took off. His dad tried his best to raise Wes and his sister without her, but ultimately he checked out when Wes was about seven and his sister was three, so Wes basically raised them both.

When I met him, he was pretty upfront about being at Everson on scholarship. His dad helped with a few things but for the most part, it's just been him and his sister. I think Dahlia has a nose for trauma or something because when I brought her home, she immediately went to Wes and curled up with him. We joke about her being a therapy dog, but I know she's brought me peace.

I get out of my truck and walk into our house, finding Wes and Dahlia together on the couch while he watches a movie. Dahlia lifts her head and wags her tail a little but I signal for her to stay where she is. She lays her head back down on Wes's leg and I head into my room.

Setting my belongings down, I begin to grab my stuff for my shift at the rec that starts in an hour. I wonder if I will see Harlow today or if she's still avoiding swimming. As I change into my uniform, Dahlia wanders into my room and jumps on my bed.

"Hi, baby. You have a good day with your Uncle Wes?" I lean over and pat her soft forehead. She looks up at me with her sweet eyes as Wes walks into my room.

"We had a great day," he responds for Dahlia. "We went on two walks, snuggled, and talked about girls." He winks at me before sitting down on my bed next to Dahlia.

"Sounds great, also, yes, please get comfy here." I roll my eyes as Wes leans back on my pillow and rests his hands behind his head.

"How did the meeting with your dad go?"

"It was actually very interesting. Speaking of girls, I found out he became a cop because of my mom. I thought it would have had something to do with a bro moment or whatever, but nope." I pick my backpack up and make sure my whistle and employee badge are inside.

"Huh. I wonder why he just now told you about that?" Wes asks as he rubs Dahlia with his foot. She flips over on her side while he gives her a massage.

"Not sure, but hey, how're your classes going? You still getting ready for midterms?" I pull a hoodie over my head before walking out of my room towards our kitchen. Dahlia hops off my bed and follows behind me, hopeful for a treat.

"Yeah, I mean, I have a few classes I need to put a little more effort into but besides that, I'm feeling good. Honestly just thankful I will have made it all four years of college without losing my scholarship," Wes responds as he makes his way out to our living room.

"That alone is a miracle," I joke with him, but I really don't mean it. I'm not surprised. In all things, Wes is diligent. He shows up and he gives his all. It's what makes him a good friend and I know it'll make him a good partner one day too. "What's the class you need to put more effort into? It wouldn't be the one you happen to share with a girl we recently met, would it?"

Wes turns his face away from me and stares at the TV. "If you're talking about Lennon, nah. There's nothing there. The date party was fun but there's really nothing else between us."

Even though he isn't looking at me, I squint to show my disbelief. But, if he says there's nothing going on, then I'll leave it alone for now. I'm not blind though, I saw the way he looked at her, and again, the man is diligent. I start to let my mind wander, dreaming about a life where I'm with Harlow and he's with Lennon. The realization of how fun that could be hits me like a ton of bricks, so I decide maybe I do want to prod.

"So you haven't talked to Lennon at all since the party?" I eye him again while rubbing Dahlia's head.

"No, I mean in class, but that's it. Why do you seem so interested?"

"Just a thought that crossed my mind. You guys seemed to get along well, and I don't know. I've never seen you act like that with a girl before."

He moves a little then turns to face me directly. "Do you mean that?"

"Yeah, man. There was a moment on Tuesday where it

felt like Harlow and I were intruding on you two, just made me think."

Wes pauses for a second then picks his phone up. "I think maybe I'll text her. See if she wants to study later or something."

"Atta boy," I shoot back. Selfishly, I'm hoping maybe I can get some secondhand insight from him hanging out with Lennon about where Harlow's been and how she's doing.

I wish I could say that I haven't been thinking about her as much as I have but that would be a lie. Not only is she making appearances in my dreams, I've been having trouble keeping my mind from wandering when I'm alone, especially in the shower.

There's something about Harlow that I really can't put my finger on, but I'm intrigued and drawn to her in a way I've never been with someone else. I think it's funny how society pretends that guys don't think about their futures or emotions and shit. Reality is, I miss Harlow when I don't see her and that sticks with me. It keeps me up at night.

I think about what Dad said earlier. It was Mom who made him change his way of thinking. She inspired him to leverage his purpose and desires for the betterment of their life together. I lean back against the counter and a shocking but clarifying thought transcends through me.

I would leverage my current plans for Harlow if it meant having her be a part of my future. But what do I do with that realization, when she's made it very clear she wants nothing to do with me?

FIFTEEN

AN OVEN MITT FLYING THROUGH THE AIR

HARLOW

The slam of the front door jolts me out of my sleep. I look around the room worried I overslept for class before realizing it's still dark and definitely not morning. I pick up my phone and the luminosity of 4:00 AM screams at me.

I tiptoe out of bed and crack my door open just the slightest to see Lennon's light still on. I can't tell if she just came in or what, but then something catches my eye. The couch is in disarray. *Oh, my, Miss Lennon, what have I caught you in?*

"Lenny!" I call out. A shadow by the bottom of her door frame freezes and I seize the opportunity to rush across our living room and push open her door.

"Harlow, wait!" she squeals.

Just as I suspected, Lennon is rocking her post hook up look in an oversized tee and very messy hair, but this time, she's got a huge hickey on her neck to sell her out. She covers her face with her hands before turning and marching towards her bed.

"Oh, don't pout because you've been caught," I taunt her. "Maybe let your sex-scapade know next time to not let the door slam on his way out."

She glares at me before crawling under her sheets. "You act like I wanted you to find out."

It's not like Lennon and I parade our sex lives—*or lack thereof*—with each other, but we also don't keep secrets about it. Over the four years of us attending Everson, Lennon's dated a few guys but she prefers to keep things casual. We usually give the other some sort of heads up if we plan to have a guy at the house, but for some reason she chose not to, and as much as I'd like to know why, I also know with Lennon not to push.

Her relationship with sex hasn't always been the healthiest. Being brought up in a strong Italian home meant attending Mass with her *Nonna* any time it was held. She struggled to understand faith and how it applied in her life as she got older, especially once she got to college. She tried to keep up with Catholicism but it usually just led to her feeling guilty about not knowing what were truly the right choices for her. She enjoyed going out, kissing boys, and having a drink every so often, but whenever she went home to visit, she was met with looming stares from her grandma.

I'm not one to really speak on religion because I understand that it holds huge significance—especially with certain cultures—but I don't believe that God wants us to be unhappy and miserable. I don't have it all figured out but I can say for certain with the few Sunday school classes I went to as a kid, we aren't supposed to judge. I've always offered myself as a safe place with Lennon because I could see it weighed on her when we first started at Everson.

I walk over and join her in bed, stroking her long chestnut hair. "I'm just giving you a hard time, Lenny. You don't have to tell me anything. But, you will have to cover that up tomorrow." I poke at her neck before getting under the covers with her. "Did you have fun at least?"

Lennon peers up at me with her warm brown eyes before bursting into giggles. "I did." Then she buries her face into my neck and we curl up into each other in bed. "I'm still waiting with him though to have sex," she whispers.

My sweet, Lenny. I kiss the top of her head. I admire that she still tries to honor the desires of her family, but it also pains me to know she's dealing with this internal battle. "Whatever you think is best. You'll know when it's right, but even then, you don't have to."

"I know," she says as she reaches over and turns off her bedside lamp. "You're sleeping with me tonight."

"Perfect. I wasn't planning on getting up anyways." The words come out lazily as I'm already dozing back off to sleep, getting comfortable next to her. "Love you, Lenny."

"More, Low."

I stir awake and Lennon is still passed out but on the other half of the bed. I look for her phone to see what time it is but can't find it so I slowly start getting up. The mattress betrays me and creaks the second I lift off of it and I hear a groan coming from her side.

"Sorry," I whisper as I make my way back into my room. I pick up my phone and roll my eyes. It's only 8:00 AM and Beckett has texted me three times, reminding me of my commitment to go with him to formal. I don't have the emotional bandwidth for him right now, so I toss my phone onto my bed and head into my bathroom.

As I peel off my sleep shirt, I turn around and look at my back. The bruises are faint now. The outline of hands are probably only still noticeable to me, anyone else would likely just see redness.

It's officially been a week since the date party and I can't put off swimming any longer. I close my eyes and try to play out any situations in my head that could lead to someone asking questions. What would my response be? I could tell them they're marks from PT? No, that wouldn't make sense. I could joke that it was a hookup gone wrong? Also, not believable. *Fuck*.

Turning on my shower, the thoughts of how to plan my practice accordingly become more pressing as I mull over the reality that the one person who I know will ask questions, will likely be there. Now I really need to think of something to say.

I get out of the shower and put on my typical uniform before heading into the kitchen to make my breakfast. Lennon has wandered out of her room and is now lying face down on the couch.

"Um, everything alright over there?"

She groans loudly and then pulls one of the couch pillows over the back of her head.

"Alright, I'll take that as a no. Do you want me to make you something to eat?"

Another groan.

"Perfect. I'm making a smoothie and some eggs. Do you want coffee?"

No response.

"Lennon!" I send an oven mitt flying through the air in her direction.

"Hey!" she yells and whips her head out from underneath the pillow. "What was that for?"

I roll my eyes at her and turn back to the fridge, getting the fruit and almond milk for the smoothie. While getting the blender from the cabinet, I feel two arms wrap around my waist and a head lay on my back.

"Do you think I messed up?" Lennon whines.

"No, Lenny, I don't think you messed up. Why do *you* think that?" Even though I know the answer, I still ask so we can have this debrief and carry on with our morning.

"I don't know. What if people find out I was with that guy and it starts something?" She taps her head lightly between my shoulders.

"Well, do you think he'd say something? And, why would that matter?" My suspicions are now raised, but I'm hoping I'll get answers without having to do research on my own.

"There are just some conflicts of interest, but no, I don't think he'd talk about us to anyone. It's just a thought I had when I woke up." She lets go of my waist then hops up onto the counter next to all the ingredients. Picking up a banana, she starts to peel it and I grab it from her hands and throw it into the blender.

"Hey!" She quips.

"Do you want to elaborate on these conflicts of interest?" Throwing the rest of the ingredients into the blender, I press the lid down and start the machine. With the loud whirring, Lennon starts to mouth words, pretending the blender is drowning out what she's saying. "Very funny," I jest.

"No, I don't want to elaborate, it's not that big of a deal. I don't know why I even said anything." She reaches behind her for the glasses and holds them out to me. I fill them up with our smoothies and she starts drinking hers while I get the eggs going.

She slips into one of the chairs and lays her head down again on the table. We continue in this silent routine of ours while I think about who was possibly in our apartment last night. She's had flings with Beckett's fraternity brothers before, so I can't see that being a problem. There's really no other circles we share except for the swim team, and there are no new prospects there for her to explore. The only possibility that pops into mind is the best friend of a certain lifeguard in my life.

I look at her again and narrow my eyes, then let out a little *hmph* before turning back to pick up our plates and set them down on the table. She perks up and looks at me with wide eyes. "What?" she asks.

"Oh, nothing. Just thinking." Sitting down and avoiding her stare, I let the silence linger for a second because I know that it will ultimately push her to keep talking.

"Are you going to tell me? Or am I just supposed to sit here and wonder because you know how that makes me feel." She pushes around her eggs with her fork.

"Just a certain someone popped into my mind that could have been here, but—"

She cuts me off, blurting out, "Who!"

The corners of my mouth pull up into a smile and I finally look her dead in the eyes. "Wes?"

A frantic look washes over her and she quickly grabs her smoothie, taking a big sip. "W-why would you think that? We aren't… We haven't talked since Tuesday?"

"You know, funny enough, I actually ran into him on Sunday, and he said the exact same thing."

Her fork drops from her hand. "Wait, he said that? Why didn't you tell me you saw him? Harlow!"

"He was on his way to meet his sister for coffee and caught me right outside Summit. It wasn't anything serious, he just asked how I was feeling because he was with you when I texted that I didn't feel good on Tuesday? Anyways, before I left, I asked him not to tell Shep he saw me, for obvious reasons, but he also asked me not to mention to you that I saw him and that you two don't talk or something."

Lennon's shoulders fall and she looks a little sad. So maybe it wasn't Wes who was here. She opens her mouth then closes it and tilts her head, letting me know she's doing some serious thinking about what she wants to say.

"Well, I'm glad you didn't say anything because like he said, and I just said, we haven't talked since Tuesday and there's nothing going on between us." She stands up and walks over to the sink, setting her dishes down, then turns on her heels. "As a matter of fact, I don't think I could ever see myself with him. What a silly thought."

I study her demeanor and there's a certain emotion emanating from her that I can't decipher, but I think I've officially pushed too far so I decide to change the subject to something I know she will gladly talk about—her major.

"Have you finished up your portfolio for your midterm?"

Lennon's pursuing a marketing degree with an emphasis on social media and content branding. Her dream is to take on some local businesses as clients. She's already helped with Everson University's swim team logo and the branding for some of our apparel.

"I know what you're doing but because I actually have exciting news, I'll bite. Yes, I just finished it and I sent it over to Boulder and Summit to see if they'd let me do a few sample posts for them on their Instagram pages. I really hope it works out because I'd love to be able to stay in Everson next year and work from home for all these cute little businesses." She stares off into the distance, her eyes glazing over in a dream-like state.

"That is exciting! Yay! I also have news. I think I'm going to finally swim today." I awkwardly smile at her and raise my eyebrows playfully.

"Oh goodie! I'm so glad you're finally feeling better." She meets me at the table and gives me a hug. "I've got to go work on a few other things for today but let me know how your practice goes—hey, that reminds me. Did you see Shep outside of the—"

"Yes." I cut her off. "I did and I really wish he wouldn't just stare at me like that. Beckett really doesn't appreciate how he keeps trying to insert himself into my life."

"Yeah, that's what I was going to say. I mean, I heard you tell him on Tuesday to leave you alone, but it doesn't seem like he really got the message."

A loud sigh leaves my mouth. I'm honestly exhausted over the entire situation and Lennon doesn't even know the half of it. I'm surprised Beckett didn't say something the other day outside Summit, but I tried to leave before he noticed Shep was watching us. I guess it worked.

I finish up my breakfast and head into my room to pack my bags for the day. I have two classes and then will head straight to the rec center for practice. Once I get everything together I stroll through the living room, giving Lennon a forehead kiss on the way out, and get into my Bronco trying to convince myself I'm ready to swim again and possibly see Shep. The thought makes my stomach flip and my chest tighten at the same time.

I spend my drive to campus thinking about the way he looked at the date party. The all black look really suited him and his eyes were so clear. Why does it always give me chills when he says my name? Plenty of people have said my name but for some reason, when he does, it unravels me. And he thought to check on me? Why do I feel like he genuinely cares about me and my wellbeing?

My music changes to a song by Sleep Token that jars me out of my thoughts and I realize not only have I already made it to campus, but I thought about Shep the entire way. What is happening to me and why do I not mind that he's occupying my thoughts?

I move through my classes on auto pilot, focusing on getting to the rec and making sure I can swiftly get into the water without risking anyone seeing my back. By the time I get there, I'm thanking my lucky stars because I don't see a familiar truck in the parking lot. Maybe Shep's schedule got changed again.

As I make my way into the locker room, I about cry with happiness that nobody else is inside. I quickly change into my suit and then throw my sweatshirt over it, grabbing everything else I need for practice. My plan is to get my cap and goggles in place, then ditch my sweatshirt on the block right before diving in.

I crack open the door to the pool deck and peer around. I still don't see Shep and I feel like I have a little luck on my side again. Darting over to the lane that's reserved for me, I get everything in place. *This is good. Things are going so well.*

Nearing the block, I place my water bottle on the edge and take a deep breath. Now is as good a time as ever. I shed my sweatshirt and turn to toss it to the side and that's when I hear it—a fucking whistle and a voice I'm starting to recognize all too well yelling very distinctly, "HARLOW SUTHERLAND. MY STAND, NOW."

I have two options. I could listen, now that everyone in the general vicinity is watching, or I could ignore Shep and dive into the pool. I decide to take my chances and go for option two.

Bad choice.

I finish my first lap and when I come up for air at the end of the lane, two tan muscular legs are standing by the block. I could just keep swimming, but at this point, I'm risking him talking to Pierce now that I know they've been in cahoots. Pulling my goggles up, I glare up at him.

"What do you want, Shep?" My tone is icy and I hope he can tell that my patience is wearing thin.

"Get out of the pool, Harlow. Now." He squats down and meets my stare. My insides do that weird flop again but I decide to test him so I push away from the wall and start to tread the water some.

"Or what?" I smirk thinking I've got him, but he leans forward and lowers his voice.

"Or I'm going to call Pierce and tell him that you've got bruises on your back that look like handprints, and they better be from some intense PT stretch he's been doing with you."

I gulp. How did I know this is exactly what would happen?

"Okay, damn." I swim toward the edge of the pool and pull my goggles and cap off letting my hair swirl in suspension around me. We meet each other's stare again and for the first time in my life, the tension with someone feels palpable. Clearing my throat, I put my hands on the edge of the deck hoping he will take the hint and back up so I can get out but instead his hands swiftly go into the water around my sides and pull me up out of the pool.

A small yelp escapes my lips as he sets me down on the pool deck and tosses me my sweatshirt. "Put that back on and follow me." The stern voice he's using is having the opposite effect on me. Instead of feeling frightened, my stomach is knotting up and I can feel heat rushing to my cheeks.

"Shep," I whisper, "this really isn't necessary."

He takes a step closer to me, our bodies almost flush with one another. "I'm not asking, Harlow. Let's go."

"FOREVER" BY NOAH KAHAN

SHEP

Harlow wasn't at the pool yesterday and I have no desire to work anymore if I don't get to see her there. Maybe that's a little dramatic, but her being there made my shifts bearable and gave me something to look forward to.

As I fumble around my room trying to get everything ready for the day, Wes calls out that he thinks Dahlia threw up in the kitchen.

I rush out of my room and sure enough, she's cowering by the couch and there's sick on the floor by her water and food bowl. Sometimes this happens, she eats too fast and it upsets her stomach. I clean it up, then walk over and crouch down by her. I hate that she thinks she's in trouble and is afraid of my reaction.

"Hey, girl. It's okay. Let me see that belly."

She rolls on her side and her tail slightly moves. I have so much to get done today before my shift starts but my focus now is on making sure Dahlia is okay.

She sulks into my room following after me while I throw on a hoodie before taking her outside. She seems okay but then gets sick again. I call the vet who helped me get her taken care of after I adopted her and thankfully he's not busy today and told me to bring her by.

I head back into the house and let Wes know that I'm not going to class today and might be calling out of work depending on what the vet says.

"Need me to cover for you? I'm on call but if you want me to go ahead and let Tom know you're not coming in, I can," he offers.

I contemplate it but a flicker of hope that Harlow might be back at the pool today has me wanting to keep my shift.

"It's okay. If anything, I'll call Mom and see if I can drop Dahlia off for the day. I'm sure she wouldn't mind watching over her grand-dog, who she loves so, so much." My voice turns into baby talk as I finish the sentence and look down at my sweet pup.

"Alright, well let me know if something changes. I hope everything's okay with our furry girl." He pats her on the head then goes into his room, shutting the door behind him.

I grab my backpack and some of Dahlia's stuff before getting her harness to lead her to my truck. She hops in the front seat like nothing is wrong, which is promising, then lays her head on the console.

I turn on "Forever" by Noah Kahan while I drive to the vet and sing to Dahlia. Thankfully she can't talk because she'd probably tell me to shut up.

An hour later at the vet, everything seems to be okay, but I call Mom anyways to see if she still wants to hangout with my girl while I'm at work just so I have peace of mind that someone's with her. Of course Mom agrees so I send Tom a text that I'll be running late to my shift.

We pull into the drive of my parent's house and Dahlia immediately perks up. While my townhouse isn't exactly small, it certainly isn't as spacious as my childhood home that sits on a chunk of property and has a huge backyard.

I wander into the house and before my own mother greets me, she's calling out for her "granddog-ter" to come see Mimi.

I roll my eyes. When I first got Dahlia, I was expecting my parents to be a little hesitant with her breed but Mom and Dad were thrilled. Dad said they've started talking at the precinct about rescuing and training some of the dogs at the shelter I got Dahlia from for emotional support care when they work with victims of sexual assault, any type of abuse, and especially with kids. Unfortunately though, they haven't found someone to head up a department like that and it's been put on pause.

"Do you want to stay for a quick bite before your shift?" Mom moves around me into the kitchen and starts to pull things out of the fridge, waving them in front of my face.

"I would love to but I need to head to the rec, I'm already running late." I walk around the kitchen island and hug her. Stepping back, I give Dahlia a rub on the head and then make my way to the front door. "Dinner tonight though, when I come to pick up my girl?"

I hear Mom's laugh echo through the house. "I look forward to the day you're saying that about a human and not a dog."

Me too, Mom. Me too.

Driving to the rec, my mind reels at the idea of bringing

Harlow home. While I realize that something draws me to her, it clicks that I still don't know that much about her besides the small things I've picked up on. I wonder what her favorite color is. What type of music does she like? Has she always loved swimming? *And the question I really want to ask,* why the fuck is she dating Beckett?

I pull into the parking lot and my heart hammers in my chest when a familiar gray Bronco comes into sight. Harlow's back. I whip into a spot and grab my things, eager to rush inside like a high schooler who doesn't want to miss the class he has with his crush. Breezing through the lobby, I bust through the door of the lifeguard office and stow away my belongings, quickly changing into my uniform. Glancing through the window, I see the locker room door open and the beautiful blonde I've been missing. She peers out before tiptoeing across the pool deck to the lane we keep reserved for her.

My gaze is transfixed on her and goosebumps erupt across my skin. Her hair is pulled up into a ponytail like usual but for some reason, it feels like I'm seeing her again for the first time. Maybe it's because I haven't seen her in a week after seeing her almost every day for the last four. I study the curves of her legs and my mouth waters at the thought of her taking off her sweatshirt, revealing the body I've been dreaming about night after night.

I notice she glances around quickly before discarding her sweatshirt onto the block. I'm halfway out the door to my stand when I see it. Two large but fading bruises on her back peek out through the keyhole of her swimsuit. Without thinking, I raise my whistle to my mouth and send a loud shrill through the rec. I let the red piece of plastic drop from my lips before shouting, "HARLOW SUTHERLAND. MY STAND, NOW."

I watch her hesitate for a second. Surely she isn't going to—nope, she is. She ignores me and dives into the pool starting her first two laps. I storm over to her lane and wait at the end of it for her to finish and come up for a breath.

Her head pops from the water and she won't even look at me. "What do you want, Shep?" She cuts her words at me but there isn't one part of me that cares if she's upset.

"Get out of the pool, Harlow. Now." I squat down to her level hoping that she can't escape my stare, but instead she pushes away from me and floats in the water, taunting me.

A smirk graces her lips. "Or what?"

I lean forward and lower my voice, ready to play the one card I know will end this game. "Or I'm going to call Pierce and tell him that you've got bruises on your back that look like handprints and they better be from some intense PT stretch he's been doing with you."

Harlow visibly gulps. "Okay, damn."

Finally, she swims toward the edge of the pool and takes her goggles and cap off. I wish I didn't notice how pretty her hair looks when it's cascading around her in the water. Our eyes meet again and I swear she blushes before clearing her throat and slowly putting her hands on the edge of the deck. I can tell she's taking her sweet time just to get under my skin.

Nope. I've had enough of this.

I reach down into the water and lightly grasp her waist, doing my best to avoid where the bruises are, then pull her up out of the pool and deposit her down onto the deck. She yelps and shock covers her face. I give her the sweatshirt she threw on the block. "Put that back on and follow me."

She nibbles on her bottom lip and I can tell I'm having an effect on her. *Good.*

She softens her voice before whispering, "Shep, this really isn't necessary."

Closing the gap between us, I speak again, steadying my words. "I'm not asking, Harlow. Let's go."

She quickly pulls the sweatshirt over her head before grabbing the things she brought out with her. I turn and start to walk towards the lifeguard office, stopping every few steps to ensure she's still trailing behind me. When we get to the office, I open the door and usher her inside, then close the blinds and lock the door.

"Shep," she starts. "Why am I here? What do you want?" Her breathing has picked up some and I can still see the flush in her cheeks.

I start pacing the room, overwhelmed by the emotions flooding my body. "What happened to your back?" I ask without looking at her because I know I'll want to touch her in some form. Every time I'm near her, I find my hands gravitating towards her.

"I don't know what you're talking about. Didn't you hear me at the date party on Tuesday?" Her tone is starting to shift back to the familiar defensive one I know all too well.

"You don't know what I'm talking about? Have you seen yourself in a mirror? I don't give a damn what you said to me Tuesday when there's visible bruises on your back. I'm going to ask you one more time, Harlow. What happened?" I turn and face her, hoping my eye contact is the pressure to make her answer me.

"Shep, nothing happened. They're not bruises, just old marks from PT." She rolls her eyes and turns to walk towards the door.

My body acts on instinct again and next thing I know, I'm reaching for her hand, pulling her back and into my body. I run my thumb along the side of her jaw and she takes a sharp breath in. I study her face and her features up close for the first time, wanting to commit every detail of her stunning appearance to memory. When our eyes meet again, she closes them.

"You've been swimming here for the last four weeks and you don't think I've memorized every inch of your body?" The words leave my lips softly and she licks hers as if tasting them. "Who did this to you?"

Her voice trembles. "You're—you're mistaken. I'm fine. It's nothing. Shep, please." She opens her eyes and a look of fear flickers across them.

I let go of her and stumble backwards. "You don't want to tell me right now, fine. Let's go and we can talk about it somewhere else."

"Uh, excuse me?" Her voice croaks. "Shep, what do you not understand about leaving me alone?"

"And how do you not understand that I can't!" I don't mean to raise my voice but I can't help it. I step towards her once more and cradle her face in my hands. "Harlow, I don't know why but I can't leave you alone. I just…can't."

We hold each other's gaze for a few seconds before she softly whispers, "Okay."

"Okay?" I parrot her.

"Okay. But, can you please let go of me." Her voice is small and it takes me too long to realize that if those bruises are from someone, every touch I've impressed upon her has likely done more harm than good.

"I'm so sorry." The words tumble out of my mouth. "Harlow, I—"

Stopping to really think about this situation and how to go forward, I realize I need to meet her where she's at if I want to ever get through to her.

"Go finish your practice like you wanted to. I'll let Tom know I need to take off early. Dahlia, my dog, was sick earlier today, so I'll just tell him I need to go take care of her. When you're done swimming, will you go with me to pick her up, and we can talk?" I hold my breath and hope that by some miracle this will get through to her.

"You have a dog?" she asks, tilting her head and looking at me pensively.

I can't help the laugh that escapes my lips. "Yes, I have a dog."

"Huh…" She chews on her bottom lip again. "I like dogs."

"So, is that a yes?" I soften my gaze at her and she looks down at her bare feet.

"Would you really tell Pierce?"

I don't want to coerce her into spending time with me but I also don't want to lie to her. The truth is, I would tell Pierce. He cares about Harlow differently than I do, but we both want to see her succeed.

"I would…feel like I'd need to." As the words leave my mouth, I hope they don't cause me to lose any of the progress I feel I've made.

"Fine, but I'm only agreeing to this because I'm not going to lose any more time being with my team." She steps closer to me and pushes a finger into my chest. "Don't let it get to you."

I nod my head quickly and smile at her. She glares at me then turns to walk towards the door. "May I leave now?" The sass returning to her voice.

"Yes, Harlow. Though, you and I both know you could have left whenever you wanted. But I guess now we also know you wanted to be alone with me." I shoot a wink giving the sass right back.

"Ugh!" she groans, before throwing open the office door and beelining back to her lane.

This girl is going to ruin me and I can't wait.

SEVENTEEN

SITTING DUCKS

HARLOW

I stomp back over to my lane before cutting a glare back at Shep. Who does he think he is? I mean, on one hand, am I really upset that he made it very clear he cares about me? No. It's the fact that I can't understand it. That bothers me.

I don't want to be a pity case for him. I know he's watched me struggle, but this feels different. In the office, it was like he saw *me*. Or even more unnerving, he saw right through me and all my bullshit. The last thing I need though is more gossip spreading through campus. If he talks to even one person about my bruises, I'm done for.

I get to the edge of the pool and sit down to let my feet dangle in the water while I get ready to swim. Did I also actually agree to leave with him? To get his dog? I didn't really see him being a dog dad, but I'm intrigued. I'm sure he's got a golden retriever or a lab. He seems like the guy to get one of those traditional frat boy breeds.

As I'm about to start my practice, something brushes up against my back. I look up to see Shep standing behind me.

"Yes?" I huff out.

He laughs before giving my ponytail a small tug. I won't ever let him know that it tugged on my heart too.

"I just wanted to offer you some privacy to take your sweatshirt off again before you get in the pool, just so nobody else sees your bruises." He speaks with no emotion, like this is exactly what he should be doing.

"O-okay." I stutter out.

"Actually, do you mind if I—here, let me." He offers his hands out and I don't know what takes over my body, but my hands levitate to meet his. He lightly grasps the ends of my sleeves before gently pulling my sweatshirt over my head and setting it next to me.

The warmth that floods me is unlike anything I've ever felt in my life. I glance up and our stare lingers. He isn't actually undressing me, but why do I feel like my soul is being bared before him somehow? I snap my gaze back to face the pool, trying to break this trance we're held in.

But then, he squats down behind me, brushing his nose against the back of my ear. My now exposed skin erupts with chills and he snickers softly.

"Careful, Harlow, you're letting your emotions show." His breath tickles the side of my neck.

Before I can counter his remark, he nudges me with his knee into the pool, but thankfully the coldness of the water is the shockwave I need to jolt me out of this. As I break the surface and wipe the water off my face, Shep gives me a smirk.

I watch him walk back to his stand before grabbing my

goggles and cap, getting everything in place so I can start swimming. That's the entire reason I'm here, but am I telling him that or myself at this point?

I decide the best thing to do today is hypoxic training—a type of training we do to help us build up our endurance, focusing on trying to take as few breaths as possible. It's not entirely beneficial towards my rehab training, however right now, it's the perfect excuse to keep me from popping my head up above the surface and having to face Shep.

I start with freestyle and a hypoxic ladder. I do two laps breathing every three strokes, then every five strokes, then every seven strokes, then try to not breathe at all. Once I get to the laps that I need to try and not breathe, I decide to do them underwater entirely. I take a deep breath then sink under, pushing off the wall with my toes to start breast-stroke. While I pull myself the distance of the lane, I focus on completing my rehab. I think about rejoining the team and not having to swim at the rec center anymore.

As the thought enters my mind, I make it to the other end of the pool and break the surface. A sinking realization hits me and has me gasping for air like I've just been punched. *Not swimming at the rec center anymore means not seeing Shep anymore.*

My chest starts to tighten and there's a knot forming in my stomach. Why does that thought make me sad? I'm sure once I'm back with the team, Shep's fixation with me will subside. Why does that also bother me? There's another thought that's been trying to circulate its way through my heart, but I refuse to entertain it one bit.

I shake off this train of thought and resume my training set. When I finish, I look over and, of course, true to his word, Shep has his bag thrown over his shoulder and he's waiting for me by the doors. Rolling my eyes, I get out of the pool and, for a second, I consider backing out of his proposition.

Do I really need to be alone with him? Do I really need to talk to him? But reality crashes back into me that he'll talk to Pierce and that will ruin everything I've been working towards for the last month. As I trudge forward, I come up with my own plan. I'll go with *pool boy* to get his dog, entertain his questions, tell him that I got the bruises from a stupid game, and then wash my hands of the entire situation.

"I need to rinse off and change, then I can meet you in the parking lot. I'm assuming given you seem to know everything about me, you know which car is mine. It's unlocked so feel free to wait there. Give me five minutes."

A small twinkle forms in his eyes. I know I'm letting him in, even just a little, and I also know that it means something to him. I don't want to lead him on, but I also don't think he deserves for me to continue to be a bitch to him when maybe he actually does care? This is all new and unfamiliar territory for me.

I find myself moving quickly to rinse off and get dressed. I'm sure anyone else would say this is excitement but no, that's not… I'm not excited to spend time with Shep. That's ridiculous.

Once I get all my stuff, I text Lennon to let her know I'll be home late because I need to run an errand. She doesn't reply right away, which is odd, but I'm sure she's just studying or something.

Approaching my car, I can see in the side mirror that Shep is holding something in his hands that after a few more blinks has me running to the car and throwing open the driver's door.

"Give me that!" I shout, snatching the soft blue piece of fabric from his hands before stuffing it into one of my bags. My breath comes out in a frustrated huff as I mentally smack myself for the oversight.

I open the door to my backseat and pop my trunk, moving anything I have back there out of the way for when we get his dog. The entire time I can feel Shep watching me, which makes my skin burn up.

Settling into my driver's seat, I ignore his presence and try to breeze past the last few minutes. Pushing my key into the ignition, Shep tries to break the silence.

"So, what—"

"Shh!" I cut him off, pushing a finger towards his mouth but not onto his lips.

He sucks his lips into his mouth trying to stifle a laugh.

"Shep! I'm serious."

He busts out in laughter.

"Ughhh," I groan while sinking down into my seat, covering my face with my hands. This is mortifying.

"I'm sorry, Harlow. Hey." He reaches out to remove one of my hands from my face and gives it a light squeeze. "I'm not laughing at you. I promise."

I let our touch linger for a second before retracting my hand and shimmying back up, straightening out my posture.

"I thought you weren't going to keep touching me." I try to change the subject.

"You're right. I'm sorry, I just can't help myself. I don't know why," he admits while rubbing the nape of his neck.

Suddenly, I'm very self conscious of who could see me

sitting with Shep in my car. I can't risk another photo being taken of me. This whole idea is honestly terrible and makes me sick to my stomach; I'm consistently trying to please Beckett *and* now trying to keep Shep from involving Pierce.

Starting up the car without further conversation, I shift into reverse and get the hell out of the parking lot. There's really only one way from the rec to get back towards campus so I start heading that way.

"Geez…" Shep says with a cheeky look on his face.

"What? We were sitting ducks and I figured you'd just start telling me where to go from here."

"Gotcha. Well yeah, just follow this road to the intersection that's by Boulder, then you can turn left going out towards the mountain trails." He opens his phone and I catch a glimpse of his home screen. It's him and who I assume are his parents. "Harlow!"

I jerk my car back into the right lane. "Sorry, I just saw your background and remembered you telling Coach Bradford about your dad being the Sheriff. I think I recognize him."

"Okay, well, eyes on the road. Yeah, that's my mom and dad." He runs a hand through his hair and tugs on it a little.

"Should I not have brought that up?" I frown at him before looking back at the road.

"No, it's fine. There's just a lot weighing on me right now with graduation and my dad being the Sheriff. Everyone thinks I'm going to just follow in his footsteps, which I am in some regards. I'm a criminal justice major, but I don't really see myself being a cop, per se."

He pauses for a second and I think he's asking for my permission to continue. "Go on," I say.

"I know I want to be involved with law enforcement, I'm just not sure how yet. I've got 'til December to pick some sort of field to volunteer in for my senior thesis and I'm struggling to figure that out." He lets out a long breath.

I know I haven't given Shep a fair chance, but I also didn't expect him to be someone who had anything to worry about. He always seems so confident and positive. However, I should be the first person to know what it's like to have to put on a brave face.

"I'm sorry, that does sound like a lot. This is probably a dumb question, but have you talked to your dad about it?"

"Yeah," a soft smile graces his lips. "I met with him a few days ago. Actually, it was the day I saw you outside of Boulder with your *friends*." The smile leaves his face and his jaw hardens. "Anyways, my dad gave me really sound advice. The problem is, it still left me with unanswered questions."

"Well I've got a few of those myself." I speak mainly to myself, but Shep hears.

"What do you mean?"

"You know what's going on with me. There are things I'm still unsure of and worried about." I can see Shep out of the corner of my eye and he's got his face screwed up like he's confused and uncertain.

"You can ask," I state. "Go ahead."

"I don't know everything. Yeah, I know you're injured. I know it happened at one of our parties—wish I was at it to be honest…can't go back now though. What I'm trying to say is, I don't know *your* story."

I don't think anyone has once made it a point to call out that I've never actually said what happened. It's all just been speculation and gossip that my team started which turned into rumors that spread like wildfire across campus. "Fair enough."

"Oh hey, don't miss this turn," Shep interjects.

"I wasn't going to, but thanks." I smirk at him before continuing. "I didn't realize you lived so far away from campus. Not that I would have known, but this is, like, the direction of the neighborhoods and stuff."

A funny look washes over his face. "Can you pull over up ahead actually?"

"Uh, sure. Is everything okay?" I didn't think I did or said anything wrong, but Shep's behavior is making me think otherwise.

"Yeah, just had a thought. Why don't we just talk right now and then you can take me back to my truck."

"I really don't mind going with you to get your dog. I'm actually kind of excited to meet her. I always wanted a pet growing up but nobody was ever home enough to take care of one."

"I appreciate that, there's just one small detail that slipped my mind."

"Okay? Is your dog like, bigger than my car? Or…" I'm wondering what could possibly be the problem. After all of this?

"My dog is at my parent's house," he blurts out.

"I'm sorry, *what*?" I pull off the road into a spot by one of the many parks and hiking trails around Everson, then turn my car off.

"I didn't even think about it. I was just so focused on talking to you that I totally forgot we'd be going to my parents' house to get her." Shep runs his hands down his face. "It's fine, Harlow. You know what, don't even worry about us talking. Just take me back to my truck. I won't tell Pierce."

I stare at him dumbfounded. A million thoughts are running through my mind right now. How did I end up alone in my car with Shep? What would happen if Beckett found out? I wonder what Shep thinks about Beckett? What would Shep do if he knew how I actually got my bruises?

But then one very powerful thought hits me. *Would Shep's dad be able to help me get Beckett to back off?*

I shock even myself as the words leave my mouth. "It's fine, just tell me how to get there."

"Harlow. You don't have to do this. You're right, you've made it clear you want nothing to do with me and I shouldn't have tried to use your injury and Pierce against you." He hangs his head in a look of defeat.

"While some of that may be true, I also for once am making a decision for myself. So, let's go get your dog." I start my Bronco up again. "Where to?"

EIGHTEEN

"YOU AND A GIRL. A GIRL!"

SHEP

"Right here." I point towards the long driveway up to my parents' house.

Harlow turns in and once we reach the top, neither one of us speaks. I know I should've thought about this before I agreed to let her come with me, but I was so focused on the bruises and wanting her to be okay, it didn't cross my mind.

"You don't have to come in, it's okay." I go to reach for the door handle when she stops me.

"Wait, what're your parents' names?" She softly smiles and, wow. I thought Harlow's eyes were pretty, but seeing them crinkled up with a glint of happiness makes me forget how to speak.

"Yoohoo, earth to *pool boy*."

I'll ignore the name calling for now. "Sorry, I just… Did you know you have really pretty eyes? They're like this really nice shade of emerald."

A blush creeps into her cheeks but then she frowns. "Shep, your parents' names?"

"Right, right. Mom will just want you to call her Mom or Momma Fords, but Laura, and then William is my dad's. I don't even know if he'll be home, but Mom for sure is."

"Okay. Let's do this then, I guess." Harlow gets out of her car and before either of us can make it to the front door, it swings open.

"Hi, can I help—oh my gosh, Shep it's you. You and a girl. *A girl!*" Mom steps out of the doorway with Dahlia running out from behind her. She makes a beeline for me.

Or so I thought.

"Hey, my girl," I start to say, squatting down to embrace her, but she breezes right past me, my jaw dropping, and immediately stops to sit in front of Harlow.

In a voice that I would've never imagined coming from Harlow, she greets Dahlia. "Oh hi, pretty girl!" She gets down to meet her and leans into the side of her neck as if giving her a hug.

I'm done for. I'm actually done for. Harlow and Dahlia, together, in front of me. I think I have died and gone to heaven.

Mom walks out and cuts a glare my way before getting closer to my two girls. "Well hi there, I'm Laura, but you can just call me Mom or Momma Fords."

I roll my eyes before snickering while casting Harlow a playful look.

"Hi, I'm Harlow." She stands up and reaches out her hand, my mom ignores it, embracing her instead. Harlow winces and I realize my mom has no idea about her injury so without raising any alarms, I quickly speak up.

"Harlow is swimming at the rec right now because she

has a hurt shoulder." I clear my throat. "She's on the college team but," I raise my voice just a little, "is injured."

I widen my eyes at her before she lets go with a small gasp. "Oh, sweetie! I'm so sorry." She smacks the side of my arm before lowering her voice, chastising me. "Maybe you should have mentioned that sooner."

Harlow, noticing the interaction, speaks up, "I'm okay. I mean, yes sometimes hugs do hurt, but it's okay. It's been over a month now since I dislocated it. I think I'm still afraid it's going to hurt more than it actually does."

"Well, I'm just so sorry you're hurt! What happened, if I may ask?" Mom looks between Harlow and myself. I shake my head, trying to sway her.

"You can ask. I think you might be the first person who has, actually." Harlow laughs softly to herself. "I had an accident at the back to school party that Chi Kappa throws. I'm not sure if you're familiar, since…" She motions in my direction.

"Oh, yes, I'm familiar. Shep didn't go this year because I was sick and his father had to work. He's the sheriff, I'm not sure if Shep mentioned that."

"I did," I cut in.

"Yes, well anyways, sometimes Will has cases that don't allow for him to come home like he might plan to. That week he was working on one of those cases while I was sick, so Shep stayed home to take care of me." Mom gives me side eye with a small smirk, and I'll be damned if my own mother isn't trying to wing-woman for me right now.

"Alright, that's enough," I stop her from continuing.

"How nice of you, Shep." Harlow raises her eyes at me

as if to show she's shocked but honestly, I don't think she is. "But yes, that party. I fell and dislocated my shoulder." Her eyes become distant when she stops speaking, as if her mind goes somewhere else.

"Well, that's just awful! I'm really sorry to hear it, but I'm glad you're getting better now!" Mom reaches out and lightly pats Harlow's hand. "Why don't you two come in? I just started dinner and I think your dad will be home soon, son. He said he'd try and finish up by six-ish."

I look at Harlow for her lead and she gives me a shy nod.

"Okay, that works for us, but also we can't stay too late since Harlow was kind enough to drive me to get Dahlia. I'll need to get back to my truck at some point." I start walking towards the house, casting a backwards glance to see my usual furry shadow trailing behind Harlow. My heart does a weird flip, but I can't fixate on that, not now.

As we enter the house, Mom wastes no time treating Harlow like it's the millionth time they've met. Harlow takes in the house and I notice she stops every few paces to look at the photos filling the space. There's a weird sensation invading my body, watching her exist in a place that's so personal to me. Maybe this is how she feels having me at the pool when she practices.

"Have you lived here your entire life?" Harlow's voice is soft.

"I have." I point to another photo farther up the hall near the kitchen. We walk to it together and she stops to take it in. It's an old photo from when I was about five. Dad has me on his shoulders and we are standing in the yard by the front door.

"That's really special," she says. "It's a beautiful home."

"Thank you!" Mom calls out from behind the wall, clearly eavesdropping on our conversation.

"Need any help, Mama?" I walk over to the sink and wash my hands. Usually when I'm home during any meal time, I'm recruited for some sort of task. I'm not great in the kitchen, but I like trying at least. I wonder if Harlow can cook.

"That's okay. You two just have a seat. I'm turning on the stove for a pot of tomato soup and I was going to make some grilled cheese. Is that okay with you, honey?" Mom grabs a few cans from the pantry.

"Yeah, that's—"

"Not you," Mom interrupts me. "Harlow, is that okay with you?"

We both sit on the bar stools by the counter and Harlow laughs, her cheeks blushing again. Seeing this side of Harlow is life altering. It's not that I thought she was devoid of human emotion, but I never expected the first time I'd see it, it would be in my childhood home.

"Yes, that's perfect. Actually, that's one of my favorite meals. I get it every time at Summit, the sandwich shop." I make a mental note of this, before catching her nervously picking at the end of her shorts. Without thinking, I reach out and place one of my hands over both of hers. She stills, but doesn't try to move me off.

"Interesting, it's one of Shep's favorites too. And, oh, we love that little shop!" Mom glances at our hands touching then gives me a look that lets me read her thoughts. Lifting my hand, I don't know what compels me to say what I do next, but the second the words leave my mouth, I'm filled with regret.

"Harlow's dating one of my fraternity brothers."

Mom drops her hands by her side and disappointment washes over her face. Harlow's body language changes immediately too, and she quickly stands up, putting space between us.

"Do you have a bathroom I can use?" Her words are so rushed, they fumble out of her mouth.

"It's just down the hall, the door should be open," Mom answers her with a polite smile.

"I can show you," I start but Mom interrupts me.

"Shepherd, I think she can find it on her own."

Damn. Now I really know I'm in trouble.

"Okay, thank you. Excuse me." Harlow quickly removes herself from the room and the second the bathroom door shuts, my mom drops the soup cans on the counter.

"Shepherd William Fords. I don't know what you just did, but I can tell you right now, that girl has no interest in whoever that guy you just brought up is." She puts her hands on her hips.

"I don't know why I said that. I guess I thought maybe after you saw me touch her hand, it would stop you from asking if we're dating or something. I didn't want you to make her uncomfortable."

"Oh no, I don't think I was going to, but you just did." She picks the cans up and turns her back to me as we both hear the door reopen. "But if she's dating someone else, what business do you have putting your hand on her like that?"

Before I can answer, Harlow wanders back into the kitchen.

"Sorry about that. Laura, did you want help with the soup?" Harlow doesn't look at me once.

"Sure! If you're okay with that, of course. I'll just get the can opener and then you can be in charge. Spice it up, make it yours." Mom opens the drawer, getting out the rest of the items needed to make dinner.

"Actually, I'd love to." Harlow takes the can opener and gets to it. I sit there in silence as her and my mom work in this unspoken routine, moving about the kitchen, handing each other things, Mom showing Harlow where something is, all while the most delicious smell fills the room.

Harlow idles by the stove, stirring the soup while Mom cleans up where she was cutting the sourdough bread to make our sandwiches. Neither of them have really acknowledged me and even Dahlia has focused on staying between them and not me.

I really messed up.

"I think everything's ready," Mom states, pulling me from my thoughts.

"Great, I'll get the bowls and plates." I stand and find my own place in the rhythm of this dinner-making experience.

As I open one of the cabinets, the front door creaks and my dad's voice calls out. "Laur, who's——" He stops speaking as he enters the kitchen and looks between Mom, me, and Harlow.

"Will, sweetie, this is Harlow." Mom greets him with a hug and kiss on the cheek before motioning to Harlow. "She knows Shep from school and the rec center."

"I see, that must be your Bronco then?" He extends a hand towards her and she shakes it tentatively.

"Yes, sir. It's nice to meet you."

"Dinner is ready! We were just about to serve ourselves and sit down." Mom changes the conversation and I watch Harlow step back as if trying to remove herself from the situation.

I don't know anything about her family, other than Pierce mentioning she has a sister, but I get the sense she feels like an outsider. Trying to regain control of the moment and also make up for my idiotic comment earlier, I butt in.

"Har, why don't you go first, since you're the guest."

Har? Where the hell did that come from?

"Uh, okay. Sure." She takes the plate from me and gets a grilled cheese off the counter before filling up her bowl with soup.

"So, are you dating my son? Or what brings you here?" Dad's words have everyone whipping their heads towards him. To Dahlia's delight, Harlow's grip loosens on the plate and her grilled cheese slides off and onto the floor.

"Oh!" Mom calls out. "Well, lucky you, miss girl." She dotes on Dahlia to distract from what happened.

I notice the look of panic covering Harlow's face so I gently grab her hand. "We'll be right back."

I guide her into the hallway by the front door. We stand there for a few seconds in silence before she pulls away.

"I'm so sorry," she finally speaks, before folding into herself. "I didn't mean to drop the sandwich, I just—"

"Hey, hey." I go to comfort her again but she flashes a look that makes me put my hands up and back away in surrender. "It's okay. I'm sorry Dad said that, but it's okay. I promise."

"I'm just so out of place here." Her words come out with a whimper. "I don't know the last time I had a meal with my family that was home-cooked, or someone asked what happened to me, or I spent time in my childhood home," she trails off.

Taking in Harlow and all that she is in front of me, my heart aches for her in a way that makes me feel helpless. There are so many sides of her I've yet to discover and I'm eager to, but I get the feeling there's so much hurt Harlow is carrying. It doesn't scare me off, but I can tell she isn't one to ask for help—much less take it. Either way, I won't stop showing up for her and reminding her she's worth caring about.

"I think you fit in just fine," I softly smile at her. "Hell, even Dahlia went to you before she did me, and that's never happened."

Harlow continues to look down, avoiding my gaze. I wish she could see herself the way I do. Before I can say anything else, Mom peers around the corner. Harlow quickly tries to fix her posture, presenting that everything's okay.

Baby, why do you do that?

"Shep, why don't you go help Dad with getting everything put together on the table? Harlow, do you want two grilled cheese triangles with your soup?"

"Yes, please." She looks at my mom and then at me.

"I'll go take care of that then." I step towards Harlow and decide to give her a small hug before turning to Mom and smiling.

"We'll be right there," she calls after me.

Just before I'm out of earshot, I hear Mom again, "Alright sweet girl, I think we need to talk."

I'm glad I don't have anything in my hands yet because I probably would have dropped it just like Harlow did earlier.

NINETEEN

ACCIDENTS HAPPEN

HARLOW

Have you ever been in a moment where if you stopped and looked around, you might think you're in a dream? It's an eerily calm feeling being somewhere that is new and unfamiliar, but also feels right—feels too good to be true.

Eating dinner at the Ford's house should have made me want to crawl out of my skin. It should have been scary or made me uncomfortable, but it didn't. It felt like I didn't just pull up a seat to their dinner table, but rather, I pulled up a seat to their family. They welcomed me in. They showed me love, and now everything with Shep makes so much more sense.

"Hey, do you think you could roll your back window down some? Dahlia likes to poke her nose out when she's in the car." Shep's voice cuts through my thoughts and I forget I'm not alone.

"Oh, yeah. Sure." I press the button and watch Dahlia poke her nose out the opening. To say I was shocked that he owned a pitbull would be an understatement. Then to find out he rescued her? So many of my little preconceived ideas I had about Shep were chipped away tonight.

"Is everything okay? You seem a little quiet. Even more than usual," Shep remarks playfully.

"Yeah, just…thinking." I keep my gaze out onto the road. It's almost 8:00 PM now, and we left the rec around 5:45 PM. I still haven't heard from Lennon and worry is creeping into my stomach. I'm sure everything's fine, but it's also not like her to just drop off the grid like this.

"So, we didn't really get the chance to finish our conversation before dinner and you having to play 20 questions with my dad. Which, I'm sorry about that." Shep laughs to himself. "I'm sure you realized it's been awhile since anyone came home with me."

Honestly, it was refreshing to have someone ask me questions to get to know me, and not just to try and find things out about me. The last few weeks have been full of people being afraid to talk to me, or ask the wrong questions, that nobody has really made an effort to just talk to me and ask me about my life.

Shep's dad was very intrigued by my interest in communications and what I would do with that major. I explained to him I always enjoyed doing public relations and before I was injured, I did a lot of public speaking for the college and our swim team. He told me the sheriff's office is always looking for people like that if I ever found myself in need of a job.

It dawned on me in that moment, I never really made plans past graduation since getting injured. I always assumed I'd go on to start training with the hopes of making it to the Olympics. Now? I'm not sure I can even swim butterfly like I used to. Maybe I should start looking for post-grad employment.

"I didn't mind it. Your parents are really nice. It was good for me." After spending a few hours in the presence of such kind and authentic people, I don't have it in me to try and put a mask on for Shep. Maybe for just the rest of this car ride, I can let myself be honest. Maybe I can be authentic with him.

"Can I ask you something?" I don't mean to blurt out my words but he flinches like I've startled him.

"Yeah, of course." He moves his hand between the gap of the seat and car door to pet Dahlia.

"Why me?"

It's another question that struck me after spending time with his parents—what would draw him to someone with my circumstances? I haven't been kind to him. I'm not warm and inviting like Laura and Will. There's nothing about me that I can really see fitting into Shep's life, so I want to know.

"What do you mean? Why have I been so persistent with you?" He looks at me pensively.

"I guess that's one way to put it. I'm just saying, you showed an interest in me without really even knowing me. And yeah, you haven't given up. I guess I'm just curious if there's a reason why." I choose to keep focusing on the road because, while I want to try and be honest with him, I never told myself it would be easy. Keeping my gaze ahead protects me from any further vulnerabilities.

"I see you for more than where you are now." He pauses and out of the corner of my eye, I can see his hands fidgeting and I know he's fighting with himself to not touch me.

Something in me wants to reach out and grab his hand. It wasn't just the time with his parents that made something shift in me, it was the realization that he doesn't touch me for his own satisfaction. No, it's like a reflex for Shep to want to be near me. He didn't have to make any effort when we sat next to each other at dinner, but his elbow would move slightly just to brush up against mine, and then his entire body would relax…

"What I mean by that," his voice pierces through my musings. "You may be injured, Harlow, and think that's all you are, but it's not. I meant what I said when we talked for the first time—I am sorry you're hurt. But, I'm not sorry that you getting injured landed you in the rec center for practice. I'm not sorry that you getting hurt, led you to me. Sure, I wish we met under different circumstances and I'm sure you can agree with that, but injuries and accidents happen."

I stir uncomfortably, but Shep either doesn't notice or doesn't care and continues to share his thoughts.

"And getting to watch you rehab and work your way back to being cleared for the team has been incredible. I can't wait to watch you compete when you're able to. But to answer your question of why, it's because the way I feel about you is different and I can't seem to shake it. And before you say anything, I don't want to shake it. I want to explore it. " He smiles at me and it's bewildering to me that rather than meet me at my best and have feelings for me then, Shep has met me at my worst and thinks I'm already worth something.

"I don't know what else to say other than thank you. I'm not very good with compliments and also the idea that someone sees me the way you do, is just… I can't comprehend it." I let out a very loud sigh and Dahlia comes and pokes her snout into my neck. "Oh, hi!"

Shep laughs. "She does that when me or Wes sighs too. I think she's got some therapy training in her and can sense distress."

"Speaking of Wes, do you know if he and Lennon have been talking? I tried to mention it to her the other day and she seemed pretty adamant that nothing was going on between them."

"That's interesting. Wes said something similar to me, but then he told me he was going to try and study with her, so I'm not really sure. I was pretty shocked though to find out your best friend is who my best friend is into."

"I've thought that too, but also, I don't think I should let much of anything surprise me lately." I make a few more turns and as we get closer to campus, I start to feel unsure about the night ending. Shep and I never did talk about my bruises and I don't want to bring it up, but I also want to make sure he isn't going to say anything to someone.

Before I can mention it, my phone starts ringing and it's Lennon. I pull into the parking lot of the rec and find a spot by Shep's truck.

"Sorry, do you mind if I pick this up actually? I haven't heard from her much today so I want to make sure everything is okay." I reach out to press the answer button on my car play screen.

"Of course, I can just hop out." He goes to reach for the door but I stop him.

"No, just one second. I want to finish our conversation before you go."

He smiles and leans back into the seat as I pick up the call.

"Hey, Lenny. You're in my car and I'm not alone. Just wanted to let you know before you say anything." I laugh.

"Oh okay, well hi, whoever is with Harlow!"

"It's Shep, actually. I was helping him with something."

He looks at me with wide eyes.

"Oh, wow, okay. Well, I don't know if you-know-who would be thrilled about that, but we can talk about that later."

In a low voice, Shep whispers to me, "Is she talking about Beckett?"

I try to wave him off, returning back to the call but he speaks again.

"Lennon, are you talking about Beckett?" His voice is sharp and I don't miss how his jaw clenches.

"Well, yeah. I mean the guy really hates you being around Harlow. I think we all learned that after the date party."

There's a sudden change in expression on Shep's face and he directs his attention to me before stating, "It was Beckett, wasn't it? That's who gave you those bruises."

My stomach drops. I open my mouth to speak but Lennon cuts in.

"I'm sorry, what bruises? Beckett did what?"

"Nothing, Len. Nothing. I'll be home in fifteen." I hang up the call before reeling on Shep.

"Are you serious?! Do you know what you just did?!" My voice is shaking.

"It *was* Beckett. You need to tell me what happened, Harlow, and I'm not asking this time. If that piece of shi—"

"Stop! Just stop!" The scream I was trying to keep strangled in my throat, slips out. "You don't know what you're talking about and I'm fine! You don't need to worry about this. I didn't ask you to step in and be my hero, Shep." I shake my head in silence. "This was a mistake. Get out of my car."

I can see the gears turning in Shep's head, but to my surprise, he doesn't argue with me. "Okay, Harlow. Good luck with Beckett." He unlocks his door then stops for a second, before turning back around and leaning towards me.

I suck a breath in, paralyzed by what's happening. His lips hover dangerously close to mine and every warning alarm that should be blaring in my head has gone silent. I close my eyes, not preparing myself for him to kiss me, but hoping that if I can't see what's happening, then it isn't really happening.

He brushes his lips on the side of my cheek near my ear, then softly states, "Your body deserves to be worshiped, not bruised."

I don't open my eyes until I know he and Dahlia are out of my car. Yet, even as I watch him drive off, knowing I'm alone, his words linger in the air and a strange feeling settles in my chest. I miss the sound of Dahlia's collar rattling every few minutes.

I miss…Shep.

TWENTY

WHAT IF...

HARLOW

The colors of the changing leaves all blur together as I speed down the road. My heart feels like it's in my throat. I don't even know how to face Lennon when I get home. I reach over into my console for my phone, reconnecting the music. I press play and the first song to pop up is "would've been you" by sombr.

As I drive and the song starts, the plucking of the guitar lulls me into my thoughts. My mind wanders to just a few hours ago when I was at Shep's, recalling the conversation I had with his mom.

"Alright sweet girl, I think we need to talk." Shep's mom moved towards me and then placed a hand on my arm. "Does Shep know?"

I squinted in confusion. Reading my expression, she continued.

"Does he know someone's hurting you?" She motioned to

the side of my body where part of my sweatshirt had ridden up and my back was exposed.

My eyes widened and panic consumed me. I quickly pulled the fabric down and opened my mouth to speak, but she stopped me again.

"I noticed it when you were in the kitchen and reached into the cabinet for a spice. Your sweatshirt came up and I'd recognize marks like that any day."

"Please..." I begged, not sure for what.

"It's that guy Shep brought up, I'm assuming?"

At this point, I decided to just not speak, nodding my head in response.

"Does anyone know?"

I shook my head side to side.

"Are you safe?"

I blinked a few times then furrowed my brow. "I don't... know." The words left my mouth in a whisper.

"I know I just met you, Harlow, but I can see a lot of myself in you. Which means if Shep is his father's son, and I know he is, he's not going to let you out of his sight." She stepped closer this time and gently caressed the side of my face. "I get the feeling you're a very strong girl."

Tears pricked the edges of my eyes and a part of my heart cracked.

"But you'll have to let someone in at some point," she continued.

I nodded my head again in response, this time the tears silently spilled over and I found myself stepping forward and resting my head on Laura's chest like a child. She brushed the ends of my ponytail with her hand while I quietly cried.

"I don't know how it got this bad," I mumbled to her before stepping back and rubbing my cheeks dry.

"That means he must be really good at it." She paused for a second and the weight of her words hit me like a ton of bricks. "What does Shep know?" she asked.

"He knows someone's hurting me. But I haven't confessed that he's right about it being Beckett, his fraternity brother." I couldn't believe I was telling her all of this, but it was like I couldn't stop.

"I see. Well, I can't tell you what to do and I certainly can't force you to get help, but guys like that…they typically escalate, and I'd be remiss if I didn't advise you to at least consider trying to get some help." Her eyes went misty.

"Was it you?" I asked quietly, not knowing how close by Shep was and if he knew the answer to the question I was asking.

"No, my college roommate went through something similar. Except, she wasn't as fortunate to be able to find help. Not to scare you, but to be honest." She softly smiled at me.

"I understand. You won't tell your husband will you?" I asked hesitantly.

"No, but I hope you know that he will be there for you if you decide to come forward." She reached out again and grabbed my hand. "You ready to go eat, sweet girl?"

My mind pulls back to the present when I hear a faint honking. The lyrics of the song confront me as if knowing my thoughts. Something about being saved and it being someone specific who could do it.

I know Shep wants to rescue me, yet I keep pushing him away. I'm starting to become more sure that Beckett isn't right for me, but trying to get away from him causes panic to creep up inside me.

Laura was being honest with me and, while I appreciated it, I also can't stop thinking about everything she said. I can't stop thinking about her roommate. She didn't say outright that she was killed, but she might as well have. I don't think Beckett would ever get to that level, but I also never imagined he would do what he did at the date party.

I decide to silence my thoughts and focus on the road ahead of me, listening to that same song on repeat. Could Shep really save me?

When I get to the apartment, I play out all the possible ways Lennon might confront me when I come in. She's probably waiting on the couch, ready to ask me a million questions, and the only question I really need to answer is with myself. *Am I going to finally tell Lennon everything?*

As I creep out of my car, steadying my breaths, a car slowly passes by, causing me to freeze. Did someone see me and Shep? Is Beckett here, ready to confront me? I don't wait any longer in the parking lot, bolting up the stairs to our apartment door.

I brace myself for what I'll find on the other side, but when I unlock the door and make my way in, Lennon isn't anywhere to be seen. I take a few more steps before I realize she's in her room. The door is shut, but I can hear her voice mumbling. It seems she's on the phone. My stomach drops at the sudden thought that she may have called Beckett.

Rushing into my room, I throw my things down and decide maybe I need to do some damage control of my own. I fish my phone out of my bag, take a deep breath, then press call.

"Beckett, hi. Sorry to just call you out of the blue."

"Yeah, what's up?"

"Oh, right. Um…"

Relief floods me that he hasn't mentioned Shep and, knowing him, it would be the first thing he'd say.

"Hello?"

"Sorry! Yeah, I was just wondering if you wanted to get dinner before the fall formal?"

Not that I actually want to, but I guess that's a good excuse for calling.

"Random, but sure. I can pick you up and then we can go to downtown Everson."

"Great!"

I know my voice is over enthused but at this point, I'm just glad it doesn't seem like any of tonight has traveled to him.

"Okay, Harlow… Bye."

I hang up my phone then fall back on my bed, letting a large sigh leave my body. Before I can even allow myself to relax, my door creaks open.

"Hey, want some company?" Lennon tip toes across my room, before sitting down next to me. She plays with my hair for a few seconds before speaking again. "We don't have to talk about what happened earlier."

I gently push myself up and turn to face her. The warmth in her chocolate eyes has always been a source of comfort to me. She's looking at me with love and concern, and I know she deserves the truth, but…

"When you're ready to talk about whatever it was that Shep brought up, you know I'm right here. But I do have to ask, what were you doing with him?"

A small laugh leaves my lips before I begin to tell Lennon all about the last few hours, minus a few details. I tell her about how apparently Shep and I both love grilled cheese and tomato soup, which makes her gasp dramatically. I fill her in on Dahlia and my total shock that Shep rescued not just a dog, but a pitbull.

We go back and forth about the night and, before I realize it, I'm beaming. My face hurts from smiling and laughing, thinking about all the little moments with Shep, and then the last few minutes with him crash back into my reality and I feel the expression melt away.

"What just happened?" Lennon asks, studying my face.

"Nothing, I just…" Leaning back onto my bed, I choose to confront the startling thoughts and emotions that have been rattling around inside me for the last few weeks. "I think I might have feelings for Shep."

"I KNEW IT!" Lennon shrieks, then rolls over to sit on top of me. Straddling my waist, she pokes up my stomach until she reaches my chest. "I knew he was finding his way in there." She taps harder where my heart is.

"Okay, okay. I get it, but there's obviously some things I need to handle with Beckett first." I push her off of me and get off my bed. Even bringing up his name fills me with panic, so I start to pace across my room.

"Yeah, that's true. People break up all the time though." She offers. "I know I've obviously been you and Beck's biggest fan, but it's not really him. It's you. I just want you to be happy, and I've never heard you talk about your relationship with Beckett like this."

Lennon asks a hundred more questions about what I'm going to do and how I plan to tell Beckett. I have no answers for her. I haven't even really accepted the fact that I admitted to maybe liking Shep, but I can't shake the electricity that hums through my body when I'm around him, or how since I kicked him out of my car, all I've wanted is to call him and apologize. But I don't even have his number.

"Am I being ridiculous?" I mumble. "Like, I had one night with Shep and suddenly I'm thinking about calling things off with Beckett and letting Shep in?" Obviously there's more to it than Lennon knows, but I still find myself wanting to please Beckett. Despite everything that's happened, everything he's done to me… Laura's words come back into my mind.

He must be really good at it.

I connected the dots that she was referring to being manipulative. I've never once thought to myself that I was in some sort of abusive relationship. I wouldn't have told anyone that either, but Shep's mom made me realize that whatever I've been doing with Beckett isn't normal and it certainly isn't healthy.

My hand involuntarily moves to my back and traces over the bruises hidden under my clothes. The movement conjures up images of my past with him and our memories no longer float through my mind like a supercut. Instead, they hover like ghosts, haunting my mind and sending chills through me.

I know what I need to do, but I'm still not ready to talk to anyone about it, except Laura. I'll have to find a way to see her again without it raising any alarms and also while still avoiding Shep, since I'm not exactly sure how I want to move forward with him.

"Hey, Low, sorry to interrupt whatever thought trance

you're in, but I was hoping we could go dress shopping this weekend for fall formal?" Lennon stands up and walks towards me then softly pinches my cheeks.

"Sorry, yeah. I think that would be really fun." I stand in the same spot of my room for a few more seconds. "I need to go shower, but yes, dress shopping this weekend. I'd love to."

She squeals then does a small jump.

"One thing though, Lenny. I'm still going with Beckett."

"I know." She smiles before continuing to skip her way out of my room. "But also, I think you really need to consider all this stuff with Shep." She stops then turns to face me. "I haven't seen you smile like that in a while."

She isn't wrong and I also can't believe the giddy feeling that consumed me while telling her about my night. How Shep and I both dipped our sandwiches at the same time. How Dahlia kept laying on my feet and when Shep would lean down to pet her, he'd let his hand linger for just a second longer near my legs, skating the length of me with his sapphire eyes. I even told her how Shep drew circles on my thigh under the dinner table…and I let him.

"This weekend, you and me. No boys. No thinking. Just dress shopping. God, I can't believe I'm saying that." I laugh as I turn to my bathroom, ready to rinse off the day.

"It's a dream come true!" Lennon's voice echoes into my room, the shutting of her bedroom door promptly following.

Shedding my clothes, I step into my shower and close my eyes. As the water crashes around me, my mind drifts off. I start to think about Lennon's words and how I should consider things with Shep. My stomach flutters at the thought of him, but in the same second, my stomach drops. Beckett will have to go.

All I have to do at this point is just get through the formal and then maybe I can reason with him about how there's really no point for us to be together. He has to see that. I mean, the way he treats me, he can't actually have feelings for me? But what if he does? I don't want to hurt him…but he hurts me.

Why is this so confusing for me! I can't believe I let Beckett get into my head and manipulate me like this. I feel so stupid, so dumb, so naive.

Mixed with the droplets from my shower, tears start to stream down my face. They burn almost as much as the water. I know this isn't the life I deserve to live. Deep down, I feel it too. I start to think about the way Shep treats me and wonder what type of person I would be if he was my boyfriend. I wonder about where I would be in my life.

I mix the tears into my face wash and work to calm myself back down. I keep going back to that mindfulness technique Margot taught me when I need to self-soothe. Focusing on the rest of my shower regimen allows my mind the reprieve it desperately needs. I work my cherry-scented shampoo into my hair and massage my fingers against my scalp. I can't help it when a groan or maybe even a moan slips out of my mouth from how good it feels. Pressing a little harder, it's like the tension is radiating out of my body.

I lean into my own touch and a flush consumes me as Shep's words replay in my mind. *Your body deserves to be worshiped, not bruised.* This time it's definitely a moan that slips out. A certain euphoria overwhelms me as I continue to massage my shampoo into my hair. My hands move from my head to my neck and as I trace my own finger along my collar bones, I imagine Shep doing it.

Just as I truly start to lose myself, Beckett pops into my mind again. My eyes snap open. "Stop it!" I yell at my thoughts and myself. I don't want to think about him. He doesn't deserve loyalty from me.

I shake off the lingering disgust and go back to finishing up washing my hair and then my body. I've never been very confident in myself or my sexuality, but something about the way Shep desires me so much is having an effect on me. I know my physique is double-take worthy. You don't swim for as long as I do and not develop a pretty sexy body. I just… never thought about what it might feel like to be truly wanted by someone. Beckett's certainly never made me feel like that.

I flick my eyes around as if there's some invisible person watching, then close them again. This time, I focus explicitly on Shep and let my mind truly wander. I think about his rippling abs. I lick my lips at the thought of what his mouth would taste like on mine. My breath quickens and my hand drifts between my legs.

What if…

TWENTY-ONE

ALL MY CARDS ON THE TABLE

SHEP

"I don't know, man. I don't really love the idea of giving you the number of the girl *I'm* interested in." Wes leans against my door frame and crosses his arms.

I've been home for maybe two minutes and I've already decided that I need to do something to stop this bullshit between Harlow and Beckett. I spent the entire drive home talking to Dahlia about all the possible ways I could run interference. Poor girl looked at me like she would rather go back to the shelter than listen to another second of my mindless rambling.

It was through those ramblings, though, that the same realization I had in the office earlier in the day hit me again. Trying to convince Harlow that she needs to open up about what's going on is never going to work. I have to continue to try and meet her where she is while she figures it out on her own. No matter how hard it might be to watch.

Involving Lennon is going to be a gamble, but I heard it

in her voice on the call when I was in the car with Harlow. She cares, and if she knew what was going on, she would probably be devastated. Is it right for me to try and involve myself with her best friend? Again, I'm not entirely sure. At this point though, I'll try just about anything.

"Wes, something is going on with Harlow and I'm pretty sure Beckett is involved. I don't know what to say, really, it all unfolded over the last few hours." I drag my hand through my hair and pull on the ends of it. Not knowing if Harlow is okay while knowing that someone is hurting her is really doing a number on me.

I know I can trust him, but I worry it could ruin any trust I've built with Harlow if I told him and she found out —not that Wes would tell anyone… God, I'm so sick to my stomach over this.

I think about the conversations I had with Harlow, her presence at dinner, and the way she floated around my house like she belonged there. I've always held on to this idea that there was something deeper going on with her. I could sense it from the first few times she swam at the rec center, I just had no idea it could be as serious as carrying the secret that someone is physically abusing her. Even thinking about it now, I can't fully wrap my mind around it.

"Is Harlow okay?" He steps forward and puts a hand on my shoulder, his concern and care grounding me. We may be best friends in this life, but I'm almost positive we are brothers in another.

"I don't know. Honestly, I don't. There are things that have happened to certainly raise some red flags, but she hasn't admitted to anything actually going on. I tried to ask her about some stuff earlier and she shut me down. I was able to convince her to come with me to pick up Dahlia from my parents' though."

Wes's eyes widen. "No shit, brother, that's where you've been? At home, *with* Harlow? Well what was that like?"

Thinking about the night makes my heart pound. There's no better way to explain how it felt to exist in the same space as Harlow other than to say it was intoxicating. I don't know what Mom said to her when I left them in the hall, but Harlow came back into the dining room looking and acting like a weight had just been lifted off her shoulders. The lightness of her radiated onto me and drew me to her like a moth to a flame.

I clear my throat before answering. "Good. It was really good. But, that brings me to my request."

Wes exhales and then walks out of my doorway into the living room. "I'm listening." He plops down on the couch.

"Beckett and Harlow are going to the fall formal together and I know that she won't change her mind about that. However, it doesn't mean that I can't still go with someone who also cares about Harlow as much as I do." Wincing as the words leave my mouth, I know this is a huge ask. Plus, Wes and I usually go to all my events together and I hate the idea that he'll be left out of this one. Maybe one of our coworkers who is also in Chi Kap can bring him.

"So, let me get this straight. You don't just want Lennon's number, you want to take her to your formal? You've gotta be kidding." His chest rumbles with a chuckle that I know is from disbelief more than it is humor. "You can't just go alone and still keep an eye on her?"

"I think having Lennon there will be helpful. I know, this

is shitty, but hear me out okay? I have a plan that you could benefit from."

Wes looks at me with curiosity, but now isn't the time for the rest of the details. It'll only be a matter of minutes before Harlow gets home and I need to intercept Lennon before Harlow does.

"Wes, please. Her number." My eyes are filled with desperation.

"Fine, hold on." He takes his phone out of his pocket and mine buzzes shortly after. "There you go."

I pull it out of my pocket and press the number right away. "Seriously, Wes, you're the best." I start to close the door and he shouts out his agreement with me on the matter.

A few rings go by before I hear the bubbly voice of Harlow's best friend on the other end.

"This is Lennon!"

"Hey, Lennon, it's uh…Shep." I hold my breath.

"Oh. Well, hi." Her voice sounds deflated.

"Not who you were expecting?"

"No, actually, I was hoping since it was an Everson number that maybe it was one of the businesses I've pitched myself to lately for social media work, but this…this seems like it will be much more inter-esting. But first off, how'd you—"

I cut her off, wanting to get straight to the point. "Wes gave it to me. But listen, we don't have a lot of time before Harlow gets to the apartment and I need to talk to you about what I said in the car before she does."

"I'm listening."

I spend the next few minutes giving her the cliff notes about my suspicions of Beckett, careful not to mention the bruises again out of respect for Harlow. She gives me a "hm" and gasps every so often, but then cuts me off mid-sentence.

"Oh shit! I think she's home, hold on."

I hear a scuffling, then what sounds like a door shutting.

"Sorry, I was in our living room. I think she's walking in the apartment now."

"That's okay. You can still talk though?"

"Yeah," she says in a hushed tone.

I close my eyes. It's time to put all my cards on the table. "Lennon, I want you to come with me to the Chi Kappa formal."

Before I can even explain my idea, she hisses into the phone. *"Are you crazy?"*

"Funny, Wes had a similar reaction." Even though she can't see me, I raise my eyebrows with anticipation for what will come out of her mouth next.

"You talked to Wes about this? About me?" Now her voice is really low.

"Yeah, remember? Who do you think I got your number from?"

"Huh, well yeah. I guess it couldn't have been Harlow given the, uh, circumstances."

"Yeah, so here are my thoughts. And just hear me out, please?"

"You've got just a few minutes before I need to go check on her. I'm sure she's freaking out right now."

I go right into it. "We go to the formal together to keep an eye on Harlow. I know she isn't going to change her mind about going with Beckett. And Lennon, I know she's your best friend and I'm sure you guys tell each other everything like most girls do," I pause, considering my choice of words for what I'm about to say next. "I'm probably really out of my depth here, but I don't think she's told you about whatever is going on with Beckett for a reason. Whether she's scared or doesn't think anyone will believe her, I'm not sure. What I am sure of though, is if either of us want to try and get through to Harlow, we have to meet her where she's at right now. And right now, she isn't in a place where she wants to talk to anyone about what's happening, but that doesn't mean we can't still keep an eye out without her knowing."

A few seconds pass and I worry maybe she hung up on me. Lennon's voice breaks through the silence, quiet and small. *"You said something about bruises in the car. Do you really think Beckett is hurting her?"*

An invisible force punches me in the stomach as another realization hits me. While I'm trying to be there for Harlow during whatever is going on, I've most definitely just rocked her best friend's world with the news of all this. Damn, I really am out of my depth here.

"I'm so sorry, Lennon. I can't imagine how this must hurt you too. But yes, I really do think Beckett is hurting her. So please, just trust me with this. Don't ask her any questions, especially about any bruises, and just let her know you're there for her when she's ready."

A sniffle echoes through the line and I'm ready to get Wes in here for back up once this call is over.

"Okay, yes. I trust you, Shep. I don't know you very well, but it's clear that you have our girl's best interest at heart. We can talk more about the formal stuff later, but I'm in."

A flood of relief washes over me. I can't believe this actually worked.

"Thank you, Lennon. Also, would you do me a small favor?"

"There's more?" She laughs quietly.

"Give Wes a chance, but don't tell him I said that. Deal?"

"Deal. Alright, I've gotta go check on Harlow. I'll text you now that I have your number."

"Sounds good. Be gentle with her for me."

"Of course. Oh hey, quick—what's your favorite color?"

"Yellow, why?"

"No reason, thanks. Bye!"

She hangs up and leaves me with a confused look on my face. I look over at Dahlia who's been laying in her crate the entire time and she cocks her head at me. "Women, huh?" She huffs as if rebuking that comment. "I know, Dahlia. You're the perfect girl." Her tail wags in agreement.

After a few seconds, Wes knocks on my door. I turn the knob and it slowly swings open.

"Well?" He looks me up and down, a glint of hurt in his eyes.

"She said yes, but listen."

He lets his head hang and I can't put my finger on why this bothers him when it's clear I'm involving Lennon only to be with Harlow.

"Talk to me, what's going on? Why's this bothering you?"

We stand there for a few minutes, a quietness hanging in the few feet between us.

"Just me being in my head." He turns to walk away and I stop him.

"What do you mean?"

Wes and I are pretty open with each other about our emotions. I think it's from all the time he's spent around my mom. She raised me to be transparent and always wear my heart on my sleeve. My dad loves my mom so much, he trusted her to raise me accordingly, with no questions or concerns that I might become too soft or whatever narrative the world is spinning these days.

"If I didn't have to come to Everson on scholarship, I would've been able to rush. I would've been able to take Lennon to the formal myself and then we all could've done this together. But, no. I'm probably just some poor schmuck in her eyes." He idles in the kitchen to distract from the weightiness of his confession by opening the fridge and focusing his attention there.

"Wes. Brother. C'mon. Do you really think that?" It hurts me that he would see himself that way. If anything, the fact he's even at Everson on scholarship despite every-thing he went through should be what makes girls want him. He's driven. He worked to get into college and not have to pay a dime. Why is being on scholarship suddenly a bad thing?

He walks over to the couch with a protein shake in his hand. Dahlia makes her way out of the room and hops up next to him.

"I don't know. I just can't help but feel a little left out." He pets Dahlia and sips on his shake.

I walk over and sit next to him with Dahlia in the middle

of us. "Well you're not. In fact, I have another idea, if you'll trust me?"

He squints at me, showing his skepticism. "Alright, fine."

I slap his shoulder and grip it a little to show him my appreciation. "Good. Now, I think you need to call and check on Lennon in a little. I didn't think about how everything might affect her and she sounded upset by the end of the call."

A twinkle takes over Wes's eyes and he's back. There's my best friend.

"Dude, that's such a good idea. Thank you."

We both relax into the couch and I turn the TV on to find a crime show to watch. Wes is messing with his phone and Dahlia has rolled over onto her back. I turn my attention back to the screen but can't focus on it for the life of me.

All I can think about is the last few minutes I was in Harlow's car and what I said to her before I left. I thought about kissing her, but I knew it wasn't the right time. She smelled so good that close to me. Thinking about it now makes me need to adjust myself. I get up once I realize this feeling isn't going away and tell Wes I'm going to rinse off.

Once I'm in my room, I shed my clothes and hop in the shower. The water runs over my body and I lean forward to rest my forearm on the wall. I can't stop thinking about her. I can't get her scent out of my mind.

Everything about her drives me wild. I know she's worked hard for her body. The commitment to her sport and fitness is an even bigger turn on. I'm sure she's noticed the way guys look at her. I hope she realizes I don't see her as just some piece of ass.

She's so much more to me than that. I meant what I said

to her. She deserves to be worshiped. She deserves to be touched with desire and affection, not man-handled by some prick who doesn't know how lucky he is to even breathe the same air as her.

Images of my girl flash through my mind and it's not just her body. It's her smile. It's how her blonde hair falls over her shoulder and cascades around her when she's in the pool. It's how she glides through the water when she swims.

I don't even realize I've closed my eyes until a groan emanates throughout me and I almost lose my footing in the shower.

I open my eyes and steady myself, then look down to see just how aroused I am. I can't help how I feel about Harlow. I use my hand to relieve some of the pressure building inside me. Thinking about her again makes me quicken my pace. I'm climbing higher and higher, then my abs clench as I finish.

I have no idea how I'm supposed to be around her now that I've allowed myself to envision her like this. In the same breath, my stomach drops. I'm still playing this huge game of "what if" with no confirmation that all my efforts aren't going to end up with no results.

I've been operating off the idea that this will work. Harlow will come around. She and I will end up together, then reality crashes back onto me.

I towel off and throw a pair of sweatpants on before falling onto my bed. Dahlia jumps up and lays down next to me. I choose to go back to my optimistic mindset, believing things will be okay. Turning my head, I look at Dahlia.

"What do you think about having a mom?"

TWENTY-TWO

THEY'RE ALL YELLOW

HARLOW

Another week passes and thankfully Shep and I don't interact much at the rec center. I'm not ready to face him after what happened. Surprisingly, he keeps out of my way too. He still smiled at me, but it was sheepish instead of confident like before.

I couldn't let myself think about it too much, because then it sent me into a spiral of thinking about him. I've had enough dreams about him and nightmares about Beckett that my mind just needs a break. Thankfully, Lennon and I agreed to go look at dresses this weekend at one of the shops downtown so it'll be the perfect distraction.

I don't love shopping the way Lennon does, but getting to spend time with her and talk about something that she loves will be exactly what I need.

We head into the store together and Lennon is already gushing about all the choices. I head towards the rack with all the black dresses, my obvious choice.

"Nuh uh!" Lennon calls out across the shop. "I'm picking dresses for you this time."

I don't have it in me to argue with her so I decide to just pick up two black dresses that I think are pretty and let her know I'm going to try those on and she can bring me whatever she wants. "Just no pink," I clarify with her before closing the curtain for the fitting room.

I start to undress and am immediately grateful for two things. First, lifting my shirt over my head no longer causes me to flinch. I'm sure it has to do with the fact that I've been putting in extra time with my rehab to keep my mind off a certain lifeguard. And second, I don't have to stress about how much skin Lennon's choices show.

I step into the first dress and shimmy it up. It's just a simple black satin dress with thin straps, a cowl neck, and a slit pretty far up the thigh. I turn and look at myself in the mirror and a soft smile forms. I made the right choice by actually doing my hair and makeup today so I can see the look all together.

I pop out of the dressing room and Lennon's nowhere to be found. I'm about to start looking for her when I hear her voice in between a rack, asking a stylist if they have anyone currently running social media for their store. I shake my head and snicker.

Turning to head back into the fitting room, a voice I was not expecting to hear catches me off guard.

"Is that my sweet girl?"

Laura Fords pops her head around the corner from the back room and my jaw drops a little. Call it divine appointment or the stars aligning, but this is the exact person I've wanted to run into lately.

"Laur—" She cuts her eyes at me. "Momma Fords!" I respond before walking towards her. She smiles and pulls me into a hug. She doesn't squeeze as tight this time, which makes me laugh recalling the other night.

"You look stunning! Do a spin for me, let me see!" She waves her finger around in the air, making a circle as I twirl around for her.

The childlike laugh that bubbles out of me feels foreign but refreshing. I've never shared a moment like this with my own mom. She couldn't really be bothered to make time for shopping trips with me.

What she was happy to show up for were my swim meets once she realized I wasn't that bad. When I was younger, I'd drink up her praise after my meets and she'd show off my medals to the other parents. Then I got to high school and realized she was just showing me off for her own gain.

My mom isn't a bad mom, but there's definitely a lack there.

"Thank you," I smile. "I'm looking for my formal dress. What're you doing here?"

"My friend owns the store and every so often I'll pop down here to help, but I'm so glad I ran into you!" She walks back around the cash wrap with me trailing behind like a little kid.

"Oh! That's nice. There's actually something I was hoping to talk to you about," I start to say before getting interrupted by another customer who walks over to ask Laura something.

She turns back to me when she's done helping. "You were saying?"

"Right, yes. I was actually thinking about what you said

at dinner the other night and I was wondering if there was anyone you knew that I could talk to?" I nibble on my lip, hoping this won't be a failed attempt at finally trying to get help.

Her eyes soften and she pulls out a sticky note from behind the counter. Scribbling on it, she passes it to me and smiles. "This is my friend, Robin. She's a licensed therapist but also does a lot of work with different support groups, should you find yourself looking for community. I should tell you though, Robin likes to meet several times the first week when taking a new client, in case that might not work with your schedule. Actually," she takes the sticky note back and writes another number on it, "here is mine as well. If you need anything, I'm just a call away."

I can't help myself as a laugh escapes. "I'm sorry, this isn't funny. I'm really grateful. It's just, I never thought I'd get your number before I got Shep's."

She shakes her head and chuckles. We continue some small talk when Lennon finally sees me. The look she casts between Laura and I tells me everything I need to know without her having to talk.

"This is Shep's mom, Laura." I answer her unspoken question.

Lennon walks over to us and introduces herself before striking up small talk with Laura. I take the opportunity to run into the dressing and stow away the sticky note with some of the most valuable phone numbers I could have. Well, sub one…

Heading back over to the counter, Lennon and Laura look deep in conversation, which strikes me as odd since they just met. What could they have to talk about? As I get closer, they both pop their heads up, looking flustered.

"Did I miss something?" I ask with a weary tone. I really hope Laura didn't tell Lennon about my bruises, but then a shocking voice of reason pierces through my doubts and tells me that I can trust Laura.

"I was just telling Laur—Momma Fords about all my social media stuff!" Lennon beams and it cracks me up that she got the same *Mom* talk.

"Very talented best friend you've got here. You know, Shep has a best friend who I think you'd get along with really well."

I let out some ungodly snort-slash-squeal before slapping a hand over my mouth. Lennon's face has turned the signature color of red I've become very familiar with over the last few weeks, as Laura just looks at the both of us, stunned.

"Was it something I said?" She glances between Lenny and I.

"You just have great intuition, that's all," I respond, smirking at Lennon.

"Well this was lovely, but we've got loads of dresses that won't try on themselves!" Then she flits away to the dressing room, leaving me alone with Laura again.

"I really hope I didn't upset her," she starts.

"No, it's just funny you say that because we both recently met Wes. Well, at least that's who I'm assuming you're referring to."

"Yes! My sweet Wesley. Are he and Lennon already an item?"

"No, but I think they've got something secretly going on."

I smile at her again and realize it's been so long since I've felt this content. "Thank you again. I'll make sure to reach out to Robin on Monday, and I'll check in with you if that's okay?"

"Of course, sweet girl. Now go try on those dresses! I'll pop my head out from the back here and there but make sure you let me know before you girls leave."

I agree to her request then head back to the fitting room. As I pull open the curtain, Lennon steps out from her room in a dress that looks like sin. She walks to the middle of the floor where there's a small platform surrounded by mirrors. She steps up and turns side to side, then faces me.

"What do you think?"

"I think that dress was made for you. Wow." I mean it too. The red silk dress hugs every curve of her body and features an open back that stops right above her waist. "You are a vision, Lenny. Wow."

She does a small dance before stepping down, remarking how easy this was and now she can focus all her attention on me, shooing me back into my dressing room.

As I shimmy out of the black dress, Lennon's hand pushes through the side of the curtain with a few dresses.

What the?

It's not the act that surprises me, it's the dresses themselves. None of them are ones I'd pick for myself and I'm at a loss for why she would even think I'd want to try them. They're all…yellow…

"Lenny, I love you, but what are these?" I say, grabbing the dresses to hang up on the rack inside the room.

"Just some other options! I'm tired of black, it's so bleh!"

"Well it may be bleh, but it never fails me!" I shoot back.

"Just try one, please!" she whines.

And I do just that. I try on all the dresses she's brought me. So many that I think I'm starting to become a dress. Just as I'm about to call it quits and fight her on letting me get the first black dress, she pokes her head in my room.

"I found one more. Please, just this last one. Even Momma Fords wants to see you in it!" she pleads with me.

Well now I really can't say no. "Okay, hand it over."

She squeals and claps her hands in delight before reaching and grabbing the dress, passing it through the small opening between the wall and curtain.

A small gasp leaves my lips as I take in the dress before me. It's once again yellow, but much softer and pale in color than the rest of the ones I tried on that were more sunshine and daisies.

I turn it around and I can't deny it's maybe one of the most beautiful dresses I've ever seen. While the back is open like Lennon's dress, it's not as low. What really takes my breath away though is, instead of thin fabric connecting the front to the back, the straps are made of pearls strung together. It's stunning.

I run my hand over the soft silk and step in. It fits me like a glove. I look at myself in the mirror, doing a small turn to look at the back of the dress. I can't believe the girl in the mirror is me.

Pushing back the curtain, I'm met with misty eyes from Laura. Then there's Lennon whose mouth is hanging wide open. They both gasp at the same time.

"Harlow," Lennon says breathlessly.

I walk towards them and step up onto the platform. I replicate the twirl I did for Laura earlier and both of them squeal. This was definitely not what I imagined the day would look like, but somehow, standing here in this pale yellow dress with two people who have made it so clear they care about me, it feels perfect. I can't help but let my mind wander to how similar this might be to another day in the future where maybe I'm trying on other types of dresses with them.

My heart jumps at the sudden hope I feel and I'm not sure what's happened inside of me over the last week, but I know for certain it has something to do with the son of a very incredible mom that's standing in front of me.

My stomach sours though as I turn and head back into the dressing room remembering who I agreed to go to this formal with. This beautiful dress for Beckett?

I hang the pale yellow dress back up and stare at it. It shocks me that the entire time I had it on, I was thinking about Shep seeing me in it, before reality smashed that dream to nothingness.

I come out of the dressing room with the yellow dress and the black dress. Lennon juts out her head with a look of confusion on her face.

"Why am I trying this hard for Beckett?" I whisper.

Lennon's shoulders drop and she slowly nods her head. "You told me this week you were still going with him."

"I know what I said but I guess the more I've thought about everything, the more my mind is changing. I can't back out now though, formal's next weekend." My familiar look of displeasure returns to my face.

"Shep will still see it," Lennon blurts out. "So get the damn yellow dress."

I think it over and realize Lennon's right. Just because I'm going with Beckett, doesn't mean I can't still dress for

Shep. The idea fills me with butterflies that are instantly chased away the second another realization hits me.

"Wait, does that mean he's going with someone?" I don't miss Lennon's wide eyes before she quickly changes the subject.

"Momma Fords!" she calls out, as Laura's head pops out from the back again.

She looks at me with the two dresses in my hands, then speaks in a high pitched voice. "Please tell me you're going to do what I think you're going to do!"

With a sudden burst of excitement, nerves, and the feeling you get when you start to have a crush on someone, I squeal, "I'm getting the yellow dress!"

The entire boutique cheers and it's in this moment another piece of my soul that I didn't even know was broken starts to heal.

TWENTY-THREE

THE ULTIMATE WING WOMAN

SHEP

"Is this actually necessary?" Wes calls out from his room.

"Yes, so shut up and put on a suit," I bark back at him while putting the finishing touches on my secret project that's taken over our dining table.

The last few days have been gone by in a blur. I finally got to talk to Harlow at the rec center the other day and she seemed different. Not a bad different, just *different*.

It hasn't helped that every time we've been in the middle of a conversation we've been interrupted. One time it was Pierce who showed up during a practice, another time her phone rang and she had to run off. I'm trying not to get frustrated, but I'm also getting impatient. Every day that I see her, my feelings for her grow.

Lennon has kept me in the loop about things, but she also won't give me any clear answers regarding how Harlow feels.

In our small talk though, Harlow did apologize for how she acted in her car the night we went to my parents. I was somewhat shocked but I've also noticed a softness to her lately that I'm not familiar with.

"Alright, alright. I'm dressed, what's the deal?" Wes whines as he walks out of his room. His eyebrows raise and he looks between the table and me. "What the hell is going on?"

A deep laugh rumbles out of me. "I told you. I have a plan if you'd just trust me."

"Right, but this doesn't really give me any answers."

As he finishes his sentence, there's a knock on the door. I give him a knowing grin and head to answer it before he can.

"Dude, seriously. What the hell is—"

"Hi," Lennon interrupts him and walks through our front door. Wes goes silent and his jaw slowly falls down.

"Lennon," he states. "What are you doing here?"

She walks towards him, her dress trailing behind her, then stops in front of the dining table near him.

"Well," she starts, "Shep here told me that you were disappointed we couldn't go to this formal together, so he told me to get ready and meet him early at your house. So, here I am."

They both turn and look at me, waiting for further explanation.

"Right, so because Lennon is helping me out and Wes, you mentioned you didn't love the idea, I wanted to do something to make things right." I point at the set up and it clicks in their minds.

With help from Mom, I got the dining table set up to look like a private restaurant setting. She helped me find the stuff to put on it and then I took care of the rest. I thought the least I could do was give Wes the opportunity to see Lennon dressed up and have this date.

"You did this?" Wes asks, raising his eyebrows. Lennon giggles next to him.

"That's correct," I head to my room and grab my keys. "The food is in the oven. I've got to go do something else before tonight, but I thought you could bring Lennon to the Chi Kappa house for me?"

"Yeah. Yeah, absolutely." Wes goes to pull out the chair for Lennon then comes over to me after she sits down. "Thank you," he whispers. I just smile back at him.

"Lennon, if Dahlia gets to be too much, Wes can put her in my room. I figured there wasn't a need for formal introductions since Harlow probably told you about her. She doesn't know you're here though, right?"

"That's correct! To both of your comments." She smiles at me then looks at Wes again.

That's my cue.

"Alright, see you guys at formal."

———

I'm on my way to Mom and Dad's when I get a call from an unknown number.

"Hello?"

There's a few seconds of silence before I finally hear the voice that makes me lose all sense.

"Shep?"

It's my girl.

"Harlow, is everything okay?" I want to ask how she got my number, but that doesn't feel important right now.

"Um, I'm not sure. Are you in Everson?"

Her voice sounds shaky and I really hope it isn't because of Beckett somehow.

"I'm heading to my parents' right now, why? Is everything okay?"

"Oh, wait. Right now?"

"Yes?"

"Shit."

"Why? What's wrong?"

Before she can answer, I turn the corner coming up on the driveway and am beyond shocked to see a gray Bronco there.

"Are you at my parent's house?" I ask in disbelief.

"Surprise?"

I see her walk out the front door then she pulls the phone away and hangs up. I hop out of my truck and head towards her.

"What're you doing here? What's going on? Is everything okay?" I lightly grab her by the sides of her arms and instinctively look her over.

She lightly giggles and it's the most beautiful sound I've ever heard.

"Shep, I'm fine," she says before swatting my hand away playfully. "Though I didn't expect to run into you here. You caught me."

She turns and makes her way back into the house like she lives here. Did I miss something?

"Momma Fords!" Harlow calls out, causing the strangest feeling to course through my body. "He's here."

"Oh goodness!" The voice of my mom rings out from farther down the hall.

When we turn into the living room, I see that apparently I'm the one intruding at my own house. It looks like Harlow and Mom were having tea or something.

"Can someone explain to me what's going on?" I raise my eyebrows, looking between the two women who both seem to be going behind my back.

"That's why I was calling you." Harlow sits back down next to my mom on the couch. "I've been talking to your mom and her friend, Robin, about," she stops for a second and chews on her bottom lip, "the stuff you're worried about."

"Oh?" Confusion floods my mind, followed swiftly by equal amounts of relief at the mention of this specific friend of Mom's.

"Your mom gave me your number, which I'm sorry it's taken so long for me to get." Harlow looks down and I glance over at my mom who winks at me. Again, I can't believe it's my own mother who's playing the ultimate wing woman here.

"Riiight…" I say before sitting down in one of the chairs opposite them. "So, what were you calling to tell me? About these meetups?" I bend down and pick up one of the small sandwiches on the table, then lean back in the chair. These two have some serious explaining to do.

"I think I'll let you two talk," Mom interrupts, then stands and gathers the empty plates before heading into the kitchen.

Harlow takes a breath, steadying herself and smiling as Mom leaves the room. "The first night I came over, you know how your mom and I talked in the hall?

I nod my head in response while chewing on the sandwich.

"Well, she told me something that helped me see things a little differently. Then I ran into her last weekend downtown and she gave me her number plus Robin's."

Harlow picks at the frayed edges of her jean shorts. Of course she's wearing the outfit that seems to be more like her uniform. Taking in her appearance, I forget we're talking about something serious and blurt out, "What're those shoes called?"

Harlow shakes her head in confusion. "My shoes? They're called Doc Martens. Why?" She gives me a puzzled look.

"You just always wear them. I like them. I remember we had an event at the fraternity house a year ago and you showed up wearing them, with some big flannel or something. I like the way you dress," I confess plainly.

Her eyes get so wide it looks like they could pop out of her head. "I didn't think anyone really noticed me that night," she mumbles.

"Oh, well...I did." I realize I'm taking over the conversation that she was trying to have with me so I try to get back on track. "Anyways, let's cut to the chase. How long have you been meeting up with my mom?"

She smiles. "We started this week. I wanted to tell you, but I've been busy with practice, class, and now therapy, all while also trying to deal with *people.*" She rolls her eyes. "But

I just wanted to thank you, and I'm going to try and put some distance between Beckett and I."

My mouth falls open some. I have so many questions. God, I have so many questions, but if I've learned anything with Harlow, it's to let her set the pace. However, my mouth works faster than my brain and before I can stop myself, I blurt out, "Baby, that's great." The realization of what I've said comes as a soft red flush takes over Harlow's cheeks. "I mean—Harlow, that's great."

She doesn't call attention to my words, which I'm grateful for. We continue talking about what she's been up to without her going into great detail. I notice a new light in her eyes and it makes me want to reach over this table and kiss her. The urge to do it has always been there, but before it was with the idea that maybe I could give her some of my own happiness. At this moment though, I want to kiss her to absorb whatever has her in this good mood.

"What were you coming here for?" She breaks my train of thought.

"Oh, I just had a suit here I needed to pick up for tonight." I'm glad she mentioned it, because I probably would have forgotten with everything that's happened in the last half hour. "You're still going with Beckett?" I hold onto a shred of hope that maybe she'll say no, but unfortunately that isn't her answer.

"I am, but after tonight I'm going to try and talk to him." She smiles softly then stands up, gathering her things. "I actually need to head out to go get ready. Lennon ditched me for something and now I have to get dressed and do my hair and makeup on my own."

My stomach drops wondering if I should tell Harlow

about Lennon and I. She was so open and honest with me and I don't want her to feel like I'm hiding something from her. I also don't want to ruin this moment by her getting upset. *Shit.*

I decide to not tell her and instead give her a different truth. Stepping towards her, I reach my hand up near her face pausing to make sure she's okay with me touching her. She nods her head softly and I tuck a strand of her hair that's fallen from her bun behind her ear. I hold my hand in place around the side of her cheek, before running my thumb over her bottom lip.

My heart is pounding and, damn, do I want to take that plump lip between my teeth and suck on it.

"You're going to be beautiful. I wish it was me who got to accompany you tonight," I whisper.

She leans into my touch then gently moves my hand off her face. It doesn't hurt my feelings. I'm sure she's still getting used to touch that isn't harmful.

"Thank you. I just have to see this through with Beckett. It'll be okay. I think it helps knowing you'll be around. If it makes you feel any better, in my mind I'm getting ready for you tonight."

My eyes widen and all Shep systems shut down. She's never talked to me like this before and I don't think I know how to handle the Harlow that actually acknowledges our chemistry.

Before I can try and play into it, she calls out to my mom that she's leaving and then smiles at me before walking out the front door. After just a few seconds, Mom pops her head out from the doorway and gives me a look.

"What?" I counter.

"How're you going to explain you showing up to formal with her best friend after *that*?" She cocks her head to the side with her eyebrows raised.

I scoff and head to my old room to grab my suit. I don't know, but I really hope it doesn't backfire.

TWENTY-FOUR

: BUT.

HARLOW

I didn't anticipate jumping the gun and getting Shep's number, but something came over me while sitting in the living room with his mom talking about my first few sessions with Robin.

After I left the shop Saturday, I called Laura that night. She told me she went ahead and spoke with Robin and she was right. Robin did want to see me back to back, so we talked about a potential schedule for me and she got it all booked. Following my practices in the week ahead, I would go straight to therapy at 6:00 PM for an hour on Monday, Wednesday, and Friday.

Laura coaxed me into meeting her at her house Monday then we rode together to the office which sat just on the edge of town. It wasn't really out of the way and I didn't mind having the support. I didn't know what to expect, but the cozy little cabin that had been renovated into a business space truly shocked me.

At the end of that first appointment, Laura was there waiting, then we went back to her house where she made me tea and we talked about how I felt. This became sort of the routine for the week.

She was also kind enough to offer her support through paying for these first couple visits until I was ready to talk to my parents about what was going on. Letting her help me like that pained me, but I also knew that there was no chance in hell I was going to ask my parents for the money or try to use my insurance.

In the past, if I'd tried to approach my parents about needing help for things, my dad was willing to listen, but it was Mom who always shut it down. It was like there was a lack of sympathy for me and maybe it was because she had spent most of it on Margot when she went through what she did in high school. Did that make it any easier? No. I was only in eighth grade when it happened, and then when I started high school, I felt like I was on my own. The years of my life where a girl needs her mom, I hardly have any memories with mine. We lived in the same house but it was like she was a ghost.

It's probably a huge reason why I've taken to Laura the way I have. As much as I want to act like the shit with Mom doesn't affect me anymore, I'm just a girl who wants to feel the love of a mother.

Trying to juggle swimming, school, and now secret meetings has been no easy feat, but with Laura's help and Lennon's quiet support of whatever I was doing with Laura this last week, I've found a new sense of courage to start putting myself first. Except with Beckett.

Today's meeting with Robin was the first one where we

finally started to talk about our relationship. While our other two meetings had more so been about my life growing up—what experiences I had, how I got along with my family, and then just talking about some of the things that were weighing on me—today, Robin finally switched lanes.

"So tell me, when was the first time Beckett laid his hands on you?" Robin spoke with a softness to her voice that mirrored Laura's and made me feel like I could tell her anything.

"I guess at our date party a little over a year ago." At first, my answers to Robin's questions were always direct-short and sweet-but that slowly changed as she helped me find my words.

"And what caused this?" She peered at me over the frames of her glasses that rested on her nose.

"I was late. But I also wasn't dressed appropriately?" My voice rose at the end almost like it was a question, because there was an uncertainty I hadn't truly addressed yet as to why Beckett did snap that day.

"I see. Can you walk me through the events of the night?" Her voice showed a slight edge to it, but if the woman was angered by what I was telling her, she was really good at keeping her face neutral.

I gave her the cliff notes version of the date party and a few times I did see her face wobble when I mentioned the way he spoke to me and how it made me feel. I was shocked that I was so comfortable telling Robin all of this, but then again, her being a stranger gave me the space to speak freely.

She told me when we first met that she is mandated by the state to report if I'm in danger, but that it's also hard to know when you'll be in danger when you're already in an abusive relationship.

When she first used that phrase, "abusive relationship," my stomach soured. Was that really what I had found myself in?

"Now, do you and Beckett have a sexual relationship as well?"

Her question pulled me from my thoughts but also took me by such surprise that I sat there with my mouth gaped open before I could process that I needed to answer.

"It's okay if you're not ready to talk about that," she continued.

Stammering, I finally pieced together a sentence that was coherent at best. "Ye–well–some…no."

She nodded her head and set down her notebook next to her on the arm rest of the couch.

"It's important that you know we don't have to talk about everything right away. However, it might be useful for you to see the different ways Beckett has mistreated you so you're able to recognize it in the future."

"But I don't want there to be a future," I rushed out as my stomach dropped.

"I know and I'm so proud of you for wanting that this quickly, but—"

There was that dreaded word: but.

"—abusers are able to manipulate their partners into feeling like they need to stay. You mentioned you've felt this way before, correct?"

Abusers? Is that really what we're calling Beckett now?

Feeling overwhelmed, I shook my head before resting my face in my hands. I wasn't dumb to think that a few therapy sessions and I'd be ready to tell Beckett to piss off and walk away, but I also didn't think the truths Robin was sharing with me would make me feel so powerless.

Working up some courage, I finally answered her question. "Yes, we've had sex. Only a few times, and it's been a while."

Robin went on to talk about the role sex can play in my situation. She also went back to the details I gave her about Beckett showing up with gifts and flowers after the date party. She said that was an act of "love bombing." A term I had never heard before, but she explained was a form of psychological and emotional abuse in and of itself as it creates doubt in the victim's mind and makes them question their feelings towards their abuser.

By the time our session was over, I felt more defeated than when I had walked in. As I exited her office door, Laura was sitting there as usual with an expectant look on her face. When I didn't meet her smile with mine, she rushed over and cradled me into her arms.

A soft cry erupted from me as she stroked my hair, whispering, "One day at a time. You'll get through this."

She asked me to wait and then popped into Robin's office, talking for a few minutes. I told Robin I was comfortable with her discussing our sessions with Laura and signed the release form for her to be my personal representative.

It was on the car ride back to her house she broke the silence and told me that I should consider letting Shep in. Not because he was her son, but because he had shown genuine care for me, and Robin agreed that a good first step in making any progress would be to let people in.

I told her I would think about it, as a different thought popped into my head.

"Do you think it's bad?" I started.

"Hm?" Laura acknowledged me but kept her attention on the road.

"Do you think it's bad that I haven't told my own parents about this? Would they be upset if they knew someone else's parent was involved, and not them?" I sighed and slumped down into the passenger seat.

"That's an interesting thought," Laura started then paused for a second. "I think if I was in their position, I'd just be happy my daughter was talking to someone. I haven't met them, but I'm sure they're lovely and their true desire, as is any parent's, is for their child to be safe and happy."

I chewed on her words until we pulled back up to the house. We walked inside and she went to get the tea started. After a few minutes of talking over my session with tea and some snacks, I made up my mind and asked her for Shep's number.

My phone buzzes and pulls me out of my thoughts and I realize I've been sitting at Lennon's vanity with the mascara wand in my hand for who knows how long. I push it back into the tube before picking my phone up and reading a text from Lennon that she'd left my dress hanging in the bathroom after she steamed it.

I still have plans to meet Beckett before the formal for dinner because of the panic-ask a few weeks ago, but there is no part of me that wants to go. Especially after today's session. I thought about canceling but, again, I don't want to poke the bear.

I finish getting ready, smoothing down my hair and grabbing a purse Lennon left out for me. As I slip into the yellow dress, a flush of nerves rises up. Thankfully, I told

Beckett I would just meet him at dinner and drive myself because I had a doctor's appointment earlier. He couldn't be bothered and I was thankful for that.

Once I feel like I have everything in place, I get in my car and head to the restaurant. I think for a second about doing something out of the ordinary. I don't care anymore about worrying what the consequences might be. I don't want to spend this drive to dinner lost in thought about all the things that've been weighing on me lately so I press the green button on my CarPlay screen and wait expectantly as the line rings.

"Hi, Harlow."

"Hi, Shep."

BEAUTIFUL, BUBBLY, ATTRACTIVE.

HARLOW

Dinner was uneventful. I couldn't have been more thankful that Beckett was in a good mood for once and that I was able to drive myself to dinner and then to Chi Kappa. I can't process the emotions I'm feeling now though as I sit in front of the fraternity house. The last two times I've been here, something has gone horribly wrong.

Beckett didn't wait for me and told me to find him once I got here. *Surprise, surprise.*

I step out of my Bronco and shrug my shoulders to get the pearl straps back in place. This dress is as beautiful now as it was when I first tried it on, but I still feel slightly out of place. Taking a deep breath, I start towards the entrance of the house, and I can't ignore how many eyes are suddenly on me. It's almost 9:00 PM, and I'm a little late, but most people don't get here until this time anyways. *Why is everyone staring then?*

At first, the dread sinks in deep that I'll likely become a

conversation piece tonight. It seems I can never escape the gossip around my injury. However, I'm shocked when I overhear one of the girls whisper to her friend how pretty I look. A new feeling erupts in my stomach and I notice everyone's heads turned towards me.

I shift uncomfortably before walking further into the house looking for Beckett, but also searching for *him*.

After a few more awkward interactions from both fraternity brothers and their dates giving me compliments, my eyes finally find the person who makes my heart hammer in my chest.

Overcome with butterflies, but not wanting to show my excitement too much, I make sure Beckett still isn't around before walking towards my lifeguard.

It's about two steps in that I come to a screeching halt, when I notice the girl next to him is wearing a dress that was hanging up in my apartment earlier today. Not only do I recognize the dress, but the girl wearing it. Lennon?

Frozen in the main room, I quickly dart off into the hall before sneaking into a bathroom. *What the hell?*

I knew Shep would be here but I didn't expect to see him with Lennon. I shouldn't be bothered, but it makes no sense. Was that where Lennon ran off to earlier today? To see Shep? But that didn't make sense either because he was at his parents' house with me. I let out a very loud groan before facing myself in the mirror.

I can't articulate the feelings that are swelling up inside me but here I am, trying to affirm my reflection that I shouldn't be insecure. It would be a lot easier if seeing Lennon in that backless silk red dress didn't make me nervous. I saw how many guys were orbiting around her. That's just Lennon—beautiful, bubbly, attractive.

Before I let my thoughts get any wilder, I grip the edge of the bathroom counter and take another deep breath. Do I actually care about Lennon with Shep? No, I don't. I can't. Even if I don't want to be here with Beckett. Even if I don't know why they're together. I can't let this get to me.

I'm overwhelmed with how quickly my emotions just fell apart. More so, how much Shep affected me. This isn't what I should be worrying about. I'm being ridiculous. I stare down my reflection and remind myself of the one goal I've been holding onto for the last six weeks: Get better and get back with your team.

I roll my eyes and put on my best poker face before exiting the bathroom and walking towards Shep and Lennon.

"Well, you two look nice." I glance over the pair of them, before crossing my arms and raising my eyebrows at Shep. A heat rises in my stomach when he makes eye contact with me. He traces down and back up my body with his slate eyes and a shiver runs through me.

"Harlow!" Lennon squeaks out. "You look stunning. Doesn't she look stunning, Shep?" I don't miss how she elbows him in the side before shoving him forward.

"That would be an understatement," he mumbles before reaching his arms out. I glance quickly and don't see Beckett anywhere. Taking a leap of faith, I step towards Shep, wrapping my arms around his waist.

Shep's hands trail down my open back before he gently pulls me into his chest. For the brief second that my nose is buried into his suit, I get a good whiff of his cologne and my body betrays me. I sag into his arms and he tightens his hold around me. I all but lose my senses when I feel him press a soft kiss on the top of my head then he drags his hands across my back before pulling away and clearing his throat.

Eyeing him up and down myself, I drink up his appearance. His hair is combed back but still messy like always. He's wearing a navy suit that compliments his eyes and he smells delicious. *Shep Fords, the man that you are.*

Lennon stands there gawking for a few seconds and it smacks me in the face what's just happened. I look around quickly to make sure nobody is paying attention and, thankfully, nobody is.

Wanting to squash all of the butterflies that are starting to overtake me, I force my gaze to Lennon. "When were you planning on telling me that you were coming to the formal with Shep?"

She starts to open her mouth but then I cut my gaze to Shep. "And you, you didn't think to mention this at the house? Hm?"

Before either of them can answer me, their faces sour and an arm snakes around my waist. "There you are," Beckett hisses.

Shit.

TWENTY-SIX

BETWEEN US GIRLS—

SHEP

Rage. Disgust. Fury.

The sneer on Beckett's face has me all but seeing red.

For once, the guy doesn't have a drink in his hand, and maybe that's why he doesn't make a comment to me like normal.

"Oh, hi. I was just talking to Lennon. She's here with Shep," Harlow says, looking down at the floor.

I don't miss the way Beckett's eyebrows rise to meet his hairline.

"Is that so?" He looks at Lennon, not me.

"Yep, that's true!" Lennon rushes out before linking her arm with mine. The entire motion is rushed and awkward, but this is a part of the show.

"Damn, Fords. You're really trying to make your way through the swim team, huh?" He turns to Harlow and whispers something to her before looking back at Lennon and I.

I start to open my mouth but Harlow cuts me off. "Enjoy the night, you two."

They turn and walk away, leaving me with a wave of nausea.

"I guess that wasn't terrible?" Lennon lets go of my arm and moves in front of me.

I'm still looking over her head at the beautiful blonde being whisked away.

"HELLO?" Lennon bobs her head up into my line of sight.

"Yeah, sure." I start to walk after Harlow when Lennon grabs my arm.

"Don't. You'll ruin the night before it even starts." She smooths down her dress and scans the crowd herself.

"Looking for someone other than my best friend? Because if so…" I start.

Lennon flushes before cocking her hip out and crossing her arms. "No, thank you very much. I'm looking to see if any other girls from swimming are here. I'll have you know that, between us girls—"

I roll my eyes.

"Your best friend is the only person I'm interested in. Currently. At the moment. Right now…" She nibbles on her lip and then sighs. "Don't say anything to him."

I raise an eyebrow before shaking my head. "I don't even have the energy to try and act like I want to know what's going on. But I will say this, he's my best friend. I'm always going to have his back."

Lennon's mouth drops slightly then she pushes a finger into my chest. "And Harlow is *my* best friend. So don't ever forget *that.*"

"Fair point."

"Let's go mingle," she says before sauntering off into the crowd.

I go to follow after Lennon but I catch sight of *her* again.

God, she's perfect.

I've never seen Harlow dressed like this and, more importantly, in something that isn't a dark color. The soft yellow is the perfect compliment to her golden skin and hair. The realization that her dress is my favorite color has me chuckling. I'm not entirely sure if it's on purpose, but I have a feeling Lennon had something to do with that. There's a twinge of pain in my stomach though when I see the open back. Flashes of the bruises that were left there a few weeks ago fill my mind and it makes my chest ache.

I need to find another moment with her to be alone. Having her in my arms for that brief second wasn't enough, but I have a feeling I'll never get enough of Harlow.

After staring at her for probably too long, I find Lennon with some of the swim team and my fraternity brothers. We make small talk while I keep my eyes on the lookout for my angel girl.

A few more minutes go by and I'm getting restless. I tell Lennon I'm going to take a walk and head towards the hall that connects to the outside.

This side of the house is where there's yard space for throwing a football and other frat stuff. It's decorated with lights and there are a few tables set up for people to talk at just like the date party. I walk over to one of the high tops and think about the car ride here when Harlow called me. I was shocked, but also pleasantly surprised.

It wasn't too long of a phone call because the restaurant

isn't that far from where she lives, but I soaked up every minute of it.

I asked her if she'd be willing to tell me more about meeting with Robin. She gave me some smaller details and I listened intently.

I didn't want to push her too far, but I asked her a question that I knew was bold. My curiosity was eating at me.

"So you're starting to feel differently about Beckett…well, what about me?"

In true Harlow fashion, she shot back, "And what about you?"

I laughed it off, then she surprised me yet again by quietly saying, "Yeah, Shep. I'm starting to feel differently about you too."

Thinking about it causes a visceral heat to flood me. Now I just have to make sure that I don't get ahead of myself and bombard Harlow with my feelings. As if my thoughts conjured her up, she suddenly peaks out of the side door and smiles when she spots me.

She glances over her shoulder, then waves for me to come towards her. I look around just to make sure she's actually motioning for me. Reading my mind, she mouths, "Yes, you. Come here."

Following a few paces behind her, she turns off into a bathroom and I hesitate. This could end so badly, but nobody is around. My feet carry me into the small space and I shut the door behind me.

"We need to talk," Harlow says through her reflection in

the mirror. She's fixing her hair when I notice one of the pearl straps is hanging off of her shoulder.

"What about?" I ask coyly, stepping towards her until her back is flush with my front. She sharply inhales. Taking the pearl strap in my hand, I slowly drag it back up to her shoulder. Her skin erupts in chills.

Not wanting to push her but feeling absolutely lost in the moment, I take my other hand and move her hair off her back and over her shoulder. I lean forward, my breath fanning on the back of her neck. "You look breathtaking," I whisper out.

I'm not sure if it's on purpose but she arches her back some which only presses her more against me. With her green eyes locked on mine in the mirror, I study her face to make sure she isn't uncomfortable. Her eyes look like they're pleading with me but for what, I'm not entirely sure.

I move slightly to the side of her face and press a soft kiss on the skin behind her ear. "Did you wear this just for me?" I purr in her ear.

"Shep," she chokes out.

I run my hands down her back until I get near her lower back and stop. My fingertips hover over the place where *his* hands were. As much as I'm craving Harlow right now, my resolve to do good by her kicks in and I realize I need to slow down. I pull my hands back and step away, then reach for her hand to turn her in my direction.

"What do you want to talk about?" I ask softly, running my thumb over her knuckles.

"I don't think I remember now," she says with a flustered look on her face. Her cheeks are the rosiest I've ever seen them.

"Maybe I can give you something else then? Maybe some insight as to why I'm here with Lennon…" I trail off.

She lets go of my hand then straightens up and crosses her arms. "Actually yes," she huffs out. "That's exactly what I wanted to talk to you about."

I run a hand through my hair, messing it up some before letting out a large sigh. "It was my idea, so don't get upset with Lennon. Not to mention, I had to basically ask Wes for his permission to bring her."

Harlow's eyes go wide and her mouth drops a little. "So those two are something then?" she asks.

"It would definitely seem that way." I laugh softly.

"So then why come together? What aren't you telling me?" She takes a step towards me and the nearness of her causes me to lose my train of thought.

"Harlow, I love that you want to be close to me, but I'm really trying to be the good guy here, and anytime you're as close to me as you are right now, I feel myself losing my resolve."

Her breath catches and I see a wicked gleam in her eye. "Oh, like this?" she taunts, before taking another step towards me. "Or how about this?" Her voice is quiet as she drapes her arms over my shoulders.

"You know, I was worried that the fire I'd seen in you a few weeks ago at the rec had been put out. Glad to see it's still there, but certainly not working in my favor." I look up at the ceiling avoiding her gaze.

"I'm waiting for you to tell me why you're here with my best friend," she whispers, her lips now just a few inches away from mine.

I force myself to look at her and give her the truth even

though I know it will ruin this moment. "I told Lennon we needed to keep an eye on you tonight with Beckett."

Her face drops and she quickly pulls her hands off my shoulders.

"Baby, wait." The words spill out of me almost as fast as I reach for her hands.

"What did you tell Lennon?" She wiggles her fingers out of mine and my chest aches.

"I'm sorry, Harlow. Please." I begin to plead with her.

"No. You didn't." The words come out strangled and I can tell I'm losing her. She puts more space between us. "Shep, tell me you didn't share any more about my bruises. Tell me you didn't tell her about Beckett."

The betrayal in her eyes cuts deep into me and I'm trying to remind myself that I had her best interest at heart. I know that I did the right thing.

"All I told her was I think Beckett is hurting you and I'm worried." I reach for her again, but she puts her hands up.

"I can't do this. Don't follow me." She turns quickly and opens the door, rushing out.

I'm about two seconds from going after her when I hear what sounds like two people bumping into each other. My stomach sinks the moment her voice echoes down the hall.

"Oh, Beckett. There you are. Let's go."

Fuck me.

TWENTY-SEVEN

HICCUP

SHEP

I wait a few more seconds before peering out into the hallway and realizing nobody is there. Rejoining the group in the main hall, Harlow is nowhere to be seen so I make my way over to Lennon, finding her in the middle of some of her friends, dancing.

Once I get her attention, I nod for her to follow me over to the back of the room.

"What?" she whines. "I was just starting to have fun."

"Shit went south," I deadpan.

She drops her arms dramatically before groaning. "What did you do?"

"She asked me why we were together and I couldn't lie to her. She's worried now about what all you know."

"Well did you tell her not much? I've been keeping an eye out like you said but, Shep, look at him. He seems fine?"

The doubt from Lennon makes my stomach knot up. This must be exactly how Harlow feels but worse. How can people really not see that Beckett isn't a good guy? What type of performance is he putting on to make Lennon of all people think he wouldn't act like that?

Both of our attentions are grabbed when we see Beckett and Harlow talking over in the corner. Beckett looks upset and has a drink in his hand now. By the way Harlow is folded into herself, I can tell whatever he's saying isn't good.

I watch as Beckett starts to guide Harlow outside by the small of her waist. I want to run over there and intervene but Lennon places her hand on my arm and whispers, "Just wait. There are so many people here, he wouldn't try something."

As if hearing what she had just said, one of my fraternity brothers and co-worker, Max, stumbles up next to us appearing to be watching the same interaction we are. He has a beer in his hand and I can tell he's already had a few drinks by the way he's teetering back and forth. "Ugh, there they go again."

Lennon and I whip our heads towards him.

"What did you just say?" I rush out, narrowing my eyes at him.

"Those two. It's the same shit every time they're here together." He takes a swig of his drink before pointing in the direction of them with his beer. "Should have"—*hiccup*—"seen the blow out they had the night Harlow got hurt."

My eyebrows shoot up so fast. Lennon gasps before placing her hand over her mouth.

I move, this time to stand in front of him and take the drink out of his hand, setting it down.

"What are you talking about, Max? You were there the night she got hurt?" My tone is clipped, but this is all news to me and apparently also to Lennon, who is turned and facing him, wholly invested.

"Damn, Fords. No need"—*hiccup*—"to take my drink." He lets out a large sigh then looks over his shoulder at the pair who are now outside by the pool. "I mean evvveryone was at that party." He points at Lennon. "Even her."

"Right, but what I'm asking is you saw them fight that night?" I urge him to continue.

"Ohhh, yeah. Big one too. Couldn't tell you what about but I saw Beckett dragging her like that outside and," he lets out a big breath, "next time I saw her, she was rushing out the door holding her shoulder. With thisss one." He tries to point at Lennon, but his finger is moving in so many different directions.

"Did you tell anyone about this?" Lennon asks this time.

"Nope"—*hiccup*—"it really all just came back to me now, seeing them and whatever." He reaches past me to grab his beer and takes another swig before his face turns serious. "Maybe I just needed to be in the same sate, *no*, state of mind to remember. Like in those crime shows, when they try—"

"Yeah, Maxy. Thanks." I push past him then turn around and take his drink from him again. "I think you've had enough. Lennon, come on."

I hear Max sighing behind me as I direct Lennon out into the hall. When we're finally alone, I look at her before asking, "Did you see Harlow get hurt that night?"

Lennon pinches the bridge of her nose. "Well, no, but..."

"You never saw her fall?" I rush out as too many gears start turning in my head.

"No, but she came up to me, and I—oh, God," Lennon lets out a wail. "He did this, didn't he?" She steps forward and starts to cry. Damn, I'm out of my depth again.

I offer her my chest to cry on, consoling her with one hand, while pulling my phone out with the other. Two rings go through before I hear my best friend's voice on the other line.

"Damn. Not even an hour in and you already—"

"I need you to come get Lennon. Now." Her head perks up at this.

"I'll be there in five. I didn't go far."

"Good man."

"Hey, pass Lennon the phone for a second will you?"

I hand it over to her and I can't hear Wes, but her cheeks turn a slight shade of red then she hangs up and gives my phone back.

"Thanks again, I'll see you later tonight." Another tear slips down her cheek. "Protect her."

I place my hands on Lennon's shoulders, squaring her to me. "I'll take care of this," I say, my voice serious.

She nods her head then turns to walk towards the front door.

I give myself a few minutes to think. So many thoughts are rampaging through my mind, but I focus on the most important one: keeping Harlow safe.

It takes all of two minutes to find the room I'm looking for after sending Lennon outside to Wes. I open the door and make my way to the computer that I know holds all the security footage archives.

I've helped with enough events at the frat house to know how to navigate this software. Sending off a text to the person in charge of our security resources that I need to look for something, he gives me the go-ahead and I sit down, typing in the date I need.

I pull up the outdoor cameras, looking for the angle that shows the scene Max described through his hiccups.

I start the footage and fast forward to a little before midnight. Everything I've heard leads me to believe Harlow's accident happened right around that time frame. I set the speed at 2x and lean back, watching for any semblance of her blonde hair. After a few minutes goes by, I start to worry this is going to be useless, then I see it. I see her.

At 11:43 PM, I see Harlow outside with a group of people. She looks happy and they all seem to be talking. No more than a few seconds pass and Beckett enters the screen.

"Shit," I say to myself.

I notice Harlow starts to pull away from the crowd and Beckett is following after her. I lose them for a second then they're back on screen but farther away.

"Oh, come on. Does this thing zoom? It has to."

I manipulate the screen and it focuses on Harlow and Shep who are now by the boulders we have behind our pool.

After another minute ticks by, my stomach drops.

"That piece of shit," I mutter to myself, before taking my phone out and recording the footage. I watch as what can only be described as a nightmare unfolds.

It looks like Harlow is trying to talk with Beckett but he's clearly upset. He throws his drink at her and when she tries to walk off, he grabs her arm and yanks her back towards him. I almost vomit when her shoulder visibly pops out of place.

Harlow collapses to the ground, immediately holding her shoulder with her hand. As if it can't get any worse, Beckett then shoves her out of the way. She lands on her hurt shoulder, then turns and throws up, probably from the pain.

Beckett looks down at her for another second before walking away.

I pause the security footage and feel tears welling up in my eyes.

It's so dark that nobody seemed to notice what was happening or maybe they were just far enough away from most people that nobody saw. Either way, my heart aches and I feel sick at what I've just discovered.

I quickly open up my messages and send the recording to my dad, Pierce, and our fraternity president, then send Wes a text as well to not leave until Harlow comes out front.

Pushing away from the desk, my hands shake and bile rises in my throat. I make my way to the main room, finding Harlow and Beckett still talking outside.

TWENTY-EIGHT

A DEER IN HEADLIGHTS

HARLOW

Standing outside by the pool, I can't help but tune out the nonsense that Beckett is droning on and on about. I don't know how long we've been out here, but all I can think about is what Shep told Lennon and how long has she known? Not to mention how reckless I was acting in the bathroom with him, taunting and flirting with him like that. Seriously, what came over me?

It could've been how good he smelled or maybe the way the suit made his eyes pop. There was also the way he ran his fingers through his hair, for a second I wanted to do it myself.

"Harlow? Are you even listening to me?" Beckett's voice cuts through my thoughts.

"What?" I respond, disoriented.

"I asked if you knew Lennon was going to be here with Shep," Beckett crosses his arms.

"Oh, no. I didn't. I'm just as surprised as you are." I

look around for them and then at Beckett again. "Can we go inside?"

Beckett starts up again about how he doesn't want to go through the same conversation we had at the date party and I should know better than to talk to Shep. At a certain point, I feel myself checking out of the conversation again then blurt out, "Can I go?"

Beckett's eyes shoot wide open. "Can you go?" He responds. "Can you go where?"

"Home? Away from here? I don't know but I really don't want to have this conversation with you anymore, Beckett." I take a breath, summoning every bit of confidence I have. "I came to formal with you because I agreed to, but after this, I think we need to stop seeing each other."

His mouth gapes open and he reaches his hand out towards my face. I brace myself for what's about to happen, when a familiar voice calls, "I wouldn't do that if I were you."

I turn on my heels and Shep is walking right towards us.

"Fords, this has nothing to do with you, so I suggest you fuck off." Beckett starts to raise his voice.

Shep ignores him, coming up to me first, "Are you okay?"

"I guess, yeah." I shrug my shoulders.

"Good. Lennon needs you, she's out front." Shep's words are direct but soft, then he physically ushers me towards the house and away from the situation. Once I'm by the door, he turns around and walks back to where Beckett is. I stop for a few seconds, looking out the window to where the guys are now alone. Beckett's mouth is moving a hundred miles a minute, meanwhile Shep just stands there with his hands in his pockets, a calm expression on his face.

I make it out front and, sure enough, Lennon is there. When I get to her though, I realize she's not alone.

"Is Shep still inside?" Wes steps towards us and asks.

"Yeah, he—what's going on here?" I look between the two of them.

Lennon opens her mouth and that's when I hear it.

Clashing, banging, and what sounds like the forming of a large crowd erupts from inside the fraternity house.

"Shit," Wes starts to take off through the front door, but not before turning and looking me dead in the eye. "Call Laura and tell her to send Will."

My stomach drops and I waste no time doing just that.

The line rings twice before I hear Momma Ford's voice on the other line.

"Sweet girl! Aren't you supposed—"

"Laura, something's wrong. Shep went to talk to Beckett and now—"

"Oh, honey, okay. Okay, I'm going to call Will. He's at the precinct, but Harlow, listen to me. Whatever you do, do not get involved."

There's a pause and I desperately want to appease her, but my words say differently, "I'm sorry, Laura. I have to go back inside and check. Please call Will."

I hang up before she can say anything else, turning to Lennon. She's frozen like a deer in headlights but I plead with my eyes for her to follow me.

TWENTY-NINE

"EXACTLY WHAT I SAID. EXACTLY WHAT YOU THINK IT MEANS."

SHEP

Willing myself not to explode on the spot, I casually walk up to Beckett and Harlow. I'll be damned if he isn't about to lay hands on her right now.

"I wouldn't do that if I were you."

Harlow turns and looks at me and I want nothing more than to pull her into my arms right now. Knowing the truth. Knowing what happened to my girl. It's overwhelming to think about the secret she's been carrying from that night.

I exchange a few words with her, ignoring Beckett completely and when she finally gives in and heads to meet Wes and Lennon, I turn and look Beckett right in the eyes.

"You're a real piece of shit you know that?"

"Excuse me?" He says, cocking his head to the side.

"You heard what I said. Thinking the way you treat Harlow is even remotely okay. Where do you get off laying your hands on her?"

"I'd keep your mouth shut if I were you. Talking about things you have no idea about," he sneers.

"Oh I think I know exactly what's going on. I just wish it didn't take me this long to figure it out."

"And what exactly is going on?" Beckett says, stepping towards me while trying to press his chest out in my direction.

"You're the reason Harlow got hurt," I say it boldly, maintaining eye contact with him.

Beckett stumbles back some before speaking again. "Oh yeah? Is that what she's saying? She's got a mouth on her."

I cut him off. "No, she actually hasn't said anything to anyone. It's what I *saw*."

Beckett stalls and I can tell he's trying to understand what I'm saying. "What do you mean you saw?"

"Exactly what I said. Exactly what you think it means. I saw. Now, if you know what's best for you, you'll leave Harlow alone and you'll take responsibility for this situation, because I can guarantee it's not going to stay under the radar." I start my walk back towards the house, leaving Beckett to stand there and mull over everything I've just said.

As I make my way through the door into the main hall, I hear Beckett catching up with me and I tell myself to not act on emotion.

"Do you think you can just make threats like that and walk away?" Beckett calls out after me. The people around us stop what they're doing and now everyone is facing our direction.

I keep walking, knowing I just need to make it to the front, leave with my people, and then deal with this later. A small twinge of regret creeps in that I probably shouldn't have confronted him tonight, but after seeing the video footage and then walking out to him almost laying hands on Harlow again, I couldn't help myself.

I turn around and am met with Beckett's fist swinging towards my face. I move out of the way, and put some distance between us. "Beckett, I think you really need to consider what you're about to do." But I can tell at this moment that he doesn't see anything other than red. His eyes are narrowed into dark slits, his pupils blown out with rage.

He comes for me again and thankfully, with the training I have, I'm able to out maneuver him and put him into a headlock. I lower my voice before speaking to him again. "I'm not gonna do this with you, Beckett. Unlike you, I don't feel the need to use violence to get my point across. If you want to talk about this, then we can, but I'm not going to fight you."

I keep him in the headlock for a few minutes until his body starts to go limp and I hear the word "fine" mumble from his mouth.

My first mistake is believing him, my second is letting go. The instant he's out of my hold, he grabs my waist and tackles me to the floor, knocking over the tables that are around us. I try to pick myself up before this gets any worse, but Beckett's fist comes down hard across my jaw, causing me to sink to the floor.

The taste of iron overwhelms me, and I see blood leaking down onto my hands, from I assume my mouth. "Seriously man, we don't need to do this." I lift my head and am met with Beckett's fist once again, this time coming across the side of my forehead. A searing pain rips through me, and I collapse to the ground again. I hear people yelling in the background, and I know this isn't going to end well. Trying to pick myself up one more time, I see Wes out of the corner of my eye running into the room and then everything goes black when Beckett delivers one more blow to the side of my head.

THIRTY

TATTERED, BLOODIED, AND BRUISED.

HARLOW

I don't wait on Lennon before pulling my heels off and rushing into the house. Pushing my way through the crowd that's started to form inside the main hall, I make out a blur of movement until I finally get up close and take in the sight before me.

Shep is knocked out on the ground, with blood coming from his mouth and his forehead. Wes is trying to keep Beckett pinned down but is taking a beating of his own.

"Someone do something!" I yell, running towards the commotion.

"Harlow, don't!" Wes shouts back at me and when he does, Beckett gets the upperhand and shoves him off.

Wes tries to scramble to his feet, but Beckett turns and kicks him in the ribs and then starts towards me.

"You!" At this point, most of the crowd has moved out of the way, but there are countless phones out, I assume recording everything.

"Beckett, please." I raise my hands in defense. "There's no need for all this. Why don't you and I just go talk somewhere."

Beckett draws his hand back and smacks me across the face. I buckle forward onto the floor, holding my cheek and hear Lennon scream in horror. He starts yelling down at me, "You did this! You lying, conniving—"

Wham!

Beckett staggers to the side and I realize, at some point in the last minute, Wes has gotten back up and managed to sucker punch Beckett to the ground. Why is nobody else helping? I start to crawl towards Shep, when finally someone from the crowd pushes forward, grabbing Beckett by the arms and dragging him away.

Wes sinks back down and out of the corner of my eye I catch Lennon running over to him. I make it to Shep, kneeling beside him and picking up his head to pull it into my lap.

"Shep, come on. Wake up. It's Harlow," I stammer, fresh tears rolling down my cheeks. At this point, most of the crowd is clinging to the walls observing with shock and horror. I can hear sirens starting to approach and realize the multiple people on their phones are not just holding them and recording. Some must have called for help too.

Abandoning any walls or defenses I had, I do what I wanted so desperately to do earlier and run my hands through Shep's hair. "It's going to be okay. I'm here," I whisper out as I meet Lennon's gaze.

Her and Wes are sitting in the middle of the floor together, with her hand clutching his cheek. How did this happen?

The sound of shoes hitting the floor becomes loud and overwhelming as the police arrive and run into the building. The next few minutes are a blur, but thankfully the one memory that's clear is the multiple hands pointing at Beckett and him being handcuffed before taken out of the room.

"Harlow, you need to let the EMTs step in," a voice appears, hazy but familiar. "Harlow, it's okay."

I blink a few times and when my vision clears, I see Sheriff Fords squatting down in front of me. I glance down and realize I've been holding Shep against my chest. I look at Will again and he gives me a soft smile before touching the side of my hand. I nod and let my arms fall to my sides. Two medics kneel down to move and start to treat him.

"Can you come with me?" Will says again and offers his hand to me. I look at it, feeling like a caged animal in the moment. Most of the people have been cleared from the house, unbeknownst to me. I glance past Will and see Wes is also being treated by a medic, Lennon still by his side.

"O-okay," I mumble. Placing my hand in Will's, he gently pulls me to my feet and then grabs a blanket from another officer, wrapping it around me.

We take a few steps towards the stairs and he helps me sit down. The officer from earlier walks over and Will says something to him, before leaving me and walking back over to check on his son. I think I'm in shock. Nothing feels real.

I gaze down at my soft yellow dress that's now stained with splotches of red. I don't know how much time passes before Will walks back over to me, looking distressed and upset. I meet his gaze and notice he also looks like he's been crying.

"Is he going to be okay?"

———

The worry that consumes me in the short amount of time during the drive from the Chi Kappa house to Everson Memorial Hospital is likely record-breaking.

Once the EMTs finished their evaluation of me and realized all I had was a small bruise, they let me go. Lennon and I rode together to the hospital and in that brief period, many earth shattering things occurred.

The first being, my parents were called and would be meeting us there. This resulted in a string of texts from not just them, but Margot as well, asking me questions that I didn't have answers for.

Then, Coach Bradford sent me an unofficial email that he was aware of the circumstances surrounding my injury and while he still wanted to speak with me in person, I was no longer required to do my practices at the rec center.

Shortly after his email, came a text from Pierce. It was at that moment, life as I knew it ceased to exist. "I saw that Beckett is the reason you're injured. I'm sorry."

Two words: *I saw*.

It didn't take long after arriving at the hospital and speaking to Shep's dad again to figure out there was a recording that had been made of the footage from the night of my injury. The realization that said recording was made by Shep came as no surprise, but how he came to find it? That's still unanswered.

Lennon and I are both sitting in the waiting room with the Fords, enveloped by an uncomfortable silence while we wait to hear more. Wes is about to be released from triage, but Shep was admitted because he clearly suffered some sort of head trauma during the fight with Beckett. The EMTs informed us Shep did regain consciousness in the ambulance and I wish I could've been there when he did.

I know I didn't do anything wrong, but I can't help feeling like this is all my fault. Whatever caused the fight to break out between Shep and Beckett, I've no doubt I was the reason.

"Harlow, you have to see this," Lennon whispers quietly, before nestling up against me. She opens her phone up and starts to play a video of the fight. It's clear that Shep tried to diffuse the situation and then Beckett blindsided him.

"Put it away, please. I can't. I caused all of this." I bury my face in my palms and Lennon rubs a hand on my back.

"No you didn't. Don't say that. Harlow, nobody could've known Beckett would react that way," Lennon offers.

"But I knew! I've known!" I choke out. "He has anger issues and I've just let it slide and kept my mouth shut about it this entire time because I was too weak to tell anyone." The words come out broken as I start to sob again.

"Okay, Lennon. I think I'll take it from here. Harlow, sweet girl, let's go for a walk?" I peer up and Laura Fords, the woman and angel herself, holds a tissue out for me.

"Do we have to?" I huff.

"Yes, we have to. Let's go before your parents get here," she whispers.

My stomach drops and I want to collapse onto the floor when a doctor appears and interrupts us.

"Shepherd is settled, and he's asking for Harlow? Is she family?"

My heart thrums with hope and I clammer up to stand next to Laura who laughs.

"Not yet," is all she says before looking at me again. "Let's go check on him, but then we really need to talk to you before your parents arrive, okay?"

"Okay," I rush out before following her and the doctor. Will joins us and we make our way to the room.

My hands begin to sweat and I realize I don't know if I can face Shep. I'm still in my dress from formal and I'm worried about what he's going to say when he sees me, tattered, bloodied, and bruised.

We turn the corner and the doctor opens the door to Shep's room. All my worries melt away when he looks past his parents at me and weakly says, "There's my girl."

THIRTY-ONE

UGH, I CAN'T WAIT FOR MY NEXT THERAPY SESSION.

HARLOW

I sit in the chair next to the hospital bed, waiting for the doctor to finish giving his final assessment to Will and Laura. "I'm sure the bruises will clear in a week, the stitches will dissolve, and as far as your concussion goes, thankfully it's minor so all you'll need to do is stay away from screens for about three days."

Will and Laura Fords stand by the other side of the bed like hawks. The protectiveness they have for their son is radiating off their bodies and it makes me feel sick. I can't begin to think about how they feel towards me, being that I'm the reason he's here right now.

Will's phone goes off and he apologizes before stepping out of the room. Laura follows, then stops and motions for me to come to her as the nurses finish checking Shep's vitals and administering more fluids.

"How are you doing?" she asks as we near the door.

"*Me?* I mean, I'm okay I guess."

"I just can't believe that young man had the audacity to do what he did. In such a public manner too. Ugh, your cheek is still red." She tuts while looking me over.

"Oddly enough, I guess it's good it happened?"

Laura raises an eyebrow at my admission before I continue, "I'm not quite sure exactly how I feel about the situation, but there is a tiny bit of relief that enough people were there to witness Beckett's behavior."

"That's a good point, but still…I wonder if that was the school calling Will. After everyone was transported here, he immediately reached out to the Dean to demand Beckett be expelled from the university." Laura peaks out the door and then pops her head back in. "Still talking."

"I don't want to press charges," I say quietly. "They asked me that after checking me out. I don't want to." I pause for a second. "Will Shep and Wes want to?"

Laura tilts her head and I can see her contemplating how to respond. "I think that one over there will want to know how you feel and then will relay the message to his best friend. That's what I think."

I turn and look at Shep who's still smiling at me.

"Laura, I need you." I hear Will's voice call out from the hall.

"I'll be just outside, sweet girl." She gives my hand a small squeeze before excusing herself.

"No charges, huh?" Shep starts.

"You heard that?" I say walking back over to the hospital bed.

"Yeah, but I'll be honest, I kinda already figured you wouldn't want to." He tries to shrug his shoulders, and I don't miss how he winces when he does.

"It's just... I think if, like your mom said, he gets expelled, that'll be enough. He won't be allowed back on campus and well, I don't think with his ego that he'd show his face anywhere around town."

"Makes sense. But hey, with Beckett out of the way now, at least we don't have to worry about being seen together or something." He closes his eyes and a soft smile adorns his bruised face. Shep's words, while optimistic, make my stomach sour. I start to think about the events of the night, the lead up to it over the last few weeks, and realize I'm no good for Shep while I'm dealing with all of this.

"I don't think—I'm sorry." I take a step away from Shep. In the time between the fight and now, I've been going over everything I've learned from Robin the last week. And while unsettling, the one thing that sticks out to me most is her saying I need to put myself first. "I don't know if that's a good idea either," I finally force the words out and I feel the bile in my stomach threatening to follow after them.

Shep opens his eyes again and I wish he wouldn't have. They're filled with hurt.

I know it would be so easy to fall into Shep and let him fix this. Let him fix *me*. But that isn't his responsibility. And so, with every ounce of courage I've gained in just a short amount of time, I look him in the eyes and come out with it.

"I think I need some space." When the words leave my mouth, it feels like the air is sucked out of the room and Shep slumps forward.

"Harlow," he starts.

"No, Shep. I mean it. I know what you're going to say and I can't let you. I know how easy it would be to ignore everything that's happened to me and focus on you, on what might be happening between us, but that's not how this needs to be done."

He nods his head silently. "What do you mean by space? Do you want to stop talking?" His lip wobbles and I really hope he's not about to start crying. I know he's in tune with his emotions-all thanks to Laura-but I don't think I can handle that right now.

While I know Shep would never use his emotions to manipulate me into making a decision, I recognize that my mind is still weak. I can feel myself wanting to please him in the same way I've developed the habit of trying to please everyone in my life. It's cost me so much and I can't keep doing it.

"I don't know how this goes, Shep. Honestly, I don't have a clue, but Robin literally told me earlier today that it's important that I learn to start setting boundaries going forward. If I want to have these healthy relationships she's mentioned…I have to try."

"Harlow, I—"

Walking towards him again, I raise my hand and gently place it on his.

"Please. I just need some time."

Shep glances down where my hand is resting on top of his, then meets my gaze again making my stomach do a flip.

His eyes are flooded with intensity and it dawns on me just how much we're connected to each other—beyond just our physical touch at this moment.

Somehow, without knowing me entirely or knowing everything that I've been carrying, Shep has embedded himself into every facet of my life that he could. He's made it so obvious he cares. I can see it. What has my heart bucking wildly in my chest though is now, I can *feel* it.

"Okay." He finally mumbles, rubbing his thumb over my knuckles. "Okay. I'll let you set the pace, but I'm telling you right now, Harlow. I'm not going anywhere."

His slate eyes meet my green ones and the passion in his stare makes me feel like I'm burning up. I withdraw my hand from his and step back again from the hospital bed.

"I'm really glad you're okay, Shep. I never meant for you to become collateral in all of this. You have to know that."

"I do, and I don't regret getting involved with you. I don't regret listening to my gut about you. I knew there was a reason I was drawn to you and I don't regret anything that's happened since the day you came up to my lifeguard stand."

My heart all but cracks in the worst and best way. Looking at the beautiful boy in front of me, even with the black eye, busted lip, and stitches running across his forehead, I can't ignore that I feel something for him too.

I know I still have so much progress to make. I know that I need to think through everything that's happened and process all my emotions about the situation. *Ugh, I can't wait for my next therapy session.*

"Thank you for saying that," is all I'm able to choke out. "I'm going to go talk to my parents and see if it's okay for me to head back to the apartment."

The thought makes me shiver as I remember all the people outside in the waiting area. I'm sure the conversations being had between my parents and the Fords are anything short of intense. When I finally got the moment alone to talk to Laura like she'd been asking, I realized it was because she wanted guidance on what she could and couldn't share.

I was so taken aback that she'd consider asking me such a thing. I told her she could be honest about knowing something was going on between Beckett and I, but to hold back on mentioning therapy. I still wasn't ready to fully immerse my parents into the reality of just how deep Beckett's claws had sunk into me, but there was no doubt they'd want to know why he personally slapped me during the fight.

"I really need to lie down," I speak again.

The adrenaline from earlier has worn off and the emotions that were also running high have dissipated, leaving me in a state of pure exhaustion. I feel like I could sleep for days. Somehow though, my feet trudge me across the room and I place a soft kiss on Shep's forehead near his cut before stepping back again.

"I'm sorry I can't just—"

"Stop, Harlow. Don't even think for one second you're doing anything wrong. I'll be fine."

"Okay," I whisper. "Oh, I just wanted to let you know that I won't be swimming at the rec anymore."

Shep's face visibly pales even more than it already was.

"Now that Coach knows what *really* happened, he said I could finish my rehab at the athletic center during team practices." I look down at the floor knowing this is the real space I was hinting at earlier.

"I understand," is all Shep responds before there's a knock on the door.

Wes walks in and gives me a sad smile, sporting a bruised cheekbone. My stomach twinges at the ugly voice in my head telling me I'm to blame for all of this.

"I'm sorry," I nod my head in a knowing direction, "for that." I turn and look at Shep, the guilt rising up in me again. "For everything."

Wes walks towards me doing what he does best and wraps his arms around me. His hug is just as awkward as it was the day we ran into each other outside of the coffee shop, but this time I welcome it.

I see Lennon behind his shoulder waiting by the door and can tell she's been crying.

Letting go of Wes, I take one more glance around the room before accepting that it's time for me to leave and hope that with my absence, a sense of normalcy will return, despite the last few hours.

"Stop it," Shep says before I can fully exit the room. "I know what you're thinking right now and you didn't cause this."

My breath hitches as the shock that this boy knows me almost better than some of the closest people in my life hits me.

Forcing myself to not cower under pressure and tell him what I know he wants to hear, I turn and give him one more soft smile. "I'll try."

THIRTY-TWO

"I MISSED YOU."

SHEP

It's been three weeks since Harlow and I have talked. I miss her so much it hurts.

I didn't realize how much she had become a part of my daily life until suddenly she wasn't in it anymore.

I know we hadn't really even started talking that much over the phone but I still wish I was able to hear from her. After a week of sitting at home, I finally got cleared to return to the rec for work but I wasn't even excited about it. What's the point if Harlow isn't going to be there?

Wes and Lennon are still hanging out, and as much as they try to hide it, it's obvious. I'm happy for the guy but it's also not making this any easier for me. Not to mention, Lennon won't talk to me either.

I know this is what Harlow needs and I want to support her, but it's seriously doing a number on me. The only relief I have is knowing Beckett is gone and Harlow is back with her team. I ran into Pierce the other day and he told me that she's doing great and they think she might be able to race in the meet coming up before Halloween.

While I'm optimistic that before then Harlow and I might start talking, I'm not getting my hopes up. I'm also not wanting to fall into the category of the guy who can't function without the girl, so I've been focusing on my senior thesis project and spending more time with Dad at the precinct, trying to narrow down what I want to do.

Lennon mentioned something the other week when she was over at our house about how Dahlia would make an incredible therapy dog. We've always joked about her being our emotional support pet, but when Lennon said that, it got me thinking.

I started doing research on what it takes for dogs to become ESAs and therapy dogs—I learned that there's a huge and important difference—and I realized that maybe this was something I could do for the precinct.

My dad had mentioned a while ago that they were interested in a program like this but needed someone to get it off the ground. I only wish it hadn't taken me until now to put it together that I want to be that someone.

When I began to look into the process for this project, I realized I was coming up short in one area. The dogs needed to have homes to reside in while doing the training. Then they'd need to be paired with handlers who'd continue their training and bring them to work when needed. This discovery led me to be where I am at this current moment: the precinct meeting room.

About fifteen cops are here and all looking at me, the Sheriff's kid, waiting to see what bullshit I'm on now. Most of these guys have known me for at least five years, some less, but they know I'm always trying to get involved.

I'm trying not to focus on the very real possibility that this idea could go nowhere and then I'll be back trying to figure out some mundane job for myself. Dahlia is lying by my feet, already setting the perfect example of what this program should be like.

I clear my throat and everyone's eyes are on me. I know I'm prepared for this, but standing in front of the room now, it's like I haven't spoken in public before.

"Right," I start. "So, thank you all for coming. I know that most of you are here because of who my dad is but I'm going to ignore that."

That warrants a few chuckles from the guys and I continue on.

"If you don't know who my dad is, I'm Shep Fords meaning, yes, my dad is the sheriff. But what most of you probably don't know is I'm pursuing my degree in criminal justice and I have to complete a senior thesis in order to graduate. Before any of you get worried that you're here to be roped into some research project, that's not the case."

As I finish my sentence, Dad walks into the room and grabs a chair in the back. I would be nervous but I already gave him this exact presentation a few days ago when he gave me the go-ahead on this idea.

"This is my dog, Dahlia." I motion down to the sleepy brown lump resting near my feet. "I rescued her from our local shelter here and she's an incredible dog. I know what most of you probably thought when you first saw her, she's a pitbull, and that's even more important to what I have to say."

I go on to tell the different guys in the room that for my senior thesis, I would like to enlist the help of anyone who is willing to foster a dog from the local shelter and be a part of helping train these dogs to create E.V.E.S.T., or the Everson Valley Emotional Support Taskforce. This garnered a lot of eyebrow raises and leaning forward on the tables.

I was clear with them that this was not to be confused with therapy dogs because that's an entirely different level of training and requirements.

"I spent the last few weeks already going over some of the more basic commands with Dahlia, who took quickly to the training. This of course is not always going to be the case, but here is an example of what we might have these dogs do. Imagine, I'm a teenager who just witnessed something horrible happen and now I'm in the precinct waiting to answer questions. This is a very high stress situation and a lot of times, adolescents don't know how to regulate their emotions yet during circumstances like this. I'm sure you all know how important it is to have the person you're asking questions be calm, and this is where one of the E.V.E.S.T. dogs would come in."

I walk over to a chair and sit down. Dahlia is still laying in the same spot and all the guys are craning to watch her and me.

"I'm going to start bouncing my knee like someone who's nervous might."

Dahlia, please don't decide this is the moment you want to stop listening to me.

"Dahlia, come." She perks up and saunters over before stopping next to me. "Sit." She does, thank God. Then I put my finger on my thigh near my knee and look at her. "Lay."

This is the moment of truth and I could cry tears of joy when Dahlia leans her head forward and lays it on my lap.

Various *wows*, *ooh*s, and even an *oh shit* ring out from the room. I wait for a few more seconds before rewarding Dahlia with a treat then have her lie down next to me again.

I look to the back of the room and Dad is beaming. I know this is such a small step, but for once I feel like I'm doing something I'm proud of. I only wish Harlow was able to hear about it.

I go over the rest of the details regarding meeting with the shelter, getting matched with dogs who seem like good candidates and how many of these dogs might be pitbulls, then speak with a few more guys before the hour is up. By the end of it all, there are four guys who can commit fully to fostering, training both at home and then once a week with the group, and would even consider becoming handlers.

"You did good, son." Dad places a hand on my arm.

"Are you sure about this? You really want to give up some of your guys to help me out?" I still want to make sure I have his blessing.

"Absolutely. I wouldn't have helped you come up with a name for the program if I didn't believe in it." He smiles. "Now go on and call your mother because she's been texting me and asking for pictures as if this was a school science fair or something."

Hugging him goodbye, I grab Dahlia's leash and start to walk out the door with her. It honestly makes me laugh how unbothered she is by her surroundings. She really never reacts to anything—

"Dahlia, wait!" Before I can stop her, she's pulled on her

leash and is racing across the street towards the other side of the road. "Dahlia, stop!"

Thankfully there aren't any cars, but it doesn't mean my heart isn't in my ass. I slow my jog and finally catch up after losing sight of her behind one of the parked cars and I'll be damned.

Rolled over on her back with her tongue hanging out, Dahlia is getting her belly rubbed by the one reason worth distracting her enough to pull away from me.

"Harlow," my voice comes out shaky. "I'm sorry. I couldn't grab her leash quick enough."

She looks up at me and her green eyes are brighter and clearer than they've ever been. She tosses her blonde hair over her shoulder before standing up and wiping her hands off on the front of her pants. Of course she's wearing a crop top and flannel with her Docs, but these ones don't have laces.

"It's okay," she says softly. "I'm glad I was able to intercept her." She laughs and my entire body feels like it could crumble to the floor.

"She was actually running to you, so that worked out." I ruffle my hair with my hands nervously, looking around to see if she's with anyone. "Getting coffee with someone?"

God, I sound pathetic.

"My sister, Margot. She's moving back here in a few months so she's been visiting more often. Especially after…" She looks down and I know she's talking about the fight.

"Gotcha, well I'm sorry to catch you like this. I hope you're doing okay." *Wrong. I hope you're doing more than okay. I hope you're getting everything you want. I just want to be a part of it.*

"Thanks. I've just been trying to keep up with life. Obviously there's a lot I'm still figuring out, but I'm managing." She smiles and it not only looks genuine, but it fills me with a warmth that lets me know it *is* genuine.

"I'm glad. Well, I'll let you go. It was good to see you." *I miss you.*

"Yeah, you too. Hey, I'm sorry I haven't—"

"Harlow, it was good to see you. Take care of yourself."

I cut her off before any type of apology can leave her perfect, pouty lips. She asked for space, I'm giving it to her. She doesn't need to apologize and I'm not going to try and end that space sooner than she wants, no matter how badly I'm craving her.

Walking away, Dahlia trots next to me and I pull my phone out to call Mom, knowing if I don't do something else, I'll turn right back around and try to talk to Harlow more.

Dahlia stops, beginning to pull on her leash again. I start to tell her to come on, when my eyes follow hers and a blur of blonde and flannel is making its way towards me at an unprecedented rate.

Before I can react, a body thuds against mine and I feel arms wrapping around my neck. The smell of vanilla spice and cherries fills my nose and I realize Harlow is hugging me. Standing there frozen, I finally wrap my arms around her and pull her tightly to my chest. I don't know what I did to deserve this, but I'm not going to argue. My heart is hammering inside my chest and every urge I've ever felt for Harlow is trying to push its way to the surface.

"I missed you," I hear her say, and I close my eyes, absorbing every ounce of her that I can before setting her back down.

She looks up at me with this gleam in her eyes that seriously takes my breath away before turning around and walking back to the coffee shop, but not without looking over her shoulder one more time and giving me the most incredible smile. That's it. I think I'm done for.

All the feelings and thoughts I've been going over for the last few weeks without talking to that beautiful girl settle in me at the mere sight of her. My heart settles. I think I love Harlow Sutherland.

THIRTY-THREE

MOMMY ISSUES

HARLOW

Holding my phone in front of me, I let out a large breath before groaning and tossing it back on the couch. "Why is this so hard for me?" I grunt out.

Robin laughs from across the room. "I'm not sure, but I will say, at first I didn't want you to push yourself, but now I think you're just afraid."

"Ugh, Robin! You're supposed to tell me that I'm staying safe in my boundaries or, or," I snap my fingers while trying to remember, "Ha, yes! Or that I'm protecting my peace."

Robin lets out an even heartier laugh. "Yes, but see, that right there tells me that you're making really good progress. You're able to see how certain actions coincide with what you've learned. I'm not going to tell you it's okay to text Shep if that's what you're hoping."

"I mean, it couldn't hurt." I frown and cross my arms.

"Harlow, you know I'll never tell you what to do. I can"

only advise and suggest, but I think you know what you want to do." Robin eyes me over her glasses. "You've put in a lot of hard work over the last few weeks."

She's right. I have.

After I left the hospital, I put my head down and started to focus on my classes, swimming, and therapy. Lennon and I got to pick our routine back up, with the slight change of me meeting up with Laura here and there for therapy.

It's been nurturing and I feel like I'm healing. Robin and I settled into a twice per week schedule following the fight, and through the last several sessions, I've learned more about myself than I have in the last ten years.

Robin was shocked to hear what happened, but not surprised. It was like Laura said, there would be no doubt Beckett would eventually escalate. I'm still processing the fact it was so public though.

Once the footage of the fight got out, more gossip on campus started up about me. This time, I decided to take it head on and I told my swim team what really happened to my shoulder and let them do the rest. After a few days, everyone was over the fight and talking about Beckett and what a terrible person he was.

Part of me felt bad, which was some of the guilt I was working through left over from his abuse. I knew that Beckett did this to himself, but the part of me that had been romantically attached to him caused my emotions to waver.

However, there is no regret in my mind for not pressing charges. I was right in that he wouldn't show his face again, but I do wonder where he went. While we had been together for over a year, we never did family introductions. He mentioned to me once that his mom lived outside of

Everson and that was it. No mention of a dad or any siblings. I couldn't help but wonder if he went back home and what that was like for him.

Robin assured me it was normal to wonder, but it was imperative to not get hung up on the *what-if*s, which was my biggest issue.

I spent the first session after everything crying to Robin about *what if* Wes hadn't been there to break up the fight. There was a very sick feeling in me that Beckett could have killed Shep, without even realizing it. The sight of him that night was terrifying. He looked like a different person. The worst part is, I only remember him having one drink, so while I wanted to try and justify his behavior with his substance abuse like I had in the past, I wasn't able to. Maybe he really was just a monster.

Robin told me after talking with Laura, Sheriff Fords had found out that Beckett had a prior offense from when he was younger but it had been expunged. I felt like everything I knew had been a lie. Who really was Beckett? And how did I get involved with him?

One of the other things that's been really hard to come to terms with is the lack of relationship I have with my mom. Apparently I have mommy issues, which makes me even more susceptible to the kind of abuse Beckett was inflicting on me. He was able to get in my head, making me want his affection and attention so badly that I was willing to overlook the bad. Apparently this was a byproduct of not getting the affection and attention I desperately wanted from my mom growing up. *How fun.*

"Harlow, I think you've come a long way. It couldn't hurt to talk to Shep. I'm sure he misses you based on everything you've shared with me, but I'm also sure that he understands the space you're wanting and will wait a little longer."

"See, but that's the thing, Robin. It's knowing he would wait longer that makes me want to talk to him. Because I know that he's a good guy and I shouldn't be afraid to talk to him…"

"But?" Robin questions me as I trail off.

"But…I feel like I'm too broken. I feel like if anyone really knew everything they wouldn't want me, and I don't want to bring all my brokenness into their life."

Robin sets her notebook down on her desk and sighs. "Harlow, listen to me. All of these preconceived notions that you have about the people in your life—Shep, and especially about the way you see yourself—are from the seeds of doubt Beckett planted in your mind. He caused you to question yourself and question your worth. We both know Shep doesn't see you as the broken girl."

Robin is right. Everyone is right. She's not the only one who's been trying to get me to see that. Even Lennon and Wes in the few times I've talked to them both have made it very clear that, while they support me taking care of myself, I really need to give Shep a chance.

Lennon and I haven't talked about what happened much at all and I think some of that is the guilt she feels for not knowing about my accident. We did talk about that the night we left the hospital though.

She asked me why I didn't tell her and the only answer I could give her, even though I knew it might hurt, was I didn't think she would believe me. I was right. It hurt her and she cried the whole night, apologizing over and over for letting me down. I did my best to assure her that wasn't the case but I know she's had a hard time accepting that.

Laura has only mentioned Shep a total of two times during the last three weeks. One was to tell me that he had been cleared to go back to work, and the second was today, when she casually mentioned he would be downtown at the precinct.

Which led me to the current moment with Robin. Do I text Shep and ask to meet him since we're both downtown?

"I really want to do it. I think I might wait though, there's something else I need to take care of first." I smile at Robin. "But you're right, I'm not the things Beckett made me feel about myself. While he may have bruised me physically and emotionally, he didn't break me."

"Ah, there she is! My star client. I'm so proud of you." Robin beams at me then checks her wrist watch. "Now, I hate to cut us right on time but I do have an old student of mine stopping by to pick up some paperwork from me, and I don't think you'll want to be here when she does."

I stop just before getting off the couch and sit back down. "What do you mean? Are you allowed to tell me? If it's just an old student—"

"Yes, I know where you're going. There's no client confidentiality. I was hoping to not have to bring this up at all because you know I'd never share your information with anyone, but I didn't realize how close we were cutting the time by."

"Okay, so…"

"Your sister, Margot." Robin says. "She emailed me this morning saying she was going to be in town getting some things in order for the university and was hoping I'd be able to get some paperwork put together that she needs since I used to teach at Everson."

"Oh, I didn't know. But never mind that. Margot is coming here? Now?" I jump up, understanding the crunch for time and start packing up my things. Laura didn't drive me today because there was something she had to do so there happens to be a rather recognizable Bronco out in the parking lot.

"Yes, but Harlow, I think Margot would want to know what's going on. I know she's your sister but she does have the licensing I do and might be more helpful than you—"

"Thank you, Robin. Really. I will take it into consideration, but I don't think now is…" My words are cut off by the sound of the bell ringing to let us know someone's walked in. My stomach drops. This office space is currently only being used by Robin so there wouldn't be any other clients here for other therapists.

"I guess now is as good a time as ever," I bite out.

Robin frowns, and I know she didn't plan for this, but I really wish she would've told me sooner. I can't help but feel a little ambushed and I think Robin recognizes that too when I don't move to leave the room.

"I can go out there and just give her the paperwork. You wait here," Robin says softly, but this is probably a true test if I've ever seen one.

"It's okay. Thank you." I smile at her then open the door and walk out to be greeted by a face that's similar to mine but just a little older, with green eyes that are just a little lighter, and long wavy hair that's just a little darker.

"Harlow?" Margot stands up and looks past me at Robin's office. "I thought that was your car out front but I couldn't be certain because I didn't know why you'd be here. Is everything okay?"

She steps forward, hugging me, and while I want to run away from this awkward moment, I choose to accept her embrace and return the gesture.

"Yeah, I'm okay. I've been seeing Robin for a little over a month now." I tuck my hair behind my ear nervously and look down at my boots.

"I didn't—How are—Never mind. Can we talk?" She reaches her hand out and places it on my arm. "Do you want to talk?"

"I mean, I guess we need to now." The memory that Shep is downtown pops into my head and I decide to go out on a limb. "We could go get coffee at Boulder?"

"Oh, sissy, I'd love that. Let me talk to Robin really fast. I can explain more about that too, I'm sure you're wondering why I'm here." She laughs before moving past me and tapping on Robin's door. Robin opens it and looks at us both, smiling.

"Robin already told me she taught you," I offer her.

Margot turns around with a look of relief. "Oh! Well then even better. Robin, could I come by later? I think I need to catch up with Harlow and want to make sure I have enough time. Will you be here late?"

Robin nods her head and they exchange a few more words while I start to head in the direction of the front door, feeling like I'm eavesdropping.

A few minutes later, Margot meets me by the door and we get in our cars to head to Boulder Brewing Co.

———

I pull into a spot on the outside of the building and get out of my Bronco. Staring at my phone for what feels like the hundredth time, I debate texting Shep and asking him if he's still downtown. I don't see his truck, but he could have also parked behind the precinct or something.

Margot somehow beat me and texted that she's already inside. I start walking towards the coffee shop when something jets out from the front of a car parked on the street and makes a beeline for me.

It only takes a few seconds for me to realize it's a dog with a leash trailing behind it, but not just any dog. It's Dahlia.

My heart leaps with the hope that fate has somehow worked in my favor, and while I'm crouching down petting the sweet puppy, her handsome owner finally appears.

When he says my name, my body turns to jello.

I look up at him and, good Lord, my breath hitches in my throat. He's wearing a white button down with navy slacks, and his hair, of course, is effortlessly ruffled. The butterflies in my stomach immediately explode and it takes me a minute to get my bearings before I can respond.

Finally standing to my feet, I brush my hands off on my pants before meeting his gaze. I can't help but smile at him. The last few weeks, while necessary, really only emphasized that I was very much enjoying seeing Shep all the time, I just didn't realize it.

"Are you getting coffee with someone?" he asks, motioning to the front door. I really hope he doesn't think I'm going on a date or something. A flash of panic sets in and one of those dreadful *what-ifs* runs through my mind. What if he's gotten over me in the last few weeks? I mean, that was what I had originally wanted, but now that I've put space between us and we haven't talked at all, I realize that I definitely do have feelings for him.

I quickly respond to let him know I'm meeting Margot and hope it's very clear that I'm not on a date.

He asks me how I am and after a few seconds of small talk and him wishing me well, I feel the need to apologize, but he won't let me. After telling me a second time that it was good to see me, he turns and starts to walk away.

When he does, I don't move. My heart is urging me to go after him and tell him that I've been thinking about him and what's been going on the last few weeks. I look inside the coffee shop and see Margot is still waiting in line, so I act on impulse and go after Shep.

Dahlia notices me first and when Shep turns around, I don't even think. I jump up and wrap my arms around him and hug him the way I've been wanting to since we hugged at the formal. I hug him the way my heart has been crying out for his affection since he looked at me the way he did in the hospital.

Every feeling, urge, thought, and desire that I've been contemplating for this man bubbles right up to the surface and I don't feel the need to fight it.

"I missed you," I finally break the silence and whisper next to his ear.

His hold around me tightens and a fire coils up in my stomach. I know that if I don't reel it in, I might do something that I'm not actually ready for, so I let him set me back down and give him the biggest smile I can.

He doesn't ask anything of me, which gives me the freedom to turn and head back to the coffee shop. But I can't stop myself from looking over my shoulder one more time and smiling at the handsome lifeguard standing on the sidewalk. The look he gives me back nearly causes my damn heart to rupture.

It's at this exact moment, when I turn and open the coffee shop door, that I realize—I could very easily let myself fall head over heels for Shep Fords. The revelation both scares me and excites me. What shocks me more is…I think I already am falling.

THIRTY-FOUR

"SWIMMERS, HUH?"

SHEP

I spend my drive back to the townhouse on another level. Harlow's scent is still trapped in my nose and I don't want it to ever go away. I completely forgot to call Mom, so I do that before heading into the house.

She asks me the questions I figured she would and I answer them as quickly as I can before bursting in through the door. Dahlia runs past me and into Wes's room. I hear not one, but two voices react.

Oh shit.

Dahlia runs out and following close behind her is Wes, whose face is beet red. He looks at me once with wide eyes then shuts his bedroom door. Deciding to entertain the circumstances, I yell out, "Hi, Lennon!"

A groan emanates into the living room and I laugh. I head into my room and start to grab some of my stuff, checking that there's nothing left to do before heading to the rec for my shift. I moved it to later tonight so I could make the meeting at the precinct.

Even though Harlow won't be there, I can hardly think about that disappointment. I'm still on cloud nine from our encounter outside the coffee shop.

I don't know what's been going on in that beautiful mind of hers since the hospital, but I hope I'll find out soon. Every time I'm around her, I just want more. I've felt like this in the past with her, but it's only grown stronger in the time we've spent not speaking to or seeing each other.

After a few minutes, I hear a knock on my door even though it's open. I look over and am shocked to see Lennon.

"Can we talk?"

Glancing beyond her, I see Wes in his doorway and he nods his head at me.

"Sure, what's up?" I start walking towards the living room, not wanting to be alone with her in my room—door open or not.

She follows me and plops down in our recliner chair, crossing her legs and leaning forward on her elbows, then comes right out with it. "How did you realize what was going on with Beckett before I did?"

Her question catches me off guard as I sit down on the couch opposite her. I turn my head to the side and look at Wes again who's trying to act like he isn't eavesdropping. He raises his hands in defense then shuts his door. *Great.*

"I'm not sure what you mean by that. How did I realize? Like when did I figure it out?" I try to answer gently because I can tell there's some hurt in Lennon's voice.

"I mean, I guess. You don't have to answer anything that you think Harlow wouldn't want me to know. I want to respect her boundaries. She's been working with Robin on that a lot, so…"

"Right," I nod my head. "So, this is probably going to sound stupid to you, but it started when she first showed up at the rec. I just got a feeling from her after seeing her there for a few days."

"You're joking." Lennon deadpans. "I've been best friends with the girl for over five years and you could tell something was wrong right away? Some friend I am!" She lifts her hands up before bringing them back down on her legs.

"No, no. Lennon. This is exactly what I didn't want to happen." I laugh a little trying to diffuse the tension. "I just meant that there was something off about the situation with Harlow. I knew about her title and ranking. She just didn't seem like the type to get drunk at a party and then get hurt so my suspicions were already raised. Then they were confirmed when I saw her bruises at the pool and then the moment in the car on speaker phone."

"Well, I believed the story," Lennon sniffs. "I mean, when she came up to me and asked to leave, she reeked of alcohol and there was puke on her clothes."

My heart drops. "Lennon, I need to show you something, but first—Wes?" I call out. He opens his door again. "Can you come here please and sit with Lennon?"

"What, why?" she asks with a puzzled look on her face.

"Just trust me." I look past her. "Wes?"

"Yeah, sure. I'm here." He walks over and motions for her to get up before sitting down and then pulling her into his lap. *Nothing going on between the two of them my ass.*

Once Lennon is settled, I pull out my phone and find

the footage of Harlow's accident. Nobody has seen this except for the few people I sent it to that night at formal. "What I'm about to show you cannot, and I mean this, *cannot* leave this room. Everyone knows what happened now, but nobody needs to know about this video."

Lennon gasps and I see Wes squeeze her hand.

I turn my phone and press play. Lennon immediately starts crying and I notice Wes is holding his breath. I can tell what part the video is at based on their reactions and when it's finally done, Lennon turns into Wes and starts sobbing.

"I'm sorry. I didn't want to upset you, but I thought this might explain your memories and, shit. I'm just sorry, Lennon. I know she's your best friend."

She continues to bawl against Wes's chest while he strokes her hair. His eyes lock onto mine and they're filled with sorrow. This isn't the first time Wes has had to take care of someone who's been in this condition, but it doesn't make it any easier for him.

Lennon finally picks her head up and glances over at me. Her red and puffy eyes make my heart hurt and I wish there was a better way to explain all of this.

"Lennon, you didn't fail Harlow in any way. I know it doesn't make you feel better, but Harlow didn't tell you for multiple reasons. The biggest being she was afraid of Beckett. That fear was able to overpower her ability to come to you as her best friend. You know that?"

She nods her head. "That's what she told me after the hospital, but she hasn't really talked about it since and it's just been bothering me. I love that she's back with the team and we're able to spend time together like before, but I can't help the feeling that we'll never actually get back to *before*."

"Maybe not, but I think that's a positive thing. These new beginnings for her and for you are good ones. Not just good ones, healthy ones. She's starting to thrive, Lennon, and she still wants you right by her side through it." I smile at her and she sniffles before rubbing the back of her hand across her cheek.

"How'd you get so smart about all this, huh?" She softly laughs and I could fall to my knees in delight that I haven't destroyed the poor girl.

"I think you know the answer to that. You've met her a few times now." I gesture to Wes who beams.

"Momma Fords."

I clap my hands together. "That's right. So, Lennon, to answer your question, it just happened the way it did. I was pushy and probably overbearing at times with Harlow, and to be honest with you, she never came out and told me what was going on. Like I said, I just put it together over time when certain things happened."

"Okay," she sighs. "If you say so. But don't get any ideas about replacing me as her best friend."

"Hey," I hold my hands up in defense, "I could say the same thing about you two." Lennon's cheeks flush as she jumps out of the chair and off of Wes.

"I was just here studying. That's it," she shoots back quickly.

"Riiight. You keep telling yourself that."

Wes snorts and then covers his face when Lennon glares at him.

"I gotta head to work but I'm glad we got to talk because hopefully, all four of us will be able to hang out soon."

"Wait, what do you mean?" Lennon perks up at this so I

decide to throw her a bone after the heaviness of the conversation.

"Let's just say I ran into a certain blonde downtown. Leggy, likes flannels, and always wears Doc Martens. You might know her? Anyways, she gave me a big hug and told me she missed me." As the last few words leave my mouth, Lennon screams and runs to Wes's room grabbing her bag and phone.

"I have to go! I need to call Harlow! Wes, I'll see you in class." She slips her sneakers on then stops and comes back over to me motioning for me to stand up. "Thank you for seeing her." She gives me a small hug and then turns and bolts out the door.

"Geez, Shep. What're you doing man?" Wes exhales then leans over and smacks me on the side of the arm. "Showing her that video?"

"She needed to see it. It's her best friend. And don't get all upset with me, it worked out in your favor." I raise my eyebrows.

"Oh don't start that shit. We were just studying, seriously. Can I be honest with you?"

"Always, what's up?" I lean back on the couch again.

"We haven't had sex." A weary look covers his face and I'm not sure if he's worried that I'm judging him or what but he should know by now that I'm not one of those guys.

"Okay, and?" I gesture for him to continue.

"I don't know. I just don't want you to get the wrong idea, especially of her."

"Damn, you really like the girl." I snort.

"Excuse me?" Wes retorts.

"I don't think I've ever heard you stand up for a girl

other than your sister. It's refreshing and I hope it works out for you. As far as the sex goes, you know I'll be the first one to tell you I've never thought that shit was super important. I think it matters, but it's not what you should be seeking out."

He nods in affirmation before leaning his head back on our recliner and staring up at the ceiling.

"You're right though. I'm down bad for that girl." He lets out a long breath before looking over at me. "Swimmers, huh?"

I chuckle before nodding my head and mumbling out in agreement.

"Swimmers."

THIRTY-FIVE

THERAPY TALK OR SOMETHING

HARLOW

"Alright, spill everything."

Margot takes a sip of her iced matcha latte and taps her freshly manicured nails on the table. I know there really isn't any reason for me to not tell her what's been going on, but the idea of trusting someone and letting them in is still a process.

"Well, I can tell you what I've told Robin or——"

"No, I want you to tell me whatever you want. We don't even have to go into detail about why you're seeing Robin. I'm assuming Mom and Dad have no idea?"

I shift in my chair. "No, they don't. Um… Laura has been paying for it, but I told her I would pay her back."

Margot chokes on her drink. "Laura Fords? Is paying for your therapy?"

"Listen, I had the same reaction but she wouldn't take no for an answer. She's friends with Robin so I'm not sure if they worked something out, but she just wanted me to start seeing someone as soon as possible."

I glance at my coffee and swirl it around in the cup. There's so much I could tell Margot but I don't want to burden her when I know there's already so much on her plate. We've always been close, but there's also been stretches where we didn't talk as much. Like when she struggled with her own demons in the past, my parents felt I wasn't old enough to really understand so they kept me out of it.

Robin's mentioned there's probably a part of my brain that has blacked out those memories or repressed them, but we've worked to rip off that Band-aid, letting the wounds breathe, and allowing my now fully developed brain to reprocess why it hurt so much to be excluded.

I do remember Margot being in therapy for years though, and that's ultimately what led her to where she is in her career today.

She reaches out and stills my anxious hand. When she smiles at me, it makes me want to cry. I put so many walls around myself over the last few years, but especially the last few months, and now that I'm starting to get past them, the people in my life mean so much more to me.

"We don't have to talk about anything you don't want to, so maybe we can just catch up? How's swimming? Any update on when you might be able to compete?" Margot suddenly sits upright and before I can try and figure out why, a voice behind me speaks.

"Look who it is, my best athlete." *Pierce.*

I spin around and, sure enough, looking delicious as always in his tight fitting workout gear, Pierce is resting his hands on the back of my chair. What really catches me off guard though is the way his gaze is locked beyond me.

I dart my eyes to the side to discover I'm caught in a very heated exchange of eye contact. The tension is palpable and even makes me feel flustered. Margot runs her hand through her hair before leaning back and crossing her arms.

I notice Pierce's grip tightens on the back of my chair, the veins in his arms popping out. I can't help but continue to look back and forth between my sister and athletic trainer who are in some sort of showdown.

"Hi, Pierce." I wave to him and redirect his attention to me. His hold on the chair relaxes and then he looks down at me and smiles.

"What's up, Sutherland? Funny running into you, I just left a meeting with Coach and I have some good news for you."

Not wanting to get my hopes up, but also feeling expectant for what he might have to say, I jump out of my seat. "What? What happened?" I draw my lip into my mouth and nervously chew on it.

"He said you're good to swim against Marymount next Friday before Halloween." Pierce reaches a hand out tentatively, but I'm so overcome with emotion, I surprise myself for a second time today by deciding to hug him.

"Oh! Wow, not quite the reaction I was expecting but this is definitely good." Pierce hugs me back before stepping away. He looks beyond me again and seeing as Margot isn't opening her mouth anytime soon; I take matters into my own hands.

"This is my sister. I mentioned her to you when we first

started training together. I don't know if you remember her, but she's moving here in January to work at Everson actually." I sit down again and glance at Margot whose lips are pursed out and her arms still crossed.

"Interesting," Pierce drawls. "Margot, right?"

"Right," is all she clips out. I shoot her a glare, wondering where the hell her manners are.

A smirk tugs on the side of Pierce's mouth. "Guess I'll be seeing both of you around."

Nodding my head in agreement, he turns and takes off. When he's a good enough distance away, I immediately reel on Margot.

"What THE hell was *that!*"

She lets out a large breath before picking up her matcha again. Slowly sipping on it, I can tell she's trying to regain her composure. I've never seen Margot rattled like this before. Well, at least, not in a very long time.

When she doesn't say anything, I continue. "Did I miss something?"

Finally she responds, "He knows my name. We were in the same graduating class at Everson. We went to college at the same time." The wavering in her voice causes me to arch an eyebrow.

"Okay, well yeah, but—"

"He knows who I am," she cuts me off. "Acting like he doesn't..." She trails off and starts mumbling something to herself.

I lean forward, motioning with my head for her to continue on.

She quickly shakes off *whatever* is happening and brings

the conversation back to me. "Tell me about Shep, what's going on with that?"

Rolling my eyes, I let out a frustrated huff. Old Harlow would've matched this ridiculous stubbornness and then some, but I'm working on New Harlow, and New Harlow decides to indulge her. "He's okay, I guess. I don't know. We haven't talked since the hospital. I told him I needed some space after everything and he's been giving me that, which is nice. I actually just ran into him outside."

Now it's Margot's turn to arch an eyebrow and give me a knowing look.

"Yeah, yeah. I like him, if that's what you're getting at. But that's where all the mess with Beckett comes in. He, uh…really didn't like that Shep and I were starting to talk. Even though it was innocent, like just passing conversations at the rec center."

My old habits start creeping in and I almost stop. But I can hear Robin's encouraging voice echoing in my mind, so I tell those habits to fuck off.

"Beckett was hurting me."

Margot's mouth drops open some and she leans forward, setting her drink down on the table between us. "I'm sorry, he was *what?*"

"Margot, can you just take what I'm saying as like therapy talk or something and not as your sister? I don't want it to turn into a big thing. It's already been hard enough to open up to Robin about it all and something about more people knowing makes me feel queasy."

She scrunches up her forehead and I can tell she's really thinking over what to say next. "When you say hurting—"

"Yes." There's no need to draw out that part of the

conversation, but to give her some sort of relief I add in, "Not that it makes it any better, but it was never massive beatings or anything like that. Just well… Ah, shit. Okay."

"What?" Margot's face pales.

"Beckett is the one who dislocated my shoulder."

Margot's mouth gapes open again and then she places a hand over it as if stifling a gag. "Harlow, that's… I—" She shakes her head before meeting my stare, her sage green eyes welling up with tears. "I'm so sorry."

"It's okay. You have nothing to apologize for. It was my choice not to tell anyone, and also, as I'm sure you understand as well, I was trapped in a cycle with him. That's mainly what Robin and I have been working on."

An invisible weight starts to lift off my chest as I disclose these secrets to my sister.

As our conversation continues, I find that talking with Margot is almost like talking with Robin, but more familiar. She does her best to not give me therapeutic advice and just listen. By the end, a new feeling of hope brims to the surface and I'm starting to look forward to Margot moving back to Everson.

THIRTY-SIX

RED LEATHER SHORTS

HARLOW

The next few days fly by and, before I know it, my first meet of the season is one day away. Pierce and I have been putting in extra time, trying to ensure that I'm comfortable racing. Marymount University is a top competitor for us, but I'm more excited than anything. There's nothing quite like the feeling of stepping up on the block and waiting for the buzzer to sound.

I'm not going to be swimming butterfly, which does make me sad, but Pierce wants to make sure I'm at one hundred percent. I know the stroke puts more strain on my shoulder and we don't want to rush anything. Either way, I'm happy to swim freestyle if it means I get to compete.

While Coach Bradford still seems reserved, I think most of that is his own guilt from how quick he was to assume the worst regarding my injury.

The amount of people who've asked me why I didn't come forward sooner about what happened with Beckett is comical. In the beginning, it was frustrating, but now I just wave them off and redirect the conversation.

Shockingly, the person who's been the most upset is Pierce. He keeps going on about how he thought, with the amount of time we've spent together, I'd have told him. No one seems to understand that there was far more at stake for me than just dropping that bomb.

And the fight at formal? Well, that blurred into the rest of the gossip on campus.

Among getting ready for the meet tomorrow, Lennon is breathing down my neck about finishing our costumes for the Halloween party on Friday. As usual, she has an elaborate plan while all I want is to wear a black dress or something with some animal ears. Call it a night.

Speaking of, Lennon saunters into my room with a bundle of fabric in her arms.

"What is *that?*" I peer over my book at her.

"*This* is your costume! If you'd just put down that damn book for more than a few minutes and let me show you what I've been working on," she scoffs before throwing down the materials. Not letting me respond, she continues, "I know you've got this new freedom and you're able to relax now that he-who-shall-not-be-named is out of the picture, but why am I not getting all your attention now?"

I set my book down, letting my head fall back in a fit of giggles. "Lennon, you've hardly been home! Are we going to talk about where you've been?"

"Studying," she retorts. "I've been studying."

"Sure…you know you can tell me if you and Wes are seeing each other, right?" I raise an eyebrow and stare her down.

"There's nothing to tell. We happened to spend some time together after the whole formal incident, but I'm not dating him or anything. And now that you've almost changed the subject, let me put you in the hot seat. What's going on with you and Shep?" She jumps on the bed next to me.

"Nothing. You know I ran into him and that's it. I haven't talked to him since, but I was thinking…"

"Yes?" Lennon beams at me eagerly.

"I might text him that I'm racing tomorrow and see if he wants to come." I pull my bottom lip into my mouth.

"I think that's a great idea! W—" She stops herself, snapping her mouth shut.

I turn my head and widen my eyes. "Hm?"

She scowls then looks away. "I'm sure Shep will know people there, that's all."

"Uh huh. Not Wes is coming to watch you and Shep can go with him?"

She waves a hand in my face then reaches down at the end of the bed for the things she brought in with her.

It takes me a few seconds to register what she's holding and my shoulders slump when it clicks. "Lennon, I'm not wearing *lingerie* to the Halloween party. You must be out of your mind."

"It's not lingerie when it's a Halloween costume! C'mon, everyone knows that!" Lennon holds up the corset to herself. "See? It's not slutty if it's for Halloweeeeeen!" Her voice rises up into a shrill pitch.

"Right, but what exactly are we supposed to be? The corset and spandex leather shorts aren't really giving off any vibes other than—"

"Shh! Enough. I'm not done yet! I just need you to try it on so I can get the vision. Here," she tosses me the clothes then stands up and starts walking towards my door. "I'll be in my room when you're changed. Indulge me."

Once she leaves, I walk into my bathroom and hold up the white corset to my body. I look at my reflection in the mirror and I've got no idea what Lennon is planning, but she's never done me wrong in the past.

Shimmying into the red leather shorts, I pull the corset over my head and tighten it. *Holy shit.*

My ass is essentially hanging out and what cleavage I do have is spilling out over the top of the white lace. I stand in front of the mirror for a few more seconds, when an odd feeling starts to coil up in my stomach. The thought of Shep seeing me in this pops into my mind and there's a jolt of excitement that shocks me.

I've been resigned to wanting to cover myself up. Hiding internal and external hurt with my wardrobe. However, with the recent change of events, it's like I've shed off that invisible layer of shame and guilt.

I decide to give Lennon the rouse she wants, so I let my hair down and ruffle it over my shoulders. I smack my lips together a few times and pinch my cheeks for an instant flush. Satisfied with my appearance, I strut into her room and throw my arms up into the air.

"Ta-da!" I shimmy my chest in her direction.

Lennon whips around and squeals. "You look amazing! This is going to be so good! Shep's going to lose his mind!" She taps her fingers tips together like she's concocting an evil plan.

"Care to explain?" I put my hands on my hips. "Like what exactly is this costume? Are we matching?"

"We are," she points to a similar outfit lying over the chair in her room. "Don't worry, I just wanted to make sure everything fit you. I'll have the rest ready by Friday."

She walks over and pushes her hands up under my boobs. "This is good," she smirks.

"Lennon," I swat at her. "Did you even consider that maybe I don't want to use Halloween as an excuse to dress up like a sex pot for Shep?"

"Hm," she pushes her pointer finger into her temple, then throws her hand dismissively in the air. "Nope! Didn't cross my mind."

I frown at her. "You're meddling, Lenny."

"Ugh! Just let me have some fun, okay? I obviously dropped the ball big time with—"

"Don't. Don't do that. You had no idea, okay? So you can't put that on yourself." I reach out and grab her by the shoulders. A twinge of guilt washes over me as I realize it's likely that Lennon's efforts are being fueled by her own. "You know what? You're right. I do want Shep to see me in this and I'm excited to see the rest of the costume."

Her eyes well up and I draw her into me. Hugging her, the wall of my own stubbornness crumbles a little more. Robin suggested something I could say to Lennon to affirm our friendship and this moment feels like the time.

I step back and place my hands around her face. "Lennon, you were as good of a friend as you could be with the amount of information I gave you. You aren't a mind reader and there was no way for you to know what was going on. Bec—*he* played his part well. Every one of his roles was believable, so much so that I even fell for the show he put on in the beginning of our relationship. It's not on you. Okay?"

She nods her head and then swipes the tears off her cheeks. "Okay."

I kiss her forehead and then ask her for some more hints about these costumes. She won't give me any details but we do come up with another plan.

Operation: Invite Shep Over After the Swim Meet.

Which involves Lennon trying to convince me to send Shep a picture of myself in this costume, and at first I immediately shut down that disaster of an idea. But Lennon has a way of twisting my arm with her overzealous attitude.

"It'll be fun! Harlow, do it!" She claps her hands, mischievously.

Taking my phone, she snaps a picture of me pouting at the camera.

"Lenny, I'm not—"

"Shut UP! That's perfect. Holy shit, you look *so* good. Look at yourself!" She squeals and shows me the screen.

I snatch back my phone and stare at the girl in the photo. I don't know why but I feel like I keep seeing myself for the first time. I study the picture and it may seem a little out of character for me to flirt with Shep, but it's never been out of my character to mess with him and give him a hard time—which is exactly what this photo will do.

THIRTY-SEVEN

THREE BUBBLES

SHEP

It's about four in the afternoon on Wednesday when my phone buzzes, and when it does, three things happen simultaneously.

One, Dahlia jumps up and knocks my phone out of my hand onto the living room floor. Two, I hear a string of expletives slip out from Wes's mouth across the room. And three, I realize that I'm in deep shit.

Wes sees my phone lying on the ground and swears again, before picking it up and handing it to me. "Dude, I think we're in way over our heads if you just got the same text I did…which I'm pretty sure you did."

When I finally have my phone in front of me, my heartbeat goes straight to my dick. A picture of Harlow from the chest up staring back at me. It's not just a normal picture though. No, no it's far from.

Harlow's wearing a very white, very lacey-looking top. Her hair looks like someone's hands have been running through it, which causes a surge of jealousy to rise up inside me. What really does it for me though, are the innocent doe eyes and pouty lips she's giving the camera.

I'm sure Lennon likely coaxed her into taking said photo. I'm not complaining one bit though.

"Hey, lover boy. I got one too from Lennon." Wes shakes his phone in my face.

We both sit there without speaking for a few seconds, staring at our screens.

"What's your text say?" I break the silence.

"Swim meet then Halloween party?" Wes responds.

"Same," I chime back. "This is, uh," I run my hands through my hair and tug on it. "These are quite the pictures. You think they're messing with us?"

Wes snorts, "Knowing Lennon, she's probably orchestrating this whole thing."

"Knowing Lennon, huh? Meaning you're going to finally admit you two are together?" I press into him, hoping he'll finally break on the matter. I don't know why the two of them won't just fess up. It's so obvious they're sneaking around.

"It's not like that. Why can't we just be friends and not be together?"

"Because I don't think *friends* send each other pictures like *that*. But hey, what do I know?" I text back to Harlow that I'll be there and she thumbs up the message. It's not huge progress, but it's progress.

"What about you? You and Harlow haven't been talking but something obviously happened," Wes snaps at me. *I've definitely pushed his buttons.*

"Nothing more than what I told you the other day, so

you might be right about Lennon pulling some strings. No complaints though. I'm excited to see Harlow race."

Wes grunts and nods his head in my direction, while squinting at his phone.

"Okay?"

"I'm trying to figure out what exactly Lennon's wearing. Should we try and match them?" Wes pops his head up.

"Match them? No. No, Wesley. I don't think we should match them," I scoff.

"Damn, not the full name. Sorry I was just trying to have some fun." He makes a face at me before standing up. "Well you're on your own then, Shepherd. Figure out your costume by yourself."

"Oh, for heaven's sake. You're so sensitive." I roll my eyes.

"You would know! I learned it from spending so much time around you."

I get off the couch and stare at him, in our own silent standoff.

I start squinting when I feel the need to blink and he pulls his shoulders back, puffing his chest out. After another few seconds go by, Dahlia barks, sensing our tension.

"See! Even Dahlia thinks this is ridiculous," I jest.

Wes relents, "Fine. We don't have to match them, but we should figure out what we're wearing."

"Um, you can find whatever get-up you want. I was just going to wear some gray sweatpants and one of *The Purge* masks leftover from last year."

Another grunt from Wes, then he turns and heads into his room. My phone buzzes again and time stands still.

HARLOW

Do you want to come over after the swim
meet?

I stare at my phone, with my mouth gaping open. I
guess enough time passes without me replying that the three
bubbles pop up again.

HARLOW

You don't have to, sorry

Yes. I'd love to

HARLOW

Okay

I'll ride with Lennon to the athletic center
then you can drive me home?

Yeah of course. Sounds great

HARLOW

My heart is pounding, then another text comes through
that has me adjusting myself through my shorts.

HARLOW

Also, I'm a little surprised for someone so
obsessed with me that you didn't have
anything to say about my picture

I laugh out loud.

Left me speechless

HARLOW

Good.

Good? Is Harlow flirting with me?

Not wanting to push my luck but curious where this might go… I decide to play into it.

Oh yeah? Well you better be wearing it for me and no one else, baby

The three bubbles pop up, then disappear. *Dammit, I went too far.* Then my jaw drops as a message finally comes in.

HARLOW:

You say that like I'm yours

Because you are

HARLOW

Am I?

See youuuu tomorrow

Oh, by the way… wait til you see the shorts that go with the top

I force myself to set my phone down, but not before biting down on my knuckle and letting out a stifled groan. I'm so worked up for this girl right now. For *my girl.*

My thoughts starts to fire off at a million miles an hour. Envisioning all the ways I can make it so very obvious she's mine. I chuckle when an idea pops into my head that will not only let everyone know Harlow is mine, but will also be playful enough to not make her uncomfortable.

"Wes!" I yell out. "We need to go to the craft store!"

THIRTY-EIGHT

ALL MY CARES TO THE WIND

HARLOW

It's race day.

I can't believe I'm finally able to say that. After feeling like I'd never compete again, I'm standing in the athletic center with Lennon and the rest of my team. I haven't felt this happy in a long time.

It's a different type of joy—getting to do the thing you love.

I just hope that all the hard work I've put in translates through my efforts today.

Lennon and I do warm ups in the pool before heading to the locker room and getting the rest of our things.

"You nervous?" She pokes my side.

"Not really. I think it'll be weird not swimming butterfly, but I know why they're doing it this way."

A few teammates pass by and wish me luck, then it's time to head back out. Once I'm on the pool deck, I glance around and my eyes find my mom, dad, and Margot in the stands.

Dad beams at me and my heart swells. Margot stands up and cheers, then quickly sits down when Pierce walks up beside me.

"Feeling good, Sutherland?"

"As best as I can. Thanks for all your help getting me back in the pool to race."

We bump fists then he walks off towards the stands. Keeping him in my line of sight, my jaw drops when he sits down next to Margot. She crosses her arms and doesn't acknowledge him.

What the hell is going on there?

"HARLOW!"

I whip my head to the side and see Lennon barreling towards me.

"What? What's wr—"

"I'm sorry. I told him not to, but he wouldn't listen!"

"What're you talking about?" Lennon grabs my shoulders and directs my attention to the far side of the athletic center and my heart drops into my stomach.

No. No. No.

Loud cheers erupt from the tall lifeguard who's walking into the crowds with a huge poster in his hands. The words "THE BLONDE ONE IS MINE" painted across it.

My cheeks burn as everyone around him watches as he holds it up and then points to me.

I cover my face with my hands, turning to Lennon.

"Lenny," I growl. "Make it stop."

"No can do! Honestly, I think it's great. Besides, there are tons of blondes here!" She bursts into laughter then her face drops, her eyes looking like they might bulge out of her head.

I turn around worried something else has happened, but find myself now bursting into laughter.

Next to my sign is another poster being waved in the air, held up by none other than Wes. His sign, however, is much more obvious, displaying 'DIBS ON LENNON' in gold paint. I double over cackling to myself.

"Look at us," I finally catch my breath. "Best friends who like best friends."

Lennon just rolls her eyes before marching over to where Wes is.

My eyes catch Shep's and a soft smile tugs on my lips. I wave to him as butterflies erupt in my stomach. My heart starts pounding when he smiles back, then mouths, "Hi, baby."

My insides do flips, cartwheels, and if I wasn't nervous before, I am now.

Something about Shep's confidence to show his affection for me, even without me returning it, is wildly attractive. It makes me want to give back the same energy. It makes me want to continue whatever *this* is with him. The quiet confidence I've been building inside myself over the last few weeks is starting to seep out. While it feels foreign and maybe a little scary, it also feels so good.

Throwing all my cares to the wind, I blow him a kiss in front of everyone. His eyes widen and I can see blush creeping into his cheeks.

I motion for him to come down onto the pool deck and start walking his way. When he steps off the last step, I throw myself towards his chest. He catches me with ease, wrapping his arms around my waist.

"Thanks for being here," I say, nuzzling my nose into the side of his neck.

"Anything for my girl," he responds, setting me down.

I pull at the end of my ponytail not sure what to do next, but Shep fills the moment by leaning down and kissing my forehead. When he steps back, I can't help but look at his lips. This growing desire in me to kiss him is becoming hard to ignore. It doesn't help that I keep having dreams about him either.

"Hey," Shep whispers, placing his hand under my chin. I snap my gaze up to his, realizing I've been staring at his mouth for a little too long. "Later," he continues, as if reading my mind. I suck my bottom lip into my mouth and nod, lost in a trance of attraction and curiosity.

He moves his thumb to pull my lip out from between my teeth, then smears the wetness across it. My heart hammers against my chest. It's as if Shep and I are the only two people in this entire arena. Whatever hold he has on me right now, I don't want it to stop. The sensation building inside of me is warm and gnawing, in the best way.

"I think I need to go," I finally mumble out.

"Yeah, you probably should," Shep says in a low, gravelly tone.

My body visibly shivers and Shep smirks.

Needing to escape the heat that's starting to overtake me, I walk briskly back to my team. It takes every bit of power I have to not look over my shoulder, because if I do, I don't know if I'll be able to stop myself from going back over to Shep.

Holy shit, I want him. I want him so bad.

"WHOAH, CALM DOWN, RAMBO."

SHEP

If there's one thing I enjoy, it's a challenge.

And Harlow Sutherland is proving to be my most favorite one yet.

Watching her find me and my sign in the crowd was a sight I've committed to memory. The shock, the flush, the light in her eyes even though she tried to hide it.

She asked if she really was mine, and I made it damn clear she is.

Somehow though, she left me in the stands feeling like I don't have the upperhand. I could tell she wanted to kiss me and, damn, did I want to kiss her too. But the thought of our first kiss being at a swim meet just didn't feel right, it doesn't do justice to the way I feel about her.

Wes and Lennon finally stopped bickering and now he and I are sitting in the stands waiting for our girls to swim. I think this may be one of the greatest moments of my life.

Wes and I are together, cheering on the girls we like, who also happen to be friends.

Lennon's event is first and Wes is locked in on her lane. I swear he doesn't blink during the entirety of her race. When she finishes in second, he still claps and cheers like she came in first.

While he focuses on her, I spend my time tracking Harlow. There's a side to her I'm getting to see that knocks me off my feet. Her passion for the sport she loves and her team is radiating off of her. I thought I'd seen her fired up before, but that was nothing compared to this version. Every so often, she sneaks glances at me which I return with winks. Her cheeks blush and she quickly darts her vision back to the pool. It's amazing.

I know we still have a lot to talk about, but I can't help but let myself fall into this bubble of what it would be like for us to date. Sometimes I forget we're not.

Mom and Dad talk about her enough like she's already part of the family. I think about her all the time. I feel things for her that I've never felt about anyone else before. She's my girl.

And right now, I'm watching my girl bounce up and down on her toes, shaking out her arms and twisting her neck around. Her race is coming up and I think I might be more nervous than she is.

"Look," I elbow Wes in the side. He yelps before smacking my arm. "Harlow's group is up next."

"Heat," Wes retorts. "It's called a heat. Seriously, didn't you do any research before coming to this?"

"I know what it's called, but it's also a group. Excuse me for not being technical." I roll my eyes.

Harlow puts her goggles on, then pulls her swim cap over her head. Coach Bradford walks up to her and my chest tightens. I swear, if I have to go down there again.

"Whoa, calm down, Rambo." Wes nudges my knee with his and I look down to see that I'm white-knuckling the edge of the bleachers.

"I'm fine. I just don't know if I trust her coach yet." But then Harlow hugs him and my shoulders relax. "Okay, maybe things are okay."

Wes laughs and rambles on about me needing to chill out. I don't think he understands the extent of Harlow's recovery that I've had a front row seat to. Sure, he knows I was always working when she had her rehab practices, but I never went into detail with him about everything that I saw. He doesn't know how many times I watched her cry or get frustrated. I also never told him in depth what happened that day during her first evaluation.

It wasn't that I didn't trust him, but even then I felt the need to protect Harlow. I could tell she didn't want anyone's pity, so I kept my cards close to my chest. I'm not sure what all Lennon has shared with him, but either way, I know how much this race means to Harlow, whether she admits it or not.

Because it's not just a race, it's a test. It's a contradiction of her deepest fears and a confirmation of her biggest hopes. It's the moment where she proves herself. She's not here for anyone other than Harlow. She isn't competing against the other athletes. She's competing with herself and damn, I hope she wins.

Harlow looks over to me as she approaches her lane. She gives me a soft smile and I give her two thumbs up just like I did the day of her evaluation. The announcer instructs them to take the starting block, and she steps up, rolling her shoulders a few times.

You got this, baby. You got this.

In a monotonous tone, the speaker states, "Take your marks."

Harlow bends down, assuming a position that looks like a track start—one leg in front and the other behind her. She grips the edge of the block, then springs forward when the buzzer sounds.

Her dive into the pool is effortless and I sit there mesmerized, watching her streamline underwater before breaking the surface. I hold my breath as she takes her first few strokes. She's only swimming the 50 meter freestyle so she won't be in the water for long, but the seconds are ticking away like hours.

Her arms move in and out of the water in a fluid motion that makes it look like she's gliding, floating through the pool. She's keeping up with the rest of her heat and as she nears the wall to finish, I can't help but jump up and scream. "Go Harlow! Go!"

It's as if she hears me and her kicks become stronger, her strokes become longer, and she's nearing first place. My stomach is in knots and I want to look away, but I can't. Just a few more pulls of her hand and…holy shit. Holy shit! She did it! She won!

I lean down and shake Wes's shoulders. "She won!"

The crowd erupts in a loud cheer, people rising to their feet. Harlow pulls up her goggles and glances around, I'm sure it's water from the pool but I wouldn't be surprised if there are a few tears mixed in with the droplets.

The announcer cuts back in, "And there you have it, folks of Everson Valley. Harlow Sutherland's first swim of the season post-injury and coming out on top! Let's hear it!"

Pride swells up in my chest and I don't even care what anyone thinks of me. I lean back and puff my chest out, yelling into the roar of the stands, "THAT'S MY GIRL!"

FORTY

IT'S ALL ABOUT PERSPECTIVE

HARLOW

As I step up onto the block, the world around me silences. I focus on the pool, the movement of the water, and try to slow my breathing down.

Everything I've done in the last few months amounts to this moment right here. I don't care about any of these other swimmers. I don't care if I lose. I just want to race without stopping. Sure, there's a chance I could win because I'm in a slower heat, but that's the last thing on my mind.

Once I'm set, I close my eyes and wait for the buzzer. When it finally sounds, I snap them open and push off the block. My streamline feels strong and the rush of adrenaline I was hoping for kicks in. I break the surface and start to take my first few strokes. There's a twinge of pain but after a few more strokes, it dissipates and I'm in the race.

With every few breaths, I can hear the crowd cheering when my ear is up to the ceiling. This isn't a long race, but every second counts. I can see that I'm keeping pace with the other swimmers, but something inside me is screaming out to push harder. To go faster. So I start to kick with everything I have left and reach my arms out as long as they'll go.

With each stroke, I let a different fear fall off of me. I leave it behind in the water and press on towards the hope of what's ahead. Chasing after the new beginnings that await me once I complete this race.

With my last few pulls in the water, I close my eyes, touching the wall and staying like that until the crowd gets even louder. I pull up my goggles and peer around the athletic center. Everyone's on their feet, roaring and clapping. I finally glance over at the scoreboard and tears rush to the surface when I see that, by just a few points of a second, I somehow came in first.

I swim over to the lane next to me and shake the hand of my opponent from Marymount, then to the other lane where my fellow teammate is. She leans over the lane rope and hugs me, the announcer cutting through the noise in the background. "And there you have it, folks of Everson Valley. Harlow Sutherland's first swim of the season post-injury and coming out on top! Let's hear it!"

As I go to pull myself out of the water, I swear I hear a voice louder than the rest that screams, "THAT'S MY GIRL!"

Coach Bradford runs over and helps me the rest of the way out of the water, then hugs me and cheers with both his fists in the air. Lennon's running in my direction and Pierce isn't far behind her.

Once the roar of the spectators settles some, I catch my breath and meet Lennon halfway. She throws herself onto me and squeals. "You did it! I'm so proud of you!"

Pierce catches up and chimes in, "Sutherland, that was awesome! Nicely done!"

I step back and feel my cheeks flush. "Thanks guys, but I wasn't even racing against my normal competitors. You put me in a slower heat." I laugh softly, trying to downplay their compliments and praise.

"Oh, who cares, Low! A win is a win!" She playfully swats at my arm.

"Yeah, I'm with Marino. Take it for what it is." Pierce gives me an awkward fist bump then leaves us to talk alone.

"I can't believe I was able to finish. I was so scared my shoulder would freeze up or something and I wouldn't—"

"None of that!" Lennon cuts me off. "We're celebrating, you deserve it."

"Lenny, I only swam one race and I'm already done for the day…I hardly deserve anything. " We walk towards the stands and she waves at my family. "I should probably go talk to them."

"Yes, you do that and I'm going to go get a slushie for us to share!"

I find my way over to my parents and Margot who still has a look of displeasure on her face.

"Well done, fishy!" Dad speaks first and sticks his arms out wide for a hug.

"Thanks, Dad." I lean into him, not worrying about the fact that I'm still soaking wet.

"Yes, well done, Harlow!" Mom agrees and gives me a pat on the back. In the past, I would have fixated on this. However, at this moment I'm just thankful to have both of my parents here supporting me. *"It's all about perspective,"* Robin's voice plays in my head.

When I step back, I turn to address Margot. "You look less than thrilled, but I'll let it go this time since I saw who came and sat by you." She rolls her eyes then reaches out and pulls me into a hug.

"I'm so proud of you. For everything." She whispers the last part, and her words hit me hard. I squeeze her a little tighter, then she steps back and sticks her finger out. As always, I boop it and then we share a smile.

"I'm really glad you were all able to come. I'm sorry I'm not racing more than once, but it means a lot that you're still here." As the words leave my mouth, I feel two arms wrap around my waist from behind.

Touch like this would usually cause panic to rise up in me, but the shocked look on my parents' faces and the smug one on Margot's tells me exactly who it is. It tells me that I'm safe.

I let Shep pull me into him and peer up to find the biggest smile I think I've ever seen from him. "Babe, you won!"

"Babe?" My mom repeats his words with her eyebrows raised.

Shep lets go of me quickly, then steps past me. "Mrs. Sutherland, hi. It's so good to see you." He hugs her, if you even want to call it that. Mom stands there with her hands pinned to her sides while Shep tries to put an arm around her.

Margot and I both stifle a laugh, Dad cutting a look at us.

"It's good to see you again, Shep," my dad speaks up and directs Shep's attention to him. They shake hands and I try not to over analyze the encounter happening before me.

"So, are you two an item now?" Mom cuts back in.

My eyes go wide and before I can figure out what to say, Shep answers. "I like your daughter, yes. And if she'll let me, I plan to try and date her." He looks to the side and winks at me. I don't think Shep has ever met an awkward moment he can't talk himself out of.

Margot butts into the conversation, "Please. You two couldn't be more together. It's obvious."

My cheeks burn and the spotlight has been on me for too long. "I, uh, gotta go find Lennon. I'll see you guys later! Oh, but Shep is driving me home. Okay, bye!" I grin awkwardly then turn around and race out of the bleachers, leaving him to fend for himself.

I walk over to Lennon who's *of course* made friends with strangers. Not just strangers, two girls from the opposing team. A curvy brunette and sporty looking redhead wearing Marymount sweatshirts are standing with Lennon next to the concession stands, talking like they're all best friends.

"Hi," I say softly, walking up to Lennon. I'm not great with small talk, so this already feels awkward for me.

The brunette turns towards me and gushes, "Hi, I'm Ava! You must be Harlow. This is my best friend, Cece! Our other friend, Rena, is around here somewhere."

"Geez, Ava. Take it down a notch before you scare the girl off." The redhead who I now know to be Cece takes a sip of her drink then smiles at me. "You had a really good race! Your friend was just telling us it's been, like, three months since you last swam."

Looking at Lennon for some context, she adds on, "We all got to talking while waiting in line."

I nod my head and the two girls smile at me. Something

about Ava and Cece is so warm and inviting. They chat a little more with Lennon while I turn and look at the concession menu, trying to decide if I want anything else while she finishes up her conversation. When they finally walk off, I turn and shake my head at Lennon.

"I swear you could make friends with the wall sometimes."

She hands me a slushie, then links her arm with mine. "You're probably right, but that's why you love me."

"One of the reasons." We laugh together, walking arm in arm back inside the athletic center, but not without being stopped by the one and only Momma Fords.

"Well I'm in luck! I was just coming to find you two. How are my beautiful girls?" She reaches out and manages to wrap her arms around the both of us. "Y'all did so well today! Harlow, I'm sure it was surreal competing again. Does your shoulder feel okay?"

"It feels great. What are you doing here?" I look around to see if she's with anyone else.

"Shepherd told me today was your first meet back, so of course I had to come watch!"

My heart feels like it's being squeezed and Lennon bumps her hip into mine when a few seconds pass and I haven't said anything.

"Thank you, Momma Fords. You don't know how much it means to me that you'd come to see me swim." I smile at her, trying to blink away tears.

"Well why wouldn't I? You know how much I love to cheer you on." She gives me an endearing look.

We all talk for a few more minutes, then she excuses herself to go find one of her friends who's also here. After a couple more stops and talking to other people Lennon recognizes, we finally make it back to the chairs where our team is. There's a handful of races left, so we settle in and watch them together. Just like old times.

"I missed this," Lennon sighs, resting her head on my shoulder.

"Me too." My voice catches.

"Hey, don't cry," she whispers, picking her head up to face me.

"I'm just really glad we have this. We have each other. I love you, Lenny." A single tear runs down my cheek.

"More," she says, reaching up and wiping it away.

Shep and I may end up together, but Lennon will always be my soulmate.

FORTY-ONE

MORE LIKE A GROWL

SHEP

I'm leaning against the side of my truck waiting for Harlow to come out of the athletic center, and my nerves are through the roof. The anticipation for our first time hanging out alone is causing my leg to bounce at an alarming rate.

A few of my fraternity brothers walk by, giving me passive head nods. I haven't done much with them since the fight and Beckett getting expelled. While it's clear he was responsible for what happened, he still has some loyal friends who think he shouldn't have gotten kicked out of school.

I've done my best to keep my mouth shut and hope that, as time continues to pass, the whole thing will be forgotten. I know Harlow is nervous about going back to Chi Kappa tomorrow for the Halloween party, but there'll be so many people there I doubt anyone will actually notice us.

I pull my phone out and mess around with it, trying to keep myself distracted.

"Hey, lifeguard. Waiting for someone?" A voice that's become a familiar melody in my life pulls my attention up from my screen.

I don't know how she does it. I don't know how every time I see Harlow, I swear she's more beautiful than before.

She's brushed out her hair and though it's still damp, it's begun to dry in messy waves. Her skin is glowing and her eyes have a twinkle in them that makes my pulse sky rocket.

Don't kiss her yet. Don't kiss her yet.

"Hello? Anyone in there?" she whispers when she's just a few inches away from me.

"Hi, yes, sorry," I clear my throat. "I'm just trying to figure out how you look like a model after competing."

She gives me a playful smirk, then starts to walk around to the passenger side.

"Whoa, hold on," I rush out, quickly trying to jog after her.

"What?" Her eyes widen.

"There's just some things you will never do when you're with me. One of those things being opening the door for yourself." I reach around her, swinging open the car door.

She rolls her eyes as she gets into my truck. "You don't have to do that, Shep."

I shut the door once she's safely inside and walk around to the driver's side. Once I'm in, I decide to push her buttons and lean over, grabbing the seatbelt. "Precious cargo," I say as I pull the strap across her chest then clip it into place. "You understand."

I plant a kiss on her forehead then start up the engine. The silence in the cabin lets me know I've been successful in my efforts and am under Harlow's skin. She gives her famous side eye then crosses her arms and huffs.

"Oh, come on, baby girl. Let me have some fun."

"Fun? I'll show you fun," she mutters just loud enough that I can hear but low enough that it sounds more like a growl than words.

"Yeah, what's your move then?" I start to back out of the parking lot, then suddenly slam my foot on the brake when Harlow's hand reaches across the center console and presses down on the inside of my thigh, inching closer and closer to the part of me that's quickly becoming hard.

"Keep pushing," she says with the same edge in her tone that drives me wild.

I raise my hands off the steering wheel in surrender and she relents.

"That's what I thought," she purrs. "Now, do I need to drive or do you still have some blood left in your *thinking* head?"

I choke on a laugh, then start to drive again. "Both heads have plenty of blood in them."

"Right," she says sarcastically. "Well, take me home, Shep Fords."

"I thought you'd never ask."

———

After receiving very condescending directions, I park in front of Harlow's building. Before we get out, she hesitates for a second and looks around the parking lot.

"Is everything okay?" My tone is laced with concern as I

watch her draw her lip into her mouth and chew on it. She's anxious.

"Yeah, I just…I'm sorry. Sometimes I get worried that Beckett's going to pop up like he used to. It's something I'm trying to work on," she shares with me in a small voice.

I try to stuff down the anger that rises up in me. It infuriates me that she's still constantly looking over her shoulder and worrying about that asshole.

"Well you're with me, so honestly, let him show up. I don't think he would try anything again."

Her shoulders relax some. "Yeah, you're probably right. Let's go."

We get out of the truck, heading up to the apartment. Harlow pushes into the door and calls out to me over her shoulder.

"Set down your stuff anywhere. My room is the one on the left if you need to use the bathroom." She drops her things by the couch. "Are you hungry? I always make pasta after a meet."

I wander in after her, placing my phone and keys on the round dining table they have in the middle of the open kitchen. I turn to give her my attention. "Yeah, that sounds great. Ever since you helped with dinner…" Harlow bends down to get a pot, her ass on perfect display. "I've been thinking about tasting you-I mean tasting your food, trying something you make."

She whips her head around and smirks. "Am I making you nervous, Shep?"

Yes.

"No, not at all, just tripped up on my words there. Can I

help?" I run a hand down my face in embarrassment when she turns back around.

"I'm okay. It'll just be about fifteen minutes."

Harlow starts moving about the kitchen, gathering different ingredients while she waits for the water to boil. Once it does, she gets to work making some sort of pasta and I watch her in awe. There's so much more to her than meets the eye and it only causes my feelings for her to grow. That same thought I had when I saw her outside of Boulder a few weeks ago pops back into my head.

Slow down, Shep.

Harlow talks to me about swimming and her race while finishing up our plates then brings them to the table. Whatever she made looks and smells incredible.

I pick up my fork and Harlow stares at me.

"Yes?"

"Oh, right. Sorry, I have this habit of wanting to see people's reactions when they take their first bite of something I cook." Her words tumble out of her mouth in excitement and that ache in my heart comes back.

Honestly, it could be the worst thing I've ever had in my life and I'd still tell her it was perfect. But of course, I take a bite and it is perfect. "Holy shit," I mumble through my chewing. "What is this?"

She squeals in delight then starts to dig in herself. "Lennon calls it 'Harlow Hug Pasta' because every bite feels like a hug. I don't really know what it is other than something I've been making since high school with my dad."

As she finishes her sentence, her eyes glaze over some and I get the feeling there's a sentiment to this meal so I decide to press into her a little. "You cooked with your Dad a lot?"

"Yeah," she chimes. "Like all the time actually. He's the one who taught me most of my kitchen knowledge. Thanks, by the way, for being so kind to him and my mom earlier. He's great, but Mom can be hard to deal with sometimes." She sets her fork down and frowns at the plate. "You know, your mom treats me more like a daughter. Which, don't get me wrong, means the world to me, but sometimes I wish I was closer with mine."

I set down my fork and reach across the small distance, placing my hand on hers. "All parents show love differently, but I'll be honest, I can see why you'd feel that way."

Harlow gives me a sad smile, then shakes her head as if clearing her mind. "Let's talk about those signs you and Wes showed up with today. Whose idea was that?"

"Mine," I say, shoveling another bite of pasta into my mouth.

Harlow's eyebrows shoot up. "No way, I would have sworn it was Wes."

"You questioned if you were mine. I needed to make sure you know who you belong to."

She giggles and I realize she hasn't pushed away my hand from earlier. Interlocking our fingers, she gazes into my eyes. "Your confidence makes me want to be confident."

"Well then I hope you know I never plan to stop making it obvious to everyone how I feel about you," I respond with a sincerity I hope she can hear.

We finish up our meals and sit at the table talking more about various things, from our majors to why I became a lifeguard and so on. I can tell something is gnawing at

Harlow though by the way she's acting. She has so many tells, I don't think she realizes it.

Every few seconds, she'll start to open her mouth to say something then close it and let out a puff of air.

"Is there something on your mind?" I decide to just cut to the chase.

"I mean, kinda, but I doubt you want to talk about it." She stares down at her empty plate while talking.

"Try me." I give her hand a small squeeze.

"The fight."

FORTY-TWO

THE ELEPHANT IN THE ROOM FOR ME

HARLOW

Shep Fords is in my apartment and with him have come a variety of feelings that I can't process. Worry, excitement, doubt, lust, fear, desire, and so many other emotions take turns working their way through me. But the one I was most scared of, panic, has yet to make an appearance.

Cooking for him was a means to take back some control of the situation. I lost it in the truck with him, when he opened the door for me and buckled me in, leaving me speechless. The way Shep cares for me makes me wonder how I ever tolerated Beckett's behavior.

Shep is kind without trying. He's gentle and protective, and his feelings for me are palpable. Sitting at my dining table with him, our hands interlocked, I'm wrestling with insecurities and lies that have taken up residence in my mind thanks to one particular asshole.

I want to be honest with Shep about how I feel and the things that I think about, but I can't until we address the elephant in the room for me. I want to know what happened the night of formal.

Details have still been sparse and, while I saw a clip of the video, it doesn't answer my questions, so I decide to be blunt and come out with it.

"I want to talk about the fight."

Shep clears his throat and lets go of my hand. Pushing the plate away from him, he rests his elbows on the table and rubs his hands down his face.

"Harlow, I don't think that's wise. Besides, there's not much to say. Was there probably a better time and place to confront Beckett? Yeah, but I was so overwhelmed with emotion after finding out he was the reason you got hurt. Are we going to talk about that?"

My stomach drops. "I don't know if I want to."

He pushes away from the table and reaches for my plate, walking them over to the sink. "Yeah, and I don't know if I want to rehash all the details about the fight."

An idea comes to my mind that seemed to work before with Margot. Maybe if I decide to be open with him, he will be open with me, so I push myself and take back the conversation.

"How did you find out it was Beckett who caused my injury?"

Shep places the dirty dishes in the sink and walks back over to me. Kissing my forehead, he looks into my eyes. "Dinner was great, thank you again."

"I'm serious, Shep. How did you find out?"

He groans and walks over to the counter, leaning back against it and crossing his arms against his chest. The action makes his muscles pop out and I temporarily lose my train of thought.

"Pierce texted me that he saw what Beckett did, so I know there's a video."

Shep's face pales. "Okay, yeah. When we were at formal, I went through our security footage from the night of the party."

I nod my head. "Well, I guess it maybe would have come out one way or another. It was so stupid too. That night? He was upset with me because I didn't want to take shots with him, but he was already hammered and I'm sure you've gathered he's not the nicest drunk."

Shep only grunts in response, clearly getting worked up.

I walk towards him and tap on his arms for him to open up. When he does, I nestle into the space between his legs, placing my hands on his chest and peer up at him. "We don't have to talk about it anymore. I just…"

"What? You might as well just say it at this point." Shep's tone causes me to pull away.

"Shit, I'm sorry, Harlow. Wait," he puts a hand behind my back and holds me in place. "I'm not upset with you, it's just talking about him and thinking about how long you were with him, it makes my mind jump to the worst conclusions about what you went through."

"Oh," I whisper. It's obvious that Shep's feelings for me cloud his judgment at times. I don't fault him for that, but it only makes the one part of the night I've been struggling with feel more confusing.

"Why didn't you fight back?" I blurt out.

"What? That's what you've been hung up on? It's not that big of a deal."

"It is to me," I respond, my tone insistent.

"Harlow, it's—"

"Why did you just take it?" I cut him off. "I don't understand."

"Because I didn't want to be like him, Harlow!" His words come out strangled with emotion and my breath catches in my throat.

"I didn't want to be like him. I didn't want you to see me the way you do him—violent and incapable of resolving things without using my hands." He tries to pull away from me and directs his gaze into the distance.

"Shep..." I move my hand to keep his on my back. I don't want him to let me go.

Letting out a large sigh, he rubs his free hand over his face and I can tell he's struggling with the confrontation.

"I could never think of you and see him." My words have him snapping his attention back on me.

"Harlow, you don't have to—"

"No, I'm serious, Shep. Let me say this."

He bows his head and I reach for him, picking his face back up to meet my stare.

"I know that I haven't been easy to deal with, okay? I know that I've been a real bitch to you at times, but it's because I couldn't understand the way you treated me. All I've known for the last couple years is manipulation and hurt and all these terrible feelings. And then you come in and make me question everything. Sure, maybe those feelings scared me too, but not the way he did. They scared me because they challenged me and made me wonder if I deserved better than what I was getting. But listen to me when I say this, I was never and will never be scared of you,

Shep. Do you hear me? I will never think of him when I see you. You are the best thing to ever—"

His lips crash onto mine and everything around us stills. I forget all the words I had practiced to say to him and I'm lost in the frenzy of his kisses. It isn't gentle, but it isn't forceful. He isn't taking, he's giving. I feel every emotion from him being poured into me.

Shep kisses me like he's trying to heal all of the hurt I've endured. Like if there was a way for him to give back every piece of my soul I've lost through his kisses, he wouldn't ever stop trying.

Suddenly he pulls back, "Harlow, wait. I'm sorry I didn't—"

This time I silence him with my lips and jump up to wrap my legs around his waist. He slips one hand under my ass and the other around the back of my neck, holding me in place against him.

I slowly move my tongue into his mouth and when his slides over mine I can't help but whimper.

He pulls away again, but this time leans forward and starts to kiss right below my ear. "You're going to drive me crazy if you keep making sounds like that, baby girl."

His words do nothing but cause another pathetic whimper to leave my lips. I've never felt like this before in my life with another guy. It's like I don't have control over the way my body is reacting, but for once, not having control feels freeing because I'm with Shep. I know I'm safe with him.

He meets my lips again and continues kissing me, while walking us towards my room. When we finally make it to the edge of my bed, he lays me down.

With his body hovering over mine, I run my fingers through his hair and tug on it to pull him into me more. A low rumble leaves his chest and he bites my lip in response.

"Harlow," he says in between kisses. "Harlow, wait."

I gaze at him wantonly. "What is it?"

"I don't want you to think I'm trying—"

I kiss him before he can finish his sentence, speaking through breaths. "I don't think you're trying to sleep with me."

He leans away and runs his thumb over the bottom of my lip that's now swollen and puffy. "I just want to make sure. I know you're still working through things and I don't want to push you."

I sit up on my elbows and press my forehead to his, closing my eyes. "I don't ever feel like I'm in a rush with you, and actually, I find that when I'm around you, I don't mind going slow."

"Good, because I want to take my time with you." Shep lays me back down and peppers my neck with soft kisses.

When he meets my lips again, I latch onto him and we stay like this for what feels like hours. Kissing each other senseless, leaving small marks on each other's necks, and intertwining our souls. When I start to lose feeling in my lips, I pull back and stare into Shep's eyes. His pupils are blown out and hazy with desire.

"Can you stay? If you want, I mean. I don't know if Dahlia's okay, but I was hoping maybe we could just sleep together tonight."

I bite my bottom lip unsure of what his response will be.

"I'd love nothing more than to spend the night with my girl."

A smile graces my lips and he rolls over onto his back, pulling his phone out of his pocket. "Let me just check with Wes that he's going to be home tonight. I'm assuming so since you're home alone." He gives me a knowing look and raises his eyebrows.

I laugh, rolling on top of him and crossing my arms on his chest. Resting my chin on my forearms so we're eye level, I study Shep's features. He still has a small scar on his forehead from the fight and it makes my stomach knot up.

As if he knows where my gaze is, he reaches out and tucks a strand of hair behind my ear. "You have to let it go." His eyes are warm and reassuring when I finally look at him. "Wes said he's good to take care of Dahlia tonight. Do you want to watch a movie or anything?"

I wiggle on top of him and can feel he's still hard. While there's a tight coiling sensation growing in my core that I really want to explore with him, I know that I need to take things slow.

"Sure, a movie and maybe some more kissing. If that's okay with you."

Wasting no time, Shep rolls me back over and his lips find mine immediately. I reach for the hem of his shirt and start to pull it over his head.

"Harlow, wait—"

"I just want to feel your body. You've got all these muscles and I've stared at them for long enough. I won't get ahead of myself," I whisper, finally tugging his shirt off and tossing it to the side of my bed.

"Okay, but…"

"Shep, I'm okay. I just want to be close to you. I've wanted this for a while and I'm ready to be with you like this." I reach down and pull my sweatshirt over my head, thanking all the stars in the universe I'm wearing a lace bra, that I may or may not have purposely packed for after the meet.

Shep groans and I watch his eyes move over my frame, licking his lips like he's ready to devour me. A shiver runs through my body at the thought and his eyes light up when he notices.

I reach for his hand and slowly move it until it's on top of my bra.

"Harlow," he groans, biting down on his lip.

"Shep." I lock my eyes with his. "I trust you."

FORTY-THREE

MY T-SHIRT

SHEP

Three words is all it takes for a fire to ignite in me that I've never felt before.

"You trust me?" I echo her words, wanting to hear them again.

"Yes, Shep. I trust you." Her eyelashes flutter as she takes a deep breath and reaches for me.

"And you're sure you want me to stay the night?" I stroke her hair with my hand.

"Yes, I…" her voice trails off.

"What is it?" I nuzzle the side of her cheek with my nose, soaking up the warmth radiating from the pinkish flush.

"I haven't really been by myself since everything went down at formal, and I guess it just makes me a little nervous to be alone at the apartment." I can see worry swimming in her eyes and I make a mental note to check in with my dad on Beckett's whereabouts as of late.

"I understand, and if that's the case, I'd be happy to take the couch," I offer, secretly hoping that she asks me to sleep with her.

"I'll think about it," she responds before leaning up and pressing a kiss along my jaw. I can't help myself as a low growl rips through me. Having Harlow be with me like this satisfies needs and desires I didn't even know I had. Every act of affection from her, every physical touch, I don't take for granted. I know it means something deeper to her and I hope I never cause her to withhold it from me.

When our lips connect again, I lose myself in her taste. Her scent ensnares me and the longer we kiss, the more my heart clings to the idea of a future with her. Of a life that's similar to today. One where I watch her swim, we kiss in the stands, we eat dinner together, and maybe we go on walks with Dahlia. A life where we continually exist together, settling down in Everson. It's all I want.

Finding the lace of her bra, I lightly trace my fingers on the edge. Goosebumps cover the soft flesh of her cleavage as I slip my hand under and palm her breast. Her breaths become shallow while I roll my hand around the sensitive skin. I do my best to be aware of any changes in her body language, but when she bucks her hips against me in response to me squeezing a little harder, the need for pleasure takes over.

Grinding my hips down into her, I align myself between her legs. A breathy moan slips out from her lips when I must hit just right the spot. So I do it over and over again, until our bodies rock together in a messy but satisfying rhythm.

Harlow wraps her legs around my waist and I don't even care that we're basically acting like two horny teenagers dry humping. Knowing that she's getting pleasure from this and clearly isn't feeling like I'm pushing her into anything only gets me more worked up. So much so that out of nowhere the sensation that I'm going to finish takes over my body.

I peel myself away from her, looking down at my sweatpants that are clearly tented. I don't know why I'm embarrassed, but I don't want to make her uncomfortable either. She must not realize what's happening because she grabs for me to come back to her level, but I stop her.

"Harlow, I'm going to finish and we aren't even having sex. I'm sorry, this has never happened but I think it's just been a while and I'm so attr—"

"What if I told you I want that?" Her gaze is heated with a gleam of curiosity as she draws her lip into her mouth.

"You want me to…"

"Mhm," she purrs.

Lying above her, my mouth gapes open. Her words aren't processing in my brain. I never doubted there was compatibility between us, but I didn't expect the sexual chemistry to be this intense.

"I've thought about it before, maybe even had a few dreams," she confesses. "You finishing because of me, and I don't know why but it excites me."

"Shit, Harlow. That's really sexy." Her cheeks flush deeper, but she doesn't break eye contact with me. If she's embarrassed or feeling shy, she's doing a damn good job of hiding it.

"If it's what you want, then I won't stop it. I just don't want to make you uncomfortable."

"I'm not, I promise. And I'd tell you if I was. I think we

both know by now that I speak my mind with you." She smirks.

"Do you care if I take my sweatpants off then? Just so after, I uh…shit sorry, I'm not trying to make this awkward." A laugh escapes my mouth.

"Shep, take your pants off."

"Yes ma'am," I move quickly to hop off the bed and slide down the gray fabric. "It's just so *after* I still have something to wear."

She nods her head in understanding, as I climb back into her bed and lower myself into the same position I was before.

"Wait," she says, putting two hands on my chest.

My stomach drops, but then she moves her hands to the side of her leggings and starts shimmying them down her thighs.

"Wait, wait, wait. What're you doing?" I lean back to rest on my calves, watching her work the tight clothing off her legs.

"Leveling the playing field." She grabs the ends, tugging them off, then throws them to the side.

She lays back on her elbows, "It is okay?"

Okay? She's fucking perfect.

Her underwear is black lace, just like her bra. I feel my mouth going dry while my eyes rake over her body. I've seen her figure before in her tight swimsuits, but this is different.

She's choosing to show herself to me and that drives me absolutely wild.

I hook my thumbs on the edge of the lace by her hips and toy with it. I'm not going to take this any farther, but it can't hurt to tease her a little.

I watch her sharply inhale, but she doesn't let the breath out. She just studies my hands as they travel along the edge of her thong, scraping the soft flesh that's right above it.

When I drag my hands down to her thighs, she finally lets out the breath she's holding. I dig my nails in gently before slowly moving one finger towards her center.

Our eyes stay locked as my movements become slow and I can tell she's getting worked up. When my finger finally makes it to the spot I desperately want to touch, I decide to torment her by letting my fingertip hover just above.

She whimpers and groans, and I almost concede to her sounds and press down on the sensitive spot. But there's no need for me to rush this with her, so I withdraw my hands and quickly move to entangle them with her hair, pushing myself back down onto her.

Her kisses become needy and as we align again, I thrust harder, hoping to give her the pressure she needs. It only takes a few minutes for me to reach the same high I was at only moments ago.

"Harlow," I groan in between kisses as the sensation builds.

I catch a glimpse of her, and the way her hair is fanned out behind her, a look of desire filling her emerald eyes, is all I need to lose myself.

Harlow senses what's happening and latches onto me even tighter with her lips, wrapping her legs around me to keep us together.

"Please," she moans out. "Please."

And that's it. Her words have me finishing into my boxers and while some people might find that embarrassing,

I'm levitating on the fact that Harlow derived some sort of pleasure from me doing that.

As I come down from the moment, Harlow doesn't seem bothered by the wetness starting to seep through and writhes underneath me. When we finally break apart, she rolls over and grabs the shirt she took off of me earlier, slipping it over her head.

She watches as I slowly stand, then blushes when she sees the stain between my legs. "I'm gonna go, uh…take care of this." I grab my sweatpants before quickly moving inside her bathroom.

As I shut the door, I hear a giggle behind me and the confidence I was feeling about three minutes ago has vanished. Looking at myself in the mirror, I shake my head. *C'mon dude, you couldn't even handle a little make-out session without blowing a load in your fucking boxers.*

There's a light tap on the door and then Harlow peers inside.

"Everything okay? I didn't hear the water start." Her eyes don't stray from mine and relief floods me that she's not looking at me any differently.

"Yeah, just getting my thoughts together," a soft laugh rumbles from my chest.

"Okay, well there are towels under the cabinet. Take your time." She bridges the gap between us and presses up on her toes to give me a soft kiss. "I'll be in the living room."

By the time I rinse off and walk out to find Harlow, she's curled up with a blanket on the couch, holding a book. My heart hammers in my chest when I see she's still wearing my T-shirt. Her hair is messy, her eyebrows drawn together while she reads. I stand in the doorway for a few seconds just observing her. For the short amount of time I've been in her space tonight, I've learned a lot about her.

She's playful, and not in the way I expected. I thought that if there came a time when I was fortunate enough to get to be intimate with her that she might play hard to get and make me work for it. Which she has, to an extent, and I'd gladly do it all over again. But this playfulness was one laced with curiosity. I could see in her face that she was trying to work out the desires between her head and her heart. Ultimately, she held the upper hand the entire time and I'm absolutely fine with that.

"Whatcha reading, pretty girl?" I call out, leaning against the door frame.

Her head pops up and she draws that bottom lip that I love so much between her teeth. "Just a romance book." She smiles. "It's about a girl who works through trauma to ultimately end up with her soulmate."

"Is that so?" I walk over to her, leaning down and pressing a kiss onto the crown of her head.

"Mhm," she nods, giving me a knowing look.

"Well, I like it then." I sit down next to her, drawing her under my arm and pulling her into my side. "Do you care if I turn something on the TV? I'll keep the volume down so you can read."

"That's fine with me." She slides down the couch, then leans back to rest her head on my lap.

I run my fingers through her hair absentmindedly while the TV plays in the background and she holds her book up to read. The simplicity of this moment lulls me into a state of comfort that I've never known. I could spend every night like this and never get tired of it, never get tired of her.

After some time, I notice the book has fallen onto her stomach and her eyes are closed. They flutter in her sleep and I try to steady my breathing to avoid waking her up. This is the most content I've ever seen her since we've met and my heart swells with pride that I could have something to do with that.

I gently move the book off her lap and grab the edges of the blanket that's started to fall off, slowly dragging it back over her body. She stirs lightly and I freeze. Once she settles again, I turn off the lamp next to the couch and lean my head back. For a few seconds, I just lay there staring at the ceiling, listening to the soft breaths coming from her.

The rhythm of her breathing becomes hypnotic and my eyes slowly start to close. "Goodnight, my angel girl," I whisper into the darkness before letting sleep take me.

"HOW DO YOU TAKE YOUR COFFEE?"

HARLOW

When I wake up, it's not being in my bed that surprises me. It's the handsome lifeguard lying next to me, with an arm hooked around my waist. Even in his sleep, it's like his default is to protect me.

I try to think back to last night and I'm not sure when I fell asleep but the last memory I do have is laying my head in Shep's lap while I read my book. The thought of him carrying me to bed makes those damn butterflies erupt in my stomach again.

There's a small flash of panic as the rest of the memories from last night flood my subconscious. I don't regret anything I did with Shep, but I'm also worried that things are falling into place a little too easily. That doesn't usually happen for me, so naturally my mind is already playing tricks on me.

Now that I'm not fighting my interest in Shep, I'm realizing how much I really do like him. I start thinking back to when he first approached me at the rec and, even then, I knew he had an effect on me. I just didn't know how to process that when my mind was so warped from all the bullshit with Beckett.

As I lie next to him, I study his features and admire all the little things I never stopped to notice. The scar on his forehead sticks out to me the most, but I really need to get past that.

His eyelashes are ridiculously long, so long that it's not fair. He has a lone freckle on the side of his neck by his ear and his hair curls at the ends, making me want to run my hands through it like usual.

"You're staring at me," his voice breaks through my thoughts and I pull my focus back to his face, having not noticed his eyes begin to peek open.

"I'm not staring. I'm observing," I quip. "Observing and thinking."

He groans and rolls away from me onto his stomach, pressing his face into my pillow. "Thinking? That's a dangerous game with you."

"Hey." I smack him on the back. "I was actually thinking good things, thank you very much."

He picks his head up and grins at me. "Oh? Wanna tell me?"

"Nope, not anymore." I hop out of bed. "Lost your chance when you decided to be mean."

"Oh c'mon, Harlow," he calls after me, scrambling out of bed.

I wave my hand in the air dismissively and head into the kitchen to start some coffee.

Shep comes up behind me and wraps one arm around

my waist and puts his other hand on my forehead to tilt my gaze back. "Don't be like that," he talks down in my direction then kisses my nose.

"I'm not being like anything," I retort, pulling out of his hold. I turn around to face him and lean back on the counter, crossing my arms.

He squints his eyes, then rolls them before walking over to the couch and plops down. "Did you sleep well?"

"Yeah, did you carry me to bed?" I ask with a hint of uncertainty in my voice because it's still not registering in my mind that Shep and I are really hanging out like this.

"Sure did. You fell asleep reading and I dozed off on the couch too, but at about three in the morning I woke up and decided to move us to your bed."

"Well, thanks. I appreciate you staying." I turn around and get to work making the coffee.

"Do you want to meet me at the Chi Kappa house tonight or what was your plan? Are you going to swim?"

"No, we always take the day off after a meet. I'm just going to hang out here and wait for Lennon to get home so we can get ready, then I'll drive us to the party. She wants to surprise you and Wes with our costumes."

"About that," Shep starts. "Care to elaborate on those?"

I spin on my heels. "If I knew, I would."

He nods his head then pulls his phone out. "I can't stay for long, there's some stuff I need to take care of before tonight, but I wanted to talk to you about something."

My stomach drops. "Okay," my voice wavers.

"I really enjoyed last night. Like a lot, but I was also hoping maybe we could hang out more too? I know you're close with my mom and it feels like I already know you pretty well because of the stuff that's happened, but there's also things about you that I don't know. Like for example…" He gets up off the couch and walks towards me, motioning with his head towards the french press on the counter. "How do you take your coffee?"

"Since you're asking, if I'm at home, I just drink it hot. If I'm at Boulder, I get their cold brew with honey, and cold foam on top." A smile breaks out on my face and he rubs his thumb along the side of my cheek. "This might be my favorite thing about you," he whispers.

"Huh?" My mind goes blank as he strokes the side of my face.

"Your smile. There was a period of time I didn't know if I'd ever see one from you. You were so sad when you started showing up at the rec center and I wondered how long it would take for you to feel happy again. Granted, I didn't know the extent of your circumstances…" His voice trails off, eyes hazy with emotion. "But then the day you had your evaluation, you smiled at me before diving into the pool and it meant the world to me."

I lean into his touch, his words soothing an ache in me that I've been trying to mend for so long. "Thank you for seeing me, Shep. I don't know what I did to deserve it, but you didn't give up. Robin and I talk about it, about you."

He nods his head urging me to continue.

"She told me that not everything has to have some grand explanation. Sometimes two people are just drawn together and rather than question it, why not embrace it? I'm trying to slowly piece together my feelings and emotions with her help, because I mean…" I nervously draw my lip in my mouth and Shep smirks. "When you talked to me that first time, at the rec, it set off something in me," I admit.

Shep's eyebrows raise and he tilts his head as if confused.

"I know, that probably doesn't make any sense because of the way I treated you in the beginning, but it's true. You had an effect on me, and my head and my heart were at war with each other. My mind was telling me that I was supposed to be with Beckett, but my heart was telling me that I needed to give you a chance."

He leans forward and presses a kiss to my forehead in silent understanding.

"I need you to know that I'm working to not get in my head about this. I don't think we're moving too fast, because reality is, I think this was a long time coming." I let out a big breath as the last few words leave my mouth. Learning to share my emotions has not come easy but damn, Robin would be proud of me.

Shep responds by giving me another soft kiss, this time on my lips. "Harlow, even if you did feel like we were moving too fast, that would be okay. You could tell me and I'd be happy to slow down. There's no rush."

I nod my head then kiss him back when a surprising thought comes to mind. "Can I teach you something?"

"Teach me?" Shep parrots my words with a confused look.

"Yeah, it's something my dad used to do when I was younger and first started swimming butterfly."

"Okay, yeah. Sure." He steps back and studies me.

"No, I need you closer. Come here," I whisper and Shep moves towards me. "Okay, now bend down some," I continue and he leans his head towards me. "Perfect, stay still."

I rise up on my tiptoes and put my face next to his, then flutter my eyelashes against his cheek. I can tell he's uncertain of what I'm doing by the way his body is tensed up, but then he relaxes after a few more seconds.

I pull away then look up and meet his stare, "It's called a butterfly kiss. Get it?"

Shep's eyes widen and he goes to open his mouth, then closes it as if recanting the words he didn't even say.

"Thank you," he finally chokes out. "Can I do it back?"

"Mhm," I chime.

He nuzzles his nose against my cheek, then bats his eyelash against it. "Butterfly kisses for my butterfly girl." His voice is so quiet, I wouldn't be able to hear him if his lips weren't right next to my ear.

My heart knots up and emotions swell inside me. Sharing this with him feels like I've shared a piece of my soul, but even though I've made myself vulnerable to Shep, I feel secure. I feel like every little bit of me that I reveal to him, he handles with the utmost care.

"Thank you," he says as he steps away from me.

I smile back at him, lost in the moment and the peace that's enveloping my heart. Maybe things will work out in my favor for once.

FORTY-FIVE

A HUNDRED PAGES AND A FEW TEARS LATER

HARLOW

A few hours after Shep leaves, Lennon finally walks in the door. Her arms are decorated with various bags from the store and she has a very smug look on her face.

"What did you do?" I ask hesitantly.

"I got everything to finish our costumes. I just need like thirty minutes, so take advantage of that time and read your book so you can give me all your attention later."

I snicker while rolling my eyes. "You're ridiculous, but okay."

She starts walking into her room then stops in her tracks, cutting a look at me. "Don't even think you're off the hook talking about your *sleepover*. I just need to do this now so I can make sure I'm not missing anything."

"Is it a costume or an arts and crafts project, Lenny?" I stand up and follow her into her bedroom.

"Ha ha. Very funny." She tosses the bags down on her bed, then turns to grab the corsets and shorts from her dresser. As her neck twists, I catch sight of a familiar mark that I've seen before in almost that exact same spot.

"Um, I'm sorry. You're tossing out comments about my very PG sleepover when you have a hickey on your neck?"

She gasps, rushing over to her vanity. "Damn you, Wesley Porter." She sneers her words as if he can hear them.

"Mhm." I cross my arms. "Well, I'll just be in my room then."

Lennon groans in response as I cross through the apartment to my room. I wonder if she's ever going to tell me what's going on between her and Wes. Not that it's any of my business, but it's strange the way she's been acting about the whole thing. Maybe they really are just friends who like to kiss a little. I guess it makes sense. They are both flirts. *Who knows.*

I fall into my bed and the memories of Shep and I kissing start playing back in my mind. I surprised myself when I told him I wanted him to finish, even if it was just from us making out. The thought of him doing that was hot and my curiosity got the best of me.

My phone buzzes and it's a picture of Dahlia from Shep. She's wearing a vest with the Everson Valley sheriff department badge and giving the camera one of those wide pitbull smiles. He told me last night what he'd been working on those few weeks we didn't talk and I couldn't believe how perfect his idea was. I was so proud of him and that he didn't spend all that time moping around, but instead, used it to create something as incredible as E.V.E.S.T.

SHEP

Trying on her "uniform" lol

What do you think?

I think she looks like the goodest, most bravest girl ever.

And yes, I hope you read it to her exactly how I would say it.

SHEP

Of course. I feel like I heard that text as I read it haha

We're going to get to the frat house around 9, does that work?

SHEP

Sounds good baby girl

Excited to see you

And especially excited to see your costume

You and me both lol

If Lennon ever finishes it

SHEP

Well keep me updated, okay?

Will dooooo

Shep hearts my message and I pick up my book, deciding to take Lennon's advice.

After about a hundred pages and a few tears later, I finish my book. Lennon still hasn't made an appearance.

"Lenny!" I yell out from my room. She hates when I do this but my bed is too comfortable to get up from right now.

"I'm coming!" Her voice carries through the living room with a heavy tone of sass, emphasized with her stomping into my room. She holds out a collection of items in her hands then drops them onto the chair in my room. "You can't rush perfection, Harlow."

"Oh, my apologies." I respond sarcastically. "Is it done?"

"It is, but we have a few hours before we need to leave so how about we discuss your night."

"I could say the same thing to you," I snap back at her.

Her eyes widen and her mouth gapes open. "Excuse me?"

"I didn't stutter." I raise my eyebrows. "I'm just saying, you were out all night and you came home with a hickey. I hardly think you're in any place to be pointing fingers."

She glares at me, her lips tightening into a thin line.

"Fine." She speaks through clenched teeth. "I slept over at Wes's last night, but seriously. It's not what you or Shep think. We're just hanging out and sometimes we kiss. Sometimes we fall asleep together. It's not that deep."

"Okay, okay." I raise my hands in surrender. "I just genuinely feel like we haven't talked about things since that one night someone snuck out of here so…"

"Right," she deadpans, realizing I've connected the dots. "Well, I'll let you know if it becomes more than what it is, but I don't think me or Wes really want to date."

Lennon can tell me all she wants that she doesn't want to date but I know her. She wants to be loved and loved well, but she's also terrified to get her heart broken. She's just waiting for someone to prove her wrong. "I get that. I think if it wasn't Shep, I wouldn't be interested in dating either."

"Oh?" Lennon arches an eyebrow. "So you two are dating?"

"No, I didn't mean—"

"Too late, you said it. Go on." She turns her ear towards me. "I'm listening."

"We aren't dating. Well, not officially. I was just trying to say that I'd be in the same boat as you if the guy was anyone besides Shep. Things are different with him."

She smirks. "I'm proud of you for finally coming to your senses."

"Oh, and we kissed," I blurt out.

The highest pitched noise I think I've ever heard comes out of Lennon's mouth. "I knew it! I knew it would happen last night!" She lets out another squeal. "I'm so happy for you! Bet you're glad you packed that lace bra." She raises her eyebrows.

My cheeks flush. "I–"

"Yeah, I saw it in your bag. Don't even try to act like you weren't hoping something might happen." She smirks.

"I can neither confirm nor deny." I giggle. "But on a serious note, he and I need to hang out more, and build a friendship too. It kinda feels like we're doing things backwards since he knows all this deep shit about me but we aren't really friends."

Lennon nods, then starts telling me about her thoughts on the situation. Despite the fact Lennon isn't in a relationship, she's a hopeless romantic—secretly, though. She wouldn't openly admit it but after living with her for the last four years, it's clear that the dream of falling hopelessly in love with someone is buried deep in her heart.

Truthfully, I always thought it would be Lennon who would find her person first. She has the personality that attracts guys with ease. Wes must be doing something right though because usually the attention isn't returned.

By the time we stop our rambling, it's getting dark outside. We start to get ready and Lennon tells me to curl my hair while she works on her makeup.

Once I'm done, she has me sit down and starts doing my makeup. She doesn't skip any details, from the dramatic false eyelashes to the cherry red lipstick she paints on me.

After my face is done up, she has me put the red leather shorts on with the white corset.

"Okay, perfect. Now let me finish your hair." She reaches for a bottle of gel she brought into my bathroom with her and squeezes a large amount into her hand.

"Uh, Lennon?" I interrupt her.

"Just trust me, okay?"

"Alright," I drawl, skepticism coating the word. I close my eyes as she works her fingers through my hair, mostly near my roots, then starts combing it back. After a few more passes, I hear the water running and open my eyes. She wets a hairbrush then drags that through the gel.

"Perfect," she says with a concentrated look on her face.

I turn and stare at myself in the mirror. "Lennon, my hair looks wet. I don't get this."

"Tsk," she holds a finger up in my face then points for me to go sit down in my bedroom. "Let me get dressed and do my hair then it'll all make sense."

After mirroring my appearance on herself, she walks out of the bathroom and grabs something I can't see from a bag. She walks towards me and tells me to close my eyes.

I shake my head but listen, and feel her place something over my head. Then she presses something into the top of the corset and claps her hands.

"All done!" she exclaims.

I open my eyes and glance down to see a red whistle hanging around my neck and a cross made of red duct tape on the corset. The whistle has a piece of paper attached to it that reads 'Blow for mouth to mouth.'

"Lennon! What on earth?!" My eyes go wide.

She lets out a devious laugh. "We're sexy lifeguards, duh!"

A cackle escapes from me and I shake my head. "You know Wes and Shep are going to lose their ever-loving minds, don't you?"

"Obviously. Where do you think I got the idea?"

"Oh, Lenny. Remind me never to question you ever again."

"I'll hold you to that," she shoots back.

Once we have everything set, we make plans to swing through a fast food place on the way to Chi Kappa.

I already planned not to drink because, with everything that's happened whenever I've been at that damned fraternity house, I'd be foolish to not stay sober.

I slip into my Doc Martens, much to Lennon's disappointment, but I had to keep a little of myself for the night. Besides, I know Shep likes them and he's the only person I care about impressing. I have a feeling, though, that won't be too hard with the way both my ass and tits are on full display.

"Alright, let's go stir some shit up!" Lennon calls out, as she walks out the door.

FORTY-SIX

GOOD OR BAD, MAYBE BOTH

SHEP

The Chi Kappa house is vibrating as the music blares at an ungodly volume. I don't mind the bass, though, and the songs are pretty good, but I won't be able to enjoy myself until Harlow gets here.

I feel like a bit of a tool wearing only gray sweatpants and this neon mask, but whatever. It's a frat party—let's be honest, I fit in. Wes decided to wear black sweatpants and a *Scream* mask. It's weird being here after formal, but thankfully the house is dark with the exception of some flashing lights, so nobody can really see me anyways.

It's a little after ten and I'm starting to grow uncomfortable that Harlow and Lennon aren't here. Mostly because Wes won't stop nagging in my ear about what he hopes Lennon is wearing. If I have to listen to his weird fantasies for another minute, I'm going to need to get drunk. Not really, but I might have to find a way to sneak off.

I don't have plans to drink more than a few beers with what happened last time I was here. I've also noticed Harlow doesn't really drink so I don't want her to feel singled out. There's also the ever present need to be on guard and I can't do that if I'm drunk. Just as I'm about to walk outside, I get a text from Harlow that they're here.

"U GOT ME" by THIEVES and CATZE starts playing and as the bass builds, so does the anticipation in my stomach. My eyes scan the room until they finally land near the front of the house.

Wes smacks the side of my arm and points towards the door. "Holy sh——"

"Shut up." I cut him off and make a beeline towards my blonde and her best friend.

As I get closer, my steps start to slow down as I'm able to really take in the sight before me.

Wes was right. Holy shit.

I lift up my mask and it takes a few seconds for her gaze to meet mine, but when it does, a very playful smirk appears on her face. She walks over to me and stops just a few inches short. My breath hitches in my throat as I rake over her body with a heated glare. Trailing up her long, muscular legs, I feel my mouth literally go dry. The red leather shorts she's wearing, if you even want to call them that, look more like bikini bottoms and not one part of me is complaining. There's a sliver of skin showing between the waist of the shorts and the bottom of the white corset and it sets off a fire in me. What really sends me over the edge is the realization of what exactly she is: a lifeguard——a very sexy lifeguard.

I pick up the whistle around her neck and read the paper attached to it, a scowl forming. "Clever."

"It was all Lennon," she responds sweetly.

I use the lanyard around her neck to pull her into me, her hands landing on my bare chest as we collide together. "Well go ahead then, why don't you put the tip in your mouth and blow?" I turn the whistle around and hold it in front of her pouty lips that are painted in a similar red.

Harlow's mouth parts just a little and a small puff of air escapes. "You're lucky I like mouth-to-mouth resuscitation," she clips, then glances around quickly before pressing her lips onto mine for just a few seconds.

When she pulls away, her cheeks are flushed and the heaviness of her breathing pushes her tits up even higher. This is going to be torture.

Wes and Lennon join us and he looks as enamored with her as I am with Harlow. They seem to be up to their usual antics, bickering and bantering over who knows what, but there's a moment where I take in the fact that all four of us are hanging out and it feels like a dream coming true.

The party plays out the way they all do. After a certain amount of time, people start getting too rowdy, I get annoyed, and Harlow seems to feel the same way since she's been clinging to my side for the last hour.

The house was set up to look similar to a haunted house, but it's really just a bunch of cheap decor covered with fake blood and various colored lights.

I don't know what it is about the whole thing, but despite being here with Harlow and our friends, something feels off. I can't explain it or figure out what exactly it is, but after the first hour of being here, I get the feeling something just isn't right.

I'm sure my continued questions to Harlow asking if she feels okay are probably bugging her, but I just want to know if she feels at all the way I do. It's probably just the fact that Dad hasn't gotten back to me about an update on Beckett and there's way too many dudes in masks here for my liking.

I check my phone and it's almost midnight when Harlow nudges into my side and asks if I'm the one who's not okay.

I don't want to scare her or ruin the night, but I guess maybe my energy isn't the best either. It would be easy to just tell her not to worry, but I don't know if she would believe me, so I settle for telling her that I just don't really enjoy parties like this. She agrees and there's a bit of relief that she takes my answer as it is.

Wes and Lennon have wandered away from us and it's just her and I outside now, leaning against some tables they have set up like usual. I watch various people spill out of the side doors, drinks sloshing out of their cups, and bodies starting to wobble. I must have a concerning expression on my face because Harlow places her hand on my arm, asking if I'm okay again.

When I turn to face her, I drink in her appearance all over again. Her emerald eyes are framed by the makeup Lennon did, her hair looks almost wet but still cascades over her shoulders in waves, and the whistle around her neck makes me chuckle.

"Yeah baby, I'm okay. I'm more than okay." I bend forward and press a kiss to the side of her head.

She gives me a soft but unsure smile, then moves her

hand down to interlock with mine. "Would you tell me if you weren't?"

"Hm?" I respond, not really paying attention because anytime Harlow touches me it causes my brain to lag.

"If you weren't okay, would you tell me?" she repeats.

I think about her question, maybe for too long because she squeezes my hand and raises her eyebrows as if to show that she's waiting for my response.

"Yeah, I think so, but I also have like this default setting to protect you or something. I don't know how to explain it, so I wouldn't ever want to worry you."

She pinches her eyebrows together and draws her lip in between her teeth. I reach out, plucking it free with my thumb. "You know you always do that when you're over-thinking something?"

"I do not," she retorts, pulling her hand from mine to cross her arms in front of her.

"You do." A laugh erupts from my chest. "It's cute, I like it."

"Well, if I'm overthinking this it's your fault, because I can tell something's wrong and you won't tell me. Isn't that a part of dating? Communication?"

Her words catch me off guard and I'm sure I look like I've forgotten how to speak. Did she just say dating?

"Yeah, it is," I reply feeling stunned. "Are we dating?"

A flustered expression washes over her face. "I don't know, are we?"

A laugh sneaks out of me again only because getting to spend time alone with her has me realizing how much I really enjoy her personality. She's witty, sarcastic, thoughtful, and sweet when she wants to be. The last few weeks have been so intense, I don't think I realized that I haven't been able to really see Harlow be Harlow. Yeah, there were moments when those characteristics peaked through her cloud of stubbornness, but I wasn't entirely sure I'd get to witness her becoming herself.

While I did my best to step up and be persistent with her, I had my moments of doubt. What if she hadn't left Beckett? What if she really never gave a shit about me? What if she got better and went back to her team and we never saw each other again?

I'd hoped that there would be a breakthrough, and there has been, but every time I get these glimpses of Harlow's true self, it truly takes me aback. She's even better than I thought.

"Yeah, I'd like to date you. Pretty sure I made that clear in front of your parents at the swim meet, but I'm also really enjoying getting to know you. Besides, I know I've said it like a hundred times and you're probably over it, but I don't want to rush you."

I say that as if I know what I'm doing. *Surprise, I don't.* My whole game plan with her has been to let her set the pace and step in when I felt like I was needed, but now that Beckett is out of the picture, I'm trying to figure out how I fit into her life.

"It means a lot to me that you think about all these things. I'm not sure what guy would kinda just," she pauses and lets out a puff of air, "take everything that's happened and be as easy going, but I feel like maybe there's still some things you don't understand that could help you know how to go about *this*." She uses a finger to point back and forth between us.

I nod my head, knowing she's right. The way I've been treating her has been based mostly on my own assumptions and I don't know if that's good or bad, maybe both.

"Well, seeing as we both don't appear to be in the party mood, would you want to just talk for a little? Until Wes and Lennon appear again?"

She chuckles. "We may be here all night then."

"That's fine with me, as long as I'm with you."

FORTY-SEVEN

STEVIE NICKS, HARRY STYLES, AND SOMETIMES TAYLOR SWIFT

HARLOW

It's almost two in the morning and we've been talking outside nonstop. I got to tell Shep about how I started swimming and why I love it. I told him about my relationship with Margot and how she knows what Beckett did. I gave him little glimpses of myself and he listened intently the entire time.

I've tip-toed around Beckett in detail but I did share with him that things weren't always so bad. It was weird trying to explain who I was prior to him and that made me a little sad.

When I first came to Everson, I didn't go out of my way to make a ton of friends because my focus was on swimming. I had Lennon in my corner so there wasn't a huge need for me to be social outside of our team.

I laughed as I shared memories from when Lennon and I first moved into the apartment we have now back in our sophomore year and the dance parties we would have in the kitchen to Stevie Nicks, Harry Styles, and sometimes Taylor Swift.

I reminisced on the wine nights we would have occasionally when Margot came to visit and how the three of us would sit around a bowl of popcorn, drink wine, and play Uno.

The more I talked to Shep about what my life was like prior to getting caught up in my relationship with Beckett, the more I realized how much I miss it. I can't ignore that there's hope blossoming in my chest for the new year when Margot is in town and us girls can start hanging out again.

Shep encouraged me to make that a priority and also said he was looking forward to the next few months too. He sheepishly revealed his dream of us being able to date and hangout with Wes and Lennon too.

I know Shep sees me and the trauma that I've endured, but I really don't want to be defined by it. I want to let it be something that gives me the courage moving forward to set higher standards for myself and better expectations. Sure, there's still damage to be undone, but why should that stop me from finding a way to carry on and be happy?

The more time I spend with Robin, and also with Shep, I start to feel more calm and relaxed. I'm able to be present and I like this version of myself I'm becoming.

"You seem to be doing great with therapy, are you still liking it? I don't know if like is the right word, but you know what I mean," Shep interjects.

"Yeah, actually I do like it. I just hope that you don't treat me differently because of it. I don't know how you usually treat girls you're interested in, but—"

"Well let me stop you right there," he stifles a chuckle. "You're not just some girl I'm interested in, Harlow."

"No, I know. I'm just saying—"

"And I'm saying that this, what we have, is different from anything I've ever had with someone. Honestly, I'm just acting on my feelings for you which sometimes doesn't work out in my favor, but I want to be real with you."

I nod my head and smile. "So what do you think?"

He cocks his head to the side. "About what?"

"Me, everything I shared with you in the last two hours."

"I think the more I learn about you, the more I like you, and I'm excited to keep getting to know you." He leans forward and wraps his arms around me, pulling me into a hug. "But I do have a few questions," he mumbles into the crown of my head.

I pull my head back and rest my chin on his chest, peering up at him. "Okay, let's hear them?"

"Is this okay? If we hug or kiss in public? Or if I want to hold your hand? How do you feel about that?"

"I'm okay with it. I'm not huge on PDA, but I don't mind little things like this." I smile up at him.

"Works with me," he presses another kiss to my forehead.

"You never know though," I drag my hands from around his back to his abs and dig my nails in a little. "I may surprise you."

Shep's eyes widen and he shakes his head. "Harlow, baby. C'mon."

"What?" I ask innocently, running my nails along the waistband of his sweatpants. "I kinda like this look, with the mask and all that. It's fun."

"Fun," he mimics me, but his voice is husky. Grabbing my hand, he pulls me behind him into the house.

"Shep," I gasp. "What're you doing?"

"Surprising you," he throws my words back in my face.

Once inside, he pulls me into a bathroom and shuts the door, locking it. Before I can speak again, he picks me up and sets me on the counter.

"Shep," I whisper as he pushes himself in between my legs, grabbing my thighs to pick my legs up and wrap them around his waist.

"If you're going to put your hands on me like that, I can't act like it doesn't affect me. Especially with this sexy little outfit you're in." He smirks at me then kisses me slowly.

His hands wander up my body and the music vibrates through the house. I swear it's the song "Make Me Feel" by Elvis Drew, which only adds to the intensity of the moment and makes me want Shep more.

As his tongue moves with mine, there's an electricity beginning to surge between us and I lose myself in him. Being with Shep feels natural and I don't have to think when we're together. I trust myself with him-and him with me-and it feels so good to let go.

I don't realize that my hips are moving against him until he pulls away, nipping my bottom lip as he does.

"You okay?" His gaze burns into me while he waits for my reassurance.

I nod my head and roll out my neck to let a shiver run down my body.

"Do you want more?" he asks in a low voice. I bite my lip, eyes widening as he continues. "What do you need, baby?"

"Your hand," I whisper.

"Where?" He reaches for mine and moves it down to the inside of my thigh. "You have to show me because you're in control here."

I feel my eyes widen and my mouth falls open some.

"Harlow, what is it?" Shep lets go of me.

I think for a second, wanting to make sure I don't ruin the moment, but also wanting to speak up for myself. I reach for his hands and put them back on my legs to keep our connection.

"You don't have to treat me like I'm fragile. You're always worried you'll do something wrong, and I get that, but I've told you this is what I want. I want you."

His hands squeeze my thighs, and he smirks when I gasp. "I'm just used to you rejecting my touch. I know, I know. Things were different then, but I just want to make sure—"

"Shep, if I didn't want you to touch me, I would've told you to stop." There's a slight edge in my tone, but I really want him to really hear this, so I grip his jaw forcing him to meet my stare. "I know you want to be careful with me, but I'm not a porcelain doll. You're not going to break me, so please stop talking and do what I've been dreaming about."

He arches an eyebrow and I roll my eyes.

"Fine—"

He silences me with a kiss and works quickly to move the skimpy leather shorts to the side. I gasp as the cool air hits the sensitive skin and Shep starts teasing me between my legs.

I moan into his mouth and buck my hips against him when he slips a finger inside me. He drags it out slowly before pushing back in with another one. He does this over and over, while I claw into his back and bite his lip repeatedly. I'm probably leaving marks on his skin, but I don't care. No one's ever made me feel like this.

A fire starts working its way up into my stomach and it's like my nerves are coiling up. I pull away, letting my head fall back overcome by all these sensations.

Shep takes the opportunity to suck on the side of my neck and presses his thumb on the spot that has me almost screaming with pleasure. I close my eyes, biting down on my lip to stifle the noise, and it only takes a few rotations of his thumb until I'm a trembling, moaning mess. Stars explode behind my eyes and I feel my body go limp in his hold as I tumble over the edge of pleasure.

"That's it. That's my girl," he coos into my ear as I ride out my high. "You did so well. You're such a good girl. Look at you falling apart on my fingers."

Shit, he has a mouth on him. I whimper as he slowly withdraws his fingers from me, a shiver wracking through my body. I blink away the lust clouding my vision, my mouth falling open as I watch him move his hand to his lips, sucking my release from his fingers.

"I've been dying to know what you taste like," he hums.

My heart hammers in my chest. There's no doubt in my mind that Shep is definitely the sexual one between us, but I can see myself exploring that more with him. Especially after that? Damn, I might actually not be able to go slow like I'd planned.

"You make me feel things I've never felt before," I admit. "It's scary, but I like it."

"You don't need to be scared. I'm not going anywhere," he responds quickly before kissing me again.

"Me neither." My words are firm and resolved.

He picks me up off the counter, setting me down, and giving me a minute to put myself back together. He even gets me a damp paper towel and wipes off my thighs. *Is he real? Was this another sex dream?*

Once I'm ready, he smiles. "I'm glad you wore your Docs, it really pulls everything together."

I follow him out of the bathroom and a flush rises in my chest wondering if anyone could hear us, but by the looks of everyone inside, they're too drunk to notice or care. I pull my phone out to see if Lennon's texted me but she hasn't. Shep must see what I do and pulls his phone out.

"They're together," he states.

"Ah." I nod my head. "Well, I'm kinda tired. Will you walk me to my car?"

"Damn, running out on me after that?" he remarks playfully but I stop in my tracks, crossing my arms.

"Don't do that." I frown.

He turns to the side and notices my expression, grabbing my hand out from under my arm.

"Sorry, baby. You always give me a hard time, figured it was time I gave it back a little. C'mon, let's go to your car."

We leave the frat house hand in hand, towards the street where my Bronco is parked along the curb.

As we walk up to my car, he turns me towards him. "I'll double check with Wes that he'll get Lennon home, okay?"

I lean against my car door and smile at him. "Brownie points for you, taking care of my best friend."

He shrugs. "You know, just trying to make sure every-one's happy."

"Well I appreciate it," I run a hand along the side of his face. "I'm happy. You make me happy, Shep."

His eyes light up and he presses one more kiss onto my lips before stepping away. "Text me when you get home, okay?"

I nod my head, and watch him start to walk towards the house and through the front door. I feel light as a feather when my phone buzzes. I pull it out smiling, expecting a text from Shep already, but my stomach drops instead.

There on my phone is a message from an unknown number. When I open the text, my phone falls from my hand onto the asphalt. I look around frantically, searching the tree line, the rest of the street, my head moving like it's on a swivel.

After another second passes, I reach down and retrieve my phone before getting in my car, locking the doors imme-diately. I look at the screen again, my hand trembling.

UNKNOWN

Attachment: 1 Image

Hope you're having fun.

Staring back at me from my messages is a photo of Shep and I walking out of the Chi Kappa house holding hands. The distance at which the photo was taken registers in my mind and I have to open my car door, the contents of my stomach spilling out.

When I'm safely locked in my car again, I open the

message and start to cry, and another pops up. It's a photo of me from just now, throwing up, the text following right after.

UNKNOWN

Glad to see I still have an effect on you.

FORTY-EIGHT

A PEACE OFFERING

SHEP

After a few minutes of trying to locate my best friend, my phone rings and I smile.

"Hey, baby. Miss me already?"

Harlow laughs nervously on the other end of the line. *"Yeah, you could say that."* Then there's a long pause. *"So I was thinking, would it be okay if I stayed at your place tonight? I'm assuming Lennon is going to end up there anyways so can I come over too?"*

My eyebrows shoot up. "Yeah, of course. Are you still here?" I start walking back outside and, sure enough, I see her Bronco down the street with the headlights on.

"Yep. I can wait and follow you to your place. Were you able to find Wes and Lennon?"

I'm already walking towards her car, when she gets out and heads towards me. We meet in the middle, with our phones still to our ears.

"No, but I found something even better," I say as a soft

smile spreads across her lips. She hangs up her phone and then throws herself into me. I wrap my arms around her and notice she's shaking. "Baby, you must be freezing. Let's go inside and see if we can't find our friends."

She nods her head into my chest and when she steps away, something is different. I don't know what, but she doesn't look as light and carefree as she did not even five minutes ago.

"Is everything okay?" I study her face.

"Yeah, I just want to be with you tonight. Is that okay?"

"Of course, angel. Let's go." I take her hand in mine, leading her back into the house.

After almost half an hour, we finally find Wes and Lennon. Once we're all together we head back outside and I text her my address just in case, watching her walk back to her car with Lenn.

Wes and I get in my truck and I can't gauge if he's drunk or not. Typically he's very chatty when he drinks, but he seems lost in thought right now. I know I could probably ask him what he's thinking but, truthfully, my mind is still reeling over the night with Harlow.

Driving back to the townhouse, catching sight of Harlow's car trailing behind me fills me with ease. I don't know how we got here, but this might be the best night ever. When we pull into the drive of our house, Wes stops me before I turn the car off. The girls haven't pulled in yet and he finally speaks.

"I messed up tonight."

I raise an eyebrow, glancing in the side mirror to watch for headlights.

"What do you mean?"

"Lennon saw me talking to a girl from one of the sororities and I guess she heard some of the talk about me from last year." His head falls and he drags a hand over his face, sighing.

Last year, Wes went through some pretty deep shit with his sister. She's only seventeen and, with the way life has gone for the two of them, he's essentially raised her. He never gave me all the details, but I know something went down at a party his sister ended up at. Wes blamed himself for what happened because they had got in a fight earlier that day and she took off, going to the party.

After he found out what happened, he started drinking more and was slipping into a bad habit of partying, hooking up with girls, and not focusing on school. It took a reckoning from my mom to get him back on track.

"She asked me if I had dated that girl or if she was just one of my hookups and because I'm an idiot who doesn't think, I laughed and said, 'I don't date.'"

"Dude, seriously?" I pinch the bridge of my nose with my thumb and pointer finger. "Is this the part where you tell me that you somehow made it up to her?"

He scoffs before laughing. "She shut me down before I could even try."

"Well, she came back to the house, so that's good… right?" Headlights beam through the back window of my truck and Wes shrugs his shoulders before opening the door and getting out.

We all head inside and Dahlia soaks up the extra attention from the girls while Wes sulks on the couch. After I walk Dahlia, we all silently split off and go to our rooms.

Harlow steps into mine and looks around with curiosity.

She cocks her head to the side when she sees my punching bag and lets out a hum of interest.

"I started boxing over a year ago."

I walk up behind her and place my hands on her shoulders. She flinches and then relaxes into my touch. "You seem a little jumpy. Are you sure everything's okay?"

"I'm just tired." She starts to put her hair into a messy bun, then looks around the room again. "Actually, can I rinse off and borrow a sweatshirt and some boxers?"

"Yeah," I answer while walking over to my dresser, grabbing her something to put on.

She walks over to my bed, and sits down next to Dahlia who's eagerly awaiting more pets. "Does she sleep with you?"

"Typically, but she doesn't have to while you're here." I offer.

"I don't mind," she says softly, petting Dahlia and looking intently into her eyes. "I feel like she gets me. Does that make sense?"

"Yeah, it does," I say, handing her my clothes. "You may have been her first unofficial case as an ESA." She chuckles at the joke, but there's also probably some truth behind it. "Speaking of cases, she had her first trial run at the precinct."

She stands up, giving me a soft smile. "Aw, I want to hear about it after I shower."

"Of course, babe." I press a kiss on her head then get her set up in my bathroom. Once she's done, I rinse off and come out to find her already in my bed and Dahlia moves to curl up next to her. I stand there for a second, taking in the sight. My two girls. Once again, peace washes over me and I get into bed with them. Then a different feeling takes over when I realize Harlow smells like me. While I love her signature scent of cherries and vanilla, something about my body wash covering her makes me feel more possessive than normal.

She lays there silently tracing patterns on Dahlia's fur. Observing her movements, I reach out and run my thumb along her cheek. "I'm really glad you're here."

When she peers up at me, her emerald eyes almost look lost, but it is after three in the morning. "I won't keep you up for much longer but let me give you the rundown on Dahlia."

"Okay," she whispers, resting her head back on the pillow and focusing on Dahlia again.

She listens as I talk about the upcoming meeting we have at the precinct with a young girl who has to be questioned as a witness to a car accident she was involved in. How we hope Dahlia will be able to help keep her calm and her parents are looking forward to it too, which is exciting.

Harlow nods as she listens and after a few minutes, she asks if I can get her some water. I kiss her forehead before getting out of bed and wandering into the kitchen. I'm shocked to see Wes lying on the couch as I leave my room.

"Damn, that bad?" I say in passing while I grab a water bottle from the fridge.

He grunts in response.

"Harlow seems a little off too. I wonder if they talked about something in the car?" I stand there for a second, feeling clueless about what's going on. "Maybe I should send Lennon into my room and let them sleep together."

"Does that mean you and I are going to share my bed?" Wes asks in a sarcastic tone.

"We can, or you can stay out here and I'll stay in your room." I walk over to his door and knock lightly, "It's Shep."

It cracks open and Lennon looks at me with an uncertainty in her eyes. "I'm not here to get involved with whatever is going on between you two. I just wanted to see if you'd take this to Harlow and maybe y'all could stay in my room tonight? I get the feeling you two need each other or something."

She looks past me at Wes then down at the water before taking it from my hand and walking out to my room.

I watch her give Wes a sad look, one that he doesn't acknowledge, before turning around and declaring, "Dahlia is staying with us too. Thanks." Then she goes into my room and shuts the door behind her.

"Alright, well I'm going to lie down in your room. You can stay out here and mope."

"Whatever," Wes clips out and my heart hurts for him, but I'm hopeful they'll figure it out.

———

At around 7:00 A.M., my body naturally wakes up, since this is usually when Dahlia starts to stir and needs to go out. I wonder if she's fine since it was only four hours ago when I walked her, but I don't want her to disturb the girls.

I quietly walk out of Wes's room and across the living room, careful not to wake the sleeping grump on the couch either. When I get to my room, I slowly crack open the door and have to hold back a laugh. Lennon and Harlow are on opposite sides of my bed with Dahlia in the middle on her back and her legs up in the air. She's in heaven.

Realizing everyone is clearly fine right now, I grab my hoodie off the door then shut it, deciding to run out and grab coffee for everyone. When I get back, Wes has moved into his room and Lennon is on the couch with Dahlia.

"I took her out for a walk, I hope that's okay," she says while petting her.

"Yeah, that's great. You didn't have to do that though," I say, handing her a coffee. I wasn't sure what she drank but figured I couldn't go wrong with a classic latte.

"Thanks," she says while grabbing the warm cup from me. "Truthfully, it helped me avoid Wes in the living room when I walked out. I didn't expect him to be there."

"Yeah, he slept on the couch last night." I sit down across from her in our recliner. "Do you want to talk about it?" I take a sip of my own coffee and watch as Lennon screws her face up, clearly thinking over what to do.

"I don't know what to say. I guess I'm confused, but it's my fault. I've told Wes that I don't want to date but I just thought...I don't know," she trails off.

"That he would try and change your mind?" I offer.

"I guess, maybe. But he said it last night, he doesn't date." She peers down at the lid of her coffee, picking at it to avoid my gaze.

"Yeah well, Wes can say some stupid shit sometimes, but I think if he knew how you felt it would change things." When she doesn't lift her head up, I decide to do a little wing-manning myself. "I don't know what you've heard about Wes, but as his best friend, I'd be happy to set the record straight. Yeah, he got around some last year, but something really shitty happened with his sister so he stopped giving a damn."

Lennon glances up and I can see a frown forming. "I don't care about his past, but I didn't know that."

"Yeah, well, don't tell him I told you. Maybe y'all can try and talk through things, I'm sure he's awake in his room listening to music or something. Take this with you as a peace offering." I hand her another cup of coffee and she smiles.

"Thanks, Shep. You know, you're a really good friend." She gets up and starts walking to Wes's room.

"That's what I keep hearing," I call out after her before getting up myself and heading into my room.

Harlow is still curled up under a blanket. It's pretty chilly now that it's officially November, so I'm surprised she was comfortable in just my sweatshirt. I walk over, putting her cold brew on my night stand, then sit down next to her, the bed dipping when I do. She stirs a little, before fluttering her eyes open.

"Hi," she says through a yawn.

"Good morning, pretty girl. Sleep okay?" I throw an arm over her, pulling her head into my lap so I can play with her hair, absentmindedly twirling the ends with my fingers.

"Mhm," she says, nestling into me. "Lenny told me you sent her in last night, that was sweet."

"Just seemed like you two needed each other, it was no big deal."

She sits up and notices the cold brew. A smile tugs on her lips. "Is that for me?"

"Of course. I wasn't sure if you'd still want this since it's cold outside but——"

"Oh, it does not matter what the temperature is outside." She interrupts me.

"Noted," I laugh, handing it to her.

She takes a sip and lets out a sigh. "Yum. We should go get breakfast. Do you and Dahlia want to come with? We can take it back to my apartment."

Once again I'm shocked by her request, but it's a Saturday so I don't have anything going on. Even if I did, I'd cancel just to spend more time with her.

"Yeah, that would be great. Do you want to check with Lennon if she's staying?"

"I'll text her that I'm leaving and can come back later if she needs me."

Harlow and I work in silence to pack up a few things of mine and Dahlia's then we head out to her Bronco. I can't help but smile watching her drive, nodding her head along to the music playing. Dahlia is curled up in the back seat and damn, I'm so fucking happy right now.

Weekends with Harlow, how did I get so lucky?

FORTY-NINE

SOME SERIOUS SCHEMING

HARLOW

It's been a little over a week since Halloween and I still haven't told anyone about the texts. Especially not Shep. How could I?

Things are finally working out for us and we've been falling into our own rhythm. I don't want to lose that, and I also don't want to let Beck-shit ruin yet another part of my life. I hate keeping this from Shep, but I know he'd make it into a big deal.

I met with Robin a few days ago and almost told her, but I don't want to feel like all my hard work has been undone. I haven't gotten any more "Unknown" texts so I'm telling myself that it was a one time occurrence. Just an attempt to get in my head and mess with me, since he no doubt blames me for getting expelled.

But just in case, I've made it work to where I'm never alone, whether Shep is at my place or I'm at his. We've spent the last week together when I haven't been in class or at practice, so I feel safe. With break coming up and our families living nearby, we planned to just stay at my apartment. Lennon is going home for the week to see her mom and grandma so it'll be just us. We haven't talked about how we're going to spend the actual day of Thanksgiving, but I'm sure it will come up.

After finishing another PT session with Pierce, I'm lying on the training table doing a few more rotations of my shoulders before I have my next evaluation to officially get cleared to swim butterfly. I'm so excited, I could jump out of my skin.

Even though I've been cleared to race, it won't feel like I'm fully back until I get to swim fly again. My last few practices, I've been able to do the stroke without stopping or feeling any pain. Coach Bradford now wants me to race against myself. He said that if I can come within five seconds of my typical race time, he'll let me swim butterfly at the next meet.

While there's a twinge of nervousness, I feel confident. I feel like I can do this. I *know* I can do this. I was made to swim butterfly.

Pierce comes back into the room with an ice pack and works to wrap it onto my shoulder. The touch of the ice sends shivers down my body and I quickly pull the sweatshirt I stole from Shep over my head.

Once I'm bundled up and ready to leave, I grab my phone and send off a text to Lennon to see if she's ready to meet up. We made plans to study at the library before practice. When I get to my car, she texts back that she's running late but will meet me there.

I'm just about to start my car when I notice someone

walking towards the sports medicine entrance. I duck down in my car, peering over the dash, watching my *sister* sheepishly go inside. There's literally no reason for her to be here, other than...*Pierce.*

My mouth gapes open and for the life of me, I cannot even begin to think of why she would be here unless something is going on that I don't know about. I half consider going back inside to see if I can catch the two of them talking, but my phone starts ringing, interrupting my scheming thoughts.

"Shep, this is not a good time."

"I'm sorry?"

"I just caught Margot going into the building that Pierce works in and there's something going on between the two of them, I just don't know what."

He laughs on the other end of the line.

"This isn't funny. I was about to do some serious scheming," I chirp back.

"Is this another fun characteristic of yours? Scheming?"

I gasp in a playful tone. "I don't know if I should answer that. I may need to use it to my advantage with you."

"Shit, I hope not." He laughs. *"I was just calling because Mom wants to know if you would like to come over for Thanksgiving."*

There it is.

"I was wondering about that," I admit.

"She said to let her know what time your family does Thanksgiving and she'll plan around that."

My heart warms at the consideration of Shep's mom. She's been such a healing presence in my life and while I have momentary flashes of guilt that I might be closer to her than my own mom, Robin assures me that sometimes we go through seasons of life where we're closer to other people than our own family, and there's nothing wrong with that.

"Okay, I'll let you know. Thanks for thinking of me."

"*Of course,*" he's quick to respond. "*You know you're basically like family.*"

I snort. "Not as your sister though, I hope."

"*God, no,*" he retorts and I can almost see his grimace through the phone.

I burst out laughing. "I know. I just wanted to hear your reaction."

"*Well, never again. I gotta run but text me later, okay? You'll come over after practice?*"

"That's the plan."

"*Great. See you later, baby.*"

"See ya."

I hang up the phone, a smile playing on my lips.

———

After a chunk of time spent buried in our books, Lenny and I pack up our things and head to the student athlete center. When we get there, Coach Bradford is waiting for me. He calls me over and I tell Lennon to go ahead to the locker room without me.

"Feeling up for a race?" He gestures to the pool with his clipboard.

"Today? Butterfly?" I stumble over my words in disbelief.

He nods his head. "Spoke to Pierce earlier and he thinks you're good to go. So if you're ready, then I'm ready."

I don't even respond, turning on my heels and darting

into the locker room. I quickly change and get my stuff, heading back out to the pool. I meet Coach Bradford by the lane where he holds up a stopwatch.

"You know your time to beat?"

"Yes, sir." I pull my goggles over my head, then my swim cap.

"Alright. Why don't you do a few laps to warm up then let's do this." He motions to the pool and walks over to sit down on one of the chairs by the back wall.

I waste no time diving into the water and start warming up. After my fourth lap of freestyle, I can't contain my excitement so I pull myself out of the pool and yell, "I'm ready!"

Getting up on the diving block, I take a deep breath. Lennon walks out of the locker room with a few of my teammates and shouts out encouragement for me.

Coach Bradford talks me through my start and the second I dive into the water, my legs start dolphin kicking. When I finally break the surface to take my first stroke, it's like my body immediately takes over and I start to propel myself out of the water with ease.

The movements of butterfly come to me with muscle memory and I feel stronger than ever. When I touch the wall and turn to swim back, I forget I'm even being timed. I'm lost in the motion of my favorite stroke, my passion, and part of me doesn't even care if I don't make it to the wall in time. Right now, I feel so good. I just want to keep swimming.

When I touch the wall to complete the race, I brace myself for the results. Lennon and my team are cheering on the pool deck still and Coach Bradford is still staring at the stopwatch.

Shit.

I lift my goggles up, resting them on my forehead and swim over to the lane rope. "How bad?" I call out to Coach.

"You did it." He grins and I don't know if I believe him.

I get out of the water and walk over to look at the stopwatch myself. "No way," I mutter, as the time stares back at me.

"You were solid out there. I don't think I've ever seen you swim that strong before. It was like your body was moving in perfect sync with your strokes." Coach Bradford beams at me and I can tell he's proud.

We finish up our practice and I'm on another level. I can't believe I get to start swimming butterfly again at our meets. As I leave the athletic center, I text Shep to let him know that I'll be at his place soon. When I get there, he's outside with Dahlia and she's wearing a pink sweater. I hop out of my car and walk over to them.

"Isn't that something," I comment, giggling.

"Guess who got it for her?" Shep responds, rolling his eyes.

"Momma?" I bend down and pet Dahlia who's always excited to see me.

"Mhm," he hums in playful annoyance.

We head into the townhouse and settle onto the couch. In addition to being a criminal justice major, Shep is also obsessed with true crime. This means that whenever we spend time together, we usually end up watching some sort of murder documentary. I find them interesting, but it does give me the heebie-jeebies at certain parts.

At some point, Wes comes in the front door but promptly goes into his room. I don't know if he and Lennon have made up since Halloween, but they haven't been seeing each other so I'm not sure what's going on there.

She told me in the car that night how Wes made a comment that he doesn't date and it only affirmed my suspicions that, despite her saying over and over again she didn't like him and things between them were "casual," there was a bit of hope inside her that he would try to prove her wrong.

I don't know much about Wes, other than the few things he's mentioned in passing and the things Shep has said, but I can see something between the two of them. It's hard to know they're likely both missing each other but just not telling the other.

When the documentary ends, Shep asks if I'll make him my Harlow Hug Pasta. He's had me make it for him more times than I can count since the first time. I don't mind, because cooking for people is like a love language for me.

While I'm in the kitchen, Shep comes up behind me and wraps his arms around my waist. Resting his chin on my shoulder, he watches me stir the noodles. We sway together in the silence and the guilt starts gnawing at me again that I haven't told him about Beckett. I've thought about maybe just going to his dad, but I don't want to involve someone else in keeping this secret.

If our feelings for each other weren't growing so much, maybe I wouldn't feel that tug of needing to be honest. There are so many things that have happened in just a short amount of time between Halloween and now that only affirm our connection and chemistry. I find myself thinking about our future together, and the fear of losing that because of Shep detaching himself to focus on finding Beckett or something, motivates my decision to just keep it to myself.

It's hard for me to understand my feelings sometimes because I have such a distorted view of relationships and even love. I would say that the way Shep makes me feel is comparable to that of the books I've read, movies I've watched, and songs I've listened to. There's an ease and simplicity to spending time with him. Falling into the routine of staying the night with one another and there's still no pressure to rush into sex which has made me feel like he genuinely likes me for me.

Even though Beckett and I didn't have much of a sex life, it was always something he used to try and validate the depth of our relationship. *"Well if you really love me, then show me."* Other comments similar to that play in my mind, and I realize that was just another way for him to manipulate me into giving him the control he wanted over me.

Shep and I have definitely gotten close to having sex a few nights because wow, the desire and attraction is definitely there, but again, the guilt of hiding something from him has kept me from being completely intimate with him.

After we eat dinner, the thought of talking to Shep about what happened pops up again and I don't know if I can actually keep this secret. The more time passes, the more it's on my mind. Hell, I've spent the last half hour thinking about it, and hardly paid any attention to Shep. He's definitely noticed something isn't right, but I've shrugged it off to something swim or school related. It hurts to know that I'm deceiving him while he so blindly trusts me.

Once the kitchen is cleaned up, we head into his room for the night. Dahlia jumps up onto the bed and waits for us to join her. I hover by his desk while Shep walks over to his dresser and starts to pull his sweatshirt over his head.

"If I haven't said it enough lately, I'm so happy you're here, Harlow."

His words crush me and I can't do it. I can't hold it in any longer and I blurt it out.

"Beckett texted me."

FIFTY

OUT THE WINDOW

SHEP

I would consider myself a level-headed person. I would like to think that most of the time, I react calmly to situations that most people would lose their heads over. However, the second I hear three words that I never expected to hear leave Harlow's mouth, all sense of logic flies out the window.

"I'm sorry, what?" I turn around and face her. She's chewing on her bottom lip and avoiding my gaze. "What do you mean he *texted* you?"

She doesn't respond for a few seconds and walks over to sit down on the edge of my bed. "Halloween night. He messaged me from an unknown number." Her voice is hushed.

"Halloween? He texted you on Halloween and you're just now telling me? Harlow, that was almost two weeks ago!" My stomach drops.

"I know! I'm sorry!" Her voice comes out strangled with emotion.

I run my hands over my face and shake my head. I have to calm down. This is not going to end well if I don't.

"Well, what did he say?" is all I manage to get out in response.

She holds her phone out to me, her green eyes watery.

Staring at the screen in front of me, reading and seeing exactly what he sent her, I can't hold in my emotions anymore.

"You're kidding me." My tone is harsh but this is insane. He was there and she didn't tell me. He was close enough to take a picture of her and she didn't mention it. "Do you even understand how bad this is? Harlow, you've put your-self in danger by not telling anyone. What was your plan?"

"I-I…" She stammers over her words. "I've just been making sure I'm not alone."

My chest tightens. All this time I thought she was wanting to stay with me and spend more time with me because her feelings for me were growing—because she was letting me in.. She was just hiding out in my apartment? And Halloween night, that's why she called me and said she wanted to come over? While a small piece of me is glad she felt she could do that, there's also an overlapping wave of betrayal that knocks me out.

"So all this time we've been spending together was just to give yourself a sense of protection?" I scoff in disbelief. "I thought you and I were actually getting closer."

She flinches at my words. "We have been getting closer," her voice barely audible.

I recognize what I'm saying is probably coming across as

hurtful, but I'm hurt. This really fucking hurts. I try to shift gears, not wanting to make this about me.

"We need to tell my dad. You need to file a restraining order or something," I insist.

"No!" She rises to her feet. "That's the last thing I want. It would only make things worse. Shep, listen. He hasn't texted me again," she continues. "I think he did it to mess with me and it's not that serious."

I widen my eyes. "It's not that serious? You're joking right?"

"I'm sorry," she repeats again. "I just felt like if I had to deal with anything related to him again, I'd be losing progress! I want to keep moving on. With you!" Her voice rises with emotion.

"You can move on and still be smart about things, Harlow." I cross my arms and her lip wobbles before a tear runs down her cheek. It takes everything in me not to walk over and wipe it away.

"I wasn't using you, Shep. I have been wanting to spend time with you and get closer to you. The guilt of keeping this from you was killing me. Especially the more I realized that my feelings for you are growing." She sits down on my bed again and pulls at the sleeves of her sweatshirt. "I really like you, Shep," she whispers, staring down at the floor.

I close my eyes and sigh. Everything she's saying is what I've been wanting to hear for so long. There's a flash of self-doubt and I wonder if I did something to make her feel like she couldn't tell me.

"I still think you need to tell my dad and let him give you his opinion." I walk over and sit down next to her, giving in and placing a hand on her leg. "This scares me, Harlow.

How can I look out for you and take care of you when I don't know everything going on?"

"I didn't want it to turn into a big deal and cause any issues between us. I know how much you don't like him and I didn't want things between us to go back to being about Beckett. But, surprise, he's found a way to weasel himself back into my life, messing things up for me." She hangs her head in defeat.

I chew on her words because part of me understands, but I still can't seem to process that she was keeping this secret from me.

"This sucks," I finally say, letting out a breath of defeat.

"Yeah. I'll go back to my apartment tonight. Lennon's home so I'll be fine." She starts to stand up and grab her things.

I should stop her, but I don't know how we're supposed to continue the night after this. Maybe the space could be good for both of us to think about things. I sit there frozen on the edge of bed while she mindlessly packs up her bag before tossing it over her shoulder.

"I really am sorry, Shep. I had a feeling too that once I did tell you, things would change, which only made me want to ignore it even more." She walks towards me and kisses my cheek. "I meant what I said. I really do like you. I even think maybe…" Her voice trails off.

"What?" I search her face but she shakes her head and turns to walk out my door.

"I'll give you some space. I'm sorry again."

I listen as she leaves out the front door and then I lie back on my bed. Staring up at my ceiling, I feel all my thoughts and feelings compound into one big mess.

I don't know if I should have let her leave, but we weren't going to agree on what to do. Maybe it's not even my place to tell her how to handle this, but I still wish I would've known. I consider everything she said about her progress and being happy, and my stomach drops. I shouldn't have let her leave.

I roll over and grab my phone, sending her a text.

> I'm sorry if I made you feel like you couldn't tell me. We can figure this out.

After a few minutes, she responds letting me know she's safely home and with Lennon, but doesn't acknowledge what I've said.

I don't want to push her any more so I set my phone down and hope maybe a good night's rest will clear both of our minds.

———

The following day, I feel like I'm operating on autopilot. I haven't heard from Harlow, and sure, I could easily text her but in the past her silence has meant she needed space which leaves me conflicted about what to do.

I thought about reaching out to my dad anyways but if Harlow found out I did that, shit would really go south.

I only had one class today and now that I'm at work, a numbness has taken over me as I watch the various people swimming. All it does is make me think of Harlow and I wish I could have a do-over of last night. I see Wes walking my way and try to perk up some.

"You and Harlow want to go out with Lennon and I

tonight? I think we're going to grab something from Summit and then take it back to the house."

While I'm glad that he and Lennon seem to be on a better note, my stomach sours that things between Harlow and I are off right now. I'm not sure she'd want to see me.

"I'll ask her, but we kind of had a fight last night."

He frowns then runs a hand through his hair. "I thought I heard the door shut, but shrugged it off to you taking Dahlia out. I realized it might have been Harlow when nobody came back in. Damn, I'm sorry. What happened?"

I hesitate, but fuck it. "Beckett texted her after the Halloween party and she didn't tell me until last night."

His jaw drops and his eyebrows shoot up. "She must have not told Lennon either because she'd have told me and you know I would have told you."

"Yeah, she didn't tell anyone. She said she's tired of him ruining shit for her so she wanted to ignore it. But it's not like he just sent her a text. It was pictures of her and I, meaning he was at the party that night."

"Okay, that's actually a big deal." Wes states and a serious look takes over his face. "You need to tell your dad."

"Yeah, that's what I said but she freaked out." I roll my eyes, feeling overwhelmed and like I really am too young to be trying to handle this.

"Well as your best friend, I'm telling you that you need to tell your dad. I don't care what Harlow says, she can be upset about it later, but that's not okay. That guy's like seriously fucked in the head."

I don't know what got into Wes but he seems genuinely concerned. Maybe it's because he's my best friend and knows how much Harlow means to me. Whatever his reasons, there's truth to his words and they mean something to me.

"You're right. I'm going to ask Harlow about coming over tonight. We'll talk about everything and I'll see if I can reason with her about meeting with my dad."

Wes nods his head then reaches up and smacks the side of my leg. "You got it. Let me know if I can help at all."

"Just don't say anything to Lennon," I rush out.

"Of course." Wes turns around and heads back to the office.

After a few minutes, I take a break and go get my phone to text Harlow about tonight. She tells me that she's going to stay late after practice to try and swim off all the over think-ing, and asks if I'll pick her up around eight since she rode with Lennon.

My heart hurts that she's clearly having a hard time with this and I feel responsible for a lot of it, but I'm hopeful things will be okay since she asked me to pick her up. Responding that I'll be there, I put my phone away, feeling a little more at ease that I'll see her tonight and hopefully we can put this all behind us.

FIFTY-ONE

ANOTHER DEEP ACHE

HARLOW

I drop my stuff next to the block. It's a little after seven now, so I know that gives me enough time to swim until I don't feel so stressed anymore.

Even though it's technically after practice hours, Coach Bradford gave me the okay to stay and told me he'd be in his office if I needed anything. Lennon also told me to call her if I change my mind but having the pool to myself is serene and I know that I'll be able to tune out the last few weeks and especially the last twenty-four hours.

I know Shep was hurt, but I also thought maybe he'd understand my position. I appreciated his text, but I just don't really know what to think. Right now, swimming is exactly what I need. Plus, it's not like it'll hurt to get in an extra practice before my first official meet swimming butterfly before break next week.

Even thinking about Thanksgiving sends an ache through me. I wonder if Shep will change his mind about wanting to spend the holiday with me. I guess it's a good thing he invited me over tonight. At least he still wants to see me and maybe we can figure all this out then.

I start swimming and after a few minutes, I slip into this peace of being able to only think about my strokes and breathing. I focus on my future and my hopes of carrying on to possibly train and qualify for the Olympics.

I think about what that would be like for Shep and I, and how it would work with his program at the precinct. It's the realization that I'm naturally including him in my future that fills me with another deep ache. I don't like being at odds with him. Why can't I just let him protect me the way he wants? I try to clear my mind again and focus on my strokes knowing we can talk about all of this when he picks me up, but his face doesn't leave my thoughts.

After another set of laps, I stop at the end of the lane to get a sip of water. The athletic center is dark except for the few overhead lights illuminating the pool deck. Shep should be here by now, but maybe he got caught up at work.

I take a deep breath and drop back under the water and swim a few more laps, hoping that he'll be here shortly. As I get towards the other end of the pool, I hear the door opening when I turn my head for a breath.

My heart jolts that Shep is here and all I can think about is jumping out of the pool and hugging him. All I want is to make up and go back to his place. I continue swimming towards the pair of shoes that are now at the end of the lane, getting more and more excited. I pop my head up out of the water and my stomach drops.

"I thought I might find you here," Beckett's voice comes out slurred and hissed.

No, no, no. This isn't happening.

I try to push away from the wall to create some distance with us, but he grabs the top of my swim cap before I can. I'm still able to pull away from him as the cap comes off in his hand, but he grabs my hair with his other, pulling me back to the edge. With his face almost touching mine, I can smell the alcohol wafting off of his breath.

"You thought you could just get rid of me?" He finishes his sentence and the next thing I know, he's shoving my head under water before I can scream out.

I immediately start to panic. Where is Shep? Would Coach Bradford be able to hear me yelling?

He pulls me up again, and I gasp for air. "You think you can just ruin my life?"

I can't even register his words as he pushes me back down under the water, but a realization hits me that if I want to try and get out of this, I need to calm down. When he finally pulls me up again, I gulp in a large breath before he shoves me back under. I can hear his garbled yells coming from above the surface and I try my best to focus on slowing down my heart while holding my breath. Maybe he just wants to scare me, but then the reality that he's drunk and I'm alone hits me.

He pulls me up out of the water again and laughs. It's dark and sinister. "You stupid bitch. Now who's going to save you?" I open my mouth to finally try screaming out for help, but he rears his other hand back and slaps me across the face. The sudden action causes me to sharply inhale and ruins my chance at getting another good breath in before he shoves me back under the water. This time, the panic starts to set in and I feel frantic.

Laura was right. I should've known Beckett would escalate. Robin told me I should consider doing more to protect myself but I didn't listen. Shep said I should've taken out a restraining order but I shut that down, and now I'm going to die because of it.

Holy shit, I'm going to die. I didn't even get to truly start my life with Shep. What about Lennon? My parents? Margot?

Suddenly everything in me kicks into fight or flight. I start thrashing in the water, smacking at Beckett, but he just pulls me out of the water and shoves me back under, faster, harder. I can't even attempt to catch my breath anymore, and on the last time, water gets into my mouth causing me to cough and choke.

Beckett doesn't bring me out of the water again and his grip on my hair becomes more forceful, my scalp prickling with pain, but then the sensations start to fade and everything goes numb. I can't feel it anymore. I can't feel...anything. I think I'm drowning.

Beckett's last words echo in my mind and clash in my head with the lyrics of the song I've been listening to over and over since my first talk with Laura.

If anyone could've saved me, it would have been Shep. It should have been Shep. But it's too late now.

And I didn't even get to tell him that I love him.

FIFTY-TWO

MY WORST NIGHTMARE

SHEP

After getting stopped by Tom to talk about my schedule for next semester, I'm finally leaving work. I send Harlow a text that I'm heading her way and when I don't get a response, I assume she's lost track of time swimming. It wouldn't surprise me.

I call Wes, letting him know I'm picking her up then will head home and start driving towards the student athlete center. It's not very far from the rec, so after only a few minutes I'm pulling in. An unsettling feeling immediately hits me though when I realize there's basically no one here. I see a truck parked in the faculty spot, Harlow's Bronco, and another car I don't recognize.

As I shut my truck off and get out, I break into a light jog, wanting to get inside sooner than later. As I push through the doors and turn towards the direction of the pool, I hear faint yelling and everything in that moment stops.

I run towards the pool deck and when I push into the arena, my heart drops. On the other side of the pool, Beckett is holding Harlow's head under water and she isn't moving.

I immediately yell and when he looks over and sees me, he lets go and takes off. I don't even have time to think about going after him. I race over to where Harlow is, stopping to pull the fire alarm to try to alert anyone else who's in the building and knowing it'll automatically call for emergency services.

I yell out for help a few times wondering if Coach Bradford is still here somewhere before getting to Harlow. Pulling my phone out of my pocket, I dial 911 before setting it on the diving block to jump in after her.

She's floating face down in the water and by the time I swim to her and get her in my arms, I can hear the dispatcher calling out from the speaker of my phone.

I try to respond while also trying to bring Harlow to the pool deck. My voice shakes as I attempt to tell them someone has drowned and we need an ambulance right away.

In the middle of all this chaos, Coach Bradford runs in. The blood leaves his face as he watches me cradle Harlow in my arms, before laying her on the pool deck and checking for her pulse. There isn't one.

"Call my dad! Call the sheriff's office!" I yell to him, panic setting in but knowing I have to calm down. This is literally what I've trained for as a lifeguard so I immediately start CPR.

After giving her compressions and mouth to mouth, the

dispatcher asks me to check again for a pulse, but I'm too scared to stop. She isn't breathing and the ambulance still isn't here.

"I couldn't get through," Coach Bradford chokes. I'd forgotten he was here. "Did you pull the alarms?"

"I was hoping someone would be here and it would get their attention," I speak through labored breaths.

Coach Bradford walks over. "Let me take over for a second. I'm trained too, son. Try calling your father again." He hands me his phone before quickly switching with me to continue giving Harlow CPR.

I call his personal number and he picks up after the second ring. "Dad," I cry out. "Harlow. She drowned. He drowned her. Beckett." My words are broken up by my sobs.

I watch Coach Bradford continually press with his whole weight onto Harlow's lifeless body. I don't even want to think about how long it's been since we started, but I know we can't stop until the EMTs arrive.

"I sent a BOLO out to all my officers. We'll find him, Shep. The ambulance should be there soon and I'll meet you at the hospital. Call her friends, I'll notify her parents."

He hangs up and by the time I go to pick up my phone, the EMTs rush through the doors. Coach Bradford quickly moves out of the way and I watch with shock and horror as they immediately pull out the AED and hook Harlow up to it.

Disconnecting with 911 now that they're here, I call Wes, who's with Lennon waiting on Harlow and I to come home. We were supposed to have a double date. We were supposed to figure things out. How the fuck did this happen!

Explaining to him what's going on feels like I'm trapped in my worst nightmare. I hear Lennon in the background crying and asking me questions that I don't have answers for. I hang up feeling more lost than I ever have.

When I turn back around, Harlow is being lifted onto a stretcher and wheeled out of the athletic center. I stand there dazed with my phone in my hand. It vibrates and Mom texts me that she spoke with Dad and she'll also meet me at the hospital.

I start to walk towards my truck, but now that the adrenaline has left my body, I collapse and let out a pained scream. Coach Bradford walks over to me and tries to help me up.

"C'mon, son. I'll drive you to the hospital." I don't argue with him and follow him out to his truck.

———

The minutes after arriving at the hospital are a blur. Everyone starts to ask me questions about what happened but all I can think about is getting to Harlow.

Mom stops me and pulls me into her. I stand there motionless for a second, before wrapping my arms around her, crying.

"She wasn't breathing, Mom. She wasn't breathing." I sob into her shoulder and I feel her body start to shake, realizing she's crying too.

"You did everything you could," she reassures me as we both stand there and cry together.

"I didn't get to…I didn't tell her I love—"

"She knew," Mom fills in my words and squeezes me tighter.

A hand grips my shoulder and I turn around to see Harlow's father, his face covered in tears.

"Mr. Sutherland, I'm so sorry." I wipe my face with the back of my hand and I feel Mom rubbing my back before she turns and walks over to speak with Lennon and Wes who've just walked in.

"Thank you for being there." His voice is hoarse and he reaches out, pulling me into a hug. While I'd hoped I'd eventually get closer to Harlow's parents, I didn't ever want it to because of something like this.

He steps away and shakes his head. "This Beckett guy, why would he do this?"

I open my mouth to speak when Margot walks up to us. "I got this," she says to me before taking her father's hand and walking him over to sit down next to their mother, who's sobbing into her hands.

For a moment, I'm left alone standing in the middle of confusion, grief, chaos, and panic. I search everyone's faces and there isn't one person whose eyes are dry. Even Wes has tear-stained cheeks and I'm sure it's because of the brunette he's clinging to who's bawling.

The wails and cries are stopped for a brief moment when someone walks out in the waiting room and calls out, "For Harlow Sutherland?"

I want to move but I can't, terrified of what this person will say. I watch her parents quickly get up and when they get closer, I try to make out the words being spoken to them.

It doesn't matter though, because when Harlow's mom

turns to her husband and starts wailing, that tells me enough. Every ounce of happiness I felt over the last few months leaves my body along with my ability to stand and I collapse onto the cold tile of the hospital floor.

She's gone. I lost her.

FIFTY-THREE

A BRIGHT WHITE

HARLOW

The sound of water sloshing next to my ears jostles me awake. I slowly open my eyes but I'm blinded by the amount of light reflecting off the water.

My senses come to me and I realize I'm floating in the middle of a pool, but where?

I bring my feet under me and my hands to my side, treading the water while I look around. I'm not at the rec center. I'm not at the athletic center.

Where am I?

As I start to swim to the edge of the pool, I take in my surroundings even more. All the walls are white, there's light everywhere, beaming in through the top of the building.

I shake my head in confusion then hear a faint laugh behind me. I whip around and there's a little girl, running on the pool deck with flippers in her hand. Her giggles are loud and bubbly and it causes an ache far down inside me.

"Hello?" I call out.

The little girl continues to run until we meet each other's gaze as she passes in front of me. When we lock eyes, she smiles before turning and continuing to run away. She doesn't just look familiar, she feels familiar.

I follow her until she dissolves into a ray of light but not before I hear a familiar voice calling after her, "Harlow! Slow down! You can't run at the pool."

Mom?

I turn my head back to where the little girl first was and I see my mother standing on the pool deck. I try to swim in her direction but as I get closer, I see she's crying.

"Mom?" I call out this time, but all I can hear are her cries, saying my name over and over again.

I go to call for her again, but hear a loud cheering behind me. I turn around and see a crowd in the stands has appeared. They're all cheering and I have to do a double take when I see someone on the diving block, getting ready to race.

I swim towards them and squint, trying to make out who's here.

"Hello?!" I call out again, confusion flooding me.

The swimmer turns and looks at me before diving into the water and disappearing. Once again, when the person looks at me, a feeling deep within me rattles and I want to make sense of this, but I can't.

It isn't until I look back over to the lane the swimmer just disappeared in and see someone coming out of the water swimming butterfly. They're wearing a swim cap with EU on the side, and dread fills me.

The people I'm seeing are myself at various stages of my

life, but that still doesn't answer where I am. Am I dreaming?

The swimmer disappears once again and I look past the pool to see my dad in the crowd, but nobody else is around him now. I try to swim over to him but every time I get to the edge of the pool, I'm back in the middle of it. I think I can hear him though. I think he's trying to talk to me. I swim closer to the edge and rest my arms on a lane rope until I can start to make out his voice.

"Hey, little girl. If you can hear me, it's Dad. Oh, Harlow. How did we get here? I'm so sorry. I'm so sorry we didn't know about any of this." Then he breaks into a sob.

"Dad!" I try to call out, but it's no use. "Daddy, I'm here!" But he can't hear me.

I push off the lane rope and towards the wall to get out, but again, it's no use. I'm back in the middle of the pool, suspended. *What is going on?*

Out of nowhere, I feel a sensation on the end of my finger. I can't tell what it is, but when I look up again, I see Margot standing on the pool deck. "I love you, sissy." The words leave her mouth and I watch her bring her finger up into the void, pressing it into the nothingness, but I feel it on mine, then she disappears.

I decide to try and swim over to the diving block, when I hear a new voice. *Lennon?*

I look over to where my dad was and see Lennon sitting on the edge of the stands. Her voice is broken up with sniffles and so I swim to the lane rope again and try to see if I can hear her.

"Harlow," then she breaks into a sob. "Harlow, please. I can't do this without you. I can't believe I didn't take things more seriously. It's all my fault. It's all my fau—" Her head falls into her hands and she bawls uncontrollably.

I go to try and say something, hoping this time someone will hear me, but before I can, the voice of Laura comes into earshot. Her voice is the loudest and I feel pressure on my hand as if someone is holding it.

"Sweet girl, it's Momma Fords. I know you're still in there."

The sensation on my hand comes back again as if it's being squeezed.

"Listen to me, you are a fighter. You're going to wake up and we're all going to be here waiting for you. I believe in you. My son needs you, Harlow. We all need you. You can't give up."

Her words slowly sink into me and I look around the pool again. The stands have faded and the surrounding area is back to being a bright white. As the water sloshes next to me, I blink a few times before flashes of my memory come back to me.

I was swimming… Beckett showed up. Then he—no. I can't be. Am I dead?

I start to swim back to the lane I was first in, ready to try and get out of the pool. I need to get back. I have to go back. As I'm getting ready to reach up to the block, a new sensation takes over me. It feels like someone is running their hands through my hair.

I reach my own hands up, but there's nothing there. I want to start crying but then I hear him. I hear Shep.

"Baby, please come back to me. I'm sorry I wasn't there sooner. I'm sorry I couldn't stop him. Please, Harlow. Stay with me. Stay with me. Stay with me."

He says it over and over until I hear another voice and it sounds like they're taking him away.

"No!" I scream into the void.

I try to pull myself up and out again, but as if stuck in a loop, I'm magically in the middle of the pool again. This time, I do feel the tears forming. I have to get back. I can't stay here. I have to fight.

I frantically look around and out of nowhere, a time clock appears on the wall. It's counting down with fifteen seconds. Quickly directing my gaze to the end of the lane, I start swimming, trying to beat it. Of all the meets, of all the races, something tells me this is the one that will matter the most.

I kick harder and pull myself through the water as fast as I can, glancing back at the clock to see it's almost at five seconds.

I'm getting closer and I'm almost there, but I'm starting to feel like I'm sinking. I can't stop though, I have to beat this clock.

I touch the wall as the buzzer sounds and when I do, I open my eyes while gasping for air. I'm blinded by lights again, but they're different than before. After a few blinks, it registers I'm in the hospital.

But all that matters to me is I'm alive. *I won.*

A nurse looks at me with tear-filled eyes before calling out, "She's awake!"

FIFTY-FOUR

A MILLION PIECES

SHEP

My dad stands at the back of the room, talking with Harlow's parents, while I watch the nurses give her something to calm her down. Since she woke up, she's been frantic and combative.

Nobody blames her. She's confused and scared, but there's a heaviness lingering between all of us who have still been existing while she was unconscious for the last few days.

I know that eventually, she'll need to hear the truth but when that moment will be, I don't know. I'm hoping more time will pass to allow for her to process what's happened, but also knowing her, I doubt she'll try and take things slow.

The nurses leave and ask for her parents to step into the hall leaving her alone with just me and my dad. They've come around lately to understand how I feel about their daughter and also with my dad's involvement as the Sheriff, they aren't putting up a fight with us being here.

"Shep," she croaks out when she finally sees me.

"I'm here, baby. I'm here," I say, quickly moving to the side of the hospital bed and reaching out for her hand.

"What's going on? I thought I died," she starts crying and I run a hand over her head, gently shushing her. "I did die," she exclaims again.

"You did," I start. "You did, but they were able to bring you back and you're still here." My own voice cracks. "I'm so glad you're still here."

"How long have I been here?" she whimpers.

"A few days now. They were able to bring you back in the ambulance but you weren't waking up. We've all been waiting for you, baby. We knew you would." I kiss the top of her hand.

"I think I heard you." She looks around the room and back at her parents who are walking back in. "I think I heard all of you. I didn't know what was going on though and I was so scared." Her voice breaks off into another sob. "It's like I was stuck and I had to make a choice to come back."

Her words shock everyone.

I look to her parents, allowing them the chance to talk to her but she keeps her focus on me. I don't know what to do in this situation, but her parents' eyes plead with me for help as Harlow only gets more upset.

I sit down next to her on the bed, leaning back against the pillows and pull her into my side. She's shaking and I'm not one to advocate for drugs, but I don't think whatever the doctor prescribed her is strong enough.

Once I have her safely tucked in my arms, she mumbles out through sobs. "He drowned me. I was swimming when he came in and I thought he was you. But he drowned me."

My heart breaks and I look again at her parents who look at me with the same brokenness. Nobody here is okay.

Suddenly, she grips onto my shirt and shudders through her tears. "What happened to him? Where's Beckett?" Her voice is shaking with fear.

This is the moment I was dreading. I glance over at my dad who shakes his head at me. I begged him to be the one to break the news but he told me it would be better if I was the one who told her. I'm seriously doubting his judgment right now, but I do my best to steady my voice before speaking again.

"He had been drinking, Harlow. A lot." My voice starts to waver and I squeeze her tighter as the emotion floods my body.

"I remember that," she whispers. "I could smell alcohol on his breath."

Her admission stuns me and everyone else in the room. We all wondered, but nobody knew what she would remember, if she did remember anything at all.

"My dad sent patrol cars after him once I found you at the pool. Do you remember that? Me showing up?"

"No," she says quietly while sniffling.

"That's okay," I press a kiss on top of her head. "I got there and saw him, but he ran off. I called 911 and waited for the paramedics, then I called my dad and told him about Beckett. A team went to look for him."

"And he was arrested?" Harlow peers up at me, her eyes flooded with tears.

"No, Harlow. I'm so sorry." I finally lose my strength

and tears of my own spill out. Not for what happened but because she doesn't need any more pain after everything she's been through.

"What?" She blinks in confusion and looks around the room. Her mom turns away, stifling a cry while her dad tries to comfort her. I wish my mom were here but she's at home with Dahlia since I've been staying at the hospital. I look at my dad one more time and barely make out the word, "Please."

Thankfully my dad gives in and walks over to the end of the hospital bed, getting Harlow's attention.

"Harlow, when my patrol cars located Beckett," he stops to sigh. "It turned into a chase. We tried to apprehend him but his driving was erratic and he wasn't stopping. I'm sorry but Beckett ran his car off the road. He didn't make it."

Harlow lets out a guttural wail before turning into me, sobs wracking through her body. I didn't know how she would take this. Despite the nature of their relationship, they still had history together and I knew him dying would have an effect on her.

"Where's Lennon?" she cries out. "I want Lennon."

An ache travels through my body, and I know it's selfish but I want to be the one who's here for her. I want to be the one who protects her now and takes care of her, but I know I don't have any say in this situation. I start to get up off the bed when Harlow grabs onto me. "You don't have to go, just someone please get Lennon."

Her mom nods and quickly leaves the room, her dad and mine following after, leaving the two of us alone for the first time.

"I'm sorry I wasn't there sooner," I whisper into her hair, kissing the top of her head again. "I'm so sorry."

She doesn't say anything, just lets me hold her and cries. Not knowing what else to do, but feeling overwhelmed with the emotions I've been wrestling with since I thought I lost her, the words that leave my mouth next come out shaky. "I love you. You're going to get through this. I'm with you."

Her body stills and she stops crying for a second. Pulling away from me, she looks up and there's a moment where I think maybe she'll say it back, instead she moves farther away. It looks like something is clicking in her head and the way her face changes, I don't have a good feeling.

"I don't think you should be with me." Her words punch me right in the gut and I can't help but let my jaw drop.

"What? What do you—"

"When Lennon gets here, I think you should leave and stay away from me." Her voice starts to shake and I climb off the bed, stepping back in shock and disbelief.

"Harlow, what're you talking about? Why would I do that when I just almost lost you?" My mind is spinning and I didn't expect this to be her reaction to me telling her how I felt. Especially when I thought maybe she felt the same.

"You don't deserve this. Any of this. I've done nothing but complicate things for you since we met. You shouldn't love me, Shep. Not someone like me. Especially now." She starts to cry and before I can protest any of what she's saying, Lennon opens the door and comes in.

She stops when she realizes something is obviously happening and looks between the two of us. "What's going on?"

"Lenny," Harlow croaks out.

I look at Lennon and I don't care that she can see tears welling up in my own eyes. This is the last thing I want.

"She said she wants me to leave."

She frowns but then nods in Harlow's direction. "I'm sorry, Shep, but I think you need to go."

I shake my head as tears start to freely fall down my face. I turn back, facing Harlow one more time who's now bawling in Lennon's arms. "I still love you." Then I walk out the door with my heart feeling like it's just been shattered into a million pieces.

NEW ROUTINE

HARLOW

It's been ten days since I left the hospital, almost twenty days since I drowned, and I don't know how I'm supposed to function normally again when my mind is working against me every second of every day.

I can't seem to process the fact that I died.

By all accounts, I was dead. And while I was brought back and am still here, the mere fact I was that close to losing everything haunts me. I thought there would be a part of me that would be thankful, or even discovered a new lust for life, but no. All I've been left with is nightmares, a fear of water, and what Margot said is likely PTSD.

I know I need to see Robin, but I'm still not ready for even that because I know her questions will be hard and confrontational. I can't handle that. I've even pushed Shep away. The one person who has consistently shown up for me, made it clear he cares, and even tried to tell me he loves me. But what did I do? I told him to stay away. When he told me I'd get through this I realized just how broken I was and nobody deserves to deal with that.

"Harlow, it's just us. You can open the door," Lennon calls out.

I guess one of them decides not to wait for me to answer anymore and the door creaks open. "Hey, sissy. It's just me." Margot tip toes into the bathroom and crouches down in front of me. I don't break my gaze from looking straight ahead. Not even when Margot puts herself in my line of sight. She's just there, but I don't see her. I see through her.

I know what they're trying to do. I know they want to help me, but they can't. I don't care that it's been almost a week since I've taken a shower or a bath. I can't do it. I can't be under the water or else I'll feel like I can't breathe. Margot places her hands on my knees and lightly jostles them.

She lowers her voice this time before speaking again. "Harlow, I'm going to turn the water off, okay?" She stands up and turns the knob. The shower silences and my shoulders slump in response. Relief floods my body, tears welling up in my eyes.

I'm weak. I'm so weak.

"I'm...I'm letting him win." The words come out broken through soft sobs. I hate to admit it but it's true. "He's dead and he's still controlling my life!" My voice cracks as I try to yell. I'm so angry and while I know it's not fair for Margot to receive the other end of these feelings, I can't help it.

The door swings open and Lennon rushes in. "I'm sorry, I can't do this anymore. I can't stand here and listen," she shakes her head, putting her hands up in the air, "I can't watch—Margot, we need to…" Her words fade as she leans closer into my sister and whispers something to her. It doesn't matter anyways. Her voice is drowned out by the pathetic wails starting to leave my lips.

This is my new routine.

I try to move forward but I can't. Which in turn, makes me feel even more fractured and broken, and then even more scared that I'll never recover from what *he* did to me. And then, I cry. I sob until I can't take deep breaths and eventually just crawl somewhere where I can lie down and eventually pass out, only to then be haunted back awake after the same nightmare.

Margot and Lennon walk out of the bathroom together and I look around at the empty space. Will I ever recover from this? Will life ever be normal for me?

I stare at the wall and try not to let the memory of what happened to me start up again. It already runs on an endless loop at night, preventing me from sleeping. I don't need it occupying my thoughts during the day too.

You hear it all the time when you're a kid that you shouldn't be afraid of the monsters under your bed. But what they don't warn you about are the ones who walk the same earth as you and then end up in your head.

Tears leak out of my eyes and my head aches from the dehydration I'm likely suffering from since I'm hardly doing anything but crying these days.

At some point, I realize I've stopped crying and am now lying on my side. The cool of the tile against my cheek has induced a shiver in me but I don't care. I don't want to move.

Out of the silence, I hear the front door to the apartment open. There's a slight commotion and sounds that I can't make out. After a few minutes, the bathroom door creaks open again, and through teary eyes, I try to figure out who's coming into the room now. My breath catches in my throat when I realize what Margot and Lennon have done.

FIFTY-SIX

I SHOULD BE HERE.

SHEP

When my phone rings and I see it's Lennon, my stomach drops. I know Harlow has been having a hard time, but it hadn't reached the point yet where her best friend reached out. I quickly answer and she explains what's going on.

My body immediately goes into action. I don't even think about what I'm doing, I just know I'm going to pack a bag, get my dog, and go see my girl.

Margot is the one in the background of the call who speaks up and asks me to bring Dahlia. At first I'm confused, but remember Harlow told her sister about the training I have been doing for E.V.E.S.T.

As I walk through the apartment door, I'm not expecting for the two girls sitting in the living room to also make my heart ache. Lennon and Margot both look like they haven't slept in days. Their eyes are the same shade of red with matching darkness underneath.

Dahlia quickly runs to Lennon, who scoops her up into

her lap and gives her the attention she wants. Margot walks over to me and when I offer my arms out for a hug, she all but collapses into them. It's evident the effects of what happened to Harlow are radiating beyond just her.

We aren't very close but there was a moment in the waiting room we shared after Harlow told me to leave. Margot was just as shocked as I was, but also explained that, with trauma, oftentimes people push away those closest to them. It's hard for them to understand why someone would want to be with them when they feel as damaged as they do.

She told me to hang in there and, eventually, Harlow would come around, but as the days passed by and I didn't hear anything other than the occasional update from Lennon, I started to worry.

After exchanging a few words with her sister, learning about what exactly has been going on since Harlow left the hospital, my chest hurts deeply. I was confused why Harlow didn't want to go home to their parents' but Margot says she made it clear the apartment with Lennon is where she wants to be.

Margot tells me that for the first week, her parents came by in shifts and everyone took turns staying up at night because Harlow's only been sleeping for a few hours at a time. I feel the blood leave my face when she goes on to explain how every night, Harlow screams herself awake at the same time. It's apparently the same nightmare on repeat and I don't miss the haunted look on her sister's face as she tells me she can't stop hearing Harlow's blood-curdling scream.

I find myself frozen in the living room, my mind reeling.

How are they all shouldering this? It doesn't seem right, and obviously nobody is going to leave Harlow alone.

With every detail Margot shares, the guilt in me rises higher and higher. I should be here. I should be a part of this group helping Harlow, especially since it's clear she's barely getting by. She isn't showering, sleeping, or eating. She's just existing in this cycle of trauma and emotions.

Margot assures me that it's best I wasn't around in the beginning and while there's likely some truth to that, I still feel every bit responsible for what happened to her sister.

It's my own nightmare I'm stuck in because she wouldn't have stayed late to the swim that night if we hadn't been at odds. I shouldn't have overreacted to her telling me about the texts. But it doesn't matter now.

What matters is this exact moment I've found myself in: picking Harlow up off the floor and trying to help her break through the fear that's paralyzing her.

I just hope she lets me stay this time.

FIFTY-SEVEN

THE GREATEST GIFT

HARLOW

"Hi, baby."

Shep's voice is soft and something inside me calms. He takes his shoes off and then sits down on the floor next to me. With one hand, he strokes my hair and then places the other one under my cheek so it's being cushioned from the floor.

He holds my face in his hand for a few seconds, not saying a single word. Just touching me softly, and coaxing me into his embrace. Then he lies down on his side, resting his head on the tile so it's right in front of mine.

We stay like this, holding each other's gaze. He doesn't ask any questions. He doesn't try to get me to talk. He just lies there with me on the floor.

After some time, he moves the hand that was running through my hair to my cheek. Cradling my face, he rubs his thumbs over my tear-stained skin. He leans forward until our foreheads and noses are touching. "What's going on in that beautiful head of yours?"

A sob croaks out from my lips. "I'm s-sorry."

"Shh," he says softly. "You have nothing to be sorry for. I'm here to be with you. We can stay here for as long as you need."

I nod my head and let him pull me into his chest. He moves to sit up, bringing me with him and leans against the wall. I fist the front of his sweatshirt and bury my face into his chest, letting all my groans and cries out.

Pressing a kiss onto the top of my head, I feel his hands moving through my hair again.

"It's a mess—my hair. It's knotted and gross. I can't..." My words are muffled by the fabric I'm pressing myself into, but Shep still hears.

"I'm not worried about it, baby. Can I try to help though?" He nuzzles his nose against the side of my head. "Will you let me try to help?"

I peer up at him and my lip wobbles. I know what he's talking about. I know what he wants to help with.

"I can't g-get in the water. I can't shower. I c-can't take a bath. I can't do it. I-I'm pathetic."

He lifts my head up to meet his gaze and the emotion in his eyes is too much. My body is already so overwhelmed. I can't handle the way he's looking at me because he's looking at me the way he always has, which means he doesn't see me any differently. It means I'm not too broken or pathetic or weak to him.

"Harlow, you may be the strongest person I know, but you're hurting and you don't have to hurt alone."

I run my hand across my nose, wiping away the snot and

tears that have accumulated on my face then sit up. The longer we hold each other's gaze, the calmer my heart rate becomes. I take a deep breath and Shep dotes on me for doing so with his smooth voice. "Good girl. There she is. There's my girl."

The words cause an entirely different sensation to flood my body and I find the ability to speak more clearly.

"How? What can you do for me that's different?"

It's a genuine question. Lennon offered to wash my hair for me in the sink. Margot even tried to use some of her psychotherapy skills to talk me through it. But it didn't matter. The second I thought about the water running over my head, my body involuntarily started to shake and then I'd break down. It was embarrassing and I don't care how many times they told me it wasn't.

"I want to do it with you," he whispers. "Together and however you want to. We can keep our clothes on or you can keep yours on and I'll take mine off." He laughs softly. "Whatever makes you feel comfortable."

While the idea stirs something in me, I doubt myself. "Shep, I don't think I can. What if I fall apart? You don't want to see me like that."

He reaches for my hands, gesturing for me to stand up with him. Like a newborn animal, I wobble upright, leaning into him for support.

"I want to see you in every way, baby. I'm here for every version of you. I know it didn't make sense to you when I said it in the hospital, but I meant what I said."

"But—"

"Harlow, I love you. I'm in love with you." Shep presses a soft kiss to my forehead, then looks me right in the eyes.

"I've been loving you for a long time and nothing is going to change that."

He still loves me.

With tears welling up in my eyes again, I nod my head in response. It's all I can give him and he doesn't protest it or require anything else in return, which is the greatest gift anyone could give me right now.

He moves me to rest against the counter, then walks towards the shower and turns the handle. Just like I knew it would, the sound of the water rushing out sends a shiver through me and my body starts to tremble.

"Hey, hey. I'm here. Look at me."

I don't even realize my eyes are squeezed shut. I pry them open and Shep's face comes into view. It's all I can see and as I focus on him, the sound of the water starts to fade.

"Do you want to try and get in the shower or do you want me to let the tub fill up some so you can sit down? It doesn't have to be higher than a few inches." Shep reaches for my hand and starts to massage it with his own. "Focus on me and what you're feeling. Not emotionally, but physically." He continues rubbing my hand and presses another soft kiss to my forehead. "The water has been running now for a minute and you're doing great."

I chew on my lip, wanting to at least try for him. That's all he's asking from me anyways—to just try. He hasn't said I have to do anything or I need to do anything. He just wants me to try.

"I want to try and sit in the tub. Is that okay?"

Shep's eyes light up. "For you, anything."

FIFTY-EIGHT

ON PERFECT DISPLAY

SHEP

I love Harlow.

I love her so much that in this very moment, I would give everything to take the pain she's feeling. It's not fair. It's not fair that she has to continue waking up everyday haunted by the damage left in the wake of a dead man.

Which brings me to another swell of emotions I'm battling within myself.

Death was too kind of a punishment for someone like Beckett.

Harlow and I haven't talked about it since she found out in the hospital, but I've seen the posts online, the vigil on the side of the road by the telephone pole he wrapped his car around.

It makes me sick.

The instance tragedy strikes, it's like everyone forgets who that person really was. I'm not heartless and, yeah, I know there are people who will grieve the loss of Beckett, but for all the people on campus who know what he did to Harlow… I just don't understand it.

I'm trying to be present for her at this moment but seeing her trembling before me, I can't stop the burning in my chest.

"Shep?" Harlow's voice pulls me out of the emotional vortex I was starting to lose myself to.

"Yes, baby?"

"I'm scared." She draws her hands together, folding them under her chin.

"I know you are, but we can do this."

Not wanting to keep her waiting in the suspension of what's to come, I shut the shower off with the stopper in the tub. Although I only let the water fill up just a few inches, I can still sense the dread starting to climb through her.

I turn back around and face Harlow. Once our eyes are locked, I pull my sweatshirt over my head, looking to her for permission to continue. She nods, so I slide down my sweatpants until I'm left in my boxers. I reach out for her wrist and slowly pull the sleeve of her sweatshirt forward. She takes her arm out and then we do the other. As I lift up the hoodie over her head leaving her in just a sports bra and pajama shorts, chills erupt on her skin.

"You okay?" I check in with her again. The urge to kiss her is overwhelming but I'm not naive to think that would be appropriate right now.

She hums in response and we stand there for a second, holding each other's gaze. I guide her towards the edge of the tub and step in. Her grip tightens and she freezes, stuck on the other side. I sense that the position we're in is an even bigger metaphor for our situation. I've always been both feet in, where she's kept herself safe behind a boundary separating us.

"You can do it," I coo. "Just one foot at a time."

She looks at me and I can tell she's paralyzed with fear. The panic spreading across her face causes my heart to twist up in pain, but I have to push all that aside. She's my priority.

I kneel down in the tub and let go of her to reach for her foot. She grips my shoulders, tension radiating into me from her hold.

As I pick up her left foot, I press soft kisses on the side of her calf and ankle. I move slowly and when my breath fans on her skin, her hold on me loosens. I glance up to her and she's closed her eyes. Watching her carefully, I move her foot over the edge of the tub and into the water. I hold my breath, waiting for her to react but she seems caught up with the continual kisses I'm giving to her.

When I settle her one foot, I move to the other to repeat the process until she's successfully stepped into the water. My emotions are rising up in me as I observe the position we're in. With her standing over me and me essentially bowing before her, my submission to her and her wellbeing is on perfect display.

"Harlow," I say in between kisses, still trying to keep her focused on my touch but wanting to make her aware of every step. "You're in the tub."

Her hold on me tightens again and I peer up to see her eyes now open, glued to me. "You don't have to move. Just stay here. Just stay with me." She doesn't speak or react. She just keeps her gaze on mine.

Cupping my hand, I take the water and start to slowly

let it wash over the lower half of her legs. I use my other hand to stroke the side of her thigh. Once we've been like this for a few minutes, I reach up to her hands on my shoulders and lift them, guiding her down towards me until she's sitting on the edge of the tub.

She looks at her hands, where the water droplets are, and then takes a sharp inhale.

"You're okay. Baby, you're okay."

She opens her mouth then closes it and lets her head fall forward instead. I really don't know exactly what I'm doing but I hope it's clear that I'm just trying to meet her where she is.

"Do you want to try and sit with me?"

Tears spill out down her cheeks and my stomach drops. I pushed her too far.

But then, she shocks me by nodding her head. There's a war waging inside her mind, I can see it. However, I can also see she's trying to fight it.

Letting her take the lead, I sit down in the tub and move to where I can rest against the back slope. She never lets go of my hands as she lowers herself down between my legs. Once her body starts to immerse in the water, a whimper escapes her lips. Even though she's facing away from me, I can tell she's starting to cry.

"You're okay," I keep reminding her. Over and over. "You're safe with me. I'm here."

At some point, she leans back and lays herself against my chest. I move our hands to the sides of the tub and then lift mine up to start cupping the water again to pour it over various parts of her body. I look at her grip which has turned into a white knuckle hold.

"Tell me what to do. Tell me what you need. Do you want to stop?" I ask softly.

She shakes her head in protest, then lifts her hand pointing to a washcloth that's hung over the side of the tub.

Moving forward to reach it, once I have it in my hands, I position Harlow to be upright. Her knees are drawn to her chest and she wraps her hands around her legs, as if hugging herself.

"Can you wash it for me, please?" Harlow asks in the smallest voice.

I look around and find her shampoo in the corner, then take the washcloth and squeeze it in the tub to soak up some of the water. Sitting behind her, I trail the wet fabric up her back trying to make her familiar with the sensation.

This is the moment that feels detrimental. Getting water on her head is the part Margot said that Harlow can't handle. I freeze and try to think how I can do this best without getting more than just her hair wet.

"Harlow…" my confidence starts to falter. "I'm going to try and not let the water run down your face but if it does, I'm sorry."

Her body tenses and I wish I could see her face at this moment. I can't imagine the fear covering it, but I force myself to press on.

Guiding her head back to where she's almost looking up at the ceiling, I bring the washcloth up to the crown of her head and squeeze it letting the water run out and down her hair. I don't even notice I'm shaking until about the fourth time I do this and accidentally get some water on her forehead.

Harlow lets out a strangled scream and my stomach knots up. "I'm sorry," I rush out. "I'm so sorry."

She doesn't tell me to stop so I just continue until her hair is wet, then take her shampoo and pour some in my hands. I work it through her hair as best as I can, all while trying to ignore that Harlow is full on sobbing now.

I use the washcloth to rinse it out, continuing my process of squeezing water into it then ringing it out over her hair.

Once the shampoo seems fully rinsed out, I lean forward and rest my chin on her shoulder. Her arms are still wrapped around her knees and so I wrap my arms around her, keeping her in my embrace. Never mind that the water has basically gone cold, we're both clothed and covered in suds. I hold her tight. I tuck her into myself and hope that she feels safe.

"I won't ever let you go." I whisper. "I'm never leaving you. I don't care if we sit in this tub all night and you just cry. I'm with you, Harlow. I'm yours, baby."

She leans into me and softly whispers back, "I know."

FIFTY-NINE

YOUR WORST, YOUR BEST

HARLOW

Shep helps me out of the tub and even though I didn't fully shower, my hair is clean and I guess that's a start. He steps out into my room leaving me to stare at my reflection in the mirror.

I pick up my brush and start to tear through my hair with it. Each pass tugs on my scalp and the prickling sensation reminds me of that day causing my brush to drop from my hands, making a loud noise that echoes through the bathroom.

Shep runs in with a sweatshirt, a look of panic spreading on his face until he sees the hairbrush on the floor. Dahlia trails behind him but darts over to me when she sees me.

"You brought Dahlia," I whisper, crouching down to pet her.

"Your sister asked," Shep responds, reaching his hand out with the sweatshirt in it. "We thought maybe she can put some of her training to use."

I stand up and turn around, pulling my wet sports bra over my head then bringing the sweatshirt down over me. Once I'm covered, I pull down the shorts I had on and walk past Shep to grab a fresh pair of underwear and sweatpants.

He walks out behind me and sits on my bed. I notice he has my hairbrush and I raise an eyebrow. Dahlia jumps up next to him, looking at me with her puppy eyes.

I crawl on top of the comforter towards the two of them, Dahlia moving to rest her head in my lap. While I rub her head, Shep shifts behind me and slowly starts dragging my brush through my hair.

I don't fight him on it because I clearly can't do it and, at this point, he seems to be the only one able to do anything for me without me freaking out.

A twinge of guilt washes over me as I think about the way I treated him in the hospital. I know he didn't deserve that.

"I'm sorry for what I said in the hospital," I whisper.

His strokes through my hair become softer and then he stops. "It's okay," he leans forward and kisses the side of my face.

"It's not," I mumble as he picks up the brush and starts to pull it through my hair again. After another minute of sitting in silence, letting him finish brushing my hair, I lean back into his chest.

He wraps his arms around me and we stay like this, with Dahlia in my lap until I hear a soft knock. Lennon slowly opens my bedroom door and when she sees me with clean, brushed hair, she starts to cry.

"I'm sorry," she says, holding a hand up to her mouth.

"It's okay." I pat the bed and she climbs onto it with Shep, Dahlia, and I.

"Thank you for calling him." I reach out and lace my fingers through hers.

"If we'd known he was what you needed all along, we would have called him sooner." She squeezes my hand with hers.

I look at Shep who smiles softly at me. I realize at this moment that while I don't know what the future looks like for me going forward, if I have Shep and Lennon in my corner, I'll be okay.

I haven't been able to think clearly since I woke up in the hospital, but something shifted in me when I got out of the tub earlier and realized I was able to get through that moment, as hard as it was.

I couldn't say for certain that I'd be able to do it again with ease, but at least I knew I was capable of doing it and that felt like a win for me.

"Is Margot staying?" I say, trying to peer out into the living room to see if she's out there.

"I told her to go home and rest," Shep says. "Lennon and I will be here with you tonight."

My stomach drops and I realize that Shep hasn't been here to witness my nightmares. My defenses start to rise but I will them away, trying to focus on the peace he was able to bring me just moments ago.

"I know about the nightmares," he says, as if reading my mind. "I'm not worried about it."

Lennon smiles and I see relief fill her eyes that this will also be a night for her to truly get some rest too. I hate how much everyone has been affected by what happened.

We all missed Thanksgiving. Lennon and Margot have hardly slept. My parents had to take off work. Everyone's lives have been disrupted because of me.

"I'll see you in the morning," Lennon leans forward and kisses my forehead then leaves my room, shutting the door behind her.

I let out a big sigh and lean back into Shep's lap. He holds me and presses kisses to the top of my head.

"I'm glad you're here," I admit and he stills. I sit back up, turning to face him and there's a pained expression on his face.

"I don't want to go back through everything because I don't think it will be good for either of us, but I want to let you know that I was really overwhelmed in the hospital when I told you to leave. And these last few weeks, I've been at my worst and I didn't want you to see me like that either."

He reaches for my face and cradles it in his hands. "I don't care if you're at your worst. I want all of you. Your worst, your best, and every bit in between. I choose you, knowing everything that might come with it and I don't love you any less. I promise that I'll keep choosing you, Harlow, because it'll always be you. In this lifetime and the next."

His words hit me just as deeply as they did earlier and I know he's telling the truth. Because who would still be here with me, after everything, if they didn't mean those words?

My mouth dries as I go to speak, knowing I'm putting my heart on the line, but I need to do it. I need to tell him how I feel. I need to let him in.

"I love you too, Shep. It was the last thing I remember thinking before I blacked out. How I was most upset that I was going to die not having told you that I love you."

A few tears spill out down my cheeks and Shep pulls me towards him, gently kissing me. When his lips touch mine, I realize how badly I needed him to be here for me during this. Was he really the key to helping me take my first step towards healing?

It wouldn't surprise me considering over the last few months, whenever I've found myself in a place that I didn't know how to get through, Shep was there to help me. He's helped me through probably some of the hardest moments of my life and I wish it didn't take until now to realize just how much I need him.

When he breaks our kiss, he looks at me with an expression that casts hope into my heart and allows me to settle into bed with a small sense of peace. Dahlia curls up in front of me and then I see Shep's hand come over my side holding something. My blanket.

He tucks it into my chest, then wraps his arm around me. As he holds me, I start to find sleep coming easier now that I'm with him and a simple but powerful thought comes to me before I allow myself to sink into the safety and protection of his arms.

For as many times as I told Shep to leave me alone, he continued to stay because he believed in us. He kept choosing me until I was ready to choose him back.

And I choose Shep.

SIXTY

THE DEAL I MADE

SHEP

Three weeks have passed since I was called over to Harlow's apartment and while it hasn't been the easiest, she's making progress every day.

Her nightmares aren't as frequent and she's starting to be comfortable showering on her own. For a while, I had to be there with her during it in case she started to have a panic attack. But my girl is a fighter, and I know she's going to get through this.

I'm waiting for her outside of Robin's office and I'm beyond thankful she finally started going back to therapy. She's back to seeing Robin three times a week. Margot has also been helping me with ways to support Harlow during her time of healing, while also giving me some support myself.

While I know that things will never be the same, I'm hopeful that this new season of life will be better because she will be healed.

We haven't talked much about things like swimming or *him*, but instead we're focusing on spending time together and with our friends and family.

I don't know if Harlow will be able to swim any time soon and while she's definitely struggling with that, she also has accepted it and is trying to make her peace with it. I'd love for her to be able to overcome her fear of being under the water in the pool, but something like what she went through isn't easily overcome.

Coach Bradford and Pierce have been meeting with her periodically to discuss her future, now that it's pretty clear she won't be pursuing the Olympics. Every so often, she'll visibly get upset, but the last meeting she had with them, Coach Bradford offered her a job to come on as the assistant swim coach at Everson next year, if she still wanted to be involved with the sport. Harlow was shocked but also excited because she didn't want to have to give up swimming entirely. Needless to say, she accepted the position.

The door opens and Harlow walks out with puffy red eyes, but it doesn't worry me anymore that she cries during therapy. In fact, we are pro-crying around here because it means she's feeling her emotions and that's progress.

"Ready?" she asks, reaching for my hand. I take it in mine, smiling at Robin who stands behind her.

We leave the little cabin and head into town. All the lamp posts are decorated with garlands and lights for Christmas and there's even a chance we might get snow later tonight.

The deal I made with Harlow is if she goes to therapy, I take her to get coffee after. It didn't take much convincing.

Once I park my truck, I walk around to open the door

and she hops out. I love winter Harlow. She looks way too good with a beanie and she also wears her Docs every day, which is my favorite thing about her. Well, one of them.

Today she's wearing a newer pair that I got for her as an early Christmas gift. I'd been keeping up with the different styles she has and Lennon helped me choose the pair she has on now. They're like her favorite ones that she typically wears, but have a thicker sole. According to Lennon, they're platforms, whatever that means.

As we walk toward the coffee shop, I notice her shoelace starting to come undone. "Hold on one second, baby," I say as I kneel down.

"What're you doing?" Her eyes go wide.

"Tying your shoe for you," I respond, putting the lace back into a bow.

When I'm done, I stand up and give her a kiss. We walk into Boulder and she pushes herself into me a little more than normal.

Once word got out that Beckett drowned Harlow, coupled with his accident, there was talk about her throughout the entire town. People would come up to her in public and offer their condolences and the first few times it happened, she had to run off to the bathroom and throw up. I know it's still not easy for her to go out in town, but it's another step in the direction of healing for her.

Once we get our coffees, we sit down in the corner on a couch together and she leans her head on my shoulder.

"I want to talk to you about something I mentioned to Robin today and see what you think," Harlow whispers.

"Okay, I'm all ears." I take a small sip of my drink.

She sits up, turning to face me and squints like she's still thinking over her words. "I want you to take me to the crash site vigil they have for…" Her words trail off.

As much as I immediately want to shut this down, I know she's trying to share something with me, so I try to do my best to listen. "Okay, and why would you want to do that?"

"I was talking to Robin today about forgiveness and acceptance. How sometimes in order for us to move on in life, we have to forgive people and accept what was done to us." She takes her lip into her mouth and starts to chew on it.

"While I don't really believe he deserves that, I'm not going to stop you from doing it. What do you gain from it? Closure?" I'm trying to make sense of what she's telling me but, damn, I'm struggling.

"Yeah, in a way. I don't know, but I feel like it's something I want to at least try." She takes a sip of her cold brew and studies me. I know my reaction to this is paramount, so I swallow my own pride about the situation and agree.

"Okay, can we go now?" she blurts out.

"Now?" I choke on my drink.

"Yeah, now. It's fresh on my mind and I want you to be with me." She grabs my hand.

"Harlow, I really don't know…"

"Please," she interjects. "For me."

I shake my head, not knowing how this is going to play out, but I agree anyways.

We get up and head back to my truck, coffee in hand, and I start up the engine before beginning the drive I'm all too familiar with.

The drive that I've taken countless times on my own

without Harlow knowing, to go and stare at the crash site of a piece of shit who almost took everything from me, cursing and swearing at the wreckage he left.

But if Harlow thinks this will help her, I'll be damned if I don't give it a try.

SIXTY-ONE

A SINGLE WHITE ROSE

HARLOW

After making a quick stop to pick up some flowers, I decided against it and asked the shop owner if I could just take one single stem instead.

Sitting in Shep's front seat, I twirl the white rose between my fingers and my stomach is a mess.

I know this was my idea and I know that it might not be a good one, but I can't stop thinking about therapy today. Robin and I don't often bring up Beckett in detail, but for some reason, today I felt like we needed to.

It's been almost two months and I still don't understand the way I feel about him dying. There's a part of me, the one that was romantically involved with him, that's sad and confused. But there's another part of me, the emotionally damaged and angry-all-the-time one, that feels relieved Beckett's gone and I don't ever have to worry about him again.

Nobody dares to ask me about him. Not my family, not

my friends, and especially not Shep. Laura is the only one who's made a passing comment and it was only to tell me that if I did want to talk about it, she was there to listen.

Lennon does have a saying though she likes to throw around whenever she can tell I'm starting to overthink things. "Your trauma is showing," she'll say playfully, but it's true and it helps bring me back to reality.

For the most part, ever since Shep came to my apartment and helped me wash my hair, I've tried to look forward and only talk about my emotions when they're overwhelming me or when I'm with Robin.

Shep will check in with me of course, but he also gives me space to come to him on my own.

As we pull up to the site, a wave of nausea crashes through me. I can see there are still flowers and a cross, which doesn't sit right with me. Besides all of those things, there's someone else here.

The truck rolls to a stop and when we get closer, Shep quickly reaches his hand across the console to stop me from moving.

"I think we should come back," he states in a serious tone.

"Why?" I try to peer around the windshield, catching sight of the side of the woman's face and she's clearly crying.

"Look, Harlow, I know we don't talk about him and what happened, but that doesn't mean I haven't kept up with what's been going on." His tone is low and I can tell he's trying to stay calm.

"Okay, and?" I ask, still confused as to what I'm missing.

"That's Beckett's mom," he states, with a stone cold expression.

I drop the rose into my lap and time stands still. I stare out the window and my mind starts running at a hundred miles a minute. At first, anger floods me and I want to spew out all the awful things I think about Beckett, but then something else comes over me as I watch her cry over her son who ultimately ended his own life because of his reckless decisions.

I don't have sympathy for him, but I do feel sorry for her.

I move Shep's hand off of me, grabbing the rose again before looking him in the eyes. "I need to do this."

I unclip my seatbelt and open the door, hopping out of the car before Shep can stop me. I hesitate for a second, but muster up every bit of courage I have and walk over to where she stands. When I get closer, she turns, and when she sees me, it's obvious from the shock and panic on her face that she knows exactly who I am.

We hold each other's stare for a few seconds, her eyes scanning over my body and then they stop on the single white rose in between my fingers. For some reason, she starts sobbing.

"I'm so sorry," her words come out pained and in this moment, I feel the grief she has. Not for Beckett, the monster who caused me so much pain, but for the mother who lost her son.

"I take it you know who I am," I whisper.

She nods, then wipes her face with the tissue she's holding. "I don't know what to say to you, other than I'm sorry.

My boy, he…" Her words are lost again to her cries and I don't know why but I reach out and touch her arm.

"I'm…" I swallow down the bit of bile that's rising in my throat. "I'm sorry."

She shakes her head, then steps away putting distance between us. "You have nothing to be sorry for. I know what he did to you and you have to know, he struggled with drinking for most of his teenage years."

I stand there for a second unsure of what to say. While what she says isn't an excuse to me, I know she's trying to make sense of what happened in her own way.

"I understand," is all I'm finally able to get out.

"Why are you here?" she asks as if it finally registers in her mind.

I laugh because a few minutes ago I thought I knew why, but standing here now, I'm at a loss.

"I'm not sure, but I felt like I needed to come out here and see this for myself. Maybe try and make peace with the situation."

I hear the ground crunching behind me and turn around to see Shep finally joining me. He wraps an arm around me and I get the feeling she also knows who he is.

"I'll leave you two," she says quickly. "Just wanted to come out here before Christmas." Her voice cracks, then she turns to walk away when something overcomes me.

Maybe it's the realization that, yet again, at the core of this is a mother who's lost her son, or maybe it's because she's about to spend a holiday plagued with grief and loss. Whatever it is, I blurt out after her, "I forgive him."

She stops in her tracks and I step towards her, Shep placing a hand firmly on my back to give me his support. I repeat the words again, this time with tears streaming down my face. I don't know if I'm saying them for her or for me, but I say it again anyways. "I forgive him."

Beckett's mom starts to cry and all she manages to mumble out is a broken, "Thank you," before turning and heading off to her car.

I stand there for another second before turning around into Shep and breaking into a sob. I don't know what for, but there are too many emotions overcoming me and unlike in the past when I'd want to shut them down, I try to actually feel them now.

"I'm so proud of you," Shep murmurs into my ear, while caressing the back of my head. "You're so strong, you know that?"

I nod into his chest, believing his words even if I don't always feel them. After a few more seconds, I step back and turn to walk towards the cross that's stuck into the earth and lay down the single white rose.

As it leaves my fingers and falls to the ground, I feel something from me leave with it. The pain and hurt I'd been nursing for far too long lifts off of me and, for the first time since August, I feel a part of my soul being genuinely restored.

I walk away leaving behind the brokenness I carried for so long and holding onto a new belief of hope and healing for what's to come.

I lace my fingers through Shep's and let him lead me back to the truck while my thoughts still unravel. I'm not the same person I was when Shep and I first met and if it wasn't for him seeing me, truly seeing me, I don't know where I'd be right now.

Sure, I wouldn't wish to go through everything I have, but I also realize that because of it, I've learned things I probably never would've. Things like how to help other people who may find themselves in an abusive relationship like I did. Things like how great therapy is and it's okay to need help. Things like life won't always make sense and it's messy, but it's beautiful, and there's so much to be grateful for.

They say to be loved is to be changed and while I stare at Shep, watching him drive us back into town, I know that statement is true. Shep has taught me what true love is and shown it to me regardless of the bruises I had—physically and emotionally.

His love gave me the freedom and grace to change at my own pace. His love encouraged me to see my ability to receive gentle love. His love embraced my struggles and helped me carry my burdens. His love moved me to realize I deserved far better than I was getting. And it's because of his love I've changed into someone who I'm proud to be, because being broken or having struggles shouldn't disqualify anyone from receiving the love we all deserve.

"Thanks for taking me," I break the silence between us. "I love you, you know?"

Shep smiles and picks my hand up to kiss the back of it. "I know."

EPILOGUE

HARLOW

"I'm almost ready!" I yell out to Shep, who's waiting patiently in my living room.

I walk back into my bathroom where my phone is set up, Lennon and Margot on FaceTime. "Are we sure about this?" I stand up on my tip-toes and do another twirl, the red lace fabric swishing.

"Yes!" Lennon screams. "We're SURE!" She claps her hands together and Margot just smiles.

"I don't know, it feels more like a you dress than a me dress." I straighten the shoulders of the long lace sleeves, attached to the bustier style mini dress that Lennon convinced me to buy for tonight's Valentine's date with Shep.

"You can always wear your Docs with it," Margot chimes in. "Make it more you."

Lennon cuts her off, "Absolutely not." She scoffs, rolling

her eyes. "Harlow, have I ever led you astray with clothing or fashion before?"

I laugh, remembering how she convinced me to buy a yellow dress for formal because she secretly knew it was Shep's favorite color—a fact I didn't learn until just recently. "No, you haven't."

"Great, then put on your heels, finish curling your hair, and go on your date!" Lennon smiles.

"Wear a red lip," Margot adds.

"Okay, okay. I'll send pictures later." I blow a kiss and then hang up the call.

A few minutes later, my heels are on, my hair is curled, and I'm painting my lips red when I hear a knock on my door.

"Baby, our reservation is in twenty minutes."

"I know, I'm—" A hand wraps around my waist before I can finish my sentence.

"Shep!" I squeal out. "You're supposed to wait until I'm ready!"

"I couldn't any longer," he growls in my ear then playfully kisses my neck.

Squirming in his grip, I manage to pull away and when I do, his eyes widen and he bites down on his bottom lip. "Damn."

My cheeks flush and I imagine they match the shade of my dress and lips.

"You look amazing, wow." He steps forward and kisses me, my lipstick smearing on his mouth.

"Oops," I giggle.

He takes my hand and walks me out towards the front

door, but not without stopping and having me do another spin for him. Shep really knows how to make a girl feel beautiful.

We get in his truck and head to the Lodge in downtown Everson, which is as crowded as I imagined it would be. It's basically the only formal restaurant in town, making it a prime spot for any special occasion.

We spend dinner talking about the rest of the semester, plans post-graduation, and where we see ourselves in the next few years. It's so easy to dream about life with Shep, and after spending Christmas with him and his family, I can't imagine my life ever not looking like that.

Our parents have even started trying to connect more for "future events," which only confirms the truth I've known since before we even started seriously dating. Shep is my person and the reason I believe soulmates exist.

When we leave the restaurant, he reaches for my hand and we walk the sidewalks of downtown beneath the streetlights—a comfortable silence between us and a crisp chill in the February air. Shep takes off his suit jacket and drapes it over my shoulders.

Once we get to his truck, he stops just before opening the door, staring at me with emotion in his eyes that covers me with a warmth and heat, making me want to shed his jacket.

"What is it?" My voice is barely above a whisper.

"You," his words are breathy. "It's always been you."

My heart starts beating rapidly in my chest and before I can say anything, he slams his lips onto mine, pushing me against his truck. We stay like this, trapped in time and lost in each other while it feels like our souls dance until he pulls away. "Let me take you home."

He steps back and opens the door, helping me in and then buckling my seatbelt for me.

We pull back into my apartment lot and he picks me up bridal style before carrying me up the stairs to my front door. I can't help the giggles that escape while I kick my feet. I never knew love could feel so good.

Using his spare key I made him, he pushes open the door and then kicks it shut behind him, heading straight for my room. He sets me down on the bed and stands over me, our breathing heavy.

"I want to show you something," he whispers as he steps back and begins to unbutton his shirt.

I draw my bottom lip into my mouth, chewing on it in anticipation for what's to come. Shep and I have been taking things slow, but that's not to say my body doesn't burn up with desire for him every time we're alone.

Once the final button is loose, he shrugs off his shirt and steps forward, rubbing his thumb over my cheek. I search his face, not entirely sure what exactly I'm supposed to be looking for, then he turns to the right, allowing me to see the side of his ribs.

Both my hands fly to cover my mouth as a gasp escapes my lips.

"Shep," I whisper, my eyes stinging from the tears that are starting to form. I reach one of my hands forward and run it over the skin that's slightly raised.

"Happy Valentine's Day." He smiles. "My gift is making sure you know I'm yours."

All words have left me as I trace over the tattoo of a butterfly on Shep's ribs.

"You did this for me?" I ask, my voice unsteady.

He nods his head, "For you. My butterfly girl. Not just because of your swimming but because of everything you've been through. Your transformation left a mark on me and this is my way of showing it."

The tears I wanted to keep from falling have abandoned my eyes and stream down my face as I jump up, throwing my arms around his neck. My soul feels so light and free and happy. "I love you, Shep," I whimper. "I love you so much."

He nuzzles his nose into my neck. "I love you, Harlow."

When he pulls away from me, my heart thrums and the connection between us feels like a blue aura of electricity. We hold each other's gaze for a moment before I tug on one of my sleeves, then the other, and let the dress fall to the floor. I watch as his eyes drink me in, skating over my naked figure and lingering on the red thong I wore to match the dress.

I step out of the pooled material and into Shep's hold, his arms running up my back and leaving chills in their wake. My hands press against his chest and when my body becomes flush with his, a fire unleashes in my stomach and into my core.

I peer up at him, my gaze wanton, and brush my lips against his bare chest. His eyes watch me like I'm the most captivating thing he's ever seen.

He bends down to find my lips with his, then trails kisses along the side of my neck and collar bones, before I realize he's lowering himself down to his knees. When he sinks to the floor, his mouth level with my waist, I drag my nails through his hair and he lets out a groan.

"I want this. I want you," my words come out so husky, I don't recognize my own voice.

He flits his gaze up to me for only a second before raising one leg in his hand, taking off my heel, then mimicking the same gesture with the other.

Once I'm barefoot, he leans towards and peppers light, breathy kisses on the inside of my thighs. We've played around like this before but something is different tonight. Something has shifted.

I don't know if it's just my heart truly healing or the tattoo marking Shep as mine, but I know tonight will be the night I give all of myself to him.

He quickly wraps his hands around the back of my legs, cupping my butt before standing and bringing me up with him. Wrapping myself around him, our mouths find each other and we kiss in a frenzy—like we can't get enough. And we can't. I know I never will.

He walks towards my bed and lays me down, sliding down his pants and boxers before climbing on top of me. The way he looks at me takes my breath away. If Shep couldn't speak, his eyes could say enough. This man loves me. Adores me. Cherishes me. He has for so long and I know he won't ever stop.

"Can I take these off, baby?" he whispers while grazing his fingertips along the edge of my thong.

I nod while sucking on my bottom lip and when he pulls down the lace fabric leaving me bare before him, I almost can't wait any longer.

"You know I have an IUD," I blurt out and then feel the apples of my cheeks flush with heat as Shep smirks.

"Eager are we?" His voice is like smoke, wrapping around me and choking me out.

I worried that the moment we decided to have sex, old habits of mine would rush in and panic would consume me. But right now, all I can sense is my all-consuming love and affection for Shep.

He brings his lips to my neck and I reach out, lightly wrapping my hand around his dick. He pulls back, blinking a few times, then looks down at where I'm holding him. I don't know what side of me he's unleashed, but this Harlow feels bold and exciting.

I stroke him a few times, before sliding my hand up to capture the side of his face. My other hand draws lazy circles on the arm that's wrapped underneath me.

"I'm ready," I whisper.

Shep leans forward to capture his lips with mine and when he does, he pushes himself inside me, and the sensation is so overwhelming, I break our kiss to cry out.

"Is it okay? Are you okay?" Shep rushes out, studying my face.

I nod quickly, rocking my hips to encourage him to move.

"More than okay. So good. You feel- You fit, so good." The words tumble out of my mouth as he picks up the pace and rocks into me.

"Oh, shit. Baby. Harlow, you're perfect." He slows down and I feel every languid thrust. "Look at you, taking me so well."

I open my eyes and follow his gaze, where he's watching himself slide in and out of me. The sight is so erotic and it drags something out of my core, setting free the version of myself that didn't feel comfortable with sex.

I moan and throw my head back, overcome with pleasure and a new sense of power. "I'm yours," I cry out, closing my eyes and Shep pushes deeper, hitting a spot that causes white spots to start appearing behind my eyelids.

"Always have been." *Thrust.* "Always will be." *Thrust.* His words spark fire in my core and I feel the tightening and pulsing of my release creeping all the way from my toes to my cheeks.

"Shep!" I nearly scream when he puts a hand under me, tilting my hips up and reaching the spot that causes me to detonate underneath him.

"Oh, fu…" he groans while I let the delicious feeling wrack through my body. "I'm going to——"

"In me. Do it in me. Don't stop," I shock myself as the pleads leave my lips, but the words are Shep's undoing and after just a few more thrusts, warmth fills me and Shep's body collapses on top of mine.

We lay there, silently, still connected while our bodies start to relax. I move some of his hair that's fallen forward and is sticking to his forehead.

"I'm really happy it's you," I whisper.

He picks his head up and places a hand along the side of my face, before letting a lazy smile grace his lips. "Yeah? I'm really happy it's you too, baby girl."

"I wouldn't want anyone else," I let a smile of my own appear before a small giggle escapes.

"What?" Shep squints, but a playfulness remains in his eyes.

"I'm just glad you didn't listen to me. Didn't let me push you away." I press a soft kiss on his lips before looking deep into his slate blue eyes. "I'm glad you didn't stay in your lane."

THE END

ACKNOWLEDGMENTS

To my mom and dad, for loving and supporting me through all phases of my life, but especially this one as an author. You've both been so encouraging and have helped me through the obstacles I faced while writing this story. Mom, your texts saying, "Go for it, baby" and Dad, your calls telling me, "You can do anything you put your mind to" are imprinted in my heart and mind. I treasure our conversations and I hope you know how unbelievably grateful I am to have two parents who love me the way you do. You both also pushed me to swim which gave me the love for this sport and be your little fishy. I love you both so much.

Katy, you said it and now I get to say it. I never want there to be a book I write that you're not apart of. Our endless texts and voice notes, heart to hearts, and conversations make me feel so loved and seen. I'm so grateful I get to call you a friend and love you almost as much as you love Twilight (because I don't know if anyone can top that) What would I do without you?

Rebecca, I quite literally would not have been able to finish this book without you and wife nights. Thank you for listening, always taking me in, and supporting me through the months of writing this story. You are a friend that I'll never not feel lucky to have.

Ciara, I don't have enough words for you. Your patience

with me through this. Your kindness and graciousness with every message, text, email, and voice memo. You really took this story and helped me edit it into a treasure. I can't thank you enough for sharing your talents with me.

Shaylene, where do I even start? You've been handling this story with as much care as I have and it's meant the world to me. Thank you for letting me send you tv episode length voice memos and being willing to take my words as I wrote them. Your role as my active alpha reader is what helped me finish this book. Your belief in Shep & Harlow helped me to believe in myself.

Bryanna, you brought this story to life with your talents. Every little sticker, bookmark, and piece of this story that you turned into something I can hold is like a treasure to me. You are a treasure to me. Thank you for being all that you are. And in case you need the reminder, that means the incredible mom you are, wife, sister, friend, and more. I love you so so much.

Ola, your words have impacted me more than you know. Na wszystko jest w życiu czas. Thank you for always encouraging me and giving me your wisdom.

Ellie girl, you came into my life on the tail coats of this book being published but it feels like we've been friends for years. I hope you know how special you are and that your kindness helped me push through to release day.

My SSS girls, you carried me through some of the darkest times while I wrote this. I love all of you so much.

To my alpha and beta team, thank you for taking the time to read the bones of my story and nurture them to grow into this book. Your feedback, comments, and support helped get this book to publication. I'm beyond grateful for each of you.

To my ARC readers, thank you for showing interest in supporting me and this story. Your role in helping to share this book means so much to be because without your support, Harlow and Shep wouldn't get to meet all the people they need to.

Lastly, to myself. You went through hell and back while writing this story and you took that pain and heartache and let it tell the story of your past journey and healing, while reminding you how resilient you are. I hope you come back to this whenever you find yourself struggling and remember that you're strong and will always be okay.

ABOUT THE AUTHOR

Elle is an indie author based in Charleston, SC. She loves writing about intense emotions, heavy feelings, and things that make her heart feel alive. When she reads, she enjoys supporting other indie authors, and loves dark romance, enemies to lovers, and relatable characters.

Elle hopes to use her passion for mental health, trauma recovery, and emotional healing in her writing to connect with other reader's souls. Her dream is to restore hearts she didn't break and make the lost feel seen.

When she isn't spending time writing, shopping for more books, or working through her endless TBR, she is snuggling her two pitbull rescues or finding a new coffee shop to work on all things bookish.

For author updates, upcoming projects, and sneak peeks, you can follow Elle on IG: @ellefsun.author

Scan the QR below to get access to the extended epilogue of *Stay in Your Lane.*

Xx, Elle

Harlow Hug Pasta

1 cup of pasta (your choice)

2 tbsp. olive oil AND 3 tbsp. butter

1 fresh lemon AND lemon pepper seasoning

garlic and onion powder

parmesan cheese

Bring your pasta to a boil, then strain the noodles.

Pour olive oil and butter into pot then stir your pasta back in. Add onion and garlic powder (a dash) then sprinkle the lemon pepper seasoning. Once you mix it all together, squeeze fresh lemon and top with parmesan cheese. Serve and enjoy!